Daughter
of the
Legend

Books by Jesse Stuart

Man with a Bull-Tongue Plow
Head o' W-Hollow
Beyond Dark Hills
Trees of Heaven
Men of the Mountains
Taps for Private Tussie
Mongrel Mettle
Album of Destiny
Foretaste of Glory
Tales from the Plum Grove Hills
The Thread That Runs So True
Hie to the Hunters
Clearing in the Sky
Kentucky Is My Land
The Good Spirit of Laurel Ridge
The Year of My Rebirth
Plowshare in Heaven
God's Oddling
Hold April
A Jesse Stuart Reader
Save Every Lamb
Daughter of the Legend

For Boys and Girls

Penny's Worth of Character
The Beatinest Boy
Red Mule
The Rightful Owner
Andy Finds a Way

Daughter
of the
Legend

Jesse Stuart

McGraw-Hill Book Company

New York   Toronto   London

DAUGHTER OF THE LEGEND

Library of Congress Catalog Card Number: 65-25553

62244

to Fern and Ben

Stuart,Jesse

Daughter of the legend

1

"TAKE IT EASY, Dewberry," I said. I looked through the windshield into the deep valley below and my body was tense. With one hand I held the truck door where the side glass had been let down; with the other hand I held on to Ben Dewberry's shoulder.

"Take your fingers off my shoulder," Ben said. He was steering the truck among the low stumps where we had cut the trees as close to the ground as we could, trying to miss a few of the big rocks that bulged above the sawbriar-and-huckleberry-covered slope.

"We'll never get over this part of the road when it rains," I said.

"Wouldn't even try to drive over it then."

What a country, I thought, as the truck slid this way and that over the dry steep mountain earth, missing this stump and hitting that one. There wasn't a foot of railroad,

electric wire, or hard road in Cantwell County. There
wasn't a telephone, a stone house, or even a brick house in
the county either.

"This may be a rough country, Ben," I said when he
had steered safely onto the flat below, "but I like it."

"I like it better than any place we've gone yet," he said.

But I knew why Ben was in love with Cantwell County.
It wasn't the rough road or the rugged mountains with
the great timber stretches around their flanks of oak,
pine, gum, beech, ash, and yellow poplars that caused Ben
Dewberry to fall in love with Cantwell County. And it
wasn't the mountains or the trees that had caused me to
love the country.

I'd lived in mountains all my life. I'd lived in the Virginia mountains within a rifle's distance of Ben Dewberry's
shack. We had mountains there covered with oak, pine,
beech, ash, and tall poplars growing in the loamy coves
where streams of cool blue mountain water poured over
the ferny ledges. We had one hard road running through
the county; we had telephones, electric wires, a branch railroad line and we had stone and brick buildings.

"I want you to meet Fern," Ben said. "Honest, I've
never seen a girl so beautiful in all my life."

Ben could think of Fern now, since he was driving
around the mountainside where there were only a few
stumps and rocks to watch.

"And I'd like to meet that girl you've been talkin' about
in your sleep," he said, putting his face forward to look
through the cracked windshield at the road ahead.

"I want you to meet her, Ben," I said. "I want you to
meet an angel."

My fear of the road had left me and I looked down at

the gorge below where a stream, flecked with foam, swirled and eddied.

"What did you say 'er name was?" Ben asked.

"Deutsia Huntoon."

"That's an odd name."

"But it's a pretty name," I said.

It was strange how I'd met Deutsia when we'd gone to Oak Hill for supplies. She was standing alone across the street from Little Tavern. I'd started to the tavern to buy a soda but stopped still in my tracks at the sight of her. I wondered how any woman in the world could be so pretty. Her hair was as golden as a poplar leaf ripened by early October's sun. It fell loosely down her back almost to her knees. I'd never seen hair that long and as October-poplar-leaf-golden as hers. She looked at me with soft blue eyes shaded by heavy lashes. Her eyes were as blue as the petals of mountain violets. Her sun-tanned face had the smoothness and color of a rope-hickory-nut stripped of its shell. She was tall and slender, straight as a sapling, with slim ankles and shapely nut-brown legs.

"My name is Dave Stoneking," I said to her.

"My name is Deutsia Huntoon," she said. Her lips parted to show two rows of perfect teeth, as white as corn grains before they begin to harden in the husk.

I had stood there holding her warm soft hand while people going toward the Little Tavern stopped to stare at us.

"Wake up, Dave," Ben said. "Have you gone to sleep?"

"I was thinking about Deutsia."

"You must have it pretty bad."

"I'm in love for the first time in my life," I said.

"What will Bonnie say when I tell her about this girl?"

Ben asked. "She expects you to marry her, doesn't she?"

"She will just have to expect," I said.

"We'll get together with our girls tonight," Ben said. "I suppose they already know each other."

I wondered if Fern would be as pretty as Deutsia.

We left the WPA road for the gravel road which was the only one that connected Cantwell to the world beyond these mountains.

"Two lumberjacks going to see the two most beautiful women in the world," Ben said, stepping on the gas.

And one of the prettiest valleys in the world, too, I thought as we rolled along at fifteen miles an hour toward Oak Hill, a village of about five hundred people built on the slope of a low rolling foothill overlooking the winding Clinch River that gorged between the high shale bluffs and the jagged overhanging rocks. The river changed its course north, east, west and south. It followed the way of least resistance, as the people that had inhabited its narrow fertile valley and the hollows and high rugged slopes had done for more than a century.

Ben drove the truck a block beyond Little Tavern and parked under a street maple's shade.

"I'm to meet Fern in the tavern," he said. "Where are you to meet Deutsia?"

"I don't know."

Ben laughed loudly. He bent over and slapped his knees with his big hands as he laughed.

"Have a date with a girl and you don't even know where you're to meet her! What happened? Didn't you agree on a place to meet?"

"We forgot it," I said.

"Are you sure this is the afternoon you're to meet her?"

"Saturday afternoon," I said.

"Maybe she's down around Little Tavern."

"Maybe," I said.

As we walked toward Little Tavern, I looked at the crowd of people that had come from the mountain slopes, coves, and the Clinch valley to do their shopping. Saturday is the big day in Oak Hill, I thought, as I watched this milling crowd of people that filled Main Street, moving in and out of the stores like honey bees going in and out of their hives when the blossom season was on. They were carrying baskets of young chickens and eggs and apples, sacks of green beans and jars of wild honey into the stores to barter for groceries and spices.

"This is a busy little village," Ben said. "I wouldn't mind to settle down here."

"Maybe we'll both settle here," I said.

I looked at the faces of young women and girls and the mothers with swarms of children following after them. I looked at the wrinkled faces of old women, lean, tall and stooped, the handsome, dark and fair faces of young men, tall and straight, and the bearded faces of men who looked at us with keen blue eyes that had faraway looks in them. And I wondered about each clean-shaven young man I saw. I wondered if he had ever seen Deutsia and if he had thought that she was as beautiful as I thought she was and if his lips had ever kissed her lips.

"Here's Little Tavern," Ben said. "Let's step inside. Maybe your Deutsia and my Fern have already gotten together."

We walked up the steps. "I hope they have," I said. "I'd like to see 'em side by side."

As we entered the crowded tavern I saw a girl standing by the fountain, and she smiled at us. Not at me, for I could tell the smile was meant for Ben.

"Fern," Ben said.

"You're a little late."

"Road's awful rough on the mountain."

"I'll forgive you, Ben," she said softly.

"Fern, I want you to meet my friend Dave Stoneking."

"Mighty glad to meet you, Fern," I said, giving her hand a squeeze.

"I'm glad to meet you," she said.

But I don't know whether she's glad to meet me or not, I thought, as I quickly let go of her hand, for it felt limp and cold. There wasn't the soft warmth and shock I had felt in Deutsia's hand when I had first held it.

"Dave is looking for a girl named Deutsia Huntoon," Ben said. "You haven't seen Deutsia around here, have you?"

Just as Ben said the word "Deutsia" the smile left Fern Hailston's face; it seemed to grow as cold as her hand had felt to me.

"You know 'er, don't you?" Ben asked before Fern had time to answer his first question.

"I haven't seen her around here," Fern said. "She never comes to Little Tavern. Oh, yes, I know her, but not very well!"

When Fern said these words more color flushed her face. The crowd of people in the tavern that hadn't noticed us at first became silent when they heard the words that Fern had spoken.

"Why doesn't she come here?" I asked.

"She just doesn't," Fern replied nervously.

I looked at Fern Hailston, the girl that Ben Dewberry had said was the most beautiful girl he had ever met in his life. She was short and buxom with big sparkling brown eyes that slanted downward toward the corners of her lips. She had thick brown curly hair that did not reach her shoulders, for it had been bobbed. Her hands were heavy and her fingers were short. She wore oxfords and blue anklets the color of her dress and her muscular legs were sun-tanned but were not as brown as Deutsia's legs.

"Where do you think Deutsia could be?" I asked.

"You might find her over around the courthouse."

"What would she be doing over there?" I wanted to ask Fern but didn't, since everybody had quit eating his ice cream or drinking his soda to listen to us.

"I'll be getting over to the courthouse," I said.

When I walked outside Little Tavern to look for the courthouse I wondered if Fern and Deutsia had had trouble with each other. I wondered why Fern didn't like Deutsia. I wondered if Deutsia and Fern had fallen in love with the same man once. And I wondered if that man was one of the clean-shaven young men I saw as I glanced over the milling crowd, searching for the courthouse.

At the far end of Main Street, I saw a two-story frame structure, painted white with green trimmings. Around it a large crowd of people had gathered. Thinking this must be the courthouse, I walked toward it. As I walked closer I saw tall, dark, swarthy, sunburned, husky figures of the earth, fair women, handsome men, bearded men with eagle eyes and old women and mothers with deep-lined faces.

And there were swarms of children of all sizes, ages and descriptions, playing tag in and out of the big two-story frame building. Children joyously screaming were hiding behind their mothers and fathers. Above the door of the peculiar structure was a sign that read "Cantwell County Courthouse."

"Lemonade, five cents a glass," a tall bearded man said, standing above a large white churn with a dipper in one hand and a glass of lemonade in another.

"Turtle-steak sandwiches, ten cents apiece."

A broken-faced old lady walked up and bought a glass of lemonade and a turtle-steak sandwich. Nearby were other stands where women and men were selling rabbit sandwiches, fish sandwiches, home-cured ham sandwiches, wine and lemonade. I wondered why these things would be sold at the outskirts of Oak Hill. I wondered why the people didn't go to the Little Tavern in Oak Hill for their sandwiches. But these were different sandwiches and drinks from the ones sold in Little Tavern.

I bought a glass of lemonade and a home-cured ham sandwich while I stood looking for Deutsia among the swirling, laughing crowd of people. Maybe Deutsia saw me first. When I spotted her she was walking toward me, looking prettier than she had the first time I saw her. She was dressed in something soft and clinging and blue that brought out the violet-petal blue of her eyes.

"Where've you been, Deutsia?" I asked. "I've looked all over town for you. I've looked in Little Tavern and down the streets."

"I've been right here," she said, smiling.

The people about us stared at each other with surprised looks and talked in low tones. I stood close to

Deutsia and held her hand, looking into her soft blue eyes as I talked, feeling the warmth and thrill of her hand go through my body.

I was again with the girl who wouldn't give me peace night or day. Not that I wanted peace. I wanted to be stirred within my heart, brain and body as I had been the first time I'd seen her.

"I'd like you to meet my friend Ben Dewberry," I said.

"Where is he?"

"He's over at Little Tavern, with Fern Hailston."

"That's not my side of town."

Why isn't it your side of town? I thought, as I stood looking at her. Fern Hailston can't compare with you.

"And Miss Fern is not my company," she said, breaking our brief silence.

"Then we won't go to the tavern. We'll go anywhere you say. If you want to, we'll stay right here. We'll do anything that suits you."

If Ben Dewberry and Fern Hailston were happy together in their end of town, I thought, Deustia and I would be just as happy together in our end of the town, where sandwiches and drinks were different and the people were happier and friendlier.

"I have something I want to do," she said. "Will you help me?"

"I'll be glad to."

"You wait here just a minute."

I watched her walk away from me. She didn't take a clumsy step like Fern Hailston. I watched Deutsia walk toward the sandwich stand, saw her buy a turtle-steak sandwich, a fish sandwich, a ham sandwich and a small bottle of wine. The tall bearded man put each in a paper sack for her. She came toward me, with two paper sacks in each hand.

"Did you get all this for me?" I asked.

"No."

"For yourself?"

"No." She smiled at my inquisitiveness.

"Come with me," she said. "I'll show you the one I got them for."

"Let me carry part of it."

We each carried two of the sacks. I took hold of her free hand and followed her down an alley. Beside our path were tall dying ragweeds and smartweeds filled with scraps of paper the wind had blown there. On each side were rows of unpainted small frame houses. We hurried toward a small squat building a hundred yards from the courthouse, a building with iron bars across the windows.

"Where to—the jail?"

"Right," she said.

"What a jailhouse. Five good men could pry it over with handspikes."

"Wait until you see the inside!"

"Do you have a friend in jail?"

"Yes, I do," she said, with a serious expression on her face.

It made me wonder if Deutsia's real lover was in jail and if she were only going about with me in the meantime. I would have to free myself of this jealousy, I thought. We walked up the steep steps into the little jailhouse.

"Jailer Jarvis Henthorne, this is Dave Stoneking."

"Glad to know you, Mr. Stoneking," Jarvis said, extending his hand. He looked at me suspiciously with cold and lifeless eyes.

I shook his soft shriveled cold hand that felt like a cold-blooded blacksnake I'd once dug from the earth in December when digging after a rabbit.

"I'm glad to know you," I said.

"So you're back again, Deutsia," Jarvis said in a friendly tone of voice. "And you've brought that worthless critter a lot of good grub."

"I'd like to take it to 'im if you don't mind."

"Do you want to take your boy friend along with you?" he asked.

"I'd like to if you don't mind," she replied.

"Is he all right?" he asked her, teasing her.

"Yes, sir."

He kept his left hand on his pistol handle, turned the key with his right hand, and opened the door. As soon as Deutsia and I stepped inside he locked the door again. We walked up a narrow dirty stairway to the upstairs, and I saw a scene I'll never forget. Here was one thin, pale-faced prisoner stretched on a dirty, ragged mattress. He was wearing a dirty pair of overall pants tied at his waist with a suspender, and a blue work shirt, clean but so filled with holes that we could see more of his pale flesh than of the blue work shirt. His feet were shoeless, sockless, and dirty on the bottoms. Houseflies were alighting on his toes and he would wiggle them in his sleep to shoo the flies away for a minute. Then they would come right back.

"Who is this man, Deutsia?"

"Don Praytor," she said.

"Is he married?"

"He's married and has five children."

"Why is he here?" I asked.

"If you live in the valley and make whiskey," she said, "you don't go to jail. If you live up on the mountain where I live and if you are even found with whiskey on you, you go to jail.

"Sheriff Ezra Pratt found a half pint of moonshine on Don Praytor," she whispered. "That's why he's here. He's been here eight months without even a trial."

"Why do they keep him so long?" I whispered. I didn't want Jarvis Henthorne to hear me.

"Remember, the jailor gets a dollar a day for every prisoner he feeds," she whispered in my ear.

"This is the dirtiest place I've ever seen in my life," I said.

I watched a row of cockroaches sliding up and down the wall preening their long whiskers at the houseflies that swarmed in and out of the paneless windows between the iron bars. The smell of the place was enough to knock a man down. The floor was dirty and the only furniture was the two old rusty iron beds. They had dirty mattresses, no sheet or pillow, and only one blanket to each bed. There was a lard bucket filled with drinking water at the head of the bed where Don Praytor was lying fast asleep. There was a battered lard can, covered with a newspaper across the top, to be used for an indoor privy. The houseflies were making good use of the drinking water, for there was a black line of flies all the way around the bucket's rim. A black cloud of flies rested on the newspaper covering the lard can.

"We'd better wake Don," Deutsia said.

"All right." I reached down and shook his leg.

"He's sound asleep."

"Wake up, fellow," I said. "The grub's here!"

He arose slowly and rubbed his blue sleep-filled eyes. They were weak, tired eyes, slow to let the light enter after they'd been closed in sleep.

"Who's this with you, Deutsia?" he asked. "Is he a lawyer that's come to try to get me outen this filthy jail?"

"No, Don, he's a friend of mine. He's a timber cutter from the Big Woods Tract."

"Oh, I see," Don said. "I hoped he was a lawyer."

"We brought you a fish, a ham and a turtle sandwich," Deutsia said. "Which one do you want first?"

"It won't matter. They're all good."

"And a bottle of wine to wash them down with," I said.

Deutsia gave him the fish sandwich. He filled his mouth until his lean jaws bulged. Four big bites and it was gone. He ate like a starved man.

"Here's the other two sandwiches and the bottle of wine," Deutsia said. "All this came from the mountain."

"Deutsia, you're an angel," Don Praytor said. "Never did a girl live that has a better heart than you have!"

"Oh, you're just bragging on me."

"No I'm not, either," he told her. "If I's not a married man, you're the girl I'd choose to marry! You've always been good to the mountain prisoners in this bughouse! You've managed to get 'em good grub and carry it in here! If you didn't, I don't know how they'd've managed to live! I couldn't live on what I'm fed here!"

"Shhh," she murmured, holding her finger to her lips.

"Let Jarvis Henthorne hear!" A tiny spark of color came to each pale cheek and a bit of fire kindled in his eyes. "I don't care if he does hear me. He'll never stop your bringing grub to me. If you bring it to me, he won't have to feed me and he'll make more money outen the dollar he gets every day for my keep."

If Ben Dewberry could see starved pale-faced Don Praytor in this dirty jail eight months without a trial for carrying a half pint of whiskey, what would he think of Cantwell County justice? Would he still want to settle down in Oak Hill?

Don Praytor ate the ham and turtle-steak sandwiches greedily. After he'd washed down each big bite with a gulp of wine, he would say, "Lord, this is good grub. You're an angel, Deutsia. I'll never forget you. Maybe I'll be able to help you someday if I live to get outen this hellhole."

"We'll have to go now, Don," Deutsia said. "I'll be back to see you."

"Goodbye, Don."

"Come again, Dave."

Hand in hand we went down the stairs. Jarvis Henthorne unlocked the door, bowed to us in a friendly way and said in a very soft sweet voice, "I hope you had a pleasant visit."

"We've had a very good visit," Deutsia said. "Thank you for lettin' us in."

"It's been an interesting visit for me," I said.

"Come back again," he invited us.

"You see that mountain?" Deutsia said to me soon as we'd walked fifty yards from the jail.

"Yes."

"We're a different people, living there," she said.

"Do you live there?"

"I do. That's Sanctuary Mountain."

"How are you a different people?"

"You'll have to learn."

"Does Don Praytor live on that mountain?" I asked.

"He does."

"Is he akin to you?" I asked.

"Not any that I know, but he's one of my people. And the people that I've fed in this jail have been from that mountain. They've been my people."

I lifted my eyes again toward the mountain. From where I stood down in the valley, the topmost cliffs shouldered against the sky. They made a foundation for the roof of the sky to rest on. Sanctuary Mountain was a giant pillar of earth with a sun going down beyond its jagged backbone, dragging a shirttail of red sky behind it. I wondered if Deutsia's people on Sanctuary Mountain were feuding with the people in this valley. She'd called the mountain people "her people," and I knew there was a difference between them. If feuding was the difference, I knew the side that I would choose. I would fight for and alongside Deutsia's people to the bitter end.

"What are you thinking about, Dave?"

"About you and your people."

"Don't think too much about us."

"But your troubles are my troubles."

"Do you mean that?"

"I mean every word of it."

We walked slowly toward the courthouse where the stands had sold their sandwiches and the big lemonade churn was emptied. The older people had gone and only a few of the children remained, still playing tag around the courthouse.

"Would you like to take a walk through the courthouse?" she asked.

"Is it anything like the jail?"

"Very much like the jail. The janitor gets his money but he doesn't sweep. Someone from Sanctuary Mountain who has to pay his fine by spending time in jail does the sweeping to cut his jail sentence to half time."

"Is the janitor a valley man?"

"The people who run this county are from the valley."

"I don't care about seeing the courthouse. Wouldn't you like to go someplace outside this town?"

"I'd be glad," she said. "But how'll we go?"

"Would you mind takin' a ride with me?"

"Of course not," she replied.

"I think Ben left the key in the truck," I said. "If it's there, we'll go."

2

❧ ❧ ❧ ❧ ❧ ❧ ❧ ❧ ❧ ❧ ❧

WE HURRIED toward the truck. I
looked inside.

"Here's the key, as I'd expected," I
said, opening the truck door. "Ben always forgets and
leaves it in the truck. Climb in!"

I stepped on the starter and we were off.

"Which way does this gravel road go?" I asked.

"Twenty miles or more. It goes to Sand Suck, and
that's on the other end of Cantwell County."

"Does the road follow the Clinch River?"

"It does."

"Do you mind riding in a truck?" I asked Deutsia.

"I love to ride beside you. I'd like to ride beside you in a
joltwagon over a rough rocky road. I'd ride behind you on
muleback. I'd ride or walk with you any place."

At these words I suddenly felt better than I ever had in
my life. I stepped on the gas and we left a swirl of soup-
bean-colored dust clouds behind us.

"I like to hear you talk like that. Sit closer to me."

"All right, Dave," she said, scooting over on the seat close to me.

"Closer."

And when she hugged as close to me as she could get, I put my arm around her, pulling her as close as possible. I felt the trammels of her golden hair between her back and my arm.

The river wound alongside the road like a white wind-blown ribbon. And the thin willow leaves, now turning brown in late September, rustled in the wind. I had the road to watch, and Deutsia's face. When she looked up at me, I had to look at her blue eyes even if it were just for a second. Deutsia was helping me watch the road, too. I don't think she was afraid, even though I was driving the truck as fast as it would go on the straight stretches of road.

"Look," she said, pointing at a car coming toward us. "I'd know that car any place."

"Whose car is it?"

"Miss Fern's car."

"And I'll bet Ben's right in there beside her. You look and see. I'm going to give them our dust and make them lay over to the ditch."

I pushed the accelerator to the floorboard, held two-thirds of the road and was moving with full speed close toward Fern Hailston's car. I would've taken off a fender if she hadn't laid over in a hurry. Behind me were clouds of dust too thick for anyone to see through. They would have to wait until the dust cleared. And just as we passed Fern Hailston's car, Ben stuck his head out and yelled, "What do you mean, you fool?"

"You shouldn't do Miss Fern that way," Deutsia said as

we passed them like a shot out of a gun. "She's a good nurse. She's the only person that will climb the mountain to deliver babies for our women. Mountain paths never get too steep for her to climb and the night never gets too dark for her to go."

"I'm glad to hear that, but I didn't like the way she acted when your name was mentioned. I wondered what she had against you."

"Don't hold that against her," Deutsia said, as I let up on the accelerator. "You must forgive people for prejudices. When someone smites your cheek, turn your other cheek and let them smite it."

"When anybody smites my cheek, I'm not turning the other cheek. I'm smiting back in a hurry. That's what I've got fists for."

I slowed the truck down until we were moving along slowly, not raising any dust at the teams hitched to jolt-wagons and buggies. These teams were tired pulling their heavy loads over this gravel road from Oak Hill. We passed many people riding horseback and muleback and many animals were carrying double, a man and his wife, a man and his son, and we passed a few horses carrying two lovers.

"When will we reach Sand Suck?"

"Just around this curve and we are there."

"What kind of a place is it?"

"A very pretty place," she said. "There's a store, post office, and four houses. Two houses are on this side of the Clinch and two are at the other end of the swinging bridge that spans the river."

Just as she finished talking we rounded the curve.

"You certainly told the truth," I said, bringing the

truck to a stop in front of the store. "This place looks like a picture in a storybook."

There was a car parked in front of the store, two bare-backed mules tied to the low-hanging limbs of a sweet gum tree and a good-looking saddle horse reined to a post of the store porch. Several old men were spitting ambeer across the porch onto the storeyard grass that was worn and trampled by feet of men and beasts. On the left of the store was a high wall of cliffs and above the cliffs a massive growth of timber slanted toward the evening sky. Pine tops were etched so closely against the sky that their green spars jabbed into its blue.

On the other side of the road was the swinging bridge built from twin sycamores on our side of the river to twin water birches on the other side. Heavy cables were wrapped midway around these trees, and small wire cables were wrapped around the big cables and dropped down to support a plank walk. There was a ladder built up on each end of this bridge. We watched a small girl climb up, then walk over the rocking, creaking bridge and climb down the ladder on our side. Beyond the river were two white cottages, not far apart, nestled under a grove of tall pines.

"This is the prettiest place I've ever seen. I wonder why it's called Sand Suck."

"Because of a swirl hole under the twin sycamores," Deutsia said. "Three men have been drowned in that swirl hole."

"Sand Suck's the wrong name for a place as pretty as this. But we won't bother to change it now."

"Never mind, you won't change the name even if you wanted to," she said. "Not many things change here."

"Are you getting hungry?"

"A little."

"Can't we buy something to eat in the store?"

"Sardines, crackers, cookies, potted ham and cheese," she replied.

"Would you like a supper in this country store?"

"I'd love it."

"Then we eat."

What is better than to eat in a country store where the old men whittle shavings and the customers come for groceries and ask for mail any hour of the night? I thought. This was the life I loved. I'd eaten at many country stores and I couldn't remember ever getting a meal that didn't satisfy me.

I slammed my door shut and walked around and opened her door and lifted her from the truck. We walked across the yard to the porch, past the old men whittling and spitting ambeer, talking about the weather and politics.

"He's been in there eight long years," I heard one old man say as we passed, "and now he's astin' fer four more long years."

The store was filled with people bartering their products for groceries, spices, clothes, cloth, hardware implements and tobacco. They were filling their baskets with store goods after they had emptied them of vegetables and produce. After each one was through with his trading he would ask if there was a letter for him. We waited our turn and the old man with spectacles low on his nose came over and asked, "What might you folks have?"

"Sardines, potted ham, can of salmon, crackers, brown sugar and a can of peaches," I said.

"A nice supper," the old man said with a toothless grin.

He got our order, opened the cans for us and placed

them on the top of a salt barrel. And then he found us two spoons.

"We don't have dishes fer ye," he said. "Ye'll both haf to eat outen the same cans. Ye won't mind, will ye?"

And then he cackled like a guinea rooster.

"No, we won't mind," Deutsia said.

We had to stand beside the barrel, since there weren't any chairs. But that was all right. I could look across at Deutsia and she could look at me. And I wondered if she saw as much in me as I saw in her sweet face, her golden hair, her fine curved lips, her pretty white teeth and eyes and her tall, shapely body.

"This is a good supper," Deutsia said.

"It tastes good to me, too."

"I'm glad you like it, children," the old man said.

The people in the store watched us while they bartered with the clerks. But we didn't have time to watch the people. We were watching each other as if it were the last time that we would be together. But neither of us, I'm sure, had any such thought, for this was an afternoon and an evening of joy, love and happiness for us, such as I had never known before.

When Deutsia ate sardines from the can, I ate sardines from the can with her. When she dipped her spoon into the salmon can I dipped my spoon into the can beside hers. People watching us laughed and I heard an old woman say in a loud whisper, "Just a young pair of fools. Wait until she gets older and bears as many youngins as I have and hoes as much corn and terbacker, and she won't be as pretty as an angel then. She'll know the price of love. And when he works as many years and as hard as my old man, he won't look like he does now."

"You're right, Martha," replied the bent old woman she was whispering to. "Time will bend 'em over like sleet bends a winter tree, and change the color of their hair as frost changes the color of the grass."

We didn't worry about the corn, tobacco, hard work, child-bearing, or Time. Deutsia winked at me as we listened to their loud whispers. We had finished the salmon, the sardines, the potted ham and we were eating our dessert. We put brown sugar on the crackers and ate them with the peaches. We must've been hungry, for we didn't leave anything.

"What a wonderful supper!" Deutsia said.

"I'm glad you liked it."

"I don't want to rush you away from here," Deutsia said. "But I wonder if your friend Ben is thinkin' we're wrecked some place."

"I don't care what he's thinking," I said. "I'm having the best time I've ever had in my life."

We left the store and walked across the storeyard to the truck, where we stood a minute and looked at the stars in the sky. There were thousands of stars but no moon. A cool September wind was rustling the turning leaves in the sycamore tops above us. It made a mournful sound, something like the lonesome singing of insects in a dew-covered cornfield on an August night.

I drove slowly all the way back and there was silence between us. I wanted the distance back to Oak Hill to be more than twenty miles. I wanted to drive and drive through the night beneath the stars with her beside me.

"I'm goin' to walk you home," I said to Deutsia when we got back to Oak Hill.

"But Ben will soon be back to the truck. He'll wonder where you've gone."

"Let him wonder."

"He's liable to drive off and leave you."

"Then I can walk home."

"It'll be tomorrow morning before you get back."

"Tomorrow is Sunday and I don't mind."

"How many miles is it to your shanty?"

"Sixteen or seventeen."

"That's some walk."

"But how far do you have to walk?" I asked her.

"Just two or three miles," she said. "Maybe four."

"Do you plan to walk home alone?"

"I've walked home alone many times."

"But you won't tonight," I said. "Aren't you afraid to walk these mountain paths at night alone when there's no moon?"

"Afraid of what?"

"Afraid you might step on a rattlesnake?"

"A rattlesnake warns before he strikes."

"You might not hear its warning."

"Yes, I would," she said. "I've never failed yet."

"What about a man?"

"I'm not afraid of a man," she said. "I can outrun any man I've seen yet."

"But I'm going to take you home anyway."

I didn't want to miss walking along a mountain path with Deutsia, where the road would be narrow and where we would have to walk as close together as two people can walk.

"You can go part of the way."

We left Oak Hill and soon as we reached the mountain path I put my arm around her and she put her arm around me gently. And the warmth and touch of her soft hand ran through me like a mild shock of electricity. If there had never been a current of electricity in Cantwell County, there was one now.

The farther we walked the steeper the path became. My wind became short. We stopped and rested long enough for me to catch my breath but Deutsia never tired. The path was crooked and dimly lighted by the mountain stars whose little rays of light filtered through small spaces between the brown September leaves and the pine needles.

"Deutsia, you know I'm in love with you. I swear it by the stars in the sky: I love you more than any woman I've ever seen."

She didn't answer me. She remained silent until we reached a ledge of stone where steps had been chiseled.

"This is as far as you'd better go," she said.

"Why can't I go on?"

"I'm afraid you couldn't find your way back. The steps on this cliff are hard to climb down on a dark night if you're not used to them. There are two more ledges above here."

"But how much farther do you have to go?"

"We've come about a third of the way."

"But I must go on with you. You can't go on home alone."

"I've done it a thousand times before. Why not tonight?"

"But I want to go on with you."

"This is as far as you can go." Her words were positive, and I agreed to let her go the rest of the way alone.

Slowly, I pressed my lips to hers and held them there, feeling her warm body against mine and her firm breasts against me.

"I love you," I said as our lips parted. "When can I see you again?"

"Saturday in Oak Hill at the same place you found me today," she said.

"All right," I said, pulling her close against me again and kissing her tenderly.

"Goodnight," I said, watching her climb the cliff.

"Goodnight." And she was soon lost from sight. I stood a minute alone looking at the turn of the trail where she had disappeared.

When I started down the mountain path that we had come I knew what she meant about climbing the mountain. It was hard for me to find my way; it was hard for me to walk without stumbling over the rocks. As we'd come up the mountain path together we'd not stumbled over a rock. I wondered if she hadn't traveled this path so many times that she knew where each rock was.

When I finally reached Oak Hill, I found Ben waiting beside the truck.

"What in the hell happened to you?" Ben asked me. "Where've you been all this time?"

"I've been to take Deutsia home."

"How far did you take her?"

"A third of the way."

"What time would you've got here if you'd taken her all the way home? It's three o'clock in the mornin' now. I've been waitin' here for you since midnight."

"I didn't know it was that late."

"It starts gettin' late at eleven o'clock when you're out with a girl," he said.

"The time passed too fast for us."

"It surely did," he said, getting in the truck, starting the motor, switching on the lights. "Where did you take this truck today?"

"Why do I have to tell you that?" I asked.

"You passed us like a bat outen hell," he said. "You nearly scared Fern to death. We thought you's goin' to take a fender off Fern's car. You left a cloud of dust thick as pea soup behind you. We had to wait five minutes for it to clear so we could see the road. A lumber truck is not made to date in."

"It's wonderful to date in," I said.

"Look at that gas," Ben said, looking at the gauge. "It's really low."

"I'm sorry about the gas, Ben."

"Get my cigarettes from my shirt pocket and light one for me."

I lifted the cigarette pack from his shirt pocket, lit one and stuck it between his lips.

"Have a cigarette, Dave."

"Thanks, Ben, but I'll smoke my pipe."

Ben looked at the graveled road ahead, pulling on his cigarette and exhaling twin clouds of smoke from his nostrils. I smoked my pipe and thought about Deutsia.

"Did you have a good time yesterday?" Ben asked me, breaking our silence.

"Never had a better time in my life."

"Are you telling me the truth?"

"I wouldn't lie to you."

"You must be in love with that gal."

"I am."

There was silence as we left the graveled highway for the WPA road. "Did you have a good time today?"

"Wonderful," he said.

"I guess you're in love, too, then."

"I am."

"You're lucky to have a girl with a car."

"Lucky to have a girl with a car? I'm lucky to have a girl with good stock in her."

"What do you mean by good stock?"

"When you buy cattle and hogs you don't buy scrub stock, do you?" he said, steering the truck from the WPA road to the mountain road we'd made to our shanty.

"But what has stock got to do with a girl?" I said, laughing at Ben's ideas about women.

"Don't fall in love with that Huntoon gal, Dave," Ben said pleadingly.

"I'm already in love with her. I love her more than any woman I've ever seen."

"You'd better lay offen that gal," Ben warned me. "I'm your friend. I'm putting you wise."

"But I'm in love with her. You'd only see her once you'd know why I'm in love with her."

"You'd better forget 'er," Ben warned me. "I'm tellin' you."

"You don't say so!" I said, smarting at his advice.

"That's exactly what I say," Ben snarled, as he steered quickly to miss a stump. "Other men have fallen in love with Deutsia before you. They had to break away."

"What in hell's this all about?" I asked Ben. "Tell me; I'm ready to listen. What's wrong with Deutsia? What's your friend Fern Hailston been feeding you about Deutsia?"

"Leave Fern outen this."

"Why should I leave her out? I could tell something was wrong by the way she acted in Little Tavern when Deutsia's name was mentioned."

"You have Fern all wrong."

"The hell I have. I've been able to do a little figuring myself. This county is divided between the valley people and the people that live up on Sanctuary Mountain. The valley people don't like the mountain people. Deutsia is a mountain girl. And she's beautiful. Fern Hailston knows she's a hell of a lot better-looking than she is. She's jealous, that's all."

"The people on the mountain and in the valley are divided, all right," Ben said. "But Fern's not jealous of Deutsia. She feels sorry for her."

"That's too bad," I said. "When it comes to looks Deutsia should feel sorry for Fern."

"Don't compare Fern with Deutsia," Ben said, his voice hard. "You'd better lay off that Deutsia Huntoon!"

"I'm not laying off," I said.

"Have it your own way. You'll live and learn."

Ben stopped the truck at the beginning of the steep bluff road.

"Since our gas is low we'd better park here and walk the rest of the way," Ben said. He was glad to change the subject. "By coastin' offen the mountain we've got enough gas to take us back to town."

We walked silently side by side up the steep bluff until we came to the cliffs where we turned left toward the shanty.

"Hezzy's got a fire in the stove to get breakfast."

I saw the yellow glow of lamplight through the shanty window.

3

𐂃𐂃𐂃𐂃𐂃𐂃𐂃𐂃𐂃𐂃𐂃𐂃𐂃𐂃𐂃

W HERE'n the hell you fellars been?"
Hezzy asked, staggering toward us as
we entered the shanty. "Nice time o'
mornin' to be a-gettin' in!"

"Oak Hill to see our girls," Ben told him.

"Sparkin' late, or is it early?" he said, with a wild laugh.

"Where'd you get your licker?" I asked Hezzy.

"Ast my ole pal over there," Hezzy said, pointing to
Mort. "He was with me. He can tell ye."

"Honey means money on the mountains," Hezzy sang
over and over.

Mort was sitting on his bunk with a gallon jug of licker
between his legs. The jug was white with a brown neck
and it was stoppered with a corncob. He sat leaning forward, with his head to one side toward the jug. The drool
that was running from one corner of his mouth barely
missed the jug.

"It's a great country here," Mort said. "We went out to

find a wild bee tree and here's what we found. Better'n any
wild honey ye ever put to your lips."

"Out to see a couple of gals, huh?" Hezzy said, looking
at Ben with watery eyes, his mouth open. "Ye fellars
oughta been with us and had fun with your old pals!"

Mort Higgins and Hezzy Blair had been cutting timber
seven years ago when Ben and I joined them. We made two
teams—Mort and Hezzy, Ben and I. We'd finished nine
tracts of timber for the Wilson-McCoy Lumber Company
and this one, called the Big Woods, would be our tenth
job. When Ben and I'd gone to the nearby towns and
found girls to date, Mort and Hezzy would squirrel-hunt in
the timber tracts where we were working; they would fox-
hunt, rabbit-hunt and trap. And in the early autumn days
they hunted for wild bee trees, since they were rich with
honey when the blossom season was over. Never had there
been a time that I could remember in the seven years we
had worked together that we didn't have wild honey and
wild meat on our table. Very often, Mort and Hezzy got a
jug of moonshine and got drunk together. They would get
drunk on Saturday night, sober up on Sunday and be fit
to use the ax, saw, wedge and sledge on Monday morning.

Mort and Hezzy could cut more timber than any two
lumberjacks I'd ever known. Hezzy was short with a bull
neck, a heavily bearded face, knotty-muscled arms and
powerful muscled legs so large he couldn't find boots to fit
them. His shoulders were as broad as the shanty door and
his gnarled, calloused hands looked like small fire shovels.
Mort was taller than Hezzy. He was well over six feet tall
with broad shoulders, long muscular arms and slender but
powerful legs.

"I found the bees a-waterin' yesterday morning," Mort said, keeping his eyes on the jug, "in that poplar cove where the water falls over the high cliff, and I hurried back and told Hezzy. And we went to find the tree.

"Coursed them to the mountaintop and found 'em in a snaggled-topped black oak," Mort said. "After we found the bee tree, we walked out a ridge path until we come to a shack. There was a little skinny man standin' in the yard and he invited us in."

"Mort and I went inside and we saw the biggest woman we've ever seen in our life," Hezzy said. "Sylvania was her name, and she was Skinny's wife. 'Did you boys come for a drink?' she ast us. 'We wouldn't mind a snort of good licker,' Mort told her. 'Draw 'em a drink, Skinny,' she said. So Skinny walks over, takes a gourd from a nail on the wall, pulls the plug outen the bunghole and draws Mort a gourd of licker. 'Good stuff,' Mort says. 'Try a gourd of it, Hezzy!' Then Skinny drawed me a gourd. And it tastes better'n honey to me. 'It's wonderful,' I said to 'em. 'I can taste it all the way down.' 'We sell it here,' Skinny says. 'How much a gallon?' Mort asks. 'Three dollars a gallon,' Skinny says."

" 'We don't have the money,' says I," Mort said, breaking in on Hezzy's story. " 'We'll take it in trade,' Sylvania says. 'See what we take in trade.' And she pointed to shotguns leaned against the wall, pistols hangin' on nails, shovels, pitchforks, mattocks, spades, hoes, double-bitted axes, broadaxes, crosscut saws, handsaws, picks, augers, braces and bits, mule harness, bridles, stoves, dishes, meal, flour, spices, even to sacks of corn and beans. And then I says, 'Would you trade us a gallon of this licker right from the bunghole of th' barrel for a bee tree we've just found?'

Skinny looks at Sylvania and she looked at 'im. I didn't see either of 'em wink. I don't know how they understood each other. But Sylvania says, 'Sure we'll trade you a gallon for a wild bee tree in the woods.' So this is how we got our corn licker."

"Sanctuary Mountain, they call it back there," Hezzy said.

"How do you get to Sanctuary Mountain from here?" I asked.

"Go to the top of this mountain and out the ridge apast where th' deep hollow cuts into the mountain flank from the ridge to the valley," Hezzy said. "Sanctuary Mountain is on t' other side of that hollow."

"Wonder how Sylvania gets by with the law?" I said. "I saw a man in Cantwell County jail from this mountain yesterday. He was jailed because the sheriff found a half pint on 'im."

"Sheriff can arrest Sylvania all he pleases," Hezzy said. "But he couldn't get her outen the shack. Skinny said his wife hadn't been outside his shack fer twenty years. Said she couldn't get through the door."

"And if she did get through the door," Mort said, "they couldn't get 'er down offen the mountain."

"You're drunk and dreaming, Hezzy," Ben said.

"I never get too drunk to know what I'm sayin', Ben," Hezzy told him. "You know I never lose my head. I'm tellin' 'em the truth, ain't I, pal?"

"You're mighty right," Mort said.

"We've found a fountain that will never run dry," Hezzy said.

Hezzy walked over, picked up the jug from between Mort's legs, held it to his lips and took four long swigs.

Each time he swigged his Adam's apple worked up and down in his throat like a tree frog scaling over sun-parched bark.

"Did you see the shacks around that ridge after you left the Big Woods?" I asked Hezzy.

"Saw all kinds of little shacks with clearin's around 'em stuck back among th' shaggy pines and tough-butted white oaks," he replied. "It's the strangest country I ever put my peepers on."

"This mountaintop is a world of its own after you leave the Big Woods," Mort said.

It must be Deutsia's world, I thought as I climbed upon my bunk to sleep. Someday I'll go to see her Sanctuary Mountain and her people.

As I lay on my bunk waiting for sleep to come, I thought over the years we had all worked and lived together. Tonight for the first time there was a feeling of tension in our shanty. There had always been good will among the four of us. And long before we had worked together, Ben and I had been friends. We were born on adjoining farms in Wise County, Virginia, and we had attended the one-room Knob Hill School together. We were classmates through all eight grades. We had slept together as boys at his home and at my home. We had hunted together, played baseball together and we had worked together. We had had double dates together when we worked in North Carolina, Virginia and now Tennessee. And this was the first time anything had ever come between us.

What has come over Ben? I wondered after we had gone to bed. First time in his life he has ever told me not to go with a girl! What's eating him? He's getting too big for his breeches!

I didn't like to think of Ben this way. If I'd ever had a friend on earth I thought that he was Ben Dewberry. Back when we were teenage boys and I was double-teamed at a pie social one night at the Knob Hill School, the only one of my classmates who stepped up to help me when I faced three men my size was Ben. Ben and I cleaned out these ruffians who had come in from Tate's Valley to wreck our pie social. Ben was a powerful man with his fists but he'd never used them unless he had to.

And one time when we were cutting timber on the mountain near Culowee, North Carolina, we went to Culowee one Saturday night to a square dance. It was a dancehall and we didn't know anybody. We asked the girls to dance since they liked us and they were friendly. But the young men weren't very friendly when a couple of woodchoppers came in and took their girls. One man started a fight with me and I floored him and kept on danc-ing. About this time, another man ran in and Ben gave him a punch in the jaw and he sprawled on the floor. Two of his pals dragged him off the floor while three more came after me. I took care of one with one lick and Ben took care of the other two. He had never stopped dancing. We danced on until after midnight, met a lot of people and made a lot of friends. That crowd of fellows soon learned we weren't the running kind. And I thought Daisy Martin, the girl I danced with that night, was beautiful. Ben encouraged me to go with her. But when the timber cutting was over in North Carolina we went to another job in Lee County, Virginia.

In Lee County, something happened that made me be-lieve until tonight Ben Dewberry was the best friend I'd ever had in my life. Ben and I were cutting the last stand of big yellow poplars on the south slope of Cumberland

Mountains that faced Powell's Valley. We had been especially chosen to cut those big valuable trees, since we were
strong young men and experienced timber cutters. If one
of the trees grew in a deep ravine near a stream, or if we
notched it close to the ground and sawed it down low, it
would fall over a high bank. That would splinter the long
heavy log, which was four to six feet in diameter and fifty
to seventy feet of body up to the first limb. So it was worth
all the precaution we could take to fell the tree without splintering its valuable body. Here is how we did it. If
smaller trees grew around one of these huge poplars, we
climbed up and built scaffolds on either side. If there were
no trees, we cut poles and built scaffolds. Then we climbed
up on our scaffolds and cut the top part of the big tree off
first. Later we sawed the bottom part of the tree down.

Once when we had scaffolded up thirty feet high to cut
a giant poplar, it didn't fall the way we had notched it. The
upper part of the tree fell against an oak, almost as large as
the poplar we had cut, and there it lodged. I was caught between the poplar log and the tree to which my scaffold was
attached. I was hurt and almost crushed, as the log of the
poplar gradually gave way when the winds blew the oak. I
would have been crushed to death had it not been for Ben
Dewberry. He scaled down the tree on the side where he
had his platform built. He climbed the tree to which my
platform was attached with his ax strapped on his body.
Then he put his legs around the scaffold tree below me,
crossed his legs and held for dear life while he used both
hands to chop the scaffold tree down and free me. Ben
Dewberry had been more than a boyhood friend of mine.
He had saved my life once.

And now what has happened to Ben Dewberry? I

thought. Why was he trying to tell me not to date Deutsia Huntoon, the prettiest woman I had ever met in my life? Then I remembered what my father once told me about bulls and men. It was after he had barely missed being gored by a four-year-old bull he had always trusted because he would follow him like a pet dog. Then for no reason this bull turned on my father without warning. My father said he could never trust a mule and now he couldn't trust a bull any longer. And I wondered if men couldn't be included. If I couldn't trust Ben Dewberry, I couldn't trust any man. I was getting to the place I wanted to fight the best friend I'd ever had on earth, because he had interfered with the love of my life, Deutsia Huntoon.

These thoughts kept whirling about in my mind. Finally, I drifted off to sleep.

4

·············

WHEN I awoke it was midafternoon. My dinner was waiting for me on the table, and a pot of coffee had been left on the stove to keep warm. Hezzy was still asleep, for he couldn't sober as quickly as Mort. Mort could get limber-drunk, sleep three hours, get up and wash his wrists, neck, face and wet the back of his head in cold water and come to life. Though it wasn't Mort's day to do the cooking, he'd sobered and cooked dinner for us and now was out in the yard filing his double-bitted ax while Ben was filing our crosscut saw and putting set in its teeth.

As I sat eating corndodger bread, fried squirrel, brown squirrel gravy and mashed potatoes, I thought of the morning when we loaded our truck with work clothes, Sunday clothes, dishes, pots, pans, silverware, cookstove, and other necessities we'd need in a shanty. Then we covered our supplies with a tarpaulin. Hezzy and I rode on the tarpaulin while Mort sat beside Ben in the cab.

That was in early August. We'd had a month's rest after finishing cutting a timber tract on Blue Mountain in Virginia. While I was resting at home, I'd gone to see Bonnie Applegate two nights a week and on Sundays. She didn't excite me a lot but I thought that I loved her enough to marry her. Little did I think then that we would cross the mountain into Cantwell County, where I would meet a girl I loved at first sight.

The road we traveled was the only one that led to the pocket of mountain world where we had come to build our shanty. We had to get ready to start cutting timber by the time the September winds began to shear the oaks of their leaves. We had seldom cut timber when it was green unless it had been a rushed job, for the massive green leaves made it a smothery world in which to work. From September until late March were the good months for timber cutting.

When we reached Cantwell County, we asked Lawyer Ott Simmons to show us the Big Woods timber tract and its boundaries. He stood on the street in Oak Hill, looked through his specs toward the mountains and pointed with his skinny hand as he talked. The south boundary was the road we'd just driven over, the north boundary was the mountain ridge and the east boundary was the deep hollow that split the Big Woods from Sanctuary Mountain. The west boundary was a small stream that flowed from the ridge down to the Clinch River. Lawyer Ott Simmons was paid by the Lawson-McCoy Lumber Company to watch over this timber tract and to protect the company's rights.

That afternoon we drove the truck back over the gravel road the way we'd come a few miles and then turned to the WPA road and drove as far as we could. There we parked the truck and walked up on the mountain to a place at about the center of Big Woods.

"Let's find as level a spot as we can near a mountain spring," Mort said.

Against a backdrop of a high wall of cliff that would serve as a barrier to the northern winds, we found a place to build our shanty. Nearby was a spring where a stream of cool water as big as Hezzy's forearm gushed from a crevice to a natural basin worn into the rock below.

"This is the place," Mort said.

For once all of us agreed. It took two weeks to clear a road of trees and brush and roll the rocks away from where we'd parked the truck to the spot we had selected for our shanty. We slept in the truck bed at night and when it rained we spread the tarpaulin over us. We set up our stove and cooked under the pines. As soon as the road was finished, we drove the truck up to the cabin site with all of our supplies.

It didn't take us long to build the shanty. We did a good job of it. Mort and Hezzy cut the shanty logs, scored and hewed them while Ben and I found a broad tree, cut and bolted the tree and rived enough clapboards to roof the little house. In two weeks we'd built our shanty, floored and shingled it. All we had to do was build a rough stone chimney with a small fireplace for the room and a flue for the lean-to that we used as a kitchen. Water was close, and we dug a hole and mixed water and clay, made a thick mud and daubed the cracks. While Mort, Hezzy and Ben did that, I put the windows in our shanty and built two bunks on each side of the cabin wall, one above the other. We were ready for winter.

Hezzy slept on the bottom bunk and Mort slept above him on their side of the shanty. And Ben slept on the bottom bunk and I slept above him on our side of the shanty.

Each man kept his clothes in his own trunk, and his tools in his own kit. And each man washed his clothes, did his sewing and sharpened his ax. But Mort did the cooking one day and Hezzy the next; Ben washed the dishes and swept the cabin, and it was my job to carry water from the spring and to cut wood for the stove. As soon as I'd finished my dinner and had eaten a dessert of wild honey with biscuit, washing it down with hot black coffee, I walked out into the cool September wind with two water buckets. I went to the spring to get water for the night. When I'd brought it up I took my ax into the woods, cut a powder-dry dead locust and chopped it into stovewood lengths. My work was done and I was ready for bed, for tomorrow we would start working on the biggest job we'd ever had.

Monday morning, after we'd eaten breakfast, we washed the dishes, swept the shanty, gathered our tools and waited for daylight. As soon as enough light streaked from the east for us to see, we climbed the mountain with our tools to the northern boundary and there we began our work. While Ben notched one white oak, I notched another. Our teamwork was perfect. But we'd never been able to cut as many feet of lumber in a day as Mort and Hezzy.

"We're in the money now," Ben said, holding his ax with one hand and wiping sweat from his brown face with his big blue bandanna. "I'm not only going to work but I'm a-goin' to save. I'm holding me back a little nest egg."

"You've had a change of heart, Ben," I said, picking up my end of the crosscut saw, getting down on my knees on the opposite side of the oak from Ben. "You've been spending all you've made."

"I expect to be livin' down in that valley one of these days," Ben said. "I expect to own a farm down there."

From where we were on our knees pulling the saw, we could look down into the valley. It looked far away to us now, miles beneath us, for we were working on the mountain crest.

"The valley land is good enough," I said.

"I'll have a good setup there," Ben said. "I can farm during summer and cut timber in the fall and winter."

"So you've made your plans?"

"I've made them in my head."

"I'll be living on this mountain."

A puff of wind came and our tree started snapping, then lumbering to the earth with a great swish in the direction of the blowing wind.

"It will be a rough life up here, fellow," Ben said.

"But that's my choice."

"Then you've made your plans?" Ben asked. We carried our crosscut saw over to the tree he had notched.

"I don't do much planning, Ben. I just let my heart be my guide."

We didn't say anything more about our plans or mention the names of our girls. I knew how he felt about Deutsia and how I felt about Fern. It will be better if we work together as we have in days past, I thought, and talk about the things we used to.

While Ben trimmed the limbs from one white oak, I trimmed the other. And we raced against each other, each trying to trim his tree first. That was the way we worked together. As soon as we had sheared the trees of their limbs, we sawed the trees into logs.

Neither of us mentioned our girls' names all day. Late

that afternoon when we saw the sun sink beyond the range
to the west, we measured the logs we had cut. We had cut
sixteen thousand feet of white oak timber. That was a good
day's work, and good pay for us, eight dollars each.

All week we worked, laughed and talked about hunting, fishing, and the good times we had had together. Never
once did Ben mention Fern and Deutsia, and neither
did I, but a lot of thoughts went through my mind. After a
hard day with the ax and crosscut saw, I would go to bed
and just lie there on my bunk and think pleasant thoughts
of Deutsia. And when I'd go to sleep, I would dream of
her.

"We've cut a hundred thousand feet of white oak this
week," Ben said on Saturday at noon, as he measured the
last logs we'd cut. "I don't mind knocking off early with
this load. Fifty bucks apiece for a week's work! Think of
it!"

"That's good going," I said. "Mort and Hezzy won't
beat us much this week."

"They had a hundred thousand feet when they began
work this morning."

"Before you move to a farm in the valley we'll beat
'em," I said, as we walked toward the shanty with our tools.

We ate our dinner, did our shanty chores, then each of
us got his shaving mug, brush, razor and pan of hot water
and stood before his own little mirror on the wall by his
bunk. We hadn't shaved all week; we'd let our beards grow
and our faces rest. I hurried so I could be first to the "bathtub," a waist-deep hole of cold mountain water in the
stream nearby.

As soon as I'd finished shaving, I hurried to the bathtub,
jumped into water so cold it nearly took my breath, soaped

myself and bathed my body. The cold water, once I was in it, felt good. Before I was finished Ben was with me waiting for the tub.

"Gettin' all set for a big date in Oak Hill?" Mort asked. He had come to take the tub over as soon as Ben'd finished.

"Yep. I'm goin' to Oak Hill to see her," I said.

"Hezzy and I have a date with Sylvania."

"Have a good time, fellows," Hezzy yelled at us. "Kiss 'em both for me."

"We don't have money," Mort yelled. "But we've found two more bee trees. Two more gallons."

"Married men have as much fun as single fellows," Ben said.

"Where do we go from here?" I asked Ben, as we parked the sputtering truck under the shade of a maple.

"I don't know where you're goin'," Ben said, "but I'm going to Fern Hailston's home as fast as I can."

"That's right," I said. "You go to one end of town and I go to the other."

Ben sat in silence and stared at me as I got out of the truck.

"Don't forget to put some gas in the truck," I said. "It's empty. And I'll be wanting to ride back with you tonight."

"I won't forget."

"And don't forget to put the key in your pocket," I said, sarcastically. "Somebody might drive it off. It's a bad habit to leave the key in the truck in this modern world."

As I walked down the dusty street, I noticed that many of the people stopped and looked at me. I wondered if they stared because I was a stranger.

"He's a nice-looking man to fall in love with Deutsia

Huntoon," I heard one old woman with a basket of groceries in her hand say to another in a loud whisper.

I thought I might say something, but I kept on going toward the courthouse as fast as I could. I was thinking of Deutsia and that I would soon be near her. I knew that she would be there.

5

ᵐᵐᵐᵐᵐᵐᵐᵐᵐᵐ

AS SOON as I saw the crowd that Deutsia had called her own people gathered around the courthouse, my eyes began to search for her. No one noticed me in this crowd, for they were too busy eating, laughing and talking.

If you ever want to see the best-looking girls in Oak Hill, never go to the Little Tavern but to the courthouse. Here you will find the tall, straight girls, dark-complexioned, light-complexioned, girls with charcoal-black straight hair and charcoal-black wavy hair, girls with long ripened-wheatstraw-colored hair and long October-poplar-leaf-golden hair, girls with shapely bodies, small waists, thin ankles, and long hands with fingers that taper like marigolds. But among those girls you will never find one as pretty as Deutsia. Suddenly, there she was.

"Where did you come from?"

"I've been beside you for a minute," Deutsia said.

"I've been searching the crowd for you."

"You've been looking at the other girls, too," she whispered.

"But none are as pretty as you."

"What would you like to do?"

"I'd like to see a show, wouldn't you?"

"But I don't go to the theater," she sighed. "I don't like the balcony seats."

"We won't get the balcony seats," I said. "We will get the best seats."

"We can't get the best seats," she said.

"Why not?"

"They are for the valley people."

"Then we won't go."

"I know something we can do," Deutsia said. "You may not want to do it."

"Anything you like."

"I know where some bees are watering," she said. "Would you like to go with me and find the bee tree?"

Deutsia put her hand in mine and we were off toward the path that wound down from the mountain into the town.

"It's halfway up the mountain," she said.

"I don't mind if we climb to the top of the mountain."

This is the first time I've ever gone with a girl to the mountains to hunt a bee tree, I thought. I'd always hunted bee trees with the lumberjacks. But this is Deutsia's idea of a good time. She has lived her life on Sanctuary Mountain. She loves it.

"I found these bees watering last Sunday," she said. "I could've coursed 'em to their tree but I thought of you."

"I'm glad you waited for us to hunt the tree together."

"Did you ever find a bee tree?"

"I've found many bee trees in my time."

"Do you like to hunt bees?"

"There's not but one thing I'd rather do."

"What's that?"

"Love you."

Now we reached the mountain path that wound like a wild grapevine around the mountainside, first going in one direction and then the other.

"This looks familiar," I said.

"It ought to look familiar. You came this way last Saturday night with me."

We put our arms around each other and slowly climbed the path toward the overhanging cliffs.

"I've climbed mountain paths all my life," I said. I stopped to catch my second breath. "But this is one of the steepest paths I've ever climbed."

"You did better the other night."

"It was in the starlight and I couldn't see where I was going."

While I filled my pipe, Deutsia pulled a goldenrod growing from the thin earth that covered a rock.

"I'm afraid one of those rocks up there might break loose and roll down on us," I said.

"I've been walking up and down this path all my life," she said. "If one's broken loose I don't know it. My brothers would know if one had, because they hunt over almost every foot of this mountain."

That was the first time Deutsia had mentioned her family.

"Are you ready to go again?"

"I'm ready."

My getting short of breath made me wonder what Deutsia thought of me. Here I was a timber cutter with

strong bulging muscles and good wind and she, a slender
woman, could beat me climbing a mountain. We stopped
to kiss many times as we walked along. I wondered if
Deutsia thought I was finding an excuse to stop to catch
my breath. It was tough climbing for me, but to kiss her I
would have been willing to climb a steeper path.

"Over there's where the bees water," Deutsia said. She
pointed to a little spring made by a small trickle of water
falling over a rock.

"Which way do we go from the spring?"

"They go east," she said, pointing.

"How do you know it's east?"

"By the sunrise."

"Now we'll find a bee tree," I said. "The sun will soon
be just right."

"An evening sun is better," she said. "But by the time
we get through coursin' 'em we'll have an evening sun."

We left the path, walked over to the pool where we
stood in silence until a bee buzzed past our heads, circled a
few times, then alighted near the water. We watched him
ease down to a sun-warmed spot of water-soaked sand and
there he drank. And when he arose, he circled slowly in the
air until he got his direction, which was opposite the sun,
and then made a straight line around the mountainside and
over a finger of mountain. He passed just over the top of a
tall pine, his tiny body between us and a white cloud.

"Let's go," Deutsia said, pulling me by the hand.

We made our way through the huckleberry vines,
sawbriars, wild snowballs and wild gooseberry vines.

"The greenbriars are rough on your bare legs," I said.

"Oh, I don't mind the briars. You'll be surprised at the
few briar scratches that I get."

We hurried to the pine tree on the finger of the mountain. Beyond this pine tree was a deep hollow in the mountain's flank and beyond this hollow was another long jutted finger of mountain.

"I hope the bees don't go to that far finger over there," I said.

"That's about where they will go."

We stood under the tall pine searching the bright air overhead for a bee flying straight to his home.

"Looks like they could find water closer."

"You don't know bees," Deutsia said. "They can find water closer but bees must find a place they like to drink, where they can drink the warm water from the soft earth or sand. Such places are few on this mountain. They must find a place where it is easy for them to come up from the ground with a load of water. I've found bees watering down in Clinch River sand and coursed them to the top of Sanctuary Mountain."

"There, see that bee," I said. I was sighting a bee between a white cloud and me. "Watch him!"

"I see him."

"Do you still see him?" I asked her after I'd lost sight.

"Yes."

"Now do you see him?" I asked after seconds had passed.

"Yes."

I looked the way she was watching but all I could see was the bright nothingness of wind between the two fingers of mountain over the deep hollow below.

"I still see a speck," she said. "Now he's gone from sight."

"Where did he go?"

"I'm afraid the bee tree is where you don't want it to be."

"Across that hollow?" I asked.

"That's where he went," she said. "I followed him beyond the hollow and lost him in the timber's shadows. Follow me. I know the way."

I followed Deutsia from one fox path to another. Though I had spent my life in the woods, I was not as clever at finding paths nor was I as quick as Deutsia. She could run like a fox and her breath never faltered. Now there were little beads of sweat on her face that glistened when the sun filtered its way through the massive leaves and vines to shine on her. Deutsia was in her mountain heaven. She talked more and laughed at everything. The dry brown white-oak leaves crunched beneath our feet and the wild grapevine leaves shimmered to the ground as we shook the strands of vines across our fox paths. Leaves, red, golden and scarlet sourwood, little thin silvered beech, light ash, red sumac, and ripe blood-red sweet gum, drifted down like many-colored raindrops with each gust of wind. The air was fragrant with the smell of early autumn leaves, ripe pawpaws, persimmons and wild grapes. It was good to breathe.

"Now we have the evening sun."

"But where is the place we're to watch for the bees?" I asked.

"Right here."

"Tell me how you know."

"See the dead top of that ash?"

"Yes."

"I lost sight of the bee there. He went into these shadows."

I stood beside her beneath the tall timber and watched above the dead ash top.

"Honey bees will look almost as large as bumblebees

now," she said. And for a while we watched and waited.

"Look, I see one," she said, pointing in the air above us. "See it?"

"Yes."

We watched it disappear among the shadows.

"See how fast he flies," Deutsia said. "That means he's close to home."

"It passed like a bullet."

"The tree is high up on this finger," she said. "Keep the sun behind you and start looking."

I looked into the tops of the tall oaks, gums and beeches as we walked slowly up the finger. I watched for a line of bees to be swarming in and out at a knothole near the top of the tree in the direction the bee had gone.

"Look, Deutsia—I've found it," I said, pointing to the top of a sweet gum. Deutsia came over where I stood.

"Those are sour gnats." She laughed until she held her sides. "Bees will be much larger."

I began to search again. I looked among the golden leaves in the tops of the tall poplars, among the thin silvered leaves of the bushy-topped beeches, among the brown leaves of the white-oak and black-oak tops, and the blood-red leaves that still clung to the sweet gum tops. I found sour gnats among the sweet leaves but I never saw a honeybee.

"Come up here," Deutsia called to me.

"Where are you?"

"On the top of the finger."

I couldn't understand how she had gone that far so quickly.

"I want to show you something," she said as I walked near.

Just above Deutsia's head on the side of an oak was a line of bees as thick as her finger going in and out at a knothole.

"How did you find them?"

"I kept looking against the sky wherever I could see an opening under the timber as I walked up the slope," she said. "I saw them swarming between the light of the sky and me."

"I would never 've found them here," I said. "I was looking up all the time. Now you get a good kiss for that." And I held her close and kissed her lips and her warm face.

"Don't forget we've got to mark this tree."

"Why?"

"So no one else will cut it," she said. "That's the law on this mountain. When you find a bee tree that is marked, you don't cut it."

"How do I mark it?"

"Cut a cross on it," she said. "That's the mark for a Huntoon's bee tree. We want to leave it until next May before we cut it and then we can save the bees. If we cut it now they starve to death."

Deutsia stood by me while I cut a cross on the tree and then I cut her initials, D.H. Beside this I cut the letters D.S. Around the cross and our initials I carved a heart.

"How do you like that?" I asked her when I had finished.

"That means everything to me," she said.

Now that the sun had gone down over the mountain and the sky was getting dirty with soft clouds, Deutsia and I started toward the hollow.

"I'm glad we found the bee tree," she said.

"You're glad because you made me do a lot of climbing."

She laughed. "You ought to see the percoon that blooms around it in early April. The ground is white as snow with percoon blossoms!"

"Deutsia and her mountain flowers," I said, squeezing her hand. "My little Deutsia knows every flower that blooms and she knows where they grow. She knows every little stream on this mountain and she knows every kind of tree, vine and briar. She knows the birds and where they build. And she knows how to find a bee tree!"

"There's a lot of things about this mountain I don't know."

"Bet that's not so," I told her.

Then Deutsia stopped, looked at the sky.

"Does the wind feel warm to you?" she asked.

"Not very warm to me," I replied. "Maybe I'm just hot."

"The air ought to be getting cool this time of day, up here."

Before we had reached the hollow there was a light glimmer that flashed upon the gathering evening dusk.

"Is that lightning?"

"Listen."

"Low rumble of thunder," I said. "Or is it the wind?"

"That was thunder."

Now that the sky was overcast and the afternoon had passed into evening, dusk had begun to change to darkness and we were far from the mountain path that we had followed from the town.

"The thunder is louder," Deutsia said.

"Where's the path?"

"Feel it with your feet," she said. "I've followed mountain paths when I couldn't see my hand in front of me."

"But you knew the path well," I said. "And it wasn't a fox path."

We walked on until we reached the next mountain finger.

"We won't be able to feel our way around the mountain," I said. "There's not even a path there."

A rugged mountain slope lay between the spring where the bees watered and the tall pine we first coursed them over.

"We'll hurry," she said. "Maybe we can make it."

Before these words had left her mouth, lightning flashed and for a second we could see the earth about us. Then thunder roared until its violence jarred the earth.

"I believe we're lost," Deutsia said. "Wait until the next lightning flash and then I can tell."

Great streaks of lightning lit up the earth, and I could see in their flash thin gray-bellied clouds just above us.

"We are lost," she said, her voice trembling. "And when a storm comes this way it's a washout."

"What will we do?"

"Watch for a cliff," she said. "Wait for a lightning flash."

We only had to wait seconds before one lightning flash followed another.

"See that rim of cliffs up there," she said. "Let's make toward it."

We hurried up the mountain, running through the brush, briars, and vines when the lightning flashed and stopping with the sudden darkness. After we reached the foot of the cliffs, we ran along the edge on a trail made by the wild foxes.

"Look under each one for a good shelter," she said. "Feel that cool wind now. It's from rain. Let's hurry!"

"Look." I pointed, but Deutsia was already looking at the cliff.

"I know that cliff," she said. "It's a good shelter."

Just as we got under the cliff all hell broke loose. I've never seen such an avalanche of rain. The rain poured over the cliff's rim in muddy torrents carrying broken limbs and bits of logs.

"We just made it in time," she said.

"Did you ever see a day turn out like this one?"

"Something happens every time I'm with you."

"Aren't you afraid out here with me under this cliff on a night like this?"

"No, I'm not afraid any place with you," she said.

"Let the storm continue," I said. "We've got a big thick roof above us. And what a cozy room." I was looking at the room during lightning flashes. "It's snug except for this entrance. And there's even a bed of leaves here."

We could stand upright in the cliff and we had space to walk around.

"Maybe this storm will be over in a few minutes," Deutsia said.

"Then we'll have to wait for the streams to run down before we can cross them."

"Do you suppose Ben will wait for you?"

"He won't be able to get the truck back," I said. "He'll have to walk home."

We stood in silence listening to the falling rain, to the

great sweeps of blowing wind and to the water pouring over the cliff's rim. It seemed as if the sky had just opened and water was pouring from it. With our arms around each other we stood and waited for the storm to pass. But it didn't pass. The storm slowed, the lightning and thunder ceased, but the rain kept falling down into the velvety darkness.

"We can't go out into this," I said.

Deutsia agreed.

"Let's sit down on the leaves," I suggested.

We felt our way to the back of our cliff-walled room until the dry leaves rustled beneath our feet.

"I guess we'll have to sleep here tonight," I said.

"We're lucky to find this cliff, and to have this bed of leaves."

I lay back on the leaves and pulled Deutsia down beside me. My arm was beneath her head and her face was close to mine. I forgot that there was a storm outside. There wasn't anything to disturb us; even if a wet fox hunting shelter slipped inside this cliff he would scurry out quickly. This cliff belonged to us, Deutsia belonged to me and I belonged to her. And the night belonged to us.

6

"D A V E, Dave," were the soft words whispered in my ear. "It's time to get up!" I felt someone pulling my hair easily and a soft hand stroking my face.

I sat up and wiped sleep from my eyes.

"Don't you know where we are?"

She was sitting beside me, and she looked as fresh and pretty as a goldenrod blossom after a rain.

"Yes, I know now." I was now almost fully awake, remembering everything that had happened the day before.

"How long have you been awake?" I asked Deutsia.

"About two hours," she said. "The mavises woke me."

"What are mavises doing in here?"

"See their nest up there," she said, pointing up toward a ledge in the cave.

"So we had company last night."

"The mavises've been to breakfast," she told me. "And they were talking to each other when they flew back in the cave."

"What were they talking about?"

"They said it was time for us to get up."

"I went outside and to a mountain stream and washed my face," she said. "And I found a piece of charcoal from a burned log and I washed my teeth."

"Why didn't you wake me?"

"I wanted to let you sleep a while longer," she said. "You did a lot of walking yesterday."

"But I can take it." I wondered if she thought that I was a weakling. Then she pulled my face down to hers and kissed me.

"You're the sweetest angel that ever lived," I said.

"Do you think so? Do you really think I am?"

"I don't just think you are," I said. "I know you are."

"Just so you say so." She wrapped her long hair around my neck and about my arms.

"What are you doing?" I asked her.

"I'm tying you to me," she said. "I'm trying to tie you to me forever."

"You wouldn't think I'd run away?"

"To tell you the truth," she said, "I've thought that you would love me and then leave me."

"What makes you have a thought like that?" I asked.

"Don't ask me that," she said. "I won't answer you."

With her long hair braided about me like strands of golden ropes we stood there looking into each other's eyes. And then we kissed again and again while the mavises made many trips in and out the cave.

"What will we do for breakfast?" I asked her. "I'm getting hungry."

"All we can find now is mountain tea berries," she said. "That's where the mavises went for breakfast. Earlier in the season we could have found wild plums and sweet anis root and pheasants' and partridges' eggs. We could've built a fire here in the cave and I could've roasted the eggs and had you a good breakfast."

"But what about coffee?"

"Cold water this morning," she said. We walked to the cave's entrance and looked below us at the mountain slope where the brush, vines and timber had been stripped of more leaves by the storm and where the trees' bodies were clean-washed, as though the world had been made over. The air tasted clean, cool and sweet to breathe. The streams sang, laughed, and murmured as they poured in swift torrents over the slopes.

As we walked around the mountain's side toward the path, Deutsia led me to a spot of ground covered with leafless huckleberry vines.

"Here's where we'll find the mountain tea berries," she said. "They're sweet and mellow this time of year."

"The mavises didn't get all of them." I picked a small handful of the rain-washed bright-red berries from their low stems among the mountain tea leaves, and gave them to Deutsia.

"Here," she said, giving me the larger handful that she had picked.

"I've cheated you," I teased her. "You've given me better measure than I gave you."

"This may not be a good breakfast," she said. "But these will stop your hunger."

"These berries are delicious," I said, mumbling my words, for my mouth was filled.

"I've been hungry on the mountain," Deutsia said, "and I've chewed the mountain tea leaves when I couldn't find any berries."

The sun was high in the sky above us and the air about us was bright and thin. The leaves had colored more. When the wind blew it rustled the leaves above us and brought them down in showers.

"We'll be going," she said, leading the way.

"Deutsia, what will your folks say about not getting home last night?"

"It won't be the first time I've slept in a cave all night when a storm caught me on this mountain," she said. "But I never slept in one with a man before. My folks won't say anything. I'll tell 'em I slept in a cave, but I don't have to tell 'em you slept beside me. Here's the path at last."

"Where do we go from here?"

"You go to your shanty," she said. "I go to my home."

"Can't I take you home?" I asked her.

"No," she said.

"Then when do we meet again?"

"Next Sunday," she said. "I have a place for us to go to."

"Where do we meet?"

"Where this path meets the graveled road."

"All right, it's a date," I said.

I watched after her until she was up the steps and beyond the cliffs and out of sight.

I wanted a hot plate lunch and coffee by the time I'd walked to the Little Tavern in Oak Hill, but since Deutsia wasn't welcome there I wouldn't stop. I would wait it out until I had walked the seventeen miles to the shanty before I'd patronize a place where she wasn't welcomed. As I walked over the last mile of mountain road in the moonlight, I felt a longing to go back to the cliff and stay again with Deutsia. Before I had always been glad to reach our shanty and to sleep on my bunk, but now the sight of it made me long to return to that one night of life and love that I had left. I hated to walk inside the shanty where I heard loud familiar voices and much laughing.

"What's kept you so long, Dave?"

"Where in the hell have you been?"

"Where did you sleep last night?"

Ben, Mort and Hezzy were sitting in chairs in the middle of the floor facing each other and my chair was between them. Where I would be sitting was a jug.

"I stayed in heaven last night," I said.

"Did you see anybody you knowed there?"

And then they laughed wild laughs.

"We'll pass the jug around on that one," Hezzy said.

"I was caught in that storm last night," I said. "And I finally found a rock cliff and slept under it on a bed of dry leaves."

"That's more like it," Mort said.

"We'll drink to your luck," Hezzy said, putting the jug to his lips.

"Hezzy and I were coming from Sylvania's," Mort said. "And we just made it to the top of th' pint when all hell broke loose. If we hadn't got here when we did, I believe there's enough water on the ground to've washed us down the mountain."

"The storm did one thing for Mort and me," Hezzy said as he licked his lips. "It washed our clothes. All we had to do today was hang 'em out to dry."

"We were warned about storms on this mountain before we left," Hezzy said. He wiped his mouth with his hand. "Mr. Wilson warned me about the storms on these mountains. Up high where they ketch the rain."

"But you forgot to tell us," Mort said. He lifted the jug to his lips.

"That's right," Hezzy said. "I did forget it."

"But Dave is safe," Mort said, scooting his tongue over his lips. "That's all that matters."

"When did you get in, Ben?" I asked.

"I got back before the storm," he said.

"Didn't you have a date?"

"But I don't go to Fern's house and stay," he said.

7

❧ ❧ ❧ ❧ ❧ ❧ ❧ ❧ ❧ ❧ ❧

NEXT MORNING we started another week's work. And I was glad that
Ben had gotten back in time to file our
crosscut saw. He'd put more set in the teeth so they'd take
bigger bites out of the pines and the resin wouldn't cause it
to bind. And he'd even ground my bitted ax and whetted it
with a stone to razor sharpness.

"I'm much obliged you did this for me," I said.

"It helps me as much as it helps you," Ben said. "Don't
thank me. We work together as a team and if you work
with dull tools, then we don't make as much. We'll have a
good week in this pine timber. "Long tall pines with a few
tiny limbs to trim. This week will be a gold mine."

Ben hadn't left anything undone. He'd brought a bottle
of kerosene along to pour on the saw and cut the resin to
make the crosscut easier to pull.

"You see, I'm goin' to need more money," he said. "I'm

going to marry Fern. I can't let 'er make more money than I make."

Never once have Deutsia and I ever talked of money, I thought. Never once have we planned a future; we have let the minutes, hours, nights and days take care of themselves. We have just lived our time together and loved each minute.

We slaughtered the tall pines, leaving their lifeless green tops piled in small heaps. We worked down under the ridge where there was more dirt on the rocks for the pines to grow. Since they were tall and easy to cut and there were not so many limbs to shear from their bodies, Ben was right in his calculations. When we measured our week's work Saturday at noon, we had set a record for the seven years we'd worked together. And for the first time in our lives we'd passed Hezzy and Mort. We had made one hundred and fifty-two dollars.

"That's money," Ben said. "Fern will be proud of me."

"You don't buy love with money, Ben."

"No, but you can hold love with money."

After we'd eaten, shaved and bathed, Ben, Mort and Hezzy started dressing in their best clothes.

"What's the matter, Dave?" Mort asked me. "Ain't you a-datin' that pretty gal you've been huggin' every night in your sleep?"

"Not today."

"Did she go back on you?" Hezzy asked me.

I didn't answer.

"That's too bad, Dave," Mort said. "I know how you feel."

"Go along with me," Ben said. "You can loaf at the Little Tavern and meet a lot of nice people."

"I'll hang around the shanty this afternoon," I said. "I need a rest anyway."

I was off on the path Hezzy and Mort had made by their trips to Skinny's and Sylvania's shack after whiskey. I was on my way to a little world that I'd heard and thought a lot about but never seen. I soon reached the ridge road where I could see farmhouses that looked as tiny as dollhouses and fodder shocks that looked like toy wigwams in the Clinch valley below.

A cool wind hit my face and rustled the tough-butted white-oak leaves above my head. I looked down upon the jutted cliffs that spread like quilts made of many pieces and in many folds. I wondered how people got anything up this mountain from the stores down in the valley, anything that they couldn't carry on their backs. No wonder this was a world of its own. In a county surrounded by a barrier of mountains, this was a pocket of land cut off by walls beneath and around it. This was Deutsia's land, the land of the sky.

I heard voices in the distance and I stopped to listen. Familiar voices! And then I knew that Skinny's and Sylvania's shack was near. I turned a sharp curve in the path and there it was. It was a rough one-room log shack with yellow clay daubing between the logs, and there was a big chimney made of fieldstones.

Around the two scrawny blackjacks that grew in the yard I saw four skinny mules without saddles on their razor backs, tied to the low limbs of a black gum tree. Two men staggered toward a patch of scrawny pines, and I heard them swearing as they hurried to hide themselves.

When I saw Hezzy running from the cabin door toward the pines, I stopped behind a cluster of oaks that grew between the house and me. I knew that Hezzy had drunk so much moonshine that his kidneys had acted up on him. After he'd made it to the pines, I hurried past the cabin listening to the roar of many men's voices coming from inside through the partly opened door. And when I went beyond this shack I found many little paths that came into the main path. I passed several of these paths before I made up my mind to follow one.

I noticed a mule's tracks. Overhead a swarm of buzzards circled and flapped their wings against the wind and then they coasted away with the speed of the blowing wind. A squirrel barked from a giant black oak top and when I looked up he ran into a knothole, stuck his head out and barked again. Crows winged over in twos toward a pine grove, cawing as they struggled against the wind.

Voices? I stopped to listen. Yes. I heard them.

The path was gradually going down, twisting this way and that way toward a cove. Just as I turned the S bend in the path, I saw a shack much the same as the one I'd seen upon the ridge, with a large chimney made of fieldstone. And I saw a man standing in the yard with two hounds at his feet, watching the children play hide and seek.

He looks familiar, I thought. When I got closer, he quit petting his hounds and stared at me suspiciously.

"Don't be afraid, Don," I said. "This is Dave."

"You're the man that come to jail with Deutsia, ain't you?" He questioned me with cold, suspicious eyes.

"Yes, don't you remember?"

"You're all right," he said. "I just want to be sure."

When I looked around for the playing children, they had gone. But I saw one stick his head around the corner of the shack, and I saw one inside the shack, standing beside his mother; both were looking out at me. She stood with the window curtain covering all but a tiny bit of her face and eyes.

"Did you get a trial?" I asked Don.

"I'd a stayed in that goddammed jail until I'd've rotted and I wouldn't've got a trial," he said. "I told you why they kept me there. Money for that son-of-a-bitch o' a jailor. There's no justice for a man from this mountain."

"Then how'd you get out?"

"I thought of somethin' and it worked. I wouldn't eat the rotten grub Jarvis Henthorne brought me," Don said. "This worked on 'im. But it wasn't all I done. Once when he was at the door, when he didn't think that I saw 'im, I started talking to myself. I pulled a plug of terbacker from my pocket and I started cutting it up in little pieces and a-runnin' over the jailhouse a-hidin' it. Every time I'd hide a piece of it I'd say, "No son-of-a-bitch will ever find that." I put a piece in each of my shoes, under the mattress, behind the door and under the lard-can privy. I talked to myself as I hid 'em. When I'd finished hidin' the terbacker, I took a coughing spell, run forward, pitchin' toward the bed where I sprawled out and laid there. Next morning old Jarvis the jailor turned me out."

"Without a trial?"

"Without a trial," he repeated. "And I'm damned glad to get back on this mountain with my family. Don't think I'll ever go down to the valley again."

"I don't blame you."

"You ain't from the valley, are you?"

"No, I'm from the mountains," I said. "The Virginia mountains."

"It took me all day to climb back up the mountain," he said. "I was so weak I could hardly walk. But I kept sayin' to myself, 'With th' help of God, I'll make it. Th' clouds'll look better below me than above me.' And I'd walk a while and rest a while. And while I rested I'd think of my wife, children and shack, and to think o' them put new life in me."

While we talked the children, five of them, like stairsteps, gathered again in the yard and started playing.

When I looked toward the shack again I saw Mrs. Praytor had come from behind the window curtain, had leaned her dark face against the window pane and was looking straight at me. Her dark face reminded me of the dark gloom of an autumn day when a cold rain is stripping the last leaves from the trees on the mountain.

And the children were all different. There were four fair-complexioned ones; two of the four had reddish hair and two were blonds. The fifth child had charcoal-black straight hair that fell about her shoulders and her face.

"Are these your children?"

"Yes, they're all my children," he said quickly before I got the words from my mouth. "We're Melungeons. Did you ever hear of us Melungeons?"

"I never did."

"Melungeons don't get justice in the courts," he said. "We're hated! Despised. We're a lost people."

That's why Deutsia doesn't go to Little Tavern or the theatre, I thought, and why she said I wouldn't love her forever. That's why Fern didn't want to be with Deutsia and why Ben told me to lay off Deutsia, because Fern had told Ben that Deutsia was a Melungeon. That's why she goes to her part of the town.

"We're called Sons and Daughters of the Legend," Don
said. "We don't know who we are. There are so many theories about where we came from that we don't know what
to believe. We've heard we're a white, Indian and Negro
mixture. You'll never know what kind of blood Deutsia
Huntoon has in her veins. I've even heard we're descendants of a people that once lived in a city called Carthage
that was destroyed by the Romans in 145 B.C. and that
some of the people fled from that ancient city to a country called Morocco where they mixed with a race called
Moors and later some of these migrated to Portugal and
then on to South Carolina and then to Sanctuary Mountain. Dave, we don't know who we are. But we do know
that we are human beings. We know we are here even if
we don't know how we got here. And whatever we are and
whoever we are we know we're a race hated and despised.
We know it's hell to be a Melungeon."

Thoughts went through my mind so quickly I felt
stunned. I was thinking about the way Deutsia had suffered
something she didn't tell me about, something I could feel
but couldn't see. I was thinking about how she spoke of her
people and how she had carried bread and wine to a man in
jail. Never in my life had I spoken of "my people," for I
didn't belong to a small group. I was just a person among
people, and that was all. I went where I pleased and when I
pleased and there were no barriers. No one had told me I
couldn't go here or I couldn't go there.

"The Melungeons live on this mountain," Don said—
maybe to break my thoughts—"and your Deutsia
Huntoon is a Melungeon."

"Well, I don't care if she is," I said. "I love her just the
same. I didn't know who she was or what she was when I

met her. I knew she was the prettiest girl I'd ever seen and I loved her from the first time I ever laid eyes on her."

"I'm glad to hear you say that," Don said, "but I want to warn you not to marry her."

"Why?" I asked.

"If you marry Deutsia you will be Melungeon," he said. "You will be one of us. And you'll always regret it. You're different. You have life with freedom before you. And you'd better hold to it."

"Then you mean I'd better not see Deutsia?" I said.

"That's what I mean," he said, getting close and speaking in low tones. "You will have trouble all your life if you marry Deutsia!"

"But I must see her," I said. "And I'm going to Huntoons' right now."

"I doubt you'll find anybody at home today."

"Maybe Deutsia'll be home by now."

"There's a closer way to Huntoons' if you'd be willin' to try it," Don said, pointing to a path winding across the cove. "See that path?"

"Yes," I said, looking the way he pointed.

"Follow that until you've passed two shacks," he said. "The third one will be Huntoons'."

"It's good to see you out of jail and back with your family, Don," I said, shaking his hand. "I'm glad I got to talk with you again."

"It's good to see you again," he said, as I walked away.

After I'd reached the path that wound up the bluff I looked back at Don Praytor's shack. I saw him standing beside his wife, and I knew that she had come from her hiding to ask about me.

The first shack I reached was deserted except for three lazy hound dogs stretched on the brown yard grass sunning themselves. They were almost too lazy to bark. They raised their heads without getting their bodies up, grunted a few times and laid their heads back down. This shack was the same as the other two, one-room with a big fieldstone chimney. There were a few clearings about the shack with chickens running all over. I noticed a cage made of close-mesh wire and I looked in to find a big rattlesnake caged. At the sound of my steps, he stuck out his tongue to catch the sound and then he rattled his tail as if he were going to strike.

Wonder why they have rattlesnakes caged? I thought. They couldn't have them for pets. I wondered if they ate rattlesnake meat and made shoes and belts of their skins, for once I'd seen a young man at the Oak Hill courthouse wearing a rattlesnake-skin belt. I looked at the window of this shack to see if anyone was peeping from behind curtains, but the place was deserted and I hurried on.

When I reached the second shack, I wondered if I'd got turned on the path and had returned to the shack I'd just left. Three lazy hound dogs were asleep on the brown yard grass, and they never even noticed me. The shack was the same. There were chickens and again a wire cage at the smokehouse with a rattlesnake in it. I moved on in the direction that I had been told.

When I had gotten out of sight of this shack, where the path had left the clearing for the tall timber, I heard the rustle of leaves. I looked toward the sound and saw a big dark-complexioned woman, whose open dress-bosom exposed her large breasts, walk from under the shell-barked hickories with a basket of hickory nuts. She was barefooted and her straight black hair fell loosely about her shoulders.

She didn't speak, but went back into the woods again. I left the woods and came into a clearing; there was Deutsia's shack in plain view. I hurried toward it, thinking that I might find her there.

I stood before a very large log shack with a lean-to built alongside it. There were four hound dogs asleep on the yard grass, and chickens were running over the yard. There was a small log barn and a smokehouse in which was a cage with two rattlesnakes in it. I looked at the front windows but there wasn't anybody at home. Standing before Deutsia's shack looking at it, I thought about the mountain world that I had seen and how, like a fly snared in a spider's web, I'd been snared into this world. I'd found something I couldn't escape, something I must stand and face, something I'd never had to face before.

8

DID YOU ever hear of the Melungeons?" I asked Ben, as we sat around the breakfast table, smoking.

"I've just been a-waitin' for you to ask me that question, Dave," Ben said. "I'm glad you're a-gettin' your eyes open at last. So you've found out about 'em?"

"Yes, I've found out about the Melungeons."

"I left that up to you," he said. "I didn't want you to think I was puttin' my jib in where I didn't have any business. I didn't want to come between you and the girl you thought you loved."

"I've asked you what you know about the Melungeons, and not about Deutsia," I said.

"You know she's a Melungeon, don't you?" Ben took another draw from his cigarette.

Mort and Hezzy sat silently on the other side of the table, smoking their pipes and listening.

"Yes, I know she's a Melungeon."

"Did you know it when you had that first date with her?"

"No, I'd never heard of the Melungeons then."

"You're not the first man that's been fooled by the beauty of the Melungeon women," Ben said. "They're so pretty while they're young that white strangers who have come into these parts have fallen for 'em before. But they've been smart enough to find out and to break away. I'm glad you're findin' out."

"I know how you found out about the Melungeons. Fern told you about them."

"Fern knows just about every Melungeon family living up on that mountain. She's caught enough of their babies. You know a doctor won't walk back on that mountain and catch a baby for nothing. And the Melungeons never have any money to pay a doctor. If you want to know more about the Melungeons, ask Fern about 'em. She can tell you. She's not only caught their babies but she's doctored 'em for the last five years. She's the first health nurse Cantwell County ever had."

"What did they do for a doctor before your gal came along?" Hezzy asked Ben.

"They doctored themselves with juices from roots, barks and berries," Ben said. "And they had faith doctors among 'em and believed in magic healing. They believed a lot in moon magic. They thought different phases of the moon had power over their lives and the crops they planted. I think they still practice a lot of their old beliefs. They distrusted Fern and her medicines at first but they're gradually comin' over to her."

"Why does Fern try to save their babies and kill their

spirits?" I asked Ben. "Why is she so prejudiced against the Melungeons?"

"They're not our equals," Ben said. "I don't care if they are a strong, good-looking race of people."

"Skinny was tellin' about his Uncle Elf Hoon," Mort said. "When he was 103 years old his mule kicked 'im in the head and knocked 'im outen his mind for a week. And when he was 107, lightning hit 'im and knocked his shoes off'n his feet. And Skinny said that his Uncle Elf said, 'My mule got tired of me and tried to kill me when I was 103, and he couldn't kill me and God Almighty must've thought I'd lived long enough and He tried to kill me with a bolt o' lightning but didn't quite do it and I guess I'll live a few years yet.' Skinny said his Uncle Elf lived to be 113 and went to his long sleep in his chair smoking his pipe."

"That's a pleasant way to die," Hezzy said. "Since the Lord couldn't knock 'im out with lightning, He put 'im to sleep." And then Hezzy laughed at his own words.

"Fern said it wasn't anything unusual for a Melungeon to live a hundred years," Ben said.

"I never heard o' Melungeons until I came here," Mort mumbled. "I wonder why. I've been a lot of places and read a lot of books."

"No wonder you didn't hear of 'em," Hezzy said. "Look where Cantwell County is! It's in the head of no place and walled in by ranges, and in the middle of Cantwell County is Sanctuary Mountain where they live. And they live right on the damned top of it. I don't see how they can even get a mule up there. You know you can't take a wagon. And an automobile would scare their youngins to death. A lot of 'em've never been off'n the mountain."

"Don't they ever move away?" I asked.

"They move away, so Fern told me," Ben said. "But they're a strange people. They move to another mountaintop. You can't get one to move down into the valley where the land is fertile. They won't work. Oh, they'll tend a few patches. But all they want to do is hunt and fish."

"I don't blame them for not wanting to live in a valley," I said, my temper rising. "Look how the people treat them. I know a little about it. I've been feeling the last few weeks what they've felt for over a hundred years. It's hell the way Melungeons are treated."

"But you don't want to go with a Melungeon," Ben said. "It's disgraceful."

"Why is it disgraceful?"

"You know about the blood in the Melungeons, don't you?"

"I don't know about their blood," I said. "But my guess is, their blood is red. It's not blue blood like the people in the valley think they have in their veins."

"If you'll listen, Dave," Ben said, dropping his cigarette stub in his coffee cup, "I'll tell you what I've heard about the blood in the Melungeons. There are four theories about how they got here and who they are. You remember Sir Walter Raleigh's Lost Colony? There was never a trace of it found. It's believed they were captured by the Cherokee Indians and brought to this mountain and here they mixed with the Indians."

"The Indians brought 'em to a good hidin' place," Hezzy said as he emptied the ashes from his pipe into his saucer.

"And here's another theory." Ben went on talking as he took another cigarette from his pack, bounced it on the table and then struck a match under the table and lit it. "There is a theory that a Portuguese ship was wrecked on the Carolina coast and the sailors rigged up a raft and reached shore, migrated inland, were accepted by the Cherokees and took Cherokee wives. Many say that it was a Spanish ship instead of a Portuguese. I don't know. I'm tellin' you what I've heard."

"Did Fern tell you this?" I asked.

"Fern told me this and any of the old settlers will tell you," Ben said. "But these are theories they don't like to believe."

"What are the theories they like to believe?" I asked, refilling my pipe as I listened.

"Many of the people believe the Melungeon is a mixture of poor mountain whites, Indians and Negroes," Ben continued. "And here is what they say. That during the Civil War, Cantwell County fought for the Union almost to a man, and that many escaped mulattoes from the Deep South were smuggled to Cantwell County where they found refuge upon Sanctuary Mountain and mixed with the poor whites."

"You can just tell by lookin' at Sylvania she's dipped," Mort said. "But Skinny doesn't show it," Hezzy said. "He's as red-faced as a mad turkey gobbler."

"And the last theory is that there is not any Indian blood in the Melungeons," Ben said, "but just a mixture of escaped slaves and trashy whites. And this is what the majority of people believe."

"It's nothing to me what their blood is," Hezzy said. "But I know they've got Indian blood in 'em. I lived with the Navahos two years at Cameron, New Mexico. Sylvania acts a lot like the Navaho squaws I used to know."

"I think Dave'd better pay heed," Mort said.

"Let Dave work out his own problem," Hezzy said. "It's all right to play around with a good-lookin' Melungeon, but he doesn't have to marry her," Mort said. He gave a wild laugh.

"What do you mean by 'playing around'?" I asked Mort.

"One you can have a lot of fun with in bed," Mort said. "One that is good to sleep with."

"I don't like your damn remarks, Mort," I said, getting up from the table.

"I didn't mean to make you mad, Dave," he said. "I's only jokin'."

"When you make a slurry remark about Deutsia Huntoon," I said, "you and I are going to tangle and pretty damned quick."

"But surely you couldn't love Deutsia Huntoon," Ben said.

"But I surely can love Deutsia Huntoon."

Then I got up from the smoke-filled room and walked out into the yard to breathe deeply of clean sunlit morning air. I'd heard so much about Deutsia's people that I wanted to think. I wasn't anything but a lumberjack with a strong body filled with knots of muscle and with at least an average brain, but to me my problem was as great as any problem could be to a man, for it concerned the destiny of my life and my happiness and the destiny and the happiness of the woman I loved.

Ben didn't understand. He was going with Fern Hailston who was somebody in Oak Hill, known all over Cantwell County because she was the Health Nurse. Fern and Ben could go any place at any time and they would be welcomed. Deutsia and I had our limitations.

"Where are you goin'?" Ben asked me. He saw me get-

ting out of my work clothes into my Sunday clothes.
"You're not goin' to see Deutsia Huntoon?"

"Yes, I've got a date with Deutsia."

"I've got a date with Fern," Ben said. "I'm going to
Oak Hill at one o'clock and I'd like to take you, but I hate
to haul you to a date with Deutsia Huntoon! I thought after you'd found out about her being a Melungeon you'd
never look at her again."

"Since when did you become owner of the truck?" I
asked, snapping words from my lips like a mad turtle snaps
his stone-hard lips. "You were just hired to drive the truck.
And you weren't given permission to drive it to Oak Hill
to see Fern Hailston, either. If that truck goes, I go with
it!"

From where we parked the truck we could see up the
graveled road to where the path came down from Hide-
away Mountain. Deutsia was standing there waiting for me.
I looked at her first and then at Ben, whose face I'll never
forget. It was frozen with hatred.

"If you don't know who she is, Ben," I said. "I'll tell
you. That's Deutsia. She's waiting there for me."

"You don't have to tell me," he said. "I know who she
is."

"I thought my telling you would keep you from staring," I said, getting out of the truck and slamming the
door.

I started toward Deutsia, held her close, and kissed her.
I didn't give a damn if Ben Dewberry, Fern Hailston, and
all the bluebloods in Oak Hill saw me.

9

WE'VE GOT a river to cross and a mountain to climb," Deutsia said. "We go over to the Clinch right here."

She led the way along the narrow footpath toward the river.

"How do we cross?" I asked. "Boat?"

Deutsia laughed at my words.

"I'll show you."

On the bank of the Clinch we stood where a tall sycamore had uprooted and had fallen across two-thirds of the width of this mountain river. We walked over the body of a giant tree that had often served as a bridge. I could tell by the way the bark was worn. We grabbed the bushy leafless top branches of the tree and held to a branch above us, then walked on as far as I thought it safe for two people to walk.

"Sit on this limb, pull off your shoes and roll your pant legs up," she said.

Deutsia started taking off her oxfords.

I rolled my pants until they were tight around my legs.

"Can you hold your shoes and mine?" she asked me.

"I think so," I said.

I held the four shoes by the strings.

"Now keep your other hand on my shoulder."

I laid my hand on her shoulder as she lifted her dress and stepped down from the sycamore top into the water.

"Step where I do," she said. "Be careful."

When I put my foot where she had just put hers, it went down on a rock. And I followed her, stepping where she stepped. She was keeping her dress dry, but her hair was dragging the water behind her.

When we reached the river bank, Deutsia shook the water from her hair and we sat on a rock and put our shoes back on.

"Come," Deutsia said gleefully, taking my hand.

I followed her up a path beneath the pines, around and over the rocks, under the bright-leafed maples, the brown-leafed white oaks and red-leafed gums.

"I want my pipe and a good smoke," I said when we reached the top where the wind chilled the sweat on our faces.

"Isn't it wonderful up here?" Deutsia said.

I struck a match to light my pipe but the wind erased the flame.

"Too much wind up here. I can't light my pipe."

"We'll fix that."

With her back to the wind she spread her dress, making it a barrier against the wind so I could light my pipe.

"You know how to do everything," I said.

She smiled.

We hurried over the wind-swept rocks where scrawny seedling pine needles stuck our legs and huckleberry vines, sawbriars and greenbriars pulled at our shoelaces. Then we came to a ridge road where we looked at the setting sun, large as a spread umbrella and the color of a hot red hollyhock.

"We'll make it on time," she said.

In less than ten minutes we came to a pine grove where dry pine needles crunched beneath our feet and where within the dense grove we could hear singing. Our road made a sharp turn and we came directly upon a gathering of people, sitting on split-log benches. The pines had been cut away, except for a few on which lanterns hung, and around the cleared enclosure that was the churchhouse were walls of the thickly studded trees. By the time we had walked down to sit on a bench, the singing had begun. We were in an outdoors churchhouse.

By the lantern light I could see many of the faces that I'd noticed around the courthouse. I also saw many strange faces. Two of the boys played a snappy tune on their guitars, almost like a fast square dance tune, while the people that faced us, and many of the congregation sitting on the benches, sang "Feasting on the Mountain."

In front of the choir the preacher stood with a rough handmade table before him, his hand upon his opened Bible. Down beside him were the wire cages like the ones I'd seen at the shacks on Sanctuary Mountain.

"What church is this?" I whispered to Deutsia.

"Holiness Faith Healers."

"What's in that cage up there?"

"Rattlesnakes."

"Why do they have rattlesnakes?"

"Wait a minute and you'll see."

As we whispered I saw eyes stare at us, telling us without saying a word to quit whispering in church. I wondered, too, if they also meant me to take my arm from around Deutsia, but I looked around and other men were sitting close to their girls with their arms around them.

Before the song was finished a fat woman in front of us jumped up, clapping her hands above her head, shouting, "Glory to God! Glory to God! We'll feast on the mountain up there!" And she pointed toward the sky when she said "up there." She danced a tune on the pine needles and shouted while they finished the song.

"Glory to God, Sister Witherspoon," the preacher said, as the choir sat down on their log seats that were just a little higher than ours. "We'll feast on the mountain up there! Glory to God!"

Sister Witherspoon sat down, her body jerking and her hands a-quiver, her face covered with drops of sweat that shone brightly in the lantern light.

The preacher stood at the table before us, dressed in his faded clean-washed overalls and blue work shirt with his sleeves rolled to his elbows and his shirt collar unbuttoned. There was a beard on his face and his hair was uncombed. When he opened his mouth he showed two rows of discolored front teeth. He was a tall man but bent over like a wind-whipped oak on the mountaintop, and his eyes looked down at us like a hawk's eyes when they look over a flock of chickens.

"I'll take my text," he said, "from the sixteenth chapter and the eighteenth verse of St. Mark."

He bent over his opened Bible and began to read, stumbling slowly over the words as a barefoot boy stumbles over rocks when he first pulls off his shoes in the spring.

" 'They shall take up serpents; and if they drink any deadly thing, it shall not hurt them; they shall lay hands on the sick, and they shall recover.' "

"That's the Word, folks," he said, his long black mustache working up and down as he spoke. "That's the Gospel for ye. And soon as we have another song, I'll give ye the message that God told me to give ye."

The choir rose from their log seats, the young men with the guitars looked at each other, one nodded a signal to the other and then there was a fast plucking of strings, a wild outburst of many-tongued discordant voices singing, "I'll Be a Holiness until I Die." I knew that this was a dance tune, for my feet began to move, to pat on the pine needles, and I looked about me and other feet were doing the same.

"Glory, glory," the preacher shouted, looking upward toward the pine-needle ceiling. "Won't we all be Holiness until we die? Until we reach that Heaven in the sky?"

"You bet we will, Brother Dusty," yelled a dark-complexioned man with a deep booming voice like a mountain wind surging down into a hollow. "You bet we will, Brother Dusty! I'm saved and sanctified and I can't sin no more, Brother Dusty!"

And he clapped his big fire-shovel hands and twitched his mouth, wiggling the horns of his black mustache as his feet patted the tune on the pine needles. After a few pats with his feet, he let out a yell. "Whoopee! Glory to God! Sing children! Sing! Glory be to God, we'll all be Holiness till we die! We'll be Holiness when we reach that Heaven in the sky! Glory! Glory! Glory be to God! Glory be to God!" he was shouting in a big voice like the wind, high above the voices in the choir. "Glory be, brothers! Glory

be, sisters! Glory be to the God that gives us power to heal
the sick and the afflicted, that gives us the power to handle
the serpents and if we are right with God, they won't bite
us! Blessed be the name of the Sweet Jesus that gives us
power to handle fire and won't let it burn us! Send us the
Light, Sweet Jesus!"

"Amen, Brother Cliff," Preacher Dusty said to the big
man, who was standing now, jerking as I'd never seen a
man jerk before.

"The serpents and the fire will test you, Brother Cliff,"
a tall woman screamed as she arose from her seat. She
waved her hands into the air above her tousled hair. "If
you ain't right with Jesus, the serpent will send his fangs
into ye and turn loose his venom and the flame will wither
yer flesh ... scorch and burn it ... Ah, the Devil is in ye
when the serpent will fang ye and the flames scorch ye ...
Ah, it's the sign that ye ain't right with Jesus!"

She danced a tune, her head thrown back, her face toward the pine-bough ceiling. Her eyes were closed, her
mouth was open and she mumbled words that I couldn't
understand. Now Brother Dusty was walking between the
rows of seated people, looking straight ahead at something
I couldn't see. His hands were spread before him and he,
too, was mumbling words I couldn't understand.

"What are they saying?" I asked Deutsia. I had to shout
to get my words above the singing and the mumbling of
many people.

"They are talking in the Unknown Tongue," she said.

"Can you understand them?"

"No."

"Listen, young man," a big man with a red beardy face

said to me in a loud voice. "I belong to the real Unknown Tongues. And I've been a-sittin' here a-tryin' to make out what they're a-sayin' and the only word that they have said that I can understand is 'sweet tater.' I come here tonight a-thinkin' they would talk in the language of my Church! But they're a-speakin' a tongue only the Devil in his hell can understand!"

Before he had finished saying these words the big woman, with her eyes closed, sprawled on the ground, her body jerking and her lips and eyelids twitching. There she lay before Deutsia and me, her dress high upon her body showing her big legs, her cotton bloomers and her red outing petticoat. She stared vacantly toward her Heaven in the sky as she mumbled her unknown words.

"Speak to Jesus, Sister Hallie," a woman said, sitting on the seat above her. "Tell Him that you love Him. Thank Him for the magic power to heal! Speak to Him tonight as you've never spoken to Him before and help Him fight the mean old Devil to a finish on this night. Tell Him to he'p bind the Devil's hands, to he'p us shet his filthy mouth, and chain him in the endless pit fer eternity."

And she jumped up and started running circles, shouting "Glory to Sweet Jesus" as she ran. Maybe she started the others; I don't know. It seemed that everybody arose from his seat but Deutsia and me. People—men, women and boys—grabbed each other and started swinging as I'd seen them swing in figure eight of an old square dance. But dancers never piled upon the floor and kicked and moaned and said words no one could understand as these people did. Amid the singing and the wild confusion of people going around and around, stumbling over the women and

men on the ground with pine needles in their hair and stick-
ing to their clothes, many young couples still sat on the
benches with their arms about each other, kissing.

Small children held babies in their laps while their
mothers and fathers shouted and rolled. I saw little girls and
little boys run madly through the crowd, stepping on
men's hands and women's tangled hair, screaming as they
went. They were afraid of all this confusion. Once I saw a
small boy run out screaming into the dark pine woods, his
hands high in the air, his heels touching his rump as he
ran.

Brother Dusty tried to preach by shouting his words
and waving his big gnarled hands to get his God-given message to his congregation above the din and roar of the
rolling, kicking and quivering people. I could hear a few of
Brother Dusty's words. "Hell is nineteen miles straight,
straight under the ground," I heard him scream as he
pointed down to the ground. I looked above me and insects
were swarming around the smoky-globed lanterns. High
on this mountain the insects, too, had found the Light and
the lantern warmth as well.

I've been to many a church in the mountains, I thought,
as I looked beneath the split wooden log we were sitting on
to see what was holding it up, but I have never seen anything like this. As I was touching the rough oak posts that
had been placed in auger holes in the bottom of the logs we
sat on, I heard a scream among the people and wild screams
among the tenor-voiced children. I got up and saw Brother
Dusty with a big rattler around his neck. He was patting
the rattler's head while it flicked out its tongue to catch and
listen to the sound of the confusion, a greater sound of
voices than a rattler ever hears when left alone free to roam

his mountain world among the rocks and wild huckleberry vines. Brother Dusty turned this way and that to show the rattler to all the people. From where we sat, I could see the rattler's tail a-quiver as Sister Hallie's lips were a-quiver on the ground beneath us.

"Sweet Jesus gives me the power," Brother Dusty said. "There ain't no Devil in this man. Not nary bit o' th' Devil in this flesh. Saved and sanctified and can't sin any more. They shall take up serpents. Ain't this the fulfillment, folks? Ain't it? Oh for that home among the stars where the angels sing and play their guitars!"

"Amen, Brother Dusty."

I wondered if only Brother Dusty would handle a rattlesnake, fondle it and coddle it and let it listen to his congregation, let it wrap itself about his neck as if it were a necktie. This giant rattler must have been heavy about his neck, it looked him in the eyes with its cold, hard lidless eyes and put wild fears into the small children who looked up at it. But the rattler didn't scare Brother Dusty. All eyes of the shouting people turned toward him, but not the eyes of the people lying on the floor jerking. Their eyes were closed and their jerks came easier. Many had jerked until they could move no more and they lay on the pine-needle floor lifeless and exhausted, with drool running from the corners of their mouths.

"That's closer than I want to get to a rattlesnake," I said to Deutsia.

When I said these words to her, I looked at her soft fair-complexioned face, her blue eyes that focused the rattler around Brother Dusty's neck, and wondered if her religion was this snake religion. I could never attend this church with her if we married, I thought. I would never trust a rattlesnake. Too many had almost got me in the timber woods. There were fangs of the mountain rattler embedded in my boots.

When I turned my face from her to look over the congregation again, I saw something that made me want to run to the pine woods as I'd seen the small boy run. I saw many men and women, with rattlesnakes around their necks and in their arms. And they were fondling them with no more fear than I would have had if I'd handled a piece of rope.

"These're Sweet Jesus' children," Brother Dusty said. "There ain't no part of the Devil in 'em. Not a chip from the Devil's tree o' sin in 'em. Not a drop of th' Devil's blood! Yes, we've had people bitten by the serpent but the serpent knows the ones that's got Devil in 'em. He knows the facts, people, for he can smell th' Devil in a man a mile away, and he can taste the Devil in 'em when he bites!"

I wondered if these little children had the Devil in them as they ran screaming when their mothers and fathers came out among the congregation with these vicious, rusty-looking rattlers around their necks and in their arms. Many women held the snakes to their bosoms.

Women came from their trances and took up the snakes. The wire-caged doors were all opened now, and I'd never seen as many rattlers in one place. Now I knew why I'd seen the snakes in cages at the shacks on Sanctuary Mountain. These people that came to this church on this night and brought their snakes had kept them in cages so they wouldn't go to sleep. For this was October, a time when rattlers should be in their winter beds.

There was so much to see. I turned my eyes toward the table that Brother Dusty had used for a pulpit, and saw women who didn't have rattlers to prove their faith standing with flaming pine torches, holding the flames to their hands, the rich heavy smelly pine smoke going up in dark heavy spirals toward their faces.

"The flame can't sear this flesh," one screamed, but I knew the flame was searing her flesh, the way she twitched.

"I know I'm a child of Sweet Jesus," a fair-haired woman screamed. "When the flame don't burn, it is the sign!"

"I feel the fire within," another screamed, "but not this worldly fire from the torch that can't sear the flesh because God won't burn His children!"

The children didn't fear the flames; they feared the ugly writhing snakes. They would gather close to watch these women stick the flames to their hands. With one hand these women held the pine torch and applied the flame to the other hand. That evening was something I would never forget. While I sat watching the women apply the torches to their flesh, I saw Brother Dusty with his rattler still around his neck. His big hand was playing with its head, and his big fingers were fingering its lips. I took my arm from around Deutsia to use if the rattler came too near, for I was afraid.

"What's the matter, young man?" Brother Dusty said as he stood before me with his rattlesnake too near for my comfort.

"Don't get that rattler close to me."

"Be saved tonight, young man," he said. "It's the Devil in you. You're possessed with seedy, vile sin."

"Keep back with that rattler," I warned him again.

"What about you, honey?" the woman said to Deutsia.

Deutsia didn't answer her, but with her soft hand she stroked the rattler's head.

"That snake acts as if it knows you," I said to her. I got up from the seat and began to back away.

"It won't bite," she said.

"They ain't no Devil in this pretty girl," Brother Dusty said.

"Let's go, Deutsia," I said, pulling her by the hand. "Let's clear out of here!"

Deutsia and I turned to walk back the way we came.

"I don't belong to this church," Deutsia said in a whisper as we started back to the rear.

"I'm glad you don't."

We faced a crowd of people standing at the rear. Many had their hands and faces bandaged.

"I don't belong to any church," she said.

"What's wrong with these people, anyway?" I asked.

"Burnt hands and bitten by rattlesnakes," she said. "They had Devil in 'em."

"What's all this crowd doing back here?" I asked in a low tone.

"They come to watch what goes on," she said. "They don't belong."

"Look to your left," I whispered.

Deutsia turned her head to look.

"See what I see?"

"Yes."

There stood Fern Hailston and Ben Dewberry among the crowd of onlookers. They were smiling as they watched the crowd of worshipers. Then I saw them looking at us, but when Ben saw me looking at them he quickly turned his head as if he didn't see me. I knew he was ashamed of me.

"Gee, I'm glad to get out of here," I said.

We were out in the pine woods now, where darkness hovered over the earth like a black brooding hen.

"How did you like this church?" she asked me.

"I've never seen anything like it."

"This is the last revival meeting before the rattlesnakes go to sleep. That's why I wanted you to see it."

"Wonder how Ben and Fern got up here?" I asked.

"I don't know," Deutsia said. "Miss Fern ought to be a good mountain climber."

"I didn't worry so much about climbing the mountain," I said. "It's the getting down."

"We'll get down the mountain easier than we got up," Deutsia said.

"We can do anything together."

"I feel strong with you," Deutsia said, "and I need you. I need you always."

We started down the mountain toward the curving ribbon of river. Down we went, away from the wind, the stars and moon.

10

FOR TWO DAYS and nights you've been on my bones," I said to Ben who was sitting directly in front of me smoking a cigarette, "and I'm getting goddamned tired of it!"

Ben knew what he wanted and he was going after it. He was going to marry Fern Hailston and he wanted more money, but his getting more money depended on how hard I worked. If one fell down on the job, both of us lost money. It was too bad for Ben that I was having to do a lot of thinking, for it was causing him to lose a lot of money.

"But I've never seen you act the way you're acting now," Ben said. He pulled a draw from his cigarette. "You act like a man that's nearly dead. You pull the crosscut saw like a woman sixty years old. When I look across the log at you, your eyes have a faraway look in 'em and I can't tell whether you're asleep or awake; I can't tell whether you are dead or alive."

"I'm thinking."

"You ought to do your thinking some place else," he

told me. "When we go out to work, we ought to work. Leave your thinking for idle hours when we're here at the shanty."

"You've been hard as hell to get along with since you saw me at church with Deutsia," I said. "You were ashamed of us."

"You told the truth," Ben snapped. "I *was* ashamed of you there with your arm around a Melungeon."

"I've just been sittin' here a-listenin'," Hezzy put in between puffs on his pipe. "It's none of your business, Ben, and it ain't none of Miss Hailston's business if Dave is in love with a Melungeon. Lawyer Eif Simmons showed 'er to me in Oak Hill th' other day. She's the prettiest gal I've seen in a long time. She's the prettiest gal I've seen in this county."

"But would you tell Dave to marry this Melungeon?"

"I'd say for 'im to marry 'er if he loves her," Hezzy said. He looked straight at Ben. "Man loves many women in the spring of his youth but the real love only comes once. And I believe the real love has come to Dave. I hear 'im a-talkin' to Deutsia at night in his sleep. I hear 'im a-cussin' this one and that one over her. I even hear 'im a-cussin' you, Ben and this Miss Hailston that you plan to marry. I don't think it's a case of the sweet-tail with Dave. I think it's a case of the real love. It's the real thing. He's more in love with his gal than you're in love with yourn."

"How do you know how much I'm in love with Fern?" Ben asked Hezzy. Ben's face was red from Hezzy's telling him that he ought to stay out of my affairs. "You don't look like you've been such a great lover in your day. I don't see you a-sittin' down and writin' a letter home to your wife every day. You do well to write 'er once a week!"

"That's just it, Ben," Hezzy said calmly. "I left my wife in Cameron, New Mexico. I listened to a fellow like you. I played along and tried to kid myself, tried to make myself believe that I didn't like the girl when my heart told me I did love her. And my heart was right. I've known it all these years. My heart still tells me that I love her. And the blood that flowed in her veins wasn't the same as the blood that flowed in my veins."

"Was she dipped too?" Mort asked Hezzy, breaking in on the argument.

"She was a full-blooded Navaho Indian," Hezzy said. "Tall and slender with coarse straight black hair and eyes so black they sparkled like deep pools of mountain water when she looked at me. She had high cheekbones and her skin was as dark as new-ground earth!"

"I'd never settle down with a tribe of Indians out in some faraway place," Mort said, shaking his head and blowing a cloud of smoke.

"I think she was an Indian princess," Hezzy went on. "She married the son of a Navaho chief. His name was Little Star. Now she's Mrs. Little Star, when she should be Mrs. Hezzy Blair. And I could've settled in New Mexico and lived with her people, hunted, fished, and trapped with 'em, and I'd 'a been happier there than I am a-livin' on this mountain, a-cuttin' timber through the week and going to Skinny and Sylvania's to get drunk Sundays."

"But who knows what kind of blood the Melungeons 've got in 'em?" Ben asked Hezzy. "Deutsia Huntoon's not the daughter of an Indian chief. She's not a Navaho. I know what people think she is."

"I wouldn't advise you to say too much, Ben," I said.

"Who gives a damn what kind of blood she's got in her

veins?" Hezzy asked Ben. I was pleased that one man in the whole damned county had taken my side. "If Dave loves her, that's all that matters. He's got enough prejudice to fight without a man who is supposed to be his best friend a-turnin' on 'im. You ought to help 'im fight his battle instead of your turnin' around and fighting against 'im."

"I can't see it that way," Mort put in. "I think Ben is trying to help 'im. I think if he goes on with that gal and gets serious with 'er, one of these days he'll look back and see where Ben Dewberry was his friend. He'll get sore as hell at 'im now, but that won't be the situation in a few years from now."

All three men were interested in my affair. Each had taken his stand. Maybe it was because they'd heard a lot of talk. I knew Ben had heard plenty and he'd seen plenty with his own eyes. Never before had the four of us argued as we argued now. We'd gotten along fine together for seven years. And now Ben had met Fern Hailston and I had met Deutsia Huntoon, and since Fern was filled with prejudices toward Deutsia and her people, she had influenced Ben to see and feel her way. Our arguments in the shanty and the timber woods were getting more violent as the days passed.

That night I didn't go to sleep until midnight. I rolled and tossed on my bunk thinking of crossing the Clinch River with Deutsia and how we climbed the mountain, how we walked along the ridge road to church and what a strange church it was. I thought of those things and this snake religion. That worried me more than the blood in Deutsia's veins.

But I did think of the blood that flowed in her veins, of

her ancestors, the vast continent from which they sprang.
... I thought of Spain, and the things I'd read about Spain
and the Spanish people in my advanced geography, my fa-
vorite subject in school in the mountains of Virginia. I'd
read where the Spaniards were dark and handsome and that
there were mountains in Spain, there were guitars and
music and much dancing, fighting and fun. And I read
where the Spaniards drank wine at their meals as we drank
coffee, water and milk. Could it be, I thought, that the
blood of the Spaniards flowed in Deutsia's veins?

Could she have come from the Portuguese? I wondered. I remembered a picture of a dark-complexioned man
with bearded lips I'd seen in my geography when I studied
about Portugal. I read that the Portuguese had once been,
like the Spaniards, a powerful nation of seafaring people,
that they took their ships to almost every port in the then
known world and did a lot of trading. And it could have
been, I thought, that one of their ships had wrecked on the
Carolina coast and that the Portuguese had come ashore
and had migrated westward to the mountain ranges, had
taken Cherokee Indian wives, and caused all this trouble
two hundred years later when I'd met one of their beautiful descendants in Cantwell County.

Could it be that Deutsia had that seafaring blood in her,
just a spark of that ancestry left, that made her roam the
mountain and know the rivers?

Maybe it was the Indian in her, I thought. The
Cherokee that made her roam the mountain, know the
trees, the birds, almost every variety of plant and flower
that grew on the mountain, the plant roots that were good
to eat and those that were poisonous, the nuts and berries
that were good to eat and where to find them, how to fish,
hunt, course the wild bee to his tree.

Maybe some of her ancestors were savages in the vast dark continent of Africa. Maybe they had known the fear of the cobra, a snake more deadly than the rattlesnake, in the dense jungle where the wind was hot and smothery to breathe; maybe they had known the scorch of the torrid sun which had darkened their flesh, maybe they had known the jungle trails and all the fears of the wild beasts that infested the jungle; maybe they had chanted unknown words while they danced to the beat of the tom-tom. Maybe blood from these savages was in Deutsia's veins.

And there must be something of my own ancestry in her, I thought, when I remembered her hair. For I'd read in a history book about the blond hair of the Anglo-Saxons. The Romans took young girls they had captured on this isle back to Rome to sell into slavery, but when the Romans saw their golden hair they wouldn't sell them as slaves. When I read about these Anglo-Saxon girls that escaped slavery in Rome, I wanted to think young Roman boys two thousand years ago fell in love with these golden-haired girls, married them and were kind to them, taught them the Roman language and the ways of the Roman people.

I'm from a race that won't be bullied, I reasoned. And that's the Scottish race. Because I loved this girl, I would fight for her and her place among others.

I had problems ahead of me. I didn't know what kind of blood flowed in Deutsia's veins, but one thing I was sure of as I tossed on my bunk: I wasn't going to let anybody shove her around. She had the same right to love and happiness everybody else had. I'd be damned if I was going to let a few people tell me the girl I should marry and the girl I should leave alone. Ben Dewberry, Mort Higgins and all the people in the valley and Oak Hill wouldn't tell me what to do. I had to be honest with myself and let my own heart be my guide, since I had found a girl I loved until love hurt me.

"Why don't you be quiet, Dave, so we can go to sleep?" Ben Dewberry said, raising up on his bunk. "Every time I doze off to sleep you kick your blanket like a mule and let out a moan. What's eatin' on ye? Sweet tail?"

"Too many people tryin' to tell me what to do," I said. "I'm in love and I've got a troubled mind."

"But what I've said to you, Dave, is for your own good," Ben said, as he lay back down. "We've been friends from boyhood, back as far as we can remember. And someday you'll thank your lucky stars you had me for a friend to give you good advice and get you to lay off that Melungeon woman. The people around here who ain't Melungeons know you're from good stock. They know you don't belong to those Melungeons. They know you shouldn't join that clan in holy matrimony, either. You and Deutsia Huntoon are the talk of the people in Oak Hill and the talk's a-spreadin' all over Cantwell County."

"Ben's right, Dave," Mort Higgins said. "You poor lumberjack, layin' there on your bunk, tossin' and a-moanin' so that you can't sleep and won't let us sleep . . . all over that Huntoon gal! I gave you some good advice too, Dave. As I've told you before, she's all right to play around with. Play with her and get this thing ye think is love, this sweet tail, outen yer system. You'll know someday Ben Dewberry and Mort Higgins were yer friends, fer they stood up to yer face and told ye the truth. It takes a friend, Dave, to tell ye the truth to yer face. Ye'll remember us, Dave, till yer dyin' day."

"Won't ye shut up, all of ye, and go to sleep," Hezzy

said. "Hell, we've got to work tomorrow. I was asleep and, goddammit, Ben, you and Mort...ye advice-givers and world-savers...waked me. Hell, let Dave alone! If he loves Deutsia Huntoon and she loves him with a love that's deep, they're lucky! They're damned lucky! Deep love comes only once. Let 'em marry and be sure ye keep your goddam bills outen their affairs. Quit peckin' at 'em. Leave 'em alone. And everybody get quiet so I can get some shut-eye!"

I didn't answer anything that had been said. I'd heard it before. There was no use to stir up an argument that late at night. It was my affair. I had to work it out. I was already worked up to the place I was ready to start swinging with my fists. I pulled my blanket back over me and I lay perfectly still. Don Praytor's words came back to me: *If you marry Deutsia Huntoon you'll have regrets always. Hold to your freedom while you have it.*

11

WEDNESDAY we cut less timber than we'd cut on any day that we had ever worked together. When I said something to Ben he would snap his words at me, like a snapping turtle fighting for his life. I would snap my answers right back at him. For I was getting to the place that I despised Ben and I knew that he despised me. Money was what he wanted most right now, and I bore down on the crosscut saw to make the sawing tough for him. I knew that it meant less money for Ben and myself. But Deutsia was not after money. And money didn't mean a hell of a lot to me. Money meant a lot to Fern Hailston and Ben Dewberry; money was their substitute for love.

On Thursday, Ben didn't speak to me all day and I didn't speak to him. If he wanted me to reach him his ax when he was in a position where he couldn't easily get to it, he would motion to me to hand him his ax and I would. And if I wanted my ax when it was on Ben's side of the tree laps,

I would motion to him to reach it to me and he would. All day we cut timber, doing our talking with signs by motions of our hands and heads.

On Friday Ben openly threatened me with his knife, drawing it from his pocket and calling me vile names. I grabbed my double-bitted ax and made for him with my ax poised ready to strike. Ben saw that I meant business and he ran through the timber woods toward the sound of Mort's and Hezzy's axes with me at his heels. When we came in sight, Ben yelled at Mort to stop me. If Mort and Hezzy hadn't caught me and hadn't taken the ax from me and begged both of us to be at peace with each other, I don't know what I would have done to Ben. If he hadn't outrun me, I would have done something.

On Saturday, when we went to Oak Hill to get our checks, get them cashed and bring back a load of supplies, Mort rode in the truck cab with Ben and I rode in the truck bed with Hezzy. That was the day several people, whom I'd never seen before, came to me and told me in nice sweet words that I was hurting myself by going with a Melungeon. Each had the same story to tell, the story they'd probably told many other young men that had come to Cantwell County and had fallen in love with a beautiful Melungeon girl, for each told the story too smoothly not to have told it many times before.

"You are a handsome young man and you are a stranger here and I feel that it is my duty to warn you about something you probably don't know about. I hope you won't feel hurt when I tell you. I want to warn you about the girl you are taking too seriously, the beautiful Melungeon girl, Deutsia Huntoon. Of course, it's none of my business but you know that she's not really our people. Of course, she has white blood in her veins but that's the catch ... it's not all white blood. And if I were you, I'd think twice before I would be seen with her again, since all the people here have noticed you with her. And everybody's a-talkin' about it and pitying you. Your good friend Ben Dewberry, who is such a nice young man, is terribly upset over it. He's about to worry himself to death over your situation."

"Lady, that's my own affair," I'd say after waiting until she was through with her story. "I don't give a damn what kind of blood flows in Deutsia Huntoon's veins just so it isn't blue blood!"

As soon as I'd say my little speech, each would take off with a sullen, hurt look, but I didn't care. I'd heard enough about blood and ancestry to go me a lifetime, and I'd made up my mind to fight for my rights and the girl I loved.

When I got my hundred and sixty-eight dollars, after I'd paid for my part of our supplies, I folded the bills and put them in my hip pocket. I didn't know when and where I would have use for this money. I'd made up my mind that I was leaving the shanty. As Ben drove back up the mountain, I knew that this would be the last time I would ever ride in this truck. I was through, and Hezzy would have to get another man to take my place to work as a partner with Ben Dewberry.

"It hurts like hell, Dave, to see you a-leavin' us," Hezzy said. He leaned against the door facing, wiping tears from his eyes with the back of his calloused hand. "It'll be hard to find another man that can use an ax like you can. It'll be hard to find another man as easy to get along with. And if you ever need work, you know where to come."

"Ben wouldn't say that I was easy to get along with." I

stood in the shanty yard, with my toolkit and my turkey of clothes.

"But don't pay too much attention to Ben," Mort Higgins said. "Ben and I both said a lot we didn't mean."

"How can I keep from paying attention to a man that tries to run my affairs?" I asked Mort. "What right has he to fight against my happiness? What right has he to call me vile names?"

"It all happened in a fit of temper," Mort said.

"He's been in a fit of temper ever since he started dating Fern Hailston," I said. "Ben and Fern Hailston have everybody in Oak Hill in the same fit of temper. I ought to know because of what happened yesterday. I know it's time for me to get out of here. I know that I'll be sleeping under a different roof."

"I hate to see you go, Dave," Hezzy said, shaking his head. "But I admire you, fellar! I don't blame you a bit. You're a-lettin' your heart be your guide. I hope everything will work out for you. I wish you a lot of happiness!"

"I got my part of the knives, forks, spoons, dishes, pots and pans," I said. "Thought I might need them."

"That's all right, Dave," Hezzy said as he walked down the shanty steps, took my big hand in his big calloused hand and squeezed it in a handshake of good friendship. Mort followed him down the steps and shook my hand.

"I hope you get along all right," Mort said. "I think you'd better think this thing over before you go ahead. You may not be a happy man to go among people not your kind. Remember Sanctuary Mountain ain't as big as the country you've had to roam over."

"I understand all that, Mort," I said. "But I no longer

need your advice. This is goodbye. It's not the time to take
any more advice from you. I know what I want. I know
what I'm going to do."

Mort and Hezzy stood watching me with blank expressions on their faces as I lifted my toolkit and my turkey
from the ground. Ben Dewberry didn't come out of the
shanty to say goodbye and wish me luck. He wasn't that
kind. Our years of friendship didn't mean anything to him
now, for he hadn't spoken to me since Friday when I ran
after him through the woods with my double-bitted ax.

As I climbed the bluff above the shanty, I dropped my
toolkit and turkey on the ground beside me once to look
back at the shanty. And there Mort and Hezzy stood in the
yard, watching me silently. I waved goodbye to Hezzy and
Mort and I was on my way. When I reached the ridge
road, I looked toward the valley where I saw fluffy clouds
that looked thick and soft as a featherbed, clouds on which
it would be good to sleep, floating lazily over the valley,
pushed along slowly by a mountain wind. I dropped my
tools, wiped sweat from my face and filled my pipe with
burley leaf. Then, I walked forward swiftly toward my
destination.

12

YOU HAVE come," Deutsia said. She met me at the door. She spoke with a tone of surprise, but didn't ask any questions.

"Yes, I've come."

I dropped my toolkit by the door, and walked into Huntoons' shack.

"Meet my mother, Dave," Deutsia said, introducing me to the shy dark woman I'd seen before.

"Glad to meet you, Mrs. Huntoon," I said. I shook her hand that had warmth, but fell limp when I held it. "It's good to see you," she said softly. She pulled away as if she were afraid of me. She was embarrassed at my coming un-invited to their shack. I could have told Mrs. Huntoon that this was not the first time we had met. I'd first seen her barefooted and with a basket of hickory nuts. The last time I saw her she had a rattlesnake pressed against her bosom and was walking up the broad aisle of the church under the pines between the rows of split-rail log seats.

"I'm glad you're here," Deutsia said, as Mrs. Huntoon walked back into the kitchen. "I think of you all the time."

"Since that night at the church," I said, "I've thought of you almost day and night. I've been through a lot since that night. Now I am here with all the possessions I have."

When I'd finished saying these words, Deutsia wiped tears from her eyes.

"I knew you'd never let me down," she said. "I knew if I couldn't believe in you, there wasn't a man in the world that I would believe. And now I need you. I need you more than I've ever needed you in my life."

Just then a door opened and a tall man, dressed in faded overalls and a blue workshirt, walked in with his head bowed so he could walk under the door. His face was covered with red beard. His eyes were blue as violets in April on the mountain and he had long horns of reddish mustache that reached almost to his ears.

"This is my father, Dave," Deutsia said.

"I'm glad to make your acquaintance, young man," he said. He clasped my hand and gave it a hearty squeeze, his blue eyes searching my eyes. He certainly looked me over from head to foot.

"I'm glad to know Deutsia's father."

He released his grip on my hand and put his arm around Deutsia and drew her close to him.

"She's been Daddy's boss girl ever since she's been big enough to follow 'im to a hunt. She used to go with me and carry the game until I had to carry her and her load."

And then he tickled her playfully with his stubby fingers under the chin and he patted her head.

"Yes, she's Bass' Deutsia all right," he said.

I had noticed that nearly all of the Melungeons' men,

with the exception of the young men, had beardy faces. Nearly all the Melungeon women, old and young, wore long hair that fell down their backs. And nearly all of them, young or old, with the exception of Brother Dusty, had pretty rows of even clean white teeth.

"Is that your toolkit outside by the door?" Mr. Huntoon asked me.

"Yes."

"You a-goin' to cut timber someplace?"

"I've been a-cuttin' timber."

"Finished?"

"We didn't get done," I said. "But I'm through with that job!"

"You've got a kit of nice-looking tools," he said. "And you've got a crosscut saw so sharp that'll eat right through seasoned locust."

"Yes sir, I keep it that way."

I wondered if Deutsia had told him about me.

"Where's Daid?" he asked, turning toward Deutsia.

"She's in the kitchen," Deutsia said.

He walked toward the kitchen door, opened it and went inside, closing the door behind him. I heard them talking in low tones behind the closed door while I looked around the room quickly. There were two big homemade beds, one in each corner of the room. They were covered with crazy-patched quilts. There was a stand table with a large white bowl and pitcher on it and there was a dresser on the side of the room opposite the stand table. It was an old piece of homemade furniture with a mirror that reached almost to the low papered ceiling. The walls were papered with newspapers and there were portraits of men with dogs and guns, portraits of old people and a few of children, portraits of the Huntoons and their relatives. The portraits of the old people looked as if they were people from a different world. The room was tidy. The floor was scrubbed clean and was spotted with homemade rugs.

"Sit down," Deutsia said. "There's no use standing when there's an empty chair."

"Does your father know that I've been goin' with you?" I asked her.

"He never asks me who I go with," she said. "And I didn't tell him."

"Does your mother know that I go with you?"

"Not until she saw me at church with you."

"How do I go about asking 'em to marry you, then?"

"You've got to ask me first," she said.

"Haven't I ever asked you?"

"Not that I remember."

"Deutsia, will you marry me?"

"Yes. My mind's been made up since the day we met."

"So has mine."

"Why should you ask my parents?"

"I thought they ought to know."

"It's all right for 'em to know," she said. Thinking a minute, she continued, "I guess they should know. But a marriage is up to two people. It's up to you and me. My mother and father married because they loved each other. Then why shouldn't I marry you if I love you and you love me? Why should my parents choose the man for me to marry after they've had their right to marriage?"

"There's not any reason," I said. I thought about how my brothers-in-law had asked my parents for my two sisters. And when I thought about them, I remembered a few marriages where the parents married their children because they were friends and got along fine together, but when their children married the marriages didn't last.

"It should take only two people to decide on whether or not to get married," Deutsia said. "Just you and I." She got up from her chair and put her arms around me.

"I feel the same way."

"But I know how some of your friends will feel."

"Let's don't mention them," I said.

"But we won't be able to escape them."

"We'll never bother them."

"But they'll bother us."

"Didn't the men you worked with hate to see you go?"

"Hezzy and Mort hated to see me go," I said. "Ben was glad that I went."

I didn't tell Deutsia that we had come to blows. I didn't tell her about the words that we'd had. And I didn't tell her about the women in Oak Hill who had come to me each with the same story, warning me not to marry her. I knew that she'd had these things to face all of her life and she wouldn't want to hear them again.

"Do they have a man to take your place?"

"I don't know. I don't care. That's their problem."

"You just packed and walked away?"

"I've come to marry you," I said. "I want you more than anything in this world."

We embraced. As lodestone is to a metal we were drawn together by an irresistible force called love. Then, we heard loud voices and much laughter outside the shack. I had just taken my arms from around Deutsia when the front door opened. All the talking and laughing was coming from the three boys and two girls who entered. Two of the boys were carrying buckets.

"Dave, I want you to meet the rest of the family." They stopped still in their tracks, looking at each other.

"This is my sister Meese." She introduced me to a tall dark-complexioned girl with long crow-wing-black straight hair, black eyes, white teeth and a shapely body.

"And this is my sister Alona." She introduced me to a golden-haired girl of about fourteen who looked very much like Deutsia.

"This is my oldest brother, Pribble." She introduced me to a tall dark-complexioned boy whom I had heard play the guitar at church. He was as dark as Deutsia's mother and he was as shy, for he barely spoke to me. He acted like a wild fox in my presence. He was all the time trying to get away.

"This is Force." She introduced me to a tall light-complexioned youth of about eighteen who was more at ease with us than Pribble, who had gone from the room.

"And this is Cress," she said. She ruffled his dark wavy hair with her hand. "He's the baby."

"I'm not a baby," he said.

He looked down at his bare feet.

"Where did you get the buckets of fish?" I asked. I had been watching them swishing in the buckets of water.

"In the Clinch."

"How did you catch em?"

"Trot lines and nets."

And before he'd finished his words, Deutsia's brothers and sisters shyly hurried into the kitchen, Cress slamming the door behind them. They were all glad to get away from me, a stranger. They didn't know I was planning to be their brother-in-law. I wondered what made them so shy of me. I wondered if they were as much prejudiced against the outlanders as the outlanders were prejudiced against the Melungeons.

Deutsia and I had the front room in the shack all to ourselves. We pulled our chairs close together where we could put our arms around each other. We used happy words when we spoke to each other. There were no barriers between us. No, not one. For not even the snake-religion of Deutsia's people could come between us. Our words dripping with wild-honey sweetness went from her lips and my lips to each other's ears, then into each other's hearts, where they stopped to stay forever.

When Mr. Huntoon opened the door his eyes were filled with surprise. I felt the blood surge to my face as I took my arms from around Deutsia and looked up at him. I couldn't tell if he was disgusted, surprised or happy, for his eyes twinkled as he looked at us. Turning around quickly, he slowly walked back to the kitchen.

"Come to dinner," he said.

I followed Deutsia into the kitchen, where a long table stood loaded with dishes of sweet-scented food. There was a stove in one corner and a cupboard in the other, where pots, pans, dippers and cups hung from nails on the uneven newspapered log walls. I saw strings of red peppers, leatherbritches beans, drying apples, squash and pumpkin hanging on the walls near the stove and in a corner behind the stove. I noticed the floor was scrubbed as clean as the clothless table where we ate. I felt hungry when I smelled this food.

"You want to wash your hands and face?" Mrs. Huntoon asked me.

"I do," I said.

"Then come out here," Deutsia said. We went out to

the porch, where there was a large wooden bucket filled
with water on a little table. There were bars of homemade
soap in a dish and a clean towel hanging to a nail on the
wall.

Deutsia dipped water with a gourd and poured it into
the pan.

"Do we wash together?" I asked her.

"If two wash together from the same pan of water and
dry on the same towel, they will be good friends forever,"
she said.

Deutsia rubbed her wet hands with herb-scented soap
until they were filled with bright soapy lather and then she
gave the soap to me. I lathered my hands and we washed
our hands and faces in the same pan of water, laughing
when the soap got into our eyes and made them smart. She
lifted the towel from the nail and we dried ourselves.

"Now you sit there," Daid Huntoon said. She pointed
to my chair.

"And this is my place," Deutsia said, sitting down in the
chair beside mine.

When Deutsia said these words she smiled. Her father
smiled, too, but Daid Huntoon didn't, nor did Pribble,
Cress or Meese. There was an expression of sadness in Daid
Huntoon's face that reminded me of a dark winter tree
asleep in a dismal rain.

I ate greedily of better food than I'd had in a long time.
We had fried river fish, wild rabbit fried crisp with brown
gravy, mashed potatoes; we had wild blackberries they had
picked from the mountains in their season and had canned.
We had squash and turnips; we had wild honey, dark and
light in the cone piled on two big dishes; we had griddle
cornpone and butter. We had coffee, wine and milk to
drink. We had wild huckleberry pie for dessert.

When the children spoke to Mr. Huntoon at the table, they called him Bass. And when they spoke to Mrs. Huntoon, they called her Daid. Though it was hard for me to call them by their first names, since I'd been taught to call my parents Mother and Father, I followed the example of their children. I didn't use the name Daid once, since she didn't talk to me while she ate. But I talked to Bass, Force and Alona. I let Pribble, Cress, Meese and Daid remain in their silence. I watched them reach and help themselves when the dishes were close enough. When the dishes were not close, they mumbled shy words to each other, asking for them.

Deutsia and I laughed and talked as if we had always known each other and eaten at the table many times together. I not only passed dishes to Deutsia but I dipped the food from the dish onto her plate and let her tell me when she had enough; then I'd add a little extra. Force and Alona laughed at our table manners. And Bass would look at us and smile. But I wondered what he was thinking and I wondered what Daid was thinking when she looked at me with her sad black eyes.

"It's the best meal I've eaten in many moons," I said. I finished my last swallow of coffee with my wild huckleberry pie. "It's certainly better than I've been eating at the shanty. Somebody here is a better cook than Mort Higgins and Hezzy Blair."

At these words a tiny smile played on Daid's lips.

As the children finished their dinner, each got up quietly and left the kitchen. When Deutsia and I got up from the table we left Daid and Bass sitting there. We went back to the front room and no sooner had we reached the chairs by the hearth when we heard the dishes rattling behind us.

"We'll soon be washing dishes together, won't we, honey?" I said.

After Daid and Bass had finished with the dishes and walked into the front room, I knew it was the right time to talk with them about my marriage to Deutsia. Bass was smoking a light burley cigar that he had rolled himself, holding it between his beardy lips and blowing clouds of smoke that feathered upward to the newspapered ceiling.

"Bass, did you ever give something that belonged to you, something that you loved very dearly, to somebody you didn't know very well?" I asked him.

I tried to let my words fall as easy as if I were speaking to Mort or Hezzy in the timber woods. I was afraid that Daid and Bass were going to walk directly through the room, if I didn't say something to hold them.

"I don't know exactly what you mean," Bass said, sitting down in a chair across the hearth from me.

"You and Daid have something that I want as much as life. I want Deutsia."

When I said these words Daid looked at Bass with her black eyes shining like deep pools of leaf-stained water glowing in the sun. Deutsia looked at Bass and Daid and then at me.

"I want to marry Deutsia," I said to break the silence and to change the puzzled expressions on Daid's and Bass' faces.

"You mean that you want to marry Deutsia?" Bass asked me, as if he were not sure of my words.

"That's what I mean."

"How long have you knowed Deutsia?"

"About two months."

My voice trembled since I couldn't understand the strange actions of Daid and Bass.

"Do you know you want to marry 'er?" Bass asked me as he blew a cloud of smoke from his cigar.

"I know I want to marry her," I said. "I'm in love with Deutsia."

"Are you in love with him, Deutsia?" Bass asked.

"I am," she replied.

"It's so sudden," Bass said. There was something more Bass wanted to say. But when he started to say it, he'd stumble for words, and he would pull harder on his cigar and blow bigger clouds of smoke into the room.

"Do you know there are prejudices against our people?" Bass asked me.

"Yes, I know it," I said.

"And then you are willin' to marry my Deutsia?"

"Yes, I'm willing."

"You mean you want to marry my daughter Deutsia, even though she's a Melungeon?"

"To me she is an angel," I said. "She's the prettiest girl in the world and I love her more than any girl I've ever seen. Yes, I mean I want to marry your daughter Deutsia."

"If you marry Deutsia, you will have to love her," Bass said, looking at the embers. "It will be a test of your love for her, because when you marry her you'll be one of us and people are not kind to us. If you do not know about us, and all the barriers against us, you'd better think this over before you jump from the frying pan into the fire."

"I know about the barriers," I said. "I've had to fight them already."

"Then it's all up to you and Deutsia," he said. "She has the right to marry the one she loves. I asked you these questions because you are an outlander and a stranger and I want you to know the facts about us. I don't think you should marry her and not know 'em. I don't have any right to make up Deutsia's mind for her. She can make up her own mind. I hope she doesn't get a husband that is prejudiced against her and her people. We've had enough to fight in our lifetime. And our children will have enough to fight. And maybe your children will have enough to fight."

Here's one who can and will fight for them, I thought.

"I'm glad you feel the way you do, Bass," I said. "Even if you and Did would've been against our marrying, we might have married anyway."

Did never said one word while we had talked. Her face and eyes gave expressions of how she felt about the things we had talked about and that was all. Now that it was all settled we could begin to make our own plans for a new life that belonged to us.

"Mom always told me to build the cage first and then catch the bird," I said to Deutsia as we sat on an uprooted pine. Here we could look over across the deep valley below. "I have the bird but don't have any cage."

"You don't have ideas about building one?"

The strong mountain wind blew across the valley toward us. It blew Deutsia's hair behind her against the pine needles.

"What do you think I brought my tools along for? I can make about anything with wood. I can make very good furniture."

"That's wonderful," she said. "I'd like pretty furniture that you made in our house."

"Making furniture is my hobby. I wish you could see

the furniture in my home in Virginia that I made for my mother."

"You've got to make us a cupboard, chairs, a bed and tables," she said. "And you've got to make us some baskets. You've got to make one that we can carry into the mountains and fill with hickory nuts."

"I'll do that soon," I said. "But let's plan what to do first. We've got to get married. And then I'll have to get a piece of land for us," I said.

"What do you mean?"

"I'll have to buy a little piece of land for our house and garden."

"No, this mountain belongs to all of us," she said. "This is our mountain. We can build where we please."

"Then we'll walk around and find a place," I said. "We'll do that before we go back to your shack. You ought to know some good places."

"I know the place," she said. "I've always dreamed I'd have a house here and that I'd live here someday."

We didn't walk two hundred yards from the pine log where we'd been sitting until we came to a level spot where there was dirt enough to cover the rocks.

"This is the place," she said. "There's a good spring in the pine grove. See that stream of water coming from the rocks?"

"I can see a stream flowing away."

"There's a big spring under the cliff."

"That's wonderful," I said. I lifted a handful of earth and let it sift between my fingers. "And this is good dirt for a garden."

"We can see in every direction from here," Deutsia said.

"There're even plenty of loose rocks here for a chimney and a foundation," I said. "And yonder's oak timber for house logs."

"Then this will be the place."

We stood watching the sunset; it was like a red wagon wheel. I put my arms around Deutsia and pulled her close. I kissed her wind-cooled lips. I knew we were standing on the place where we would see many suns sink, over the mountain. Here we would be near Heaven.

13

NO TWO people could have been happier than we. Deutsia went barefooted so she wouldn't spoil her slippers on the dew-moist autumn leaves that drifted onto the path. She wore wild flowers in her hair and a soft white voile dress with lace and ruffles at the neck and sleeves.

I wore my oxford gray suit, soft gray felt hat, new tan shoes. I knew the world would soon belong to me. We would soon have a license to marry; then we would go to Flem Reeder, Squire of Oak Hill, and have him marry us.

"There's the courthouse, Deutsia," I said. "It looks better to me than it has ever looked before, honey."

"Yes, I know we're close," she said, her voice shaky.

"What's the matter, honey? You're not afraid, are you?"

"No, I'm not afraid," she said with a smile.

"Just nervous, like I've been all morning. This morning I forgot to shave one side of my face. I didn't know it until I looked into the mirror."

"I'm forgettin' something," Deutsia said, looking at her feet.

She placed her hand on my shoulder, brushed the damp sand grains from one foot and then the other and put on her hose and her slippers.

"Now I'm ready."

"I couldn't sleep last night for thinking of today," I said. "I kept Pribble and Force awake about all night. Once I raised my arm and hit Force across the face. Once Pribble woke me trying to lift my leg from over him."

"Sounds like you slept in the middle!"

"I did."

"How do I look?" Deutsia asked me.

"You look just the way I want the girl I'm going to marry to look, so beautiful you take my breath away," I told her. I was afraid to tell her she was pale and her lips were trembling.

We walked briskly up to the courthouse steps, trying to miss the tobacco quids and puddles of ambeer spittle. I could feel the fear run through Deutsia's arm like a current. She was as shaky as oak leaves in an autumn wind.

Though we were early, there were many people standing in the clerk's office waiting to be served. Behind the partition that ran across the room two secretaries worked busily. One would ask this man what he wanted and he'd say he wanted to know something about a deed to his land, and then she would say, as she opened a little gate for him to enter into their side of the partitioned room, "You'll have to go back and see Mr. Woods. You'll find him in the first room on your right." We dropped into the long line of people and waited impatiently.

"Something for you?"

"We want a marriage license," I said.

All eyes turned upon us as we watched the secretary, a tall girl wearing a tan suit, her blond hair crinkled with waves, walk toward a cabinet, pull out a drawer and return with a paper decorated with wreaths of roses.

"Your name, please?" she asked me while she unfolded the flowery scroll.

"Dave Stoneking."

"Your age?"

"Twenty-six."

"Have you been married before?"

"No."

And then she asked me the date of my birth, my mother's and father's names and the names of my grandparents.

"Kate," the other clerk who was short and fat called to her, "come over here a minute."

Kate walked over and the short clerk whispered something. We could see her painted lips moving but I couldn't tell the words they were saying. When they'd finished, we saw Kate draw her lips tightly and an ugly frown came over her face.

"You'll have to come inside to see Mr. Woods."

She opened the little door for us and we followed her. She seemed to be in a hurry to get through with us as soon as possible.

"Mr. Woods, here are two people wanting to get married," she said.

We faced a man dressed in a gray suit, wearing a stiff celluloid collar and a broad bow tie. There was a pencil and a fountain pen in his front coat pocket, and several pencils lying on the highly varnished desk he sat behind.

"What's wrong, Kate?" he asked. He looked up from a paper on his desk.

"The girl's name is Huntoon, sir," she said. "I thought it was a problem for you to decide."

After she had said these words, she hurried out of his private office.

"Huntoon, huh?" he said, glancing up at Deutsia and then looking back at the paper on his desk.

"Where are you from, young man?"

"Virginia."

"A stranger in these parts, huh?"

"No, I'm not a stranger here."

"Then you know about the Huntoons?"

"Yes, I know about the Huntoons."

"After knowing about the facts, you want to marry this girl?" he asked, his face getting red.

"Yes, I want to marry her."

"Did you know there's a law that prohibits my issuing you a license?"

"What do you mean?"

"Did you know she's a Melungeon?"

"Yes. What do you know about the Melungeons?"

"I know Melungeon means dark race," he said. "Dark races and white races don't mix here. There's a law against it, thank God."

"But who knows who these Melungeons are?" I said. "They could be Phoenicians mixed with Indians."

He hit the table with his hand. I looked at Deutsia as she tried to turn her face from me. Tears were streaming down her face.

"You can't get a license here," he said. "No, never."

"I thought this was a free country."

"Don't argue with me," he warned, his voice contorted with anger. "Don't argue with me if you want to go out of here alive. You may be a big strong man but I have the difference right here in my desk."

He pulled the desk drawer open until I could see he meant business. I saw the long, bright shining barrel of a .38 Special.

"Young woman, I'd sell you a license any time to marry one of your kind," he said, easing his hand over the handle of his revolver.

"I don't want trouble," I said. "I didn't come here for trouble. We want to get married."

"But you can't get married here," he said, the muscles in his jaws tightening. "Only one white man ever got a license here to marry a Melungeon. He was so ugly he couldn't marry one of his kind, so he cut the woman's arm he was to marry and drank some of her blood and swore he had Melungeon blood in his veins. We knew what he'd done before we took his oath on the witness stand. We issued the low-down a marriage license."

"I don't want to hear about it," I said.

"But your case is similar," he said. "I thought you ought to know these things."

"Remember one thing," I said, as I followed Deutsia, who was pulling at my hand. "If you'll leave your difference in the drawer and come outside with me, I'll show you what a 'difference' is!"

"I warn you," he said, "that you won't be able to get a marriage license in any of the adjoining counties."

With one hand on his revolver, he sat looking at the paper on his desk. We walked out of his office, faced the cold eyes staring at us as we went out the way we'd come in. Everybody had been listening to the words Mr. Woods and I had said.

"I sometimes wish I was dead," Deutsia cried when we got outside the courthouse.

"Don't feel that way."

"I can't help it," she said, crying as though her heart would break.

People stopped and looked at us on the street as we left town.

"Why was I ever born?"

"You were born for me."

"I never told you that *I* didn't sleep last night," she sobbed. "I didn't know whether to go today or not. I wasn't sure that we could get the license. But I want to marry you."

"Don't worry, honey."

"But you could've married some other girl," she said. "You wouldn't've had all this trouble. You'd have been much happier."

Deutsia stopped to wipe the tears from her eyes so she could see the path.

When we reached Huntoons' shack, Deutsia ran inside and threw her arms around Bass' neck and sobbed until her body trembled. Daid stood nearby with tears running down her clay-colored cheeks. Meese, Alona, Pribble, Force and Cress gathered into the room and stood silently as Deutsia wept.

"We couldn't get . . ."

"I understand, Deutsia," Bass said quickly before she had time to tell him. "I know what happened. You don't have to tell me."

"But it hurts to know. . . ."

"I know, I know, my Deutsia," Bass interrupted quickly. "It's too bad it must be like this, my child. Don't grieve too much. Don't waste too many tears. You have too many good days before you."

Deutsia's face was hidden in her hands as she leaned against Bass, sobbing. With one of his powerful arms around her shoulders, he drew her close to him and with his big hand he stroked her golden hair gently.

"What will we do now?" Deutsia asked him, sniffling.

"My child, this night will be a happy night for you. For every tear you've shed you will laugh once. And when you have laughed you'll've forgotten much that has been said to you! Now hush your crying! You're a woman and you must face the world!"

As I stood wondering what Bass was going to do, Daid wiped tears from her eyes with the corner of her blue-checked apron. Her face brightened at the words Bass had spoken.

"Daid, put on every big and little pot," Bass said. "Prepare a midnight feast."

"What are you going to do, Bass?" she said.

"Never mind what I'm going to do," Bass told her. "Do as I tell you. Meese, you and Alona help Daid. Cress, you keep stovewood and water in the kitchen fer 'em! Put up the best we have to eat and something of everything we've got. Give the best we have on this night."

Deutsia took her hands from her face and looked up at Bass with tear-stained eyes.

"What does this mean, Bass?" she asked.

"Never you mind, my child," he said, looking at Pribble.

"Pribble, you get on the mule and ride until dark askin' everybody to come tonight to an all-night dance and midnight feast. You go toward Sylvania and Skinny's shack. Go to all the shacks down on the fingers o' the mountain. Don't miss a shack. Invite everybody. Invite every man, woman and child."

"What do you want me to do, Bass?" Force asked.

"You go out the ridge road toward Treadways' and Leffersons' and invite everybody out that way," Bass ordered him. "Don't miss a shack. If you do and the people hear about what went on here tonight, they'll be mad at us for a long time to come."

We watched Pribble and Force hurry toward the barn. Force went out the gate, his steps getting faster as he hurried along the dusty ridge road while the midday sun was high in the sky.

"And you," Bass said, looking at Deutsia and then at me, "I'm going to make it lighter on you, since you will be the groom and bride. I want you to gather wild flowers and decorate this room for tonight."

"Sounds like there's going to be a wedding here tonight," I said.

"You didn't miss it," Bass said, with a twinkle in his blue eyes, "We won't be whipped."

"But they didn't get. . . ."

"Never mind, Daid," Bass said before Daid had time to finish. "There'll be a wedding here tonight. You do your part and the rest will be done. The people are right now being invited here tonight. The church meetings are all over now and they don't have any place to go. You can look for them here tonight."

Daid didn't ask another question, but hurried into the kitchen.

"Hadn't we better move the furniture from the front room?" Deutsia asked.

"Expect you'd better. And you'd better get into some old clothes." Bass pulled a cigar from his vest pocket and left the shack.

14

"LOOK AT THESE, Dave," Deutsia
said. She stooped to pluck the Queen
Anne's lace that grew just outside the gate.
"Wild flowers right in the door."

Deutsia and I gathered an armload of Queen Anne's
lace between the gate and the smokehouse. The last flower
I plucked was beside the wire cage that had once held two
rattlesnakes.

"What did Daid ever do with her rattlesnakes?"

"Put 'em behind the rocks in the cellar," she said.
"They stay in the cellar during the winter. They awake
with the thundershowers in late March and April."

"When the snakes get to sleep, the big revivals are
over," I said. "When the snakes awake in the spring, the
big revivals start again. Is that the way it works?"

"That's right," Deutsia replied, as we walked toward
the shack carrying our first armload of wild flowers.

When we carried the flowers inside the front room, we

heard Daid in the kitchen rattling pots and pans and giving orders to Meese, Alona and Cress. Everybody was working at Huntoons'.

"We've a lot more flowers to gather," I said.

"And I know where they grow. We'll get some gold-enrods now," Deutsia said. "I know where there's a field of them."

Her lithe brown legs ran up the path before me.

"This morning I wanted to die," she said. "I wished deep in my heart I was dead. This afternoon, I want to live forever, and live with you! We'll pick wild strawberries in the spring together. I'll make you good wild strawberry jelly, strawberry preserves, and I'll can them for you. Win-tertime is rough up on this mountain. We will need wild canned fruit and berries."

"And I'll raise a garden, truck patches, make furniture, cut wood and I'll hunt and carry home wild game. I'll fish in the rivers with your brothers and father. I'm not a Melungeon, but I can make a good one. Won't it be fun to be married and living together in a little place of our own where we can work for each other?"

"If we can only do half what we plan," Deutsia said, her face beaming with happiness. "I want to dream and to plan. I've got all sorts of plans."

"Look at the goldenrods," I said. We came to a little clearing where goldenrods grew as close as tangled saw-briars around a rock cliff. "Look what a field of gold up here under a white cloud."

"We'll soon have our arms full."

She began to pluck the goldenrods and lay the stems across my arm until I had a load. Then I laid my load down until I plucked an armload for her.

As soon as we'd carried the goldenrods to the shack, we went to the woods and found sourwoods in the deep hollows where the winds hadn't stripped them of leaves. I climbed into a sourwood tree and carefully broke the leafy boughs and dropped them down to the ground. Next we gathered pine boughs so we would have the green boughs mingled with the flaming red sourwood leaves. And we gathered tough-butted white-oak boughs filled with clusters of autumn-brown leaves.

Then we gathered blossoms from a cove; milkweed blossoms where a mountain spring seeped near a clearing's edge and purplish-red ironweed tops. We found wisps of the yellow butterfly weed, and clumps of blue violets hidden away under the leaves. We found a few wild lettuce blossoms and mountain tea stems with many ripe red mountain tea berries. We even brought a few sawbriars filled with little clusters of blue berries. Deutsia found a patch of late phlox flowering among the rocks by a little creek that wound through a cove.

After we'd gathered the flowers and leaves for decoration, Deutsia and I took the beds and dresser apart and moved them into the back room. Then Deutsia arranged the flowers and leaves while I drove nails into the walls for the wreaths she arranged.

All afternoon we worked to get the room ready for our wedding and the big dance to follow. If Deutsia didn't like the place where I'd driven a nail, I'd pull it out and drive it where she said. She wanted to contrast the wreaths she'd made of the different flowers, leaves and boughs.

"We must get it right," she said. "Make it look as pretty here as in this mountain world where it grew."

"We can't spend too much time on this room," I said. "We've got to get ready. And we've got to dance tonight. We can't be tired before the night begins!"

We had just enough time to get dressed and get back into the room we had decorated when Add Sizemore and his wife came. Daid came from the kitchen to the front room to greet them.

"What's this all about?" Add asked. He put a gnarled hand on each horn of his mustache to push it back to his ear. "I told Belle before we started that I'll bet it was a wedding and a big shindig afterwards."

Sport Moore, his wife Effie and three children came a few minutes later. He wore a white shirt, a bow tie and his Sunday suit. And Effie wore a long sweeping black dress with a shawl about her thin shoulders. Time, childbearing and mountain climbing had stooped her thin body.

And then Ben Daniels came and brought his wife Nettie, his dark-complexioned son and his fair-haired apple-cheeked daughter. As they came, Deutsia introduced me. At first they looked at me suspiciously. But after we'd met, we were soon talking about hunting and fishing.

Lonnie Eversole, his wife Lottie and their five children came; Sham Revelett, who was broader across the shoulders than Hezzy Blair, came and brought his wife and oldest son and daughter; Don Praytor came and brought his shy dark wife Doshie, and their five stair-stepped children.

"Deutsia's a fine girl," Don whispered to me. "You remember our talk, don't you?"

"Yes, I remember."

"I hope it all turns out for the best," he said. "I didn't

know whether you meant what you said that day or not.
Now I know you meant every word of it."

"Where's Bass?" Don asked Deutsia.

"He went away and said he'd be back," she said.
"We're looking for 'im any minute."

The front room was soon filled with people shaking
hands and talking and laughing in a friendly manner. They
were pleased to get together and to talk about how pretty
the room looked, about religion, crops, weather, hunting,
fishing, trappings, ginseng, roots, herbs, hides, dances, marriages, births and deaths. The shy children stayed close to
their mothers and others ran into the kitchen, where Alona
and Meese were still getting the midnight feast ready. And
the young men and women got together, looked into each
other's eyes and said foolish things and giggled.

"When will Bass come?" I asked Deutsia. "What do
you reckon is keeping him?"

"I'm not uneasy," she replied. "He'll be here."

Just then Brother Dusty Tackett and Bass walked in.
Brother Dusty came with a Bible in his hand. Behind them
came Elic Lefferson with a banjo, Mat Mahan with a fiddle, Ed Greenwood and Jad Dee with guitars. And behind
them came their wives bringing more children.

"I'll bet everybody's come that was invited," I said
to Deutsia. "Look at the people! This place is full and run-
nin' over!"

These were the people I'd seen at the courthouse in
Oak Hill and upon the mountain at the last revival. Many
were dressed in their Sunday clothes and many were
dressed in their overalls and boots.

"Folks, give me your attention a minute," Brother
Dusty said, holding his hands up, touching the ceiling.

"We're going to have a wedding first. And we're a-going to rejoice afterward. Will th' young couple that's to be married step right up here?"

Deutsia held my arm as we moved slowly through the crowded room.

"Make way, folks," Brother Dusty said. "Let 'em through!"

People's eyes were turned upon us as we passed them. I cannot describe my feelings, except I was proud to walk beside Deutsia and to hear the old and young women, the old men and young boys whispering to each other and talking in low tones about us.

"I started to ast ye to hold hands," Brother Dusty said, "but I see ye are already a-holdin' hands. That's fine, children. Ye must go on through life a-lovin' one another like this."

When he said this everybody stopped talking but the children, and I heard their mothers trying to get them quiet.

"In the presence of God Almighty," Brother Dusty said, "and before you people, we're gathered here to join this young woman and young man in holy matrimony. If anybody here thinks this should not be done, let him speak up now."

"We think it should be done," everybody screamed, and then there was so much talking Brother Dusty had to ask them to be quiet.

"Dave Stoneking, will you take this woman Deutsia Huntoon, to be thy wedded wife, to love her, to comfort her and keep her, forsaking all others?"

"I will."

"Deutsia Huntoon, will you take this man Dave Stoneking, to be thy wedded husband, to love him, to comfort and obey, forsaking all others?"

"I will," Deutsia said.

"Ain't Stoneking a funny name?" I heard a woman whisper.

"It ain't a name among our people," I heard a woman answer her.

"I now pronounce you man and wife," Brother Dusty said, shaking Deutsia's hand. "May God bless ye!"

"May God bless ye, Dave," he said to me as he held my hand.

There was so much talking among the people I couldn't understand what anyone was saying.

"And may ye both be happy!"

Then the people crowded about us and shook our hands and wished us much happiness. I'll never forget the expression on Don Praytor's face as he shook my hand.

"I hope everything goes all right for you and Deutsia," he said.

Daid wiped tears from her eyes but didn't say anything.

Bass shook my hand and put his arm around Deutsia.

"My child," he said, and that was all.

"Now we must start the music and the dance," Hunt Mallicoat shouted. "Come on, boys, with the music."

"Goodnight, folks," Brother Dusty said, as he started toward the door with Bass beside him.

"Goodnight, Brother Dusty," everybody said in unison.

Elic Lefferson, Mat Mahan, Ed Greenwood and Jad Dee seated themselves in chairs at one end of the room and began to tune their fiddle, banjo and guitars.

"While they get ready with the music, couple off,"

Hunt Mallicoat said. "Every man get his partner. We've got enough room for three sets. And every married man get his wife."

Everybody laughed.

"I want you old people to dance," Hunt shouted again, looking down upon us. "I didn't mean old. I mean you young men with the long gray beards. Every one of ye. Hear me! I mean it. Let this be a night of enjoyment! Let us feast and be happy tonight! Like a tough-butted white-oak that grows on this mountain, we will not be whipped! But by the music we will be moved! Don't ye doubt it."

"All you small children too young to dance move over against the wall," Bass said. "Make room for three sets."

There were couples among us not more than twelve years old and some of the couples were seventy.

"Now when you want something to eat or drink," Bass said, "you'll find it on the table in the kitchen. Any time you are thirsty, drink. You will find plenty to drink— anything from water on. And when you are hungry you go eat. There is plenty of grub for everybody."

When the music started, the couples hit the floor and Hunt Mallicoat called the figure eight. I had never seen such dancing.

Hunt Mallicoat couldn't jump up and crack his feet together three times as he called the set, for his head hit the ceiling. I could see all colors of petticoats as the men swung their wives and the young men swung their girls. The coarse brogans hit the floor with loud cracks and the dust went up from the floor and came down from the ceiling. Our dancing even jarred the wreaths from the walls. But the little boys would run from where they were sitting by the wall and jerk the flowers from the floor and the dance went on. The music was fast and furious and the dancers' feet made movements almost too fast to see.

"Swing your partners, and I mean swing 'em," Hunt shouted louder than Brother Dusty could preach.

At the end of the sets when the people stopped to catch their breath, they hurried into the kitchen to get a drink and to eat. The dining table and kitchen table were loaded with good things to eat and plenty to drink.

"A body's throat gets dry when he calls for a dance," Hunt Mallicoat said as he finished a big gourd of moonshine.

"Let's go back to the dance while th' night is still young," Hunt said.

"Just another swig, Hunt," Mat Mahan said. "I need it to make me bear down on my fiddle."

All night we danced. Hunt Mallicoat called every set. Hunt's booming voice sounded like a wind blowing down in some deep hollow. And all night long I danced with Deutsia. I held her close enough to kiss her each time we Waltzed the Hall. She was light on her feet and she never tired. Daid and Bass never missed a set. Daid could dance well, though she was too big for Bass to lift from the floor when he went whirlygiggin' around.

Many mothers who couldn't dance fed the children when they got hungry. They laid them across the beds in the back room in rows when they got sleepy. Many of the men got so limber their wives had to swing 'em. Many men got beyond dancing and had to go outside the room to get some fresh October wind to revive them. But the dance went on until the morning hours. Many could hardly walk outside the shack they were so full of drink and so tired from dancing. And many we heard yelling until they were far around the ridge. Wives had trouble getting their children and their husbands started home. But it was a night that would go down among the mountain people and be talked about for years to come.

15

TUESDAY afternoon, Deutsia, Pribble and I went to the mountaintop. She carried my ax while I walked beside her with my toolkit on my shoulder. Pribble walked behind us with the crosscut saw.

"It's wonderful to think about," Deutsia said. "We are goin' to build us a place to live."

"It's a good time to start work," I said. "This is good weather for chopping."

"How long will it take you to get the logs ready?"

"Not very long," I said, thinking that Pribble, strong-looking as he was, could use the ax and crosscut saw well, and be a great help.

When we reached the saplings near the site we'd chosen, I began to notch a tall, straight, almost limbless sapling. Pribble and Deutsia stood by watching my sharp double-bitted ax eat into the wood.

"Now, Pribble," I said, "let's get down on our knees and saw it off close to the ground."

But Pribble didn't know anything about sawing down a tree. I had to show him and then he rode the crosscut saw. I didn't mind, since it didn't take long to saw down a sapling with a sharp-toothed heavy crosscut saw. Deutsia watched us saw the tree down, watched it break from the stump and lumber clumsily to the ground, smashing the underbrush and vines beneath it.

Then I measured the thickness of the log by hacking little notches into the bark.

"What are you doing?"

"The walls of our shack must be square and smooth," I said. "I'm lining the log so I can score and hew it. I don't want any round logs in our home."

She watched me when I showed Pribble how to walk along on top of the log and sink his ax into the sides of the tree to the lines I'd made.

"Be sure you don't cut deeper than the lines," I warned Pribble.

But Pribble cut into the log like he was cutting stove-wood.

"I'll tell you what we'll do, Pribble," I said. "You just help me saw down the trees. This afternoon I'll score and hew the trees myself, then you can help me saw the tree into logs."

"All right," he said, since he was a man of few words.

That afternoon, with Deutsia watching us, we sawed down the straightest, prettiest white oaks, black oaks, chestnut oaks and red oaks we could find on the mountain-top. Pribble moaned and groaned, for he didn't like to work, but I held him until we got the trees cut down. He complained that his back hurt him, that his hands were blistered.

"The only way to build a house is to start it," I told Deutsia when we quit work at sunset.

"You can certainly use an ax and a crosscut saw," she said.

"I wish I could do everything as well as I can chop. We're going to have our house built and be living in it before the snow falls."

"That won't be long. Snow comes early to this mountain."

Each morning I went to score, hew and bark logs before daylight. I would hurry to Huntoons' for dinner, eat in a hurry and then rush back to work. Not one of the Huntoon men helped me, for they were always in the woods with their dogs and guns. They hunted by day and they hunted by night. And when they weren't hunting they were fishing. Once Bass went out to help me, but he was awkward with an ax and I didn't like his work. I told him nicely that I would rather finish the logs by myself so that when he had time from his hunting he could help me do the things that it would take more than one man to do, such as rolling the foundation stones in place and putting the logs upon each other. Bass was pleased, for he wanted to get back to the woods and the rivers.

While I worked to make the logs for our home, Deutsia made quilts and gathered things we would need when we moved in to start housekeeping. She gathered wild grapes and made wild-grape jelly. But often she came to the woods where I was working to look at the logs. She'd ask me how I could smooth the sides of a log with an ax until it looked as if it had been sawed by a mill. She couldn't understand how I could do it, for it had never been done on this mountain before.

I'd never eaten more wild meat, more fish, wild honey and good food than I ate at the Huntoons' table. We had turtle steaks, rabbit, possum, squirrel, groundhog, coon, pheasant, woodcock, dove and quail. And we had fried or broiled fish every day. We had as good food as I had ever eaten. I'd thought after I'd eaten the first meal in their shack that it was put on the table for me because I was a visitor and they didn't know that I intended to become a member of the family. But every meal was as good as that one and many were better. And at each meal or any time we wanted it, we had homemade wine to drink.

In the evenings, around a blazing fire, the men told their stories about the game they had killed that day. One night Force told us how he'd found three rabbits a-sittin' by looking for the tips of their ears above the leaves.

"But how do you keep from scaring them up from their sleep?" I asked Force. "The leaves are so dry when you step on them it makes sound enough to wake a rabbit."

"But I walk on my tiptoes," he said. "I never wake a rabbit from sleeping."

"How do you find their ears?" Bass asked him. "They are brown like the leaves they nest in."

"I look carefully in a place where I think a rabbit is sleeping," he explained. "I look for a little brown V. His ears grow close together on his head but they spread apart when he's asleep."

"You're making a fine hunter," Bass said. "I used to hunt 'em that way."

The men told Deutsia where they had killed each animal and bird, for Deutsia had hunted with them and knew each cove, hollow, each patch of timber and almost every cliff. Often Meese would hunt with them during the day, and sometimes she went at night. Even Alona went hunting with them when they didn't hunt too far during the day. I'd hunted a lot myself, but I'd never known people in my lifetime to hunt like the Huntoons.

While Force and Bass talked about hunting and fishing and the traplines they planned to set before the first snows came to the mountain, Meese popped cappers of corn over the fire. She'd pop a capper of corn and pour the white fluffy grains into a big pan. As soon as she had it filled with popcorn, she poured a jar of clean wild honey into the pan and she and Alona made honey popcorn balls for us. Then Alona took out the sweet potatoes she had roasting in the ashes and we had roasted sweet potatoes and honey popcorn balls. The evenings before the Huntoons' fireside were made cheerful by much talking, laughing and eating. Even Daid smiled when Meese passed the popcorn balls to her. She was not as shy of me as she had been. But Pribble wouldn't listen when Deutsia and I spoke of building our house. He would rather hear Force talk about the game he had killed that afternoon.

Since becoming part of this family, I understood why Deutsia knew the mountains so well. I often wondered when I was working on the logs if Deutsia wouldn't be as happy hunting with her people in the woods during the day and beneath an October moon at night as she would be settling with me behind the smooth-hewn walls of a log house. I wondered if she would be as happy with me as she had been when she hunted with her father, brothers and sisters.

When this work is done and Deutsia and I have a home of our own, I thought, we will take to the mountains to hunt with Bass, Pribble, Force, Cress, Alona and Meese. We will go because I know how Deutsia loves the life they are living.

By November eighth I not only had the logs finished for our shack, but I had riven white-oak clapboards to roof it. My only problem was getting someone to help me cut the board trees and to saw them into bolts. Finally, I persuaded Bass to quit hunting and fishing long enough to help me do this sawing, and Pribble long enough to help me saw the trees I had scored and hewed into house logs. I dragged the logs with Bass' mule to the spot we'd selected for the house and then I hauled the clapboards on a sled.

Force helped me lay the foundation, for I promised him enough money to buy traps for a trapline of his own if he would. On November twelfth we had a house raising and twelve men came to help us raise the logs into the walls. We put one log upon the other, notched them carefully at the corners, so they would fit close. On that day, the men's wives went to Huntoons' to help cook and we feasted at dinner and supper. In the evening, we had a big dance to the fast tunes of fiddle music.

Then I hired Don Praytor to help me roof the house and to saw places in the walls for the windows, case them and fit the sashes. I hired him as long as he would work, and that was as long as it took us to daub the cracks, build a big chimney and lay a hearthstone. The rest of the work I did myself, splitting puncheon floor from dead mountain chestnuts and planing the tops of the puncheons. I partitioned the house into three rooms, a front room with the fireplace, and a middle room between the front room and kitchen. It didn't take me long to build a flue of small rocks; there were plenty of rocks on this mountain. I bought a secondhand stove, a bed and a table from Sylvania, and Skinny hauled them to our home. I would make new ones later. We wanted to move into our own home as soon as we could. We were ready to move in on November twentieth, and lucky for us the autumn had been late.

16

WITH a table, bed, stove, two chairs, with bedding and quilts Deutsia had made, dishes and kitchen utensils she had gathered and the ones I had brought from the shanty, our house was furnished. We sat before our own fireplace where the bright crackling flames threw out enough heat to warm us and to light our room.

"This is the prettiest place on this mountain, Dave," Deutsia said as she looked over the room where light and shadow played on the smooth walls. "I'm proud of our home."

"It's better than a rock cliff. Maybe this house will inspire them to make better ones."

"Sure it will," she said. "They'll be trying to build one like ours. You wait and see. They'll ask you why you built a place like this."

"I'll tell 'em I had to have a pretty cage for a pretty bird."

"Oh, it's heaven to be in our own home!"

"Your folks were kind to us," I said. "I never stayed at a place in my life where I was treated nicer and had food that I liked better."

"I like to hear you say that, Dave," Deutsia said, her face beaming with joy. "I'm glad to hear a kind word spoken for my people, but there's not any place in the world like your own home."

"It's well anchored against the wind here," I said. "The big chimney will help hold us, and the logs are well notched. If the wind turns us over our house won't come apart."

"Then you're afraid of the storms up here?"

"I am after seeing that one the night we found the cliff," I said. "I'll never forget that night."

"Neither will I," Deutsia said. "That was the first night we spent together."

My chair was close to Deutsia's and our arms were around each other as we watched the bright tongues of flame leap from the dry cedar logs, rich resined pine knots and dry-seasoned yellow locust sticks.

"Now I'm going to put one bed you make for us right over in that corner," Deutsia said. "I'm going to put a stand table over by the window. I'm going to put the cedar chest over on this side. I know where I'm going to put everything you make. When are you going to start making our furniture?"

"Tomorrow."

"What are you going to make first?"

"Some good chairs. And when I get the chairs made, what do you want me to make next?"

"The cedar chest, so we can put things in it."

"And then?"

"A walnut bed."

"I've already got the trees spotted," I said. "They are dead trees already seasoned."

"I've always wanted a pretty home," Deutsia said. "And when spring comes I'll show you how to make it prettier here. You wait until I gather my wild flowers and bring them in here and put them in this yard."

"I want to help you."

"Dave, there is something I want to tell you," Deutsia said, turning her eyes from the flaming fire. "I'm going to give you a present next spring. . . . I mean it, Dave," she said, before I could start my question.

"Why didn't you tell me before?"

"I wasn't sure," she said. "But I'm sure now."

"Oh, that's the best news yet," I said. "I'm really going to kiss you for this good news."

Before the fire, in our own little smooth-walled room, I pulled her carefully over to me, her face beneath mine, her hair streaming down to the floor, and I bent over until my lips met her lips. I held her there and kissed her fondly while the light of the dancing flames flickered over her hair and the dry wood crackled.

"We moved just in time," I said. "Look out the window."

"That looks like a deep snow," Deutsia said. She raised her head from the pillow, looked out the window at a mountain world changed from dark and brown to white. "It's a pretty world. I like the changes of the seasons here, white, green, brown and"—her voice trembled—"dark, all are pretty."

"This won't bother me from my work," I said. "I've got my wood here to make the chairs. I've got my tools here. I can work inside."

"That will be better. You'll be closer to me."

"And we've got dry wood to burn."

"If the snow stays on very long and we get short of supplies," Deutsia said, "we can get them from Bass and Daid. They always store and can for the winter, in spring, summer and autumn. They know what winter means here."

"If we were to run out of supplies and couldn't get them up here," I said, "we'd never be able to get off the mountain now."

"Not when there's this much snow on the ground," she said. "It always drifts down by the second cliffs. I've seen drifts twenty feet deep there."

"Why do we mind the weather?" I asked Deutsia. "We've built walls and a roof against it. Why should we even talk about the weather? We're snug in our little place. We can even sleep as late as we want to on a morning like this."

Then Deutsia lay her head on my arm, pulled up close to me, and I pulled the quilts upon us. Though a gray morning light had come to the white mountain world, we would not rise at an early hour on that morning.

Before the great snow had melted and gorged the mountain streams I had finished our chairs. I had made two rockers and six straight chairs.

While I worked, Deutsia would cook meals for us and we'd eat at our little table together. After we'd eaten, I'd go back to my whittling, planing, and sandpapering, and putting arms and legs together. As soon as Deutsia was through with the dishes she would help me. She would hold the pieces while I bored small holes with brace and bit to pin the pieces together with wooden pins or bored holes to fit rungs into the legs.

When the snow had melted, leaving drifts here and there, I went with my ax to the dead seasoned black walnuts and wild cherries that I had found on the mountains. I chopped these trees down, trimmed their branches and topped them. And then I chopped two straight dead cedars that would split easily. I got Bass' mule and dragged these logs to the house so I would have plenty to do when another snow fell.

17

❧ ❧ ❧ ❧ ❧ ❧ ❧ ❧ ❧ ❧ ❧

"DEUTSIA, I'm wondering what to do with this money I'm carrying around in my pocket," I said. "Now that the big snow has melted I've been thinking about going down to Oak Hill, to get some supplies before another big snow comes."

"There are some things we can't get at Sylvania's and Skinny's," she said. "When January comes it will be almost impossible to go down or climb Sanctuary Mountain for the ice and snow. You should go now and bring back some of the things we can't get here."

"I'll bring all I can carry up the mountain," I said. "We have oil lamps, but we don't have any oil."

"Oil is heavy to carry."

"But wouldn't you love the glow of light again from our oil lamps?"

"I certainly would."

First thing I wrote on the list was kerosene.

"Now Deutsia, tell me what you want the most."

"I want five yards of outing flannel to make dresses for our baby," she said. "And I want needles and spools of fine and coarse white and black thread. Be sure to get all this down. And I want about twelve or fifteen yards of white muslin for sheeting and pillow cases. Ask the clerk to help you pick out material for window curtains. Get a little printed pattern for the kitchen ones."

"Wonderful," I said, writing as fast as I could.

"Oh yes, embroidery floss. Get pink and blue," she said.

"Why pink?" I said. "He's going to be a boy."

Then Deutsia laughed loudly and I laughed with her.

"And you won't mind if I add a few things to these?" I said.

"Not if you want to spend the money and carry them up the mountain."

When Sylvania and Skinny ran out of kerosene on the mountain we did without oil for our lamps. I'd been in many of the cabins on the mountains and I'd seen the dark smoke stains on the paper. They had come from pine torches used to light the cabins. We kept pine torches ready but had never used them, because we didn't want to smoke our walls. I was a little different from the Melungeons. I was more afraid of burning our house down. Kerosene was a necessity as far as I was concerned.

"Now what about some store groceries?" I said. "What do you want?"

"Dave, I've been craving fruit," she said. "I'd like some oranges, bananas, and I want a coconut."

"You'll get them," I said. "I'm craving them, too, and I'm not going to have a baby."

Deutsia laughed again. "Oh, we mustn't forget coffee,"

she said. "Get some white sugar, too. Wild-honey sweetening is good but it can't take the place of white sugar. Get us some candy, too."

"You shouldn't have asked for candy," I said. "I was going to bring it for one of my little surprises. Now what kind of a surprise can I think of for you?"

"You'll think of something," she said. "What are you going to get for yourself?"

"Oh, a lot of little things," I said. "You know where I'll go for mine. I'll have to go to the hardware. I've got to get a saw-filing set, files and blades for my wood saws. I'd better write these down, too, for I don't want to forget them. I've got to have blades for my planers, and I've got to get some finishing nails."

"Hardware is heavy," she said. "It won't take much to make you a load."

"It takes a lot to make fifty pounds," I told her. "I can carry fifty pounds up the mountain. When I was a boy and old pack peddler John used to come to my home in Virginia he'd drop his pack on our floor, open it and our whole family would gather around and look at the nice things he had. You know how many pounds he carried?"

"No, I've never seen a pack peddler," Deutsia said. "I've heard about them. One never climbed up on Sanctuary Mountain. Maybe because he was warned down in the valley that the road was steep up here to us and that we didn't have any money."

"You've missed something, Deutsia, by not seeing one of the old pack peddlers," I said. "Old peddler John carried over a hundred pounds in his pack. He might have carried two hundred pounds. The ordinary little man couldn't lift one of the packs the old peddlers carried. I can come up

Sanctuary Mountain with all my small items in a sack plus a two-gallon can of kerosene in my hand. I'll go down to Oak Hill and back tomorrow."

When the roosters began crowing at four o'clock, I got up. Deutsia was awakened, too, and she got up with me.

"I'll take some sassafras tea this morning," I said. "I don't want any of that parched corn coffee."

The Melungeons were wonderful on finding substitutes for almost everything. They had been forced to do it. When they didn't have coffee and couldn't get it on the mountain, they substituted parched corn.

"Tonight we'll have some real coffee," I said.

After a breakfast of fried eggs, slab bacon and sassafras tea, I got one of the pine torches we kept in the cabin for emergency and searched for a long white meal sack in the press.

"I wish I could go with you," Deutsia said. Tears welled up in her eyes. "I'd like to see Oak Hill again and I'd like to visit with my friends at the courthouse."

I pulled Deutsia close and kissed her. "I wish you could go with me, honey," I said. "Remember, it won't be long until you'll be able."

I took the lighted pine torch and was on my way.

The morning sky was clear and filled with stars. A soft, gentle wind pulled at the flame on my pine torch and made it sputter. The starlight was almost enough to light my path until I could see my way.

I'd traveled over this path many times. I'd been over it so many times now I knew where the big cliffs were and where my path angled down. When I reached the first cliffs, I put out the blaze on my torch and laid it on a rock.

I had left home at six. Now I could see the first light streaks from the east coming up on Sanctuary Mountain, and I heard the voices of winter birds searching for their breakfasts on a mountain where there was little food. With my eyes better adjusted to the starlight, I walked on, taking broad steps like a trotting fox, for my feet felt sure of the places when I put them down. I felt proud of myself. But I was not as good as Deutsia following a mountain path. Sanctuary Mountain will be something to climb with a fifty-pound load, I thought.

In less than an hour I'd reached the bottom cliffs and before nine I had reached Oak Hill. Oak Hill is a lazy little town, I thought. I've come from the top of Sanctuary Mountain down to Oak Hill and I have an hour to wait before the stores open. Since I didn't like to loaf around, there was something I could do before the stores opened. I could see if Circuit Judge John Palmer was in his office. Ever since I had met Don Praytor in the County Jail, there was something I wanted to ask Judge Palmer. I walked over to the courthouse.

"Say, fellow," I asked the bearded man sweeping, "is Judge Palmer in his office yet?"

"How would I know about him?" he said. "He sentenced me to jail for six months, since I couldn't pay my fine. I was caught with a half pint of herbs. I can reduce my fine in half if I clean the courthouse. So when I go, another will follow me and reduce his fine the same way." He leaned on his broom and looked at me. "Ain't I seen ye some'eres?"

"I don't know," I replied. "Are you from the mountain?"

"That's it," he said. "Ye jined us. Ye married the Huntoon gal."

"How long did you wait in jail before they tried you?"

"Oh, I can't grumble about that," he said. "I only had to wait three months. Hell, too many from the mountain have to wait six months and longer. Since you're one of us, go upstairs and you'll find old Judge Palmer's office first door on your left. He's an early bird, lives a few miles out of town on a farm in the Clinch River valley. He gets up with the cows and chickens. He's allus in a hurry except when it comes to tryin' one of us from Sanctuary Mountain who has been caught carryin' or sellin' honorable herbs. Say, the only two people ever to beat county, state and Federal laws"—and he laughed loudly—"is dear Sylvania and her little husband Skinny."

"Yes, I know," I said. "My name is Dave Stoneking."

"I'm glad to meet a man who has the guts to join us," he said. "I'm Bud Mahan and I've been down here in jail while you've been up there on our Sanctuary Mountain."

"Well, you know we don't come down here very much after the snows arrive," I said. "I'll have to be going, for I have a full day ahead of me. I want to see Judge Palmer, then shop at the stores and get back home tonight."

"Tell 'em upon the mountain you saw old Bud down here and that he was sweeping the courthouse floors so hard to pay his fine he was about to break his broom handle."

"I'll tell 'em, Bud."

"Be sure and tell Deutsia," he said. "She's my first cousin."

"I'll tell her."

When I reached the head of the stairs, the first door on my left was open and I looked in. There stood a man by his desk looking and sifting through a handful of letters. I walked in and stood before him.

"Something I can do for you, young man?"

"Yes, there is."

He was about sixty, tall, clean-shaven and fair-skinned. He wore a high white collar with his necktie wrapped around it. There was a stickpin in his tie. He wore a dark suit and across his vest was a gold watch chain with a watch fob suspended from the chain.

"What is it I can do for you?"

"Judge, why is it when a man from Sanctuary Mountain is caught drinking, possessing or selling illegal moonshine whiskey he has to lay in jail six months before he is given a trial?"

"To answer you briefly, quickly and to the point, it is none of your affair," he said. "That concerns the law."

"Isn't the jailor paid from the taxpayers' money for feeding the prisoners?"

Judge Palmer's face flushed.

"Just how well do you know the people who live on Sanctuary Mountain?" he said. "I know you're not one of 'em for you don't have the looks!"

"I am now," I said. "I married one."

We stood in silence, looking at each other.

"Yes, now, I know," he said, breaking our silence. "You're the lumberjack from Virginia that married old Bass Huntoon's girl."

"Yes, I married Deutsia Huntoon."

"No, you didn't marry her legally, for you didn't get a license," he said. "It's what we call a common-law marriage, which is a common practice up on that mountain. You look like you came from a fine family. How can you betray your people?"

"I haven't betrayed my people. I married the woman I love."

"Are your parents still living?"

"Yes, they are. But what has this got to do with it?"

"Would you invite your parents up there to your home on Sanctuary Mountain? Would you?"

"My parents couldn't climb up there," I said. "If you'll see that this county or this state will build a road up there so people can go to the top in a car, I'll invite my parents to my home and show them the finest-looking people in the world."

"Yes, fine-looking all right, but how do they live?" His voice shook with feeling. "They're an ignorant people. They have no morals either and . . ."

"Judge Palmer, they are educated in their way," I interrupted him. I couldn't stand for him to talk this way about them. He was the one who was ignorant. "They don't have book education because they've been denied schooling in the Valley and the missionary teachers, outsiders called Presbyterians who believe Melungeons are God's children too, walk up that mountain and teach them up to the eighth grade in pitiful log-shack schoolhouses while Valley children can go to high school and then on to college. No, they're not educated in books like you, but they know Sanctuary Mountain and everything that lives and grows on it and they know the streams and the rivers and signs in the skies. They know when and how and where to plant their patches and to harvest them, where bee trees are and how to find them and where wild game is and how to catch it for food. They know the holes in Clinch River where the big fish live. I'm married to a Melungeon and I know how smart they are."

"You're not married to one," he corrected me sternly. "You're living with one."

"Don't say that again, Judge," I warned him. "I'm married to one under the laws of God and man. To hell with the license. If I'm not married to Deutsia Huntoon, there's not a married couple in the United States."

"Why did you come in here?" he said. "Did you come to threaten me? Now, you listen to me," his voice was cracking with anger, "I'm circuit judge here."

"Now, Judge," I interrupted again, "the law says that a man shall be given a fair and a just trial. I'm not a lawyer but I know there's a law against holding a man too long in jail before he's given a trial."

"Would you mind leaving before I have you arrested?"

"No, I don't mind going. Be sure to speed up the trials for the men on Sanctuary Mountain."

I turned around and left his office in a hurry. He was a man who would have had me arrested, and what would I have done in Cantwell County Jail with Deutsia upon Sanctuary Mountain heavy with our child? If the jail was still in the same condition as it was when Deutsia took me with her to see Don Praytor, I would have lost my mind confined there.

When I got to the foot of the stairs, Bud Mahan came with his broom.

"I heard it," he said in a low voice. "I heard what you told him. You've got guts and you're right, but get out of this courthouse in a hurry before he has you arrested. Nobody on earth ever talked to old Judge Palmer like you did. I'll bet he'll do some thinkin' after this."

I never stopped walking as Bud followed me to the courthouse steps. There was a big smile on his face and his eyes looked like they were laughing.

The stores were open now. I went into Blackburn's Drygoods Store, the only drygoods store in Cantwell. There were two women clerks. One was about my age and one about my mother's age.

"Something for you?" asked the older woman in a soft voice.

"Yes, my wife gave me a list of things to get," I said.

I pulled the list from my shirt pocket and began to read off the items. The older clerk got the muslin while the younger one got my needles and embroidery thread. "Now show me that bolt of blue with the yellow design in it up there on the right-hand side," I said to the younger clerk. She got it from the shelf and opened it out so I could see. It's just the color of Deutsia's eyes, I thought. "How many yards will it take to make a dress for a woman about your size?"

"Three and a half yards will be plenty," she said.

"Well, give me four yards," I said, thinking how well Deutsia would like a new dress to wear after the baby came.

Then I started looking around for another pattern, for I thought she would like a change. "Would you help me pick out another pattern?" I said to the young clerk. "Something like this only a little different."

She showed me three or four bolts, and after much thinking it over I decided on a pale green with white and yellow daisies in it.

"You've made a good choice," said the smiling clerk.

I didn't tell her how well Deutsia liked the mountain daisies.

"Can I show you something else?" she asked.

"Yes, there is something else," I said, looking at my list. "I want something to make window curtains."

"Well, you're the first man to buy window curtain material," she said.

"I'd like something the color of the earth or the sun," I said, thinking of our house.

"I have it," she said, getting a bolt of something tan that looked like a burlap sack only softer, like a coarse hand towel.

I took enough for four windows. But for the kitchen window I got a print that had little checks in it the color of our dishes. "Add this all up now," I said, looking at my list again.

"Oh, my goodness, I'm leaving out the most important thing," I said. "Outing flannel for the baby's clothes."

"It comes in pink and blue and white."

"Well, I'll take a little bit of all," I said, wondering which color to get. "About four yards of each . . . ah, better make it five for good measure."

I was so pleased with my purchases that I wanted to get home to Deutsia with them. Then I bought towels, washcloths, Christmas wrapping paper, and ribbon and colored twine to use for tying packages.

"Now, that's all," I said.

My purchases came to twenty-seven dollars. After the packages were wrapped and I'd begun to put them in my sack the older clerk said, "You must not live very close?"

"That's right," I said.

"Have you a long way to go?" the younger clerk asked me.

"Yes, to the top of Sanctuary Mountain."

Then the smiles left their faces. They must have become suspicious of me when I began loading my sack, because that was the way our people on the mountain took home the supplies they couldn't get from Sylvania and Skinny. They didn't thank me or say goodbye, and I didn't say goodbye to them. I put my sack over my shoulder and walked out.

I walked down the dirt street to L. C. Songbird's Hardware. Many times before I had purchased items here. I was not long finding all the things on my list. Here I bought a two-gallon can and had it filled with kerosene. There was a table in the center of this store filled with Christmas items. On it was a varied assortment of colors and designs of glass dishes, pitchers and glasses. I bought a blue pitcher and a set of glasses that I knew Deutsia would like, and I had them wrapped carefully and put in a box. Now, with my sack fuller and with more weight, I went over to Mullins' Grocery Store, a place where Deutsia and I had been together.

I remembered Deutsia told me that Maurice Mullins and his wife ran this store and that they had been very nice to her. When I went in they didn't pretend to know me, but I could tell that they did. When I bought eight pounds of coffee they knew I lived upon Sanctuary Mountain where coffee was hard to get. I bought only four pounds of white sugar, because we had better substitutes for sugar than we had for coffee. I bought two pounds of striped stick candy and a dozen bananas, six oranges and two coconuts. After I paid for my groceries, I placed each item carefully in the sack while Maurice Mullins looked on silently. Now I had everything I'd planned to get. I'd go to Little Tavern for a bite to eat and then I'd be on my way up the mountain. I was getting hungry, for it had been almost seven hours since I had eaten.

I wondered if Spooly Holderby would know me. His

first name wasn't "Spooly" but it was Spool. He was named after his mother's people, the Spool family who owned a lot of Clinch River valley land and they had accumulated more than most other families. But back in Wise County, Virginia, I remembered three or four people who had more wealth and family background than the Spools and they didn't go around like the Spools with their noses so high in the air their nostrils caught the rain. So the people in Oak Hill and Cantwell County looked up to young Spool. They called him "Spooly" for a pet name, because he was a cross between the Spools and the Holderbys. Spooly was an apple-cheeked, soft young man, plump but not overweight, usually dressed in white pants and shirt and black bow tie. He was operating Little Tavern and was a very important person. Maybe he would know me, maybe he wouldn't, I thought, as I walked toward Little Tavern with my sack across my shoulder and a two-gallon can of kerosene in my hand. Ordinarily I wouldn't go into Little Tavern, since Deutsia wasn't welcome there, but I really had a yen to see if Fern and Ben were there. When I pushed the door open and set my sack down against the wall and my kerosene can beside it, there were only four people eating there.

"Now just a minute, lumberjack." Spooly stood before me. "Where do you think you're goin'?"

"I'm comin' here for some grub and coffee."

"Who says so?"

"I used to eat here," I said. "I can carry the sack and the oil outside if you don't want them in here."

"Now don't try to change the subject," he said. "I don't care about the sack and the oil can. What I care about is something bigger than a sack and an oil can. Sure you used to eat here. But that's when you belonged to us and not to them. That was before you betrayed your people. Now you see what I mean, don't you? Sure I know you. And you thought you'd slip back here. Not while I'm around here will you ever slip back. Now be a good boy, and go back to your people on the mountain."

"You ..." I said.

"No trouble, lumberjack," he said with a forced grin as he backed away from me. "Don't start anything. You don't have a chance."

He is right, I thought. I don't have a chance.

Here was a man I would have liked to have had my hands on. But I put my sack over my shoulder and picked up my can, while two couples in booths looked on. I didn't know these people, but they were from the valley. I knew where Spooly had gone. He'd gone over to the cash register to get his gun. But he wouldn't have to shoot me; I was already out and on my way.

I walked back toward Mullins' Grocery Store. I can spend my money in the stores, I thought. I could spend a thousand dollars buying items to make living easier in the valley or up on the mountain. Yet I couldn't sit down in Little Tavern and eat. Why would I be tolerated in the stores and not in Little Tavern? Why was Little Tavern such an important place? It simply didn't make sense.

Maurice Mullins knew something was wrong when I bought a pound of brown sugar, a tin of sardines, a pound of sliced bologna, a pound of cheese and a large box of crackers. I wasn't going to get that good cup of coffee which reminded me to buy more coffee to take home. I got six more pounds. I had the money, so why not spend it? I had another idea. I got six pounds of cheese in pound packages. And I got a half dozen pound boxes of assorted candies. Maurice Mullins was pleased the way I was buying. Then I got a box of cigars and three cartons of cigarettes, each carton a different brand. I didn't make the mistake of waiting to eat in Mullins' Grocery Store. After I'd paid Maurice Mullins, I loaded my new purchases into the sack.

"You're goin' to have a good load," he said.

"Not too much. About fifty pounds. Maybe a few pounds under or over, but it doesn't matter."

He didn't ask me how far I had to go. He already knew.

"I wish I's a strong a man as you are," he said.

"Something I'm forgetting," I said. "I want a soda pop to wash my lunch down with. Just any kind will do."

He brought me a soda pop.

"Open it," I said. "Push the cap back lightly so it will stay on a while."

He did what I told him. He was pleased that I'd not asked him to stay in his store and eat. And I was pleased to be on my way home to Deutsia.

After I had walked to the foot of Sanctuary Mountain I set my can down, laid my sack on a large rock, and sat down. I pulled the food from my pockets and had a real meal. I was on Sanctuary Mountain and I was free up here. The food tasted wonderful and I washed it down with swishes from my large bottle of soda pop. The December wind cooled my face. And the music of the wind in the barren branches of the oaks was sweet music to me. I knew now why Sanctuary Mountain was so dear to the Melungeons.

Soon I was on my way again, and I didn't stop until I

reached the first wall of cliffs. I had to take my sack up and then come back and get my oil can, since I had to use one hand to hold to bushes and rocks to get up the cliffs. Then I walked on to the second walls of cliffs and here I rested a little longer. When I started out with my load I wasn't sure that I was carrying fifty pounds, but now I knew.

Anyone who climbs Sanctuary Mountain climbs it in three parts. Now I was climbing the third part. I was getting up closer to the sky and I could swear I was carrying maybe seventy-five pounds and I sometimes felt like I was carrying one hundred pounds straight up to the clouds. The day had worn on and the sun had set when I reached the last wall of rocks. Here I rested again, and then I filled my pipe for the first time while climbing the mountain. Smoke tasted so good up here. Then I found my old pine torch and I relighted it. I was on my last lap of the journey.

I'll soon be seeing her, I thought, quickening my steps. I don't belong to the valley people any longer. I belong up here. Sanctuary Mountain is my home. Deutsia will see my torch flame sputtering in the wind and she will come with open arms to meet me.

18

I S A W the shadowy outline of the neatest
log cabin on Sanctuary Mountain. At the
door I set down my can of kerosene and
dropped the sack off my shoulder onto the floor. Deutsia
came running to me with her arms high, her lips ready for
our kiss and her tear-filled eyes smiling.

"Dave, how I've missed you," she said. "Dave, Dave,
Dave..."

She took her lips from mine and looked into my face
with her arms around my shoulders. "Dave. Dave. My
Dave." Then she put her lips back on mine and I held her
close. Sweat was running down my face and my shirt was
soaked. I was very warm, and though I felt tired before I
reached our cabin, I felt rested now.

After our kiss, Deutsia said, "What have you got in
that sack?"

"You'll be surprised."

"And you've brought kerosene. Change into dry

clothes and come before the fire, Dave," Deutsia said. "I've got a good fire. If you want to bathe, there's water in the big bucket, soap there and a washcloth and towel."

I went into the room between our kitchen and front room. I bathed my body with a washcloth, using the lye soap Deutsia had made from wood ashes and fats the way Daid had taught her. I didn't like this soap very well. I liked my store-bought soap better. But I had made this big water bucket from a cedar tree that grew on Sanctuary Mountain. And right now another idea came to me: I would make something more for us and for Huntoons. A great portion of the cedar tree lay where I had cut it to get planks that I ripped with my saws to line our clothes press and to make buckets. Now I would work that tree up into useful things for Christmas presents. I knew something that we and the Huntoons needed very much.

After I dressed in dry clothes and walked into our living room before the blazing wood fire, I felt like a new man in a new house. I thought I was back in my mother's and father's clean farm home in Wise County, Virginia. Oil for our lamps! But only one was lighted. Deutsia had filled the lamp, trimmed the wick and the soft yellow light meant even more to me than the morning sunlight on Sanctuary Mountain.

"Tell me, Dave, how everything went with you in Oak Hill."

"Well, the merchants let me spend my money with them."

"Didn't you see anybody you knew?"

"Yes, I saw Spooly Holderby at Little Tavern."

"So you went there for your lunch?"

"Yes, I went there but I didn't eat."

"Why? You're not a Melungeon."

"Guilt by association, honey," I said. "And I don't mind, if you don't."

"But I hate it . . ."

"Now, now," I interrupted. "Don't you talk like that. Remember, when I married you I took you to be my wedded wife, and you and I promised we would be as one."

"They'll say down there we're not married because we didn't get a license."

"Let them talk. We're married by the union of our hearts and our minds. No one can be more married than we are."

"I know you mean it, Dave, but I cannot help feeling for you. You could have married a girl from Wise County. You could have married one of your kind where there are no Melungeons and the blood is pure . . ."

"Deutsia, Deutsia," I interrupted her. "I didn't eat with Spooly and I got him told off and he got me told off. I ate food from Mullins' Grocery Store on the big flat green-lichen rock, just a few yards upon the mountain."

"Yes, I sure know where that rock is," she said, smiling. "I've stopped and rested there many a time. About everybody on this mountain has sat on that rock."

"Deutsia, I'm about to forget to ask you if you know Bud Mahan," I said.

"I ought to know him, he's my first cousin," she replied. "Dave, I know he was caught with moonshine whiskey and has been held in jail without a trial. Just like Don Praytor. I never could get to the jail to take him sandwiches."

"Well, I saw him today."

"Were you over to the jail?"

"No, but I was over to the courthouse. Bud's out of jail now. He's cutting his fine in half by cleaning the courthouse. He calls Sanctuary Mountain Heaven, and he's homesick for up here. He wants to get back home."

"Dave, what were you doing at the courthouse?"

"I went there to see Circuit Judge John Palmer," I said. "I had some questions to ask him."

"You mean you went to his office and talked to him?" she said. "I'll bet he knew you'd married me, a girl from the mountain."

"He might not have known I married you before I talked to him but he knew I'd married Deutsia Huntoon before I got through talking to him," I said.

I repeated the whole conversation to Deutsia and she said, "You might have made it harder on the Melungeons."

"Well, I didn't get anywhere with him, and if I'd stayed in his office five minutes longer, he would've had me arrested and thrown in jail. We will never forget what we said to each other. But, Deutsia," I said, pulling her again into my arms as we sat before the fire she had made, "The merchants in Mullins' Grocery Store, Blackburn's Dry-goods Store and in L. C. Songbird's Hardware were different. They waited on me as long as I stayed with them. It's funny about these eating places. Funny about a fellow like Spooly Holderby. I'll bet young Spooly couldn't chop a tree down with an ax. Yet he thinks he's something special on a stick because he's from the Spool and the Holderby families."

"I wish I could have been with you," she said. "You

wouldn't have gone to the courthouse to see Judge Palmer and you wouldn't have tried to take me to Little Tavern. So you wouldn't have had all this trouble."

"I am a citizen of Sanctuary Mountain and I will fight for my wife and her people as long as I live."

"I keep wondering what is in that sack."

I carried the sack to the middle of our front room and poured its contents into a heap in the middle of the floor.

When I poured out what I had brought home, it made a heap larger than what the old pack peddlers used to bring to our house. Deutsia came over with a smile on her face. She sat down on the floor very awkwardly and began to examine packages in the stack.

"I didn't know you carried so much," she said. "Dave, you're strong to have carried this much. Candy, cheese, cigarettes, nails, saws, files.... Oh, how pretty!" she sighed. "Material for our window curtains! Somebody helped you select this, Dave?"

"Yes, the clerk," I said.

"Outing flannel, pink, white and blue! Dave, you're so different from our men on this mountain. You do things the right way. And you're so nice to me. Oh, and what is this?"

"A dress for you," I said.

"I've never seen anything so pretty! How beautiful!"

Then Deutsia examined the spools of thread and the assortment of needles I'd brought along.

"Soap, and towels and washcloths," she said. She held a bar of the soap up and smelled of it. "Smells so good. Smells so much better than the soap I make. What are we going to do with all these things?"

"Open that last flat package," I said. "You'll see."

"Christmas wrapping paper and colored twine and ribbon," she sighed. "Honest, you've thought of everything."

"Yes, Christmas is getting close on us," I said. "We want our first Christmas together on this mountain to be a great one. We want it to be a Christmas your folks and we will remember!"

19

❦❦❦❦❦❦❦❦❦❦❦❦❦❦

DEUTSIA didn't know what I had been
doing with the remainder of my big cedar tree until Christmas Eve. Since the
weather had been fair for the last ten days, I had gone to
the cedar tree and worked. I had made two cedar water
buckets for Daid and Bass. These were really simple to
make. But I had made a cedar pitcher and bowl, for Daid
and Bass too, just like the ones I'd made for Deutsia and me.
Then I made two cedar dough trays, one for Deutsia and
one for Daid. I made each one two feet long, hollowing
them from the cedar log into things of beauty.

Then I did something else that I hoped might spread
over the mountain and make living conditions better for
everybody. I'd not seen any signs of where anyone bathed
in winter. In Daid's and Bass' home, I didn't see a washtub
with soap and bath towels around as we used to have in
the smokehouse at my home in Wise County. Now I'd
ripped pieces from my cedar log with my ripsaw. Cedar

wood is soft, pliable and easy to work and I tongue-and-grooved those boards until they fit so snugly they were almost leakproof. I made two cedar bathtubs, one for us and one for the Huntoons.

I made each tub alike and the same size. I made one end of the tubs square so it would sit flush in the corner of a room. One end I slanted, like the end of a small boat. I bored a hole and made a stopper for a drain which could be opened or kept closed. I thought the Huntoons might like my idea. When I carried our tub to the house, Deutsia met me as usual at the door, and said, "What on earth is that you're bringing home this time?"

"A cedar bathtub," I replied. "Unless it's burned in a fire it will last a hundred years. This is a Christmas present for us," I said.

We had a cedar bathtub in our house two days before Christmas. And I told Deutsia that I would later find hollow sourwoods to make wooden pipes to carry the bathwater from the tub.

Deutsia was as happy as a child with a new toy. "First time I've ever been in a house that has a bathtub," she said. "I know Daid and Bass and my sisters and brothers will just love the one you've made for them."

I carried the bathtub, which weighed about a hundred pounds, very close to the Huntoon shack. It was very early on Christmas morning before they were out of bed. I left it in a thicket of pines near the path. I thought it safest to hide the tub, because someone might stir early on the path and not know what it was and do something to it. After hiding the tub I hurried back.

Deutsia had arranged the presents and put them in my sack.

I laid the big sack across my shoulder and then I picked up a large basket that had two water buckets, the cedar bowl and pitcher and the dough tray Deutsia had wrapped in colored paper and tied with colored string. We started along the path to the Huntoons'. There were well-worn paths between all the shacks on top of Sanctuary Mountain. Now that the leaves were off the trees, and no snow or frost on the ground they looked like the strands of a big spider web, with Sylvania's and Skinny's place the center of the web.

When we arrived at the Huntoons' they had finished breakfast. They were sitting in a half circle around a blazing wood fire.

"Christmas gifts," I said, when we entered.

"All right, boys, we'd better get a Christmas tree," Bass said.

"It's on Christmas morning the tree should be up in the house," Daid said.

"Daid, we'd better start getting the trimming for the tree," Meese said.

It was agreed that Alona would pop the corn and Daid would help her string it while Meese and Force would go to the woods to gather trimming and Pribble and I would go cut the Christmas tree. It didn't take us very long to find a Christmas tree on Sanctuary Mountain. We cut a cedar, with a beautiful round top and just as high as I was tall. I carried it to the house on my back and laid it down in the yard. There I nailed crossboards over the end of the trunk so it would stand up on the floor. I tied the top of the tree to a nail in the ceiling to steady it. Our tree was very pretty without trimming.

After the Huntoons got started, it didn't take them

long to do something. Meese and Force came back with red dogwood berries, those the robins hadn't found. They came with mountain tea stems with clusters of red mountain tea berries; they had some branches of reddish leaves still clinging to the tough-butted white-oak boughs. They had stringy, green-leafed vines of wild honeysuckle, boughs of rhododendron and mountain laurel. Then Force reached into his coat pocket and took out a clump of mountain daisies and one of violets.

"Where on earth did you find the daisies and violets on this mountain in December?" I asked.

"We know the cove where they grow," Force said. "Winds blow leaves over them. All we have to do is rake the leaves away and find the flowers."

Then Daid and Alona came from the kitchen with a dishpan of popped corn that they had laced onto red thread.

Deutsia, her sisters and her mother decorated the tree with white streamers of fluffy popcorn lying all over the cedar's green boughs. They put the mountain tea stems and the dogwood branches among the cedar's green needles. They used the rhododendron leaves, wreaths of laurel and the stringy wild honeysuckle vines by putting them over the cedar and contrasting a light and a darker green until I'd never seen a prettier tree.

And now Deutsia took the presents from our baskets and laid them on the floor under the tree. I emptied my sack onto the floor, and Deutsia placed the presents under the tree so each name on the package would show.

"Say, I never saw anything like this," Bass said. "That many presents and all wrapped in that pretty paper with fancy ribbons and strings! What's going on here? We're changing on this mountain! I wish all our neighbors could see this."

Tears welled up in Daid's eyes. "I am so glad you married our Deutsia," she said. She laid her hand on my shoulder. "You're so respectful to a woman. You look out for everything."

At first Daid had been fearful of me. And when she was fearful she didn't show her genuine warmth and affection. She had to love me to get close enough to lay her hand on me. And when she touched me with her hand I knew she loved me.

"Our presents for you are not wrapped like this," Meese said.

"They're not store-bought either," Daid sighed. "They're from the mountain."

Meese and Alona began carrying the Huntoon presents from another room and putting them under the tree. From Bass and Pribble, Deutsia and I got a fox-skin rug to go before our fireplace. There were four fox pelts sewed together. Alona gave Deutsia a cocoon that was fastened to a briar. "In the spring you'll have a pretty butterfly come from this," Alona said. "And before then you will be a mother yourself." Daid had knitted me a pair of heavy socks to wear with my boots; she had knitted a sweater and cap for her first grandchild to be. I got a big last year's hornets' nest from Force. Pribble and Force gave us a jar of wild honey. Meese and Alona gave us two clusters of blooming violets they'd found under the leaves, dug up and transplanted in rich loam they had put into an old bucket. They had a clump of wild daisies planted in another old bucket that they gave us.

"Keep them before the fire and they'll bloom for you a while longer," Meese said.

Now, when Daid, Bass, Meese, Alona, Pribble, Force and Cress got down on the floor around the tree, Deutsia and I stood by to watch them open their packages. Bass tore into one of his first. "A hammer and a hatchet," he said. "And I need them. Ain't they purty?"

"Coffee, coffee," Daid said. "Real coffee, and not parched corn coffee and not sassafras tea. We'll have real coffee for our Christmas dinner."

"Stick candy for me," said Cress.

"And for me, too," Alona said. "And, look, a doll cradle. You made it, didn't you, Dave?"

"Yes, I did."

"And what is this?" Daid said, looking at another thing I'd made.

"It's a dough tray," I said. "You can mix your cornmeal and your dough in that. It's made out of cedar and will last two or three lifetimes."

"Cedar water buckets," Bass said. "They're dandies."

"And a cedar wooden bowl and pitcher," Daid sighed. "Dave, your hands have made me happy."

"Cloth for a dress for me," Meese said. "Look at the daisies printed on it! I've never seen anything prettier!"

"Towels and washcloths," Daid said.

"A box of cigars," Bass said. "I'll try one of these factory-made cigars right after dinner. I'll be getting up in the world."

"And store-bought cigarettes for me," Pribble said. "I won't have to crumble the weed into pieces of any kind of old paper when I roll my own. Store-bought cigarettes."

"And for me, too," Force said.

I had never known people who liked to smoke or chew tobacco like the Melungeon men. And many of the women smoked clay pipes.

"Cheese, cheese," Daid said. "I'm so hungry for cheese!"

"We're sharing the things with you I brought up from Oak Hill," I said.

"Tell me what kind of a load you carried up the mountain?" Bass said.

"Fifty pounds, more or less."

"Too much, too much. That toting will make an old man of you before your time."

Now there was a package for Deutsia. It was a package she hadn't wrapped. When she opened the box there was a blue pitcher with six glasses to match. Deutsia, her mother and her sisters fondled the glasses and pitcher and spoke of them as the most beautiful things they'd ever seen. If I ever got back to Oak Hill, I knew I would bring Daid the same kind of pitcher and glasses.

"Needles, thread, thimble," Daid said. "I'm sure needin' these right now. They'll come in handy."

"You will excuse me," I said. "I'll be back in a few minutes."

I got up and left the house while they still had more packages to open. I walked out to the pine grove where I picked up the cedar bathtub, laid it over my shoulder and came around the path and up to the house, where I laid it on the porch. Then I opened the door and carried it in.

"What on earth is that?" Bass asked.

"It's a bathtub, Bass," I said. "See how it will fit into the corner of the room."

Then I explained how it could be set up and how they

could drain the water away with a pipe or they could dip the water and carry it out before they got the pipe. Every one of the Huntoons gathered around it.

"We've had one for two days," Deutsia told them. "And it works. It's wonderful!"

"We'll use this thing, won't we, boys?" Bass said, winking at Pribble and Force.

"It's best to use it every day," I said. "You'll keep the wood soaked and there won't be any danger of its leaking."

"It'll never leak," Bass said. "I'll fill it with warm water and I'll sit in it until I soak myself to the bone."

While we set the bathtub up, Daid came to the door and told us our Christmas dinner was on the table. From early morning things had been cooking. I had smelled them in the front room.

Bass took his place at one end of the table and Daid sat at the other.

After we had got in the chairs at our places, Pribble reached for a dish, and I said, "Would you mind if we say a few thankful words to God for all these things we have? Let's all hold hands around the table."

Little Cress and Alona thought it was strange to hold hands around the table. Bass and Daid had surprise written on their faces, too. But we held hands, and I said, "I'm not very good, God, at asking a blessing, but we have so many things to be thankful for. We've got Sanctuary Mountain to live on and we've got homes up here, fires to sit before, beds to sleep on and roofs to cover us. And, God, from the looks of this table, the Huntoons have plenty of good grub for this Christmas dinner. God, we thank You that we are all alive, that we are able to talk and laugh and to give presents to one another. Thank You, God, for so many won-

derful things You have given us and for all this food before
us. Amen." Slowly all hands let go, and as heads were lifted
all eyes were on the table before us.

We had fish stacked up on a big fish fry before us. We
had wild pheasant and wild turkey.

"Force and Pribble went on a long hunt to get the turkeys for Christmas," Bass said.

There were two dishes of wild turkey and one was
moving up one side the table while the second dish moved
down the other.

"They went over into the Black Water country and the
Clinch Mountain ranges in Old Virginny," Bass said.
"More wild turkeys there than here. Yes, we've thinned
'em out here."

"We were gone six days on that hunt," Force said. "We
never had no trouble stayin', for we were in Melungeon
country."

"Yeah we stayed with Melungeons but we took hard
rationin' and quilts for beddin'," Pribble said. "We wanted
to get away from the Melungeon country, for they are
hunters and they live mostly on wild game."

"I'm afraid they rob the wild turkeys' nests of their
eggs, too," Force said. "Wild eggs for breakfast are awfully
good."

Everybody was helping himself to two kinds of wild
meat and fish, heaping his plate, taking something from
each dish on the table. And there were many dishes on the
table. There were sweet potatoes and Irish potatoes, boiled,
baked and fried, turnips and turnip-top greens. And we had
cabbage too. We had dried fish, dried beans, shelled soup
beans, dried pumpkin and dried apples. We had wild
honey and maple syrup. We had sassafras tea and real

coffee. No one was drinking the tea but everybody, even to little Cress, was drinking coffee. And we had cornbread baked in a pone and biscuits cut with the top of a glass and baked brown in the oven. What a dinner we had before us! But around the Huntoon table sat some big eaters. And I was one.

"It's great, ain't it, Daid, to have our youngins and our son-in-law Dave around our table on this Christmas day, breakin' bread and partakin' o' the grub with us?"

"Yes it is, Bass," Daid said in a soft voice.

Bass was eating a drumstick of wild turkey.

"I can't get over that cedar bathtub Dave made," he said. "We got a lot of wonderful presents but that's the finest."

Around the Huntoon table there was talk and laughter.

"Now I want you to eat all you can," Bass said. "Eat until you feel satisfied. Don't go away from this table hungry."

"Save a place for the pie and more coffee," Daid said.

After we had finished, we had our choice of strawberry, apple, peach, pumpkin or wild huckleberry pie. I took wild huckleberry pie and more coffee.

"Daid, what'll our people think of us having a bathtub up here on Sanctuary Mountain?" Bass said.

"I'll tell you what they'll think, Bass," Force said. "They'll be wanting one, too. It's goin' to work Dave to death."

"There might come the time in the years ahead when everybody on old Sanctuary has a bathtub," Bass said, and he washed a bite of peach pie down with a swallow of hot coffee. "And we can say it started first in Deutsia Huntoon Stoneking's and in Bass and Daid Huntoon's houses."

After we had finished with our dessert I felt as heavy
with food as a toadfrog sitting in a yellowjackets' nest swal-
lowing each one that came up from the hole in the ground.
I didn't want to move. I took my tobacco pouch from my
pocket and filled my pipe. Little Cress went to the living
room and fetched Bass' box of factory-made cigars. He
tore into the box, took out a long cigar and admired the little gold paper band around the center. Then he bit the end
off that he put into his mouth, struck a match under the
table, lit his cigar and blew a big cloud of smoke toward
the ceiling.

"It tastes wonderful," he said. "Boys, have one."

He passed the cigars over to Pribble and Force. Each
took a cigar, bit off the end and struck a match under the
table and lighted it just as their father had done.

Daid opened a pack of cigarettes, took one from the
pack, and since I was sitting close I lighted it for her. Then
Deutsia, Meese and Alona took cigarettes from the package
and began to smoke. The Huntoons were a happy family.
They had love for each other and they were as free as
mountain winds. I thought of my home in Virginia. My father and mother didn't believe in smoking and they certainly didn't believe in drinking. We lived better than the
Huntoons, but we never had as much fun as they had. Now
the kitchen was filled with smoke, for everybody was
smoking but little Cress, and if he had asked for a cigarette,
I believe Bass and Daid would have given it to him.

"It's time you men folks cleared out so we can ridden
the table," Daid said.

When we got up from the table, Bass stretched and
yawned and put the flat palms of his hands upon the newspapered ceiling. Slowly we walked into the living room
where we sat down before the fire.

"The only trouble with Christmas is it doesn't come but once a year," Bass said. "We need four or five days like this out of every year."

Then Bass asked Cress to bring his box of cigars.

"One's not enough," he said. "Best cigar I ever smoked."

When he lighted his cigar, he reached over and slapped me on the shoulder.

"Daid and I have a wonderful son-in-law," he said. "We love you, man! You've jined us from the heart and we are with you all the way. We love you in this family and our people all over this mountain love you."

"No man like you has ever married one of us," Pribble said. "Our people have heard of you over on Black Water."

"Yes, over among the Clinch Mountain ranges," Force said. "Melungeons we met over there ast about you. They wanted to know why you married a Melungeon and accepted the problems of our people."

"Did you tell them?" I asked.

"I told 'em I had a pretty sister Deutsia and you loved her at first sight and you married her come hell and high water," Force said.

"Then you told them the truth," I said.

20

NOW CAME the succession of winter days when snow fell and hugged close the rocks and frozen dirt and then more snow came and heaped into drifts that reached the low limbs of the squat spread cedars. Even the deep crevices between the rocks and deep mountain hollows were smoothed over with snow. During these January days I finished making our furniture, made the set of chairs for Daid and went on many trips with Pribble and Force following their trap lines.

When the weather faired for a day or two, I worked building a cellar and chopped piles of stove wood and firewood. I carried the firewood to the chimney corner and stacked it there for the cold days when the wind would feel like a sheet of ice against my face, days that Deutsia didn't go outside for fear of falling on the slick snow-crust and ice-hugged rocks. On those winter evenings we supped cold wine before a roasting fire, popped corn to make wild

honey popcorn balls, talked about people living on the
mountain and planned our days ahead. She told me about
the schoolteachers the superintendent of Cantwell County
schools had sent upon the mountain. They hated to come
and the only reason one ever would was because he
couldn't find a school any place else.

"I'll never forget Miss Rose," Deutsia said. "Don
Praytor and Willis Shell had to go to Oak Hill to help her
up the mountain. She was a big fat woman and it took her
all day to climb the mountain. They had to take her by the
hands and pull her up to the first cliffs. There Don held
both her hands and Willis got behind her and shoved and
they finally got her up the steps."

"Was she a good teacher?"

"We liked her better than any teacher we ever had,"
Deutsia said. "She brought leaves, blades of grass and wild
flowers into the schoolhouse and asked us to name them."

"Did she know their names?"

"You bet she did," Deutsia said. "That's how I learned
them. I don't believe there was a tree, plant or flower that
grew on this mountain she didn't know. She'd send the
boys out to gather them for her. And then she taught us
their names. She taught us what a canyon was, she took us
from the schoolhouse and showed us a deep narrow valley
where the water poured down from between the rocks.
'This is a canyon,' she told us."

"Where did she live while she was here?"

"She stayed with us."

"Was she like the people down in the valley?"

"No, she loved us, helped us, taught us, and we loved
her."

"Where is she now?"

"She never went back from this mountain after she came up here," Deutsia said. "She died at our house and is buried in our graveyard. Our people chiseled a big rock and put her name on it and these words:

" 'Rose Fox, without malice in her heart for anyone and the best-liked teacher that was ever on this mountain to teach our children, sleeps here.'

"Each spring the school children take baskets of wild flowers and decorate her grave on Decoration Day. All of us who knew her will love her as long as we live. She did more for us than anybody we've ever known. She taught the old people to read and write. She didn't want a school down in the valley. She wanted to come up here and teach us."

"How long did you go to school to her?"

"I never went to another teacher," she said. "I went to the eighth grade, which was as far as I could go on the mountain. She didn't believe in our having snakes at our religious services. She had some foreign kind of a religion called Presbyterian." And then Deutsia told me of the teachers they had sent since she had quit school. They had had as many as five teachers in one year because the teachers didn't like to board in one of the shacks and they didn't like the people.

She told me about the families that made moonshine on the mountain and sold or traded it to Sylvania and Skinny. She told me about the good hunters and the poor hunters and how one family would steal the catch from another family's traplines. She told me how they dug ginseng, May apple roots, and yellow roots in their seasons and laid them up to dry and sold these roots in Oak Hill to the merchants. She told me how they picked wild huckleberries,

blackberries, strawberries, and raspberries and sold them to
the people in Oak Hill, and how they gathered sacks of
walnuts, butternuts, hickory nuts and hazel nuts and sold
them in the valley.

"What do the people do with their furs?" I asked
Deutsia.

"They sell them to the merchants in Oak Hill," she
said. "They usually trade them for clothes."

"What month do they take their furs to market?"

"Next month," she said. "Trapping season ends then."

And now I learned the ways of Deutsia's people, how
they trapped the winter long and saved and cured wild animal pelts to make money to buy their clothes. And I
learned the low prices they were paid for them. We talked
about these things before the fire on blizzardy winter evenings before we went to bed.

"Come, come," Deutsia said, holding her hand to her
body. "Put your hand where mine is. Feel that movement
within me?"

"I feel it."

"Life stirring within life," she said. "Isn't that strange?"

"It's yourself and myself."

"It fluttered like a bird."

And I held my hand on her until the tiny movements
stopped.

"Our child."

"I hope it's a boy," I said. "I hope he will look like you.
You must be careful now not to step on any ice."

"You watch me too carefully," she said. "I can't stay
inside all the time. I just have to get outside."

"But I don't want anything to happen."

"Women on this mountain go out in the mountains and pick berries. They hoe in the patches two days before their babies are born," Deutsia said. "They chop wood. Mattie Collins had a baby in the huckleberry patch."

"But you're not doing that," I warned her. "I'll cut the wood, pick the berries and hoe the garden."

"We'll have a son and a daughter," Deutsia said. "But what if this one is a daughter?"

"Then we'll have a son."

"What if the next one is a daughter?"

"Then we'll have a son."

"What if we have seven daughters?"

"The eighth will be a son."

Then Deutsia laughed as I'd never seen her laugh before.

Now Deutsia was beginning to change shape. She was shy when people came to visit us. Often she would go into the kitchen and stay until the visitor left, even though he was one of the men on the mountain she had known all her life. She was shy when Bass and Daid came to see us. She was shy when Pribble, Force, Meese, Alona and Cress came. Often she was shy with me and wouldn't let me hold her and kiss her. I noticed for the first time the somber autumn mood in her face that I had first noticed in Daid's face. As the days passed and our baby grew, Deutsia's mood became as somber as the mood of winter's dark trees that stood leafless and barren in the wind.

I wondered if the cause were not Deutsia's staying so close inside the shack on these short winter days and long winter nights. In summer when I met her she was happy. And now in the bleakness of winter, after she had felt life within her, she had grown depressed.

"Was that somebody knocking at the door?" Deutsia asked, as we sat before the fire one February evening sipping our wine.

I listened.

"Yes, it is."

"Wait a minute before you open the door," Deutsia said, as I started toward it.

While she hurried back to the kitchen, I heard the rap-rap-rap again and the faint voice of a man yelling, "Hello! Hello! Is anybody at home?"

Now that Deutsia was hidden in the kitchen, I opened the door.

"Skinny, what are you doing here this time of night?"

"I've come to tell you . . ." He couldn't finish his words for crying.

"What's wrong, Skinny?"

"Sylvania is dead." He burst out into loud crying.

"When did she die?"

"About two hours ago."

"Just you with her when she died?"

"Mort and Hezzy were there," he said. "They heard the last breath leave her body. I want you to come tomorrow and help with 'er coffin. It'll be a hard 'n to make. I've heard you're a good carpenter. And I want 'er put away in a nice box."

"I'm sorry to hear she's dead," I said.

"Tho' she ain't been out of the shack since she was a girl," Skinny wept, "th' Master came last night and took 'er spirit home."

"I'll bring my toolkit and come tomorrow," I said. "What time must I come?"

"In the mornin'," he said between sobs. "I've got oak

lumber stored in the barn to make the box. Mort and Hezzy will do this. And they'll have help. All I'll want you to do is line the coffin with cedar boards."

"I'll be there in the morning," I said. "Won't you come in and warm your hands before you go?"

"No, I must go on," he said, his voice sobbing like the winter wind in cedar tops at night. "I must tell all our friends about Sylvania's death."

I watched this skinny man, almost thin enough for the wind to blow away, walk hurriedly from our shack. I closed the door and went back to the kitchen.

"Sylvania is dead," I said.

"What? Sylvania dead?" Deutsia was surprised that Sylvania could die, since she was as fixed a part of Sanctuary Mountain as any cliff or tree.

"Skinny's going around to tell our people."

"He'll have to go to every house on this mountain," she said. "And he'll have to go to many houses in the valley. But he'll have friends who will help him."

"How do they have friends in the valley?" I asked.

"In Prohibition days she sold moonshine to all the county officeholders in Cantwell County," she said.

"Hezzy and Mort talked about her all the time," I said. "I never saw her but once and that's when I bought the stove. She's the biggest woman I ever saw. If they couldn't get her out of the house alive, how'll they take her out dead?"

"I wonder," Deutsia said. "I'm trying to make myself believe Sylvania's dead."

21

❧❧❧❧❧❧❧❧❧❧❧❧

I'M NOT GOING there today with you," Deutsia said.

"Deutsia, people have to die. Death is as natural as birth."

"I don't want to see people and I don't want to be seen," she said. "You go with Daid and Bass. I'm going to stay home."

There was no use begging her to go with me.

"This is a time when Skinny needs you," Deutsia said. "There will be a big crowd there this morning. People will come up from the valley."

"I must be on my way," I said. "I'll go with Daid and Bass. Why don't I ask Meese to come over and stay with you?"

"But I don't need anybody to stay with me."

I kissed Deutsia goodbye. Then I was on my way over to get her folks.

Sylvania picked a good time to die, I thought. It was a warm winter day. The snow had melted and had run from the mountain in clear, bright streams. A soft warm wind was blowing over the mountain, lifting the dead leaves from the ground.

When I reached Huntoons' shack they were up, had eaten their breakfasts and were ready for the big day.

"Where is Deutsia?" Daid asked.

"She wouldn't come."

"Is she sick?" Bass asked.

"No, she said she didn't want to see anybody or be seen."

"I understand," Daid said. "Sometimes the unborn baby is marked by its mother looking at the face of a dead person. Meese, you said you didn't want to go to the buryin', so why don't you go over and stay with Deutsia until Dave gets back home?"

"I'll be glad to go stay with Deutsia," Meese said. "I don't want to see Sylvania dead and in her coffin. I won't leave Deutsia until Dave comes back home."

I felt much better that Meese would be staying with Deutsia. Maybe I didn't understand women in their pregnancy. I didn't know whether all women were like Deutsia or not, but she was giving me cause to worry. I didn't tell Daid and Bass. Maybe Daid was worried, too, and that was the reason she suggested that Meese go stay with Deutsia until I got back.

Bass puffed a cloud of smoke from his cigar close to my nose.

"You know that smell?" he said. "That's one of the factory-mades you brought me for Christmas. I'm keeping some for special occasions like births, deaths and the special church services when Brother Dusty will test his flock by the serpent to see who's backslid into a Devil's hell."

"It smells good, Bass," I said.

"I smoked one in Sylvania's presence and she had me stand and blow smoke into her face, she liked it so much," Bass said. "Poor old soul over there a-layin' a corpse! Well, one thing about it, she won't be smellin' any brimstone and black curlin' smoke from a Devil's hell. Brother Dusty tested her with the serpent right in her own shanty. Skinny took off and wouldn't be tested."

"We'd better be a-goin', children," Daid said. "The winter sun is risin' and we'll be late."

Bass led the way, a cigar in his mouth, a stream of smoke flowing back over his shoulder, for we faced the blowing wind. Daid was at Bass' heels and I was behind her with Pribble, Force, Alona and Cress following me in single file.

"Look at the tracks on this path," Bass said. "There will be some crowd there today."

When we came out into the clearing near Skinny's and Sylvania's shack, we knew Bass had been right. There were horses and mules, with and without saddles, tied to trunks and branches of trees all over the place.

"I told you they'd be here," Bass said. "Sylvania has been a mighty tree amongst us. And now that mighty tree has fallen. Sylvania will go to the Sanctuary Mountain graveyard to sleep forever, but her spirit will be with us."

"Poor old soul," Daid said.

"Is the school year over on the mountain?" I asked Alona.

"No, we've got two more weeks to go," she said. "But our schools, the Rose Elementary School, Sanctuary Mountain Elementary, Blackwater Elementary have all been shut down for today."

"There'll never be her like again, youngins," Bass said.

Now we were getting closer to the shack. There were people everywhere. And there were little groups standing with their heads close together, talking. There was laughter and loud talk among the people and the smoke went up in tiny swirls from their pipes, cigars and cigarettes and thinned on the high mountain wind. Dry leaves were carried over our heads up here like flocks of wild birds. When the air cleared we could look up higher and see the buzzards circling. About twenty buzzards had gathered.

"I don't like the looks of them birds," Bass said, pointing. "Look up there, won't you. I should have fetched my gun."

"But there ought'n to be no shootin' around here in a time like this," Daid said.

"And there should be no turkey buzzards up there, either," Bass told her.

Now we walked up to Sylvania's and Skinny's shack.

"Mort," I said. He came out of the door and Hezzy was behind him. "It's good to see you."

Mort and I shook hands with feeling.

"Put 'er there," said Hezzy, extending me his hand with warmth.

"It's wonderful to see both of you," I said.

"We think about you," Mort said. "The shanty is lonesome with just us. We miss you and Ben. But we know women have a great power over men. Look at poor old Skinny a-floppin' around here this morning like a chicken with its head cut off."

"Yeah, like a little addled rooster," Hezzy said. "When he lost Sylvania he about lost his own life. Ah, how well I knowed dear old Sylvania! She was a blessed old soul."

Hezzy pulled his red bandanna from his hip pocket and wiped the tears.

"Here, I want you to meet my folks," I said. "I want you to know Deutsia's father, Bass Huntoon, and this is her mother, Daid. And here's her brothers, Pribble, Force and Cress. This is her sister, Alona."

"Where is your wife today?" Hezzy said.

"She's home today," I said. "And her sister Meese is with her. You see, we've got a little one on the way."

"So you have?" Mort said.

"Yes, and I thought Deutsia's coming here today might upset her too much."

"You're a-goin' to be helpin' make the coffin down at the barn," Hezzy said. "Skinny told us he wanted you to put the finishing touches on the last restin' place for his dear wife. Atter you go in and pay your last respects come down to the barn. We'll be down there getting started. I know it's early but we'll have to have it ready by noon. He wants Sylvania buried by high noon."

When we went inside the one-room cabin, which was big enough to divide into four rooms, there was hardly standing room among the people. They had gathered around the only bed in the room, a homemade bed with big posts where Sylvania lay with a sheet over her and pennies on her eyes. Women, children and men looked at this mountain of a woman and wept.

"We were a-sittin' there in front of the fire," Skinny said. "We had been talkin' and laughin' and Sylvania let out a little squeal and then she gave a long sigh, like one wind bein' chased by another wind, and she was gone. She fell back against the back of her chair. Old Death come and took her spirit in the twinklin' of an eye."

Then Skinny began to weep. He covered his face with his hands and sobbed until his body jerked. "In the twinkle of the eye," he sobbed, "she was gone and left me here alone."

"Easy, fellow, easy," Bass said. He laid his big hand on Skinny's shoulder to steady him so he wouldn't pitch over onto the floor. Bass led him to a chair and got him seated.

"Sylvania's never been out of this house since she was a girl," Daid whispered to me. "She growed up here. Her Pap and Ma, George and Hallie Hoons, lived here. They sleep near where Sylvania will sleep. She will sleep near Skinny's Pa and Ma Waters. Sylvania is the last of her family. All big people and fine-lookin' and they're all gone now." Then Daid leaned over and whispered in my ear, "How will we get a coffin in this shack? How will we ever get her out?"

Although the people were deeply grieved, this funeral was a get-together for everybody. Everybody was talking and shaking hands, and there was much laughter. This funeral was a lot different from those I'd attended in Wise County, Virginia. Bass introduced me to more of our people on the mountain. I also met Lonnie Pennix and Bert Prat.

"They're from the valley," Bass said proudly. "Bert was Cantwell County sheriff back in the dry valley days and he used to come to us on Sanctuary Mountain and we treated him with respect. He treated us with respect, too."

"Don't forget I was Bert's deputy and I walked up here with him," Lonnie said. "I was allus a friend to you and yer people, Bass."

"Right," Bass agreed.

"I let many a man get away up here," Lonnie said.

"Shot my pistol up in the air when the man I didn't want was on the ground a-runnin' through the bresh. I never shot toward the sound. I shot at many a man on Sanctuary but I never hit a one. And I'm a good shot, Bass. How did I miss 'em?"

Lonnie laughed at his own words.

"Come on Lonnie," Bert said. "I'm in charge of digging the grave. Before you go to the barn to work on the coffin, Mr. Stoneking, get Bass to show you the Sanctuary Mountain graveyard. It ain't fur from the barn."

Then Bert hurried through the crowd with Lonnie at his heels. They picked up their picks and shovels at the door.

Bass introduced me to only a few of the people in the shack. There were many there who, I'm sure, had come from Oak Hill and the valley, people Bass didn't know, but I could tell they were not our people by the pale coloring of their faces and the way they acted. They had come just to see how a woman too big to get through the door in life would be taken out in her coffin in death.

"Bass, tell everybody to clear out of the shack," Daid whispered. "Floria, Vie and me will have to bathe Sylvania and prepare her fer burial."

"All right, everybody, will you now leave the shack," Bass commanded in his loud voice. "The women folks will have to prepare Sylvania fer burial. It's warm outside. The Lord has been kind to send this warm day up here for our dear Sylvania's burial."

"Now we must take a quick look at the Sanctuary Mountain graveyard," Bass said to me. "I want you to see where we sleep up near the sky where the wind is allus blowin' over."

Bass pulled one of the factory-made cigars from his pocket, lighted it with a match he struck on his hatband, and smoke clouds trailed us past the barn and over the ridge road until we came to the Melungeons' city of the dead. Each grave had a little house built over it and the house was painted white. Since the Melungeons didn't have money to buy paint they used a white clay for paint. Here were acres of little houses, row on row and close beside, with little paths between. The place was clean and well kept with a pine tree here and there. What surprised me was that the Melungeons took better care of the little houses that covered the graves of their dead than they did the shacks where they lived.

As I looked Sanctuary Mountain graveyard over I thought, here is the place Deutsia and our children will sleep someday. The name Stoneking will be on a stone here, but it will never be carved on a crude field stone. I will see that it isn't, even if I have to tote a small tombstone up Sanctuary Mountain.

"It's a pretty place here," I said.

"Yeah, a good place to sleep when we take that last long journey to a prettier and a better mountain. Come now, let's go over here where we'll lay Sylvania to rest."

Over on the far side of this clean and beautiful city of the Melungeon dead there was a small army of men digging Sylvania's grave.

"Stop here a minute," Bass said. "See."

Under the shadow of a pine in the bright winter sun-light were the Huntoons.

"Grandpa, Grandma, Pa and Ma, all of us are here to-gether in the end," Bass said. "And here is space for the rest of us. I saw to that."

"Funny thing about a buzzard," Bert said, looking up at

the sky when we walked over where the gravediggers were. "He knows when anything dies in the mountains. I've often wondered if a buzzard could smell."

"Must be a buzzard can smell," Lonnie said. "Look up there at that cloud of 'em."

"Look out there, Lonnie, at that crowd around the shack," Bert said. "More are a-comin'. We started up here long before daylight and we saw the crowd at the crack of dawn, going by pine torchlights over the mountain paths."

Out in the clearing around the shack and the barn more mules and horses were being tied to the garden palings and the little blackjack saplings in the front yard. Where they were tied too close, they lunged and bit at each other. Now, overhead the buzzards were circling lower.

"Shoot into 'em, Lonnie, and shoo 'em away," Bert said. "And you fellows keep on digging. When you feel hot and winded you step out and let the second crew step in. See, Bass, we got three crews. We're a-goin' to relay this work."

"Don't reckon the crack of my pistol will disturb the peace of the funeral as much as the buzzards will," Lonnie said. "They're up there in the air a-pilferin' around where they got no business."

Lonnie pulled his pistol from his hip holster. He leveled it toward the turkey buzzards and pow-powed five times.

"Ye damned brazen buzzards," Lonnie said.

"There comes Skinny outside the shack, boys," Bass said.

"Shootin' around here, and my wife a corpse!" Skinny shouted. "Getting the mules and the horses skeered to death! It ain't good manners, boys."

"Just shootin' away the buzzards, Skinny," Lonnie said. "See 'em takin' off over the mountain yonder. Brought one down, fer I saw 'im floppin' among the black oak tops."

"That part is all right, boys," Skinny answered. "Buzzards are a perfect nuisance at a time like this." Then Skinny went back inside the shack.

Amsbury Johnson came up out of the grave, leaned on his long shovel handle and wiped sweat from his red beard with a blue bandanna.

"Sylvania is a big woman," he said. "They guess her weight to be 650 pounds. I think she's heavier. A circus man carried scales up here once and weighed her when she was younger and she weighed 650 then. But she wouldn't go to the circus with him. Dick and Rachel Waters wouldn't make the door bigger to get 'er out. They didn't want 'er to go off and travel as the fat woman with a circus. So she married Skinny, a little hundred-pound man who has made her a lovin' husband. Her Pa and Ma moved out so they could have the house. See, if they'd moved Sylvania out they'd've had to've torn the house down."

"But she'll have to come outen there today," Remus Wolf said. "God knows how we'll get her out. Might haf to tear the house down. Might haf to saw the door out bigger."

"Might haf to take the floor up and bury her under the floor," Estill Valence said. "We'd just have the furniture and the barrel to move out."

"You're a-gettin hot, Estill," Bert said. "Come up outen the grave. Let another man swing that mattock."

"We can't bury her under the floor," George Fannin said. "Skinny might want to jump the broom again. He wouldn't want his first wife, a powerful woman like Sylvania, buried under the floor when he was a-merrymakin' with his second wife on the floor above."

"You're right, George," Remus said. "It would cause a lot of disturbances atterwards."

"We want no disturbances," Bert said with tears in his eyes. "I've come here and got moonshine when the country was as dry as a bone. I was right here when the Revenooers were atter Sylvania. It was before I was elected High Sheriff of Cantwell County. They come and bought some from her barrel and then showed her the badge. She just laughed at them. 'You'll haf to get me outen the house first,' she said. 'Atter you get me outen the house, how are you a-goin' to get me down off the mountain?' All they could do was pour out a barrel of Sylvania's good licker. It wasn't no time until Sylvania had the barrel replenished and we were going back again."

Then Skinny came walking up where the men were digging the grave.

"Just want to see how you are getting along," he said.

"Right here under this pine is where Pa and Ma are buried and it's where I want my Sylvania to sleep. Bert, you see to the diggin' of her grave."

"Don't you worry, Skinny; I'll attend to it," Bert told him. "You don't have to worry. We'll get this grave dug and it will be plenty big for the coffin."

Skinny turned around and walked back toward the barn. His head was down and he was looking at the ground.

"I'd do anything fer old Skinny," Bert said to the men digging the grave. "He's in bushels of misery just now."

"I'd do anything for him, too," Rodney Fitch said. "There was never a better woman than Sylvania. When she sold you a gallon of moonshine you got a gallon of un-adulterated moonshine and not two quarts of moonshine with a quart of water and a quart of carbide all stirred up well and shook before drinking. I don't know what we'll do without her. We won't have no market fer our corn up here."

"They say," Tom Hankas said, as he let his pick fall against the hard mountain earth, "that you'll never miss your mother until she's gone. I say we'll never miss Sylvania until she's gone. She's been a mother to all of us."

"Well, I hear the hammers and the saws over at the barn," I said. "Bass, don't you think we'd better be getting over there?"

"Yes, I do," he said. "Come along, boys," he said to Pribble, Force and Cress.

In the big barn where Skinny kept hardware, seeds, grains, foods and other items to sustain life on the mountain, stored to sell or trade to our people, we found Mort and Hezzy hard at work. They had a crew of workers helping them make the coffin.

"That coffin looks big enough for a whole family," Bass said.

"We'll never get it through the door," Pribble sighed.

"Purty black oak wood we're a-makin' this coffin outen," Hezzy said. "Some say black oak ain't as good as wild cherry."

"Just put two in the ground fer fence posts, gentlemen, and see which lasts the longest," Mort said.

"You ever plane a cedar board, Pribble?" I said.

"Never did."

"Then here's where you learn," I said. "I'll let you use a plane too, Bass."

"I'll be glad to try it. I've never used one either."

"Yes, we're ready fer the cedar linin'," Hezzy said. "See all the good cedar boards Skinny's got in this barn."

Pribble and Bass were awkward with the planes but they could smooth the soft boards well enough. I helped them plane until we got some boards ahead and then I went to lining the big coffin. I got right into it so I could get the bottom lined first and then the sides. I did the lining while Hezzy and Mort made the coffin lid. While we worked making the coffin in the barn I heard a pistol pow-pow five more times. I thought it must be Lonnie shooting at the buzzards again. I heard Skinny out in that yard, "Stop that shootin' down there!"

"Well, I guess you know about our old friend Ben Dewberry, don't you?" Mort said.

"No, I've not heard from him since we quarreled that day in the timber woods." I felt a wave of excitement and sadness at hearing Ben's name.

"Well, he married that Hailston woman," Hezzy said. "You know, that county health nurse."

"No, I didn't know he was married," I said. "But I think it's wonderful that he is."

"Yeah, I guess they're just as happy as an old she and he coon in a hollow log," Hezzy said. "And you're happy, Dave?"

"Yes, as happy as a man can be," I said. "I hope Ben is as happily married as I am. He's a good man and deserves a good wife." I really meant what I said. I'd often thought of Ben, and now that my anger had cooled I felt unhappy about losing the best friend I'd ever had.

"Where does Ben live now?" I asked.

"He went to that big bottomland farm with all that dairy herd down there in Clinch River valley," Mort said. "No more timber-cuttin' fer old Ben. I guess he married into aplenty."

"I hear tell down in Oak Hill they've got money to

burn," Bass said. "The Hailstons are akin to the Spools, Holderbys and old Judge Palmer. They're the people who run this county."

When Bass mentioned Holderby and Palmer I almost froze in my tracks. In my heart I would always be fond of Ben, but I'd never warm up to the Holderbys and the Spools.

"You see Ben pretty often?" I asked.

"Only once or twice a month," Hezzy said. "See, we're still lumberjacks. We're not up amongst 'em here."

"You're up higher than I am," I said. "Spool Holderby wouldn't let me eat in the Little Tavern when I was down in Oak Hill before Christmas."

"Hush yer mouth, man," Mort said. "You don't mean that?"

"Yes, I do mean it."

"Why wouldn't he let you eat there?"

"Guilt by association. I'm a Melungeon now. And I'm proud to be one."

Bass, Pribble, Force and little Cress remained silent while I talked to Hezzy and Mort. I wondered what they were thinking. But I could not help saying what I had said.

"Well, she's finished and she looks like a house," Hezzy said, changing the subject.

"Let's take her to the house, fellows, for Skinny to see," Mort said. "Gather around and give a hand."

It took Hezzy, Mort, Pribble, Force, Bass, Amos Chitwood and me to carry it. Bert Madden walked along to take hold if one of us got tired.

Skinny walked out of the shack to see the new coffin. He looked at the black oak boards gleaming in the winter sun.

"It's a nice job, boys," Skinny said as his bony hands tried to shake it.

"Take a look inside at the cedar lining," Hezzy said.

Hezzy and Mort raised up the lid so Skinny could see.

"Oh, it's so purty," he said. "Sylvania would like this. It's a nice house for her, but it won't have no winders nor a door."

"We have the grave ready," Lonnie said when he walked up. "See the boys coming out the ridge path."

"They're so wet it looks like they've all jumped in a rain barrel," Flora Fitch said.

Skinny walked back inside the shack.

"The grave's ready," Bert said, wiping sweat from his face with his bandanna. Then he squeezed the sweat from the bandanna with his big hands. "We had a time getting through that dry sandstone. I had to plug five buzzards too. Hope I didn't skeer you none."

"A little shootin' won't bother us none," Flora answered. "What's a-goin' to bother us is when we start to take the coffin in and take Sylvania out of the house in the coffin."

"Can't we saw the door bigger?" Rodney Fitch asked.

"Just as well take one side the house out by the time you make the door big enough to take that coffin out," Vie Bostick answered.

"Bert, ask Skinny about it," Rodney Fitch said. "Tell 'im that's the only way to get her out."

Bert went inside the shack to speak to Skinny. The crowd of sweaty gravediggers waited outside. They held their working tools in their hands. The yard was filled with people now gathering in closer from the graveyard, barn and the woods. The horses and mules tramped around the blackjack saplings and swished at the flies the warm winds and winter sun had brought to life.

"I'll tell you men it was a job to get Sylvania ready for burial," Vie said. "It'll take six powerful men to put her in the coffin."

Bert came to the door.

"Boys, tear down that chimney," he said.

Bert was the first to climb the wall. Lonnie climbed up after him. They stood on the clapboard roof and rolled the rocks off the chimney. Lum Tremble reached Bert up a coal pick. Bert pried the rocks loose from the daubing where they were stuck.

"Soon have it done, boys, the way you're rainin' the rocks down here," Rodney Fitch said. "Stand in the clear, fellers, and see that the rocks don't roll on your toes."

The chimney was lowered to a flat pile of cornfield rocks. The hole was big enough to take the coffin through.

"All right, boys, let's take the coffin in and get Sylvania," Abraham Pitts commanded. Three men got on each side and one on each end of the coffin. Over the chimney rocks they tugged it into the shack.

"Set 'er down easy, boys, on these poles now," Abraham Pitts said. "Don't ketch anybody's finger now."

The coffin was placed on three poles. The poles were placed on rocks so the men could get their hands under them. Sylvania was upon the bed now, a great heap in a flowered dress.

"About six of you strong men lift her," Bert ordered.

The women stood and looked on. They could not begin to lift Sylvania. They'd strained their backs trying to roll her onto the big flowered dress they had spliced so it would fit her.

The men, one holding each leg, one holding each arm,

one at the head and one at each side, lifted her from the bed.

"Couldn't 'a made a better fit," Lonnie Fitch said.

"It was my wife's request that she didn't have her funeral preached nor no songs sung," Skinny said. "See that barrel over there? It's the last my wife made. It's all fer you boys. And there's the dipper over there. What you can't finish today you can finish tomorrow when you come back to help me make my new chimney."

"Fellers, I'm a little thirsty," Bert said. "Let me to that dipper."

"Just takes another dipper to cool my throat," Lonnie said. "I'm as hot as a lizard in a new ground fire."

The thirsty men stood around the barrel and drank like cattle around a water hole.

"I patronized Sylvania in life and I'll patronize her in death," Bert said. "Take your last long look at Sylvania, boys, while Lonnie gets the nails and hammer."

Strong men, tanned by the sun where their flesh was not hidden by the beards on their faces, looked at Sylvania and wept. They pulled their handkerchiefs and bandannas from their pockets and wiped their eyes.

"Just a lot o' drunk men crying," Rodney said. "It'll be awful before we get her to the grave. They'll all be crying. Ought to 'a had the licker last."

"Who is conducting this funeral, me or you, Rodney?" Skinny asked. "I'm doing what Sylvania requested. I'm going through with it if they all get down drunk."

"Ouch! That damn big-headed hammer," Lonnie yelled. "I couldn't hit the side of a barn with it. Lord, I nearly mashed the end of my finger off trying to drive that nail."

"Let me have that hammer," Rodney requested. "I can

still drive nails. Hit some people with a sour apple and they get drunk. They can't take their licker."

Well, after what I was seeing and hearing, I was glad Deutsia hadn't come with me.

Rodney shaped the coffin lid and spiked it down while the men, women and children looked on.

"Come away from that barrel," Bert demanded. "Do you fellers want to get down drunk and leave the corpse in a shack that has the end outen it? Get under these poles. What do you think today is, your birthday?"

Two men got under each end of the three poles. "Get in front, Rodney," Bert ordered. "I'll get behind and tail the coffin."

I counted fourteen men around the black oak coffin. They walked slowly out at the end of the house where they'd torn the chimney down.

"Just like picking up a house with a family in it," Rodney groaned, as we walked across the yard and out the path toward the tall pine in the Sanctuary Mountain graveyard. The crowd was noisy now. The women and children walked behind as the men carried Sylvania to her grave. Before we reached the fresh heap of dirt under the tall pine tree, Bert pulled his pistol from his hip and shot into a cloud of buzzards.

"Put two big poles across the grave," Bert ordered. "There they lay already cut."

The men carried the green hickory poles and laid them across the grave.

"All the rest of you back to your places now," Bert ordered. "Let's lift the coffin onto the poles."

"Let's wind a minute," Eif Turnstile said. "I'm about pooped."

"Wish I was planted by 'er side," Skinny moaned.

"No use to feel that way, Skinny," Lonnie consoled him.

"Take it easy, Skinny," Bert said.

"Eif, you've had time to get your wind now," Lonnie said. "What do you say we lower this coffin, men? Get the plowlines under it. Two get hold of the end of each line."

The men placed ten plowlines under the coffin.

"Ready now, boys," Lonnie said. "Heave ho! Heave ho! Heave ho!"

"Let's pull these poles from under the coffin," Bert ordered. "Four men to each pole."

The men took the poles from under the coffin while twenty men held it up with the plowlines.

"Let 'er down," Bert ordered.

Now the men, women and children were weeping loudly as Sylvania's big coffin dropped slowly while two men strained at each end of ten ropes. They pulled the ropes from under the coffin. It was all over.

"May God rest Sylvania's soul," Bert said, wiping tears from his eyes with his bandanna.

Two men took Skinny toward the shack while clouds of gray dust swirled above the busy shovels. There was a peace in the lazy wind's rustling of the green pine boughs above us and the leafless branches on the mountain black oaks. It was now past high noon, and everyone either went to his mules and horses or began his journey on foot over the paths or began the steep descent of the mountain into the valley. I was very hungry and hoped Deutsia would have supper on the table waiting for me when I got home.

22

❦ ❦ ❦ ❦ ❦ ❦ ❦ ❦ ❦

DEUTSIA and I never got lonely in our shack. Daid and Bass came nearly every day to see us. Daid was no longer shy of me. She would come to our shack and go over the rooms admiring the smoothness of the walls and the furniture I had made for Deutsia. Often she and Deutsia would go into the kitchen and talk in low tones while Bass and I sat before the fire.

Pribble, Force, Cress, Meese and Alona came bringing us gifts. Pribble brought Deutsia a red fox skin for a muff. Force brought us a jar of wild honey taken from a hollow oak in which he'd found bees when he'd cut it to get a coon. Cress brought us a pair of fox squirrels' pelts for gloves. Meese brought us a big rug she had woven from rags with percoon blossoms woven in the center. It was a beautiful rug that Deutsia placed in the middle of our front room. Alona brought me a hunting satchel that she had made from a gray fox's skin.

When the snow melted and there was no longer any danger that Deutsia might fall, we'd go to Huntoons' to spend the day. We never went there without taking them something—a basket, birdhouse, or a squirrel cage for the young squirrels they'd catch in February. I'd never lived among friendlier people, nor had better neighbors, than the Melungeons.

Hunt Mallicoat came to our shack to trade me red fox skins for a gunstock he wanted me to make for him from black walnut. Cliff Lochees came to get me to make a coffin for his little girl who was burned to death. He had seen the big coffin I had lined for Sylvania and admired its beauty. Wolf Altwahs came and wanted to trade me wine and animal pelts for beds and baskets. The Leffertsons, Mahans, Cades, Coves, Coyes, Doves, Tacketts, Treadways, Snowwaters, Dees, and Greenwoods came, to see our house and to trade with us. They brought us wine, rugs, nuts, roots, barks and animal pelts to trade us for chairs, tables and beds.

So many came that if I had taken all their orders, I would have had to work two years ahead, and I wouldn't have had any time to hunt and fish with the Huntoons. My reputation had grown. But never did I refuse to make their coffins. I made seven after they had seen Sylvania's big one.

I had found my place in a world I loved. The Melungeons accepted me and no longer feared me as an outlander. I showed them how to pack their animal pelts, their roots and barks, and told them where and how to ship them. They walked across the mountains twenty miles to ship them from Rose Hill, the nearest railway station.

I did as much for the Melungeons as I could, for they were my people. I couldn't stand to see them cheated by the people who wouldn't sell us a marriage license. As the winter days wore on toward spring, I was thinking about a place for them to sell their wild strawberries, huckleberries, raspberries, blackberries and wild honey.

I would not only fight for the woman I loved and her right to live and be respected, but I would fight for all the Melungeons. I would fight against the barriers that encircled us to the bitter end. I would fight to break the barriers, for soon we would bring a child into the world, and I wanted him to have the freedom that I had enjoyed in my youth.

In late March, I borrowed Bass' mule and plow and I plowed our garden and a patch for potatoes. With a harrow made of two short logs with two rocks for weights upon it, I harrowed the garden and leveled the earth into a soft, smooth bed. As I plowed and harrowed, Deutsia stood and leaned against an oak tree watching the cowbird, blackbird, sparrow and robin follow the mule and me.

While I was working I looked up and there stood Bass leaned against a white oak near Deutsia. When I drove the mule to the end of the garden I stopped to see what Bass wanted.

"Go ahead with your harrowin'," Bass said. "You're doin' a good job and I like to watch a man work. But I have been wonderin' if you plant when the signs are right so your garden will be fruitful," he said. "We let the moon do a lot of our work up here. Dave, you know the moon has great powers."

I tightened my lips to keep from laughing. I knew how clannish the Melungeons were. They had to be clannish and hold together or they couldn't survive. But they didn't have to be as superstitious as they were. They were the most superstitious people I'd ever known. My Deutsia wouldn't go around a tree on the opposite side from me. She always went back through the same door she used when she left the house. If a black cat crossed a path in front of her, she turned and went back. Bass and all the Huntoons and all the Melungeons I knew were the same way.

"But I don't know about the signs, Bass," I said. "When I prepare the ground and if the season is right, I plant."

"But that's not right, if you want to get good yield and some extra help from the moon," he said. "It pays a man to take advantage of all the help he can get. Why work, break your back and sweat for nothing when you can call on the moon and he will help you. Just be kind and obedient to the moon."

All the Melungeons believed the moon had great influence on their lives. Every Melungeon shack on the mountain had an almanac, and if the Melungeon could read, he went by the signs. If no one in the family could read, someone read his almanac for him. The moon had the greatest influence on Melungeon life, and next came the sun and then the wind. When I rove the clapboards to roof our cabin, I was told that I was doing it right, for I was doing it in the dark of the moon, which meant they would never curl up on a cabin roof in the summer sun. The sun was a great source of light, and warmth that made the plants grow. The sun was a mother to all vegetable life. How many times had I heard that "the eye of the sun is upon us." They talked about the sun as if it was a great powerful god in the sky looking down upon their crops, their timbered lands and upon them.

The wind was something that carried them messages.
The wind told a Melungeon when there would be rain and
how much rain to expect. The wind told him when there
would be frost and snow. It warned him not to plant too
soon where his good seeds would lie in the cold ground and
never sprout. All Bass had come to tell me was very funny,
but I wouldn't let myself laugh. I had not married Deutsia
to change her way of life. I had married her because I loved
her. The only changes I would ever make among the
Melungeons were for them to see what I had done. If they
liked it well enough to follow me, all right.

"I'll take all the help I can get from the moon or from
you, Bass," I said with a smile.

"You can get more from the moon than you can get
from me," he said. "Right now I don't like the looks of
things. Apple, pear, peach trees are blooming in the dark of
the moon. Fruit very likely will all be killed by frost and
freeze. Even the wild plums that bloomed in the dark of
the moon.

"Yes, it pays, Dave, to go by the signs in the seasons,"
Bass said, flapping his suspenders with his thumbs. "Now,
we can't control when the wild fruit and the wild berries
blossom but we can plant our vegetables at the right time.
Best time in the world to plant beans is when the signs are
in the arms and feet. You'll grow beans as long as your
arms and in clusters likes the fingers on your hand. Plant
cucumbers when the signs are in the arms and sow cabbage
when the signs are in the head. Want a cabbage head as big
as yourn, don't you? Sow beets when the signs are in the
knees so they will bulge."

"What about corn?" I said.

"Dark of the moon," Deutsia replied.

"Yes, dark of the moon," Bass said. "It won't all turn to stalk trying to reach the moon. Plant in the dark of the moon and the roots go down and the corn will have good ears. And let me warn you, don't plant anything that grows above the ground but flowers when the signs are in the bowel. Deutsia, warn Dave to plant taters in the light of the moon just before the first quarter so they won't grow so deep in the ground. Warn him to set all plants that are hardy when the moon is going down. Set them any time from full moon to new moon.

"Yeah, plant in the light of the moon and the eye of the sun will be on it from the time it breaks through the ground," Bass said. "And that old sun up there has a powerful eye. Not anything can escape the eye of the sun.

"Since you were gettin' your garden ready, Dave, I thought I'd drop over to see how you were gettin' along," Bass said. "I must be gettin' back home."

"Thank you for your advice, Bass," I said.

"Just one more thing," he said. "I can warn you so you won't do it again. But you have plowed your garden in the dark of the moon. Plow your ground in the light of the moon. If you do, it won't clod and it will be mellow and nice to work. And you warn him, Deutsia, about these signs. You know when and how to plant."

"I'll warn him, Bass."

Bass went up the path.

"I want to help plant the garden," Deutsia said. "Soon as you are through with getting it ready."

"Then you can help me this afternoon," I told her.

"I love the smell of fresh dirt in the spring."

"I like to plow the land, too," I said. "And it's a lot easier than using an ax."

"I have always dropped seeds in our garden every spring since I can remember."

"Then you can drop this spring."

"And next spring?" she said.

"Our son will be able to drop them next spring."

Deutsia laughed.

I furrowed rows through the garden after I'd harrowed the ground.

That afternoon Deutsia dropped two rows of peas through the garden and I walked behind her and covered them with a thin layer of dirt. We planted two rows of sugar corn and I made an onion bed and Deutsia carried me the onion sets.

"I'd like to help you set these in the ground in the little rows," she said. "But it's very hard for me to sit down. I feel uncomfortable."

The birds followed us as we worked. Often the cow-birds and the blackbirds would quarrel over a worm and we would laugh at their troubles. We didn't have troubles. The only thing that made me remember bitter days was when the wind blew from the Big Woods toward us carrying the sounds of axes. Then I'd remember the days that I had spent there. I would think about the advice Ben and Mort had tried to make me swallow.

Before March had ended we had planted all the seed in our garden that could grow in an early season.

23

‰‰‰‰‰‰‰‰‰‰‰‰‰‰‰‰‰‰

I DON'T WANT to stay here to-
day," Deutsia said. "I want to get out and
walk over the old paths."

Since she was getting heavier with our child, it would
soon be almost impossible for her to walk the mountain
paths, cross the streams, and climb the rocks. There were
beds of percoon she had told me about that blossomed in
April and looked like banks of snow. Last October she had
shown me this spot of earth where she had come each
spring. I knew she would want to see them in bloom again,
and she would want to find some trailing arbutus, trillium,
wild snowballs, sweet williams, and baby tears.

"Then we'll go today," I said. "The sun is bright and
the mountain wind is not too cool."

"I'll fix us a lunch and we'll spend the day."

Deutsia came to the door with the lunch basket in her
hand. I didn't know whether or not it was carrying our
baby that made her so beautiful.

I put the wine bottle on top of the lunch and carried the

basket with my right hand so Deutsia could hold to my left arm. And we were off.

"Where do we go first?"

"Out the ridge where the percoons are in bloom."

As we walked along the ridge path, we saw the gray lizards scurry up the scaly-barked hickories. They were sunning themselves, mating, playing and catching green flies. A few feet in front of us walked a terrapin with his little stone-hard snake-egg-shaped head high in the air.

"Wonder where he's going?" I said.

"He's looking for his mate," Deutsia said.

A crow flew over our heads with a worm in his bill.

"Look Deutsia," I said, pointing to the crow.

"I've seen crows work like that so many Aprils on this mountain," she said. "They build in the pine grove yonder every spring."

There was a smile on Deutsia's face. Her face had always been alive, even when she sat before the fire on winter evenings and dreamed; but now it was even more so. She'd been confined in the house during the bleak winter months, but now that April was here and she was out walking over her mountain all the glory of life had come into her. She was happier than I'd seen her in months.

"Look, blacksnakes in love," Deutsia said, finding them on the path before we stepped on them.

"In love or mating?"

"Both."

They were wrapped around each other, lying on a bed of dead leaves the April sun had warmed for them. Their eyes looked into each other's lidless eyes and their tails made quivering music on the dead leaves.

"That's the first time I've ever seen snakes mating," I said.

"I've seen them many times before," she said. "Look how pretty they are in their new spring skins."

"You can see all sorts of birds, animals, and snakes mating on this mountain in April," Deutsia said. "I've seen it ever since I can remember. I wouldn't miss April for anything."

"Now that the snakes are out, the spring revivals will soon start," I said.

"Yes, it'll soon be time for everybody to get religion again," she said. "But my religion is to be out under the moon, and stars at night, and to hear the wind blow. Religion to me is terrapins, mating snakes, and wild flowers blooming on the mountain."

We walked along the ridge path until we came to Skinny's and Sylvania's shack. I was quite warm. We didn't see any mules hitched to the yard trees or hear any voices.

"Is this the place where we leave the ridge road?" I asked Deutsia, after we'd walked a long way slowly, facing a strong wind.

"We go down the first mountain finger on the right and not the left," she said, laughing at my forgetting distances and directions so easily.

Twice before we reached the finger on our right, we stopped and picked clumps of wild blue violets. One clump grew by a rock, the other by a half-rotted pine stump. When we reached the spot for our turning, had Deutsia been blindfolded I believe she would have turned at the right place.

"See that little fox path?" she said. "That's the way we go."

"I'll go in front and push the brush back for you," I said.

"You don't have to do that. But you can pluck that wild Indian turnip bloom for me over there by that log."

After I'd brought back the blossom to Deutsia, I walked in front and parted the briars where they lapped across our little path.

"Look, look," she pointed. "There they are!"

Before me I saw a white mass of percoon petals that covered the earth like a light fluffy late October snow.

"I'm so glad to be here again," she said. "Percoon blossoms don't last any time. They're here today but they'll all be gone by next Sunday. I wish they bloomed the year around."

Deutsia, a little tired from our long walk, leaned against a budding dogwood.

"Would you like to sit down?"

"I wouldn't mind."

"Look, over there by our bee tree," I said. "There's a bed of last year's dry leaves and the sun is shining on them."

We walked over and looked at the cross and the initials carved within a heart. We stood in silence, remembering the October day we found this bee tree, the storm that overtook us and our night on the cliff.

I set the picnic basket down at the roots of the bee tree, and then I held Deutsia's hand, for it was a little hard for her to get down and to get comfortably seated on the leaves. Above our heads the bees buzzed as they worked, flying from their knothole to the patch of snow-white percoon and back to the knothole again. After watching the bees a while I leaned over backward on the comfortable bed of leaves.

"Why not try lying down on this good warm comfortable bed beside me, Deutsia?"

I helped her down beside me on the leaves where the warm glow of sun filtered through the thin dogwood leaves. She pillowed her head on my arm and we lay there and talked and drank in good breaths of mountain wind... With Deutsia's head pillowed on my arm, her golden hair spread over the bed of leaves, with the sunshine in our faces and the cool clean air blowing over us, we slept.

24

✕✚✚✚✚✚✚✚✚✚✚✚✚✕

WE TOOK a long walk each evening out the ridge road from our shack. Deutsia waited until evening before she would go. She was afraid we would meet somebody on the road. When we did see somebody walking along the path toward us, we would turn from the path and walk into the woods, hiding ourselves until the person walked past us and out of sight.

"Since time is getting near for his birth, I think you ought to go to the hospital," I said.

"Hospital?" she said. "You don't think I'm going to die?"

"No, but women nowadays go to the hospital to have their babies."

"I never heard of such!"

"You would be with good doctors," I said. "I wouldn't worry about you then."

"Where would I go to a hospital? Where would one have me?"

"Knoxville," I said. "They'd take you there. Some day

we might leave Sanctuary Mountain. We'll go among other people."

"But my kin would visit me," she said. "Being a Melungeon will follow me. I don't want to hide it."

"But you ought to go to a hospital to have our baby."

"I think that's funny," she said. "Imagine my getting off this mountain now. You'd have to carry me down. Imagine taking me to a place I'd never been before to have our baby."

"We could do it."

"But I'm not going," she said positively. "Women on this mountain would laugh at me for generations to come. What would the women in the valley think of a Melungeon going to the hospital to have her baby?"

"To hell with what they think," I said. "Some of them go to the hospital to have their babies."

"But look how Melungeon women have their babies," she said. "They never have a doctor. Miss Fern is all they have. Sometimes we don't get her."

"What do they do for a doctor?"

"Nearly any woman on this mountain can deliver a baby."

"But I don't want any of these women to deliver our baby," I said. "If you won't go to the hospital, I'm bringing a doctor upon this mountain."

"Doctors won't come up here. You know that."

"If I pay one enough, he will come."

"No, he won't."

"But he will. I'm going to try, anyway. I'm not going to take any chances with you up here."

"You think birth is so hard," Deutsia said. "Our women have had their babies in the berry patches. They've had them along a mountain path. I've never known but two women to die of childbirth."

"But you could be the third."

"I don't have any fears," she said. "You will see that I'll not have any trouble."

But I knew in my mind that I was taking chances. Since she wouldn't go to the hospital, I was going to have a doctor come to her.

Again I was forced to go down into the valley. I had said that I would never go to Oak Hill again, for I had bitter memories of the last time that Deutsia and I had come down this mountain together. And I had bitter memories of my last trip down just before Christmas. But I would get a doctor for her, if money would bring one.

"Dr. E. B. Pratt" was printed on the door of the big white frame house. And below his name were these words: "Please knock before entering." I walked up the steps and rapped on the door.

"Good morning, sir," said a sweet-voiced young woman dressed in a white uniform. "Do you want to see Dr. Pratt?"

"Yes, ma'am."

"Come in and have a seat," she said. "He's busy now. He'll be ready to see you in a few minutes."

She went back into Dr. Pratt's office where I heard someone yelling, "Oh, Doc...oh...oh..." And then came a coarse voice, "Now this won't hurt you. Just take it easy." I listened to more screams of a woman and in a few minutes an old woman came out at his office door holding a blood-splattered handkerchief over her mouth. He had been pulling her teeth.

"Come in," the young girl said.

"What can I do for you, young man?" Dr. Pratt asked. He looked at me from behind his black-rimmed spectacles. In his hand he still held his tooth-pullers; his arm and hand were shaking nervously. And there were spots of blood on the white apron he wore.

"My wife is going to have a baby," I said. "I'm hunting for a doctor."

"I'm your doctor," he said with a smile. "I've brought more babies into this world than any doctor in these parts."

"You're the doctor I want, then."

"Where do you live?"

"Up on the mountain."

Then I saw his face change its expression and the young girl that had spoken so sweetly to me at the door looked at Dr. Pratt and then at me.

"You don't mean that you live up on Sanctuary Mountain?"

"That's where I live."

"I can't stand the walk up there."

"It's not much of a climb up there," I said. "I walk it all the time."

"I never went up there as a young man," he said. "I'm sure not going to try it now."

"But I have to have a doctor."

"Women up on that mountain never did have a doctor when their babies were born."

"But they've started something new," I told him. "I want a doctor with my wife."

"Who is your wife?"

"Deutsia Huntoon."

"Oh, yes," he said, looking at the floor. "No, I can't go."

"But money doesn't stand in my way," I said. "I have the money."

"But I can't make that trip," he said. "Go down and see Dr. Clifton. He's a younger man than I am."

"Mrs. Ben Dewberry might go up there," the young girl said.

"Yes, the Cantwell County health nurse does a lot of work upon the mountain," Doctor Pratt said, looking coldly at me. "Why not have her?"

"I don't want her."

"She's as good as any doctor."

"I still don't want her," I said. "I want a doctor."

"I have patients waiting to see me, young man," he said. "No use for us to waste our time arguing. I can't go."

"I'll give you a hundred dollars if you will."

"I wouldn't go for a thousand."

I put my hat on and walked out. I didn't say another word. I understood. Everywhere in this town it was the same.

"Dr. Clifton, I'm from Sanctuary Mountain," I said. "My wife is going to have a baby. . . ."

"Young man," he interrupted me. "I'm a busy man. I've got more than I can do now. Go see Dr. Pratt."

As I walked back up the mountain, I was as mad as I'd ever been in my life. For the first time, I felt badly toward Deutsia because she wouldn't go to a hospital. I was not only mad but I was deeply hurt, and felt for the first time that my fight was a useless one. The county clerk wouldn't issue us a license to marry but we'd married anyway. And now Deutsia was going to have a baby and I couldn't get a doctor. If we can marry without a license, I thought as I walked up the mountain toward our shack, we can have our baby without a doctor. I knew that we would have to.

25

⌢⌢⌢⌢⌢⌢⌢⌢⌢⌢⌢⌢

A S THE DAYS of April swiftly passed into May, Deutsia acted more strangely than ever. She wouldn't talk about the birth of our baby; she wouldn't take walks in the evening, though the wild flowers were in fullest bloom; the blooming red buds glowed like patches of fire among the green leaves, and dogwood blossoms rustled in the wind like white sails. I thought I knew Deutsia as well as any one could ever know his wife. Now I wondered if I did. For she was living in a world I couldn't understand. I was worried now when I looked at her face.

Once I went over to talk to Daid about her. And when I told Daid how strangely Deutsia had been acting toward me, she only said, "I understand. I understand."

I finally decided to talk to Deutsia about it.

"Deutsia, when I came in from chopping wood for the stove why did you hide from me in the kitchen?" I asked her.

We were sitting before our fireplace where flames

leaped up among the dry locust wood and light and shadow flickered on our walls and ceiling.

"I don't know, Dave," she said. "I just don't want to be around anybody. I don't like for anybody to see me like this . . . not even you."

"I think you're prettier than you've ever been in your life," I said. I pulled my chair over closer to hers and I put my arm around her shoulder and pulled her gently over closer to me.

"You're a wonderful armful," I said, after I'd let her go. "I don't want you running from me and hiding in the kitchen when I bring a load of firewood in at the front door. Hear me?" I said, smiling, and I tickled her gently under the chin. "Promise me you won't?"

"No, Dave," she replied, smiling faintly. "I can't help it, Dave. Maybe I'm just plain worried."

"About having our baby?"

"No, that's not it," she said.

Then there was silence between us, for I was trying to think what was depressing my wife. I thought maybe there was something she wouldn't talk to me about. Once down in Oak Hill on a Saturday when some of the valley people were trying to tell me not to date a Melungeon girl, one told me about the man who cut his wife-to-be's arm and drank some blood so he could say he had Melungeon blood in him and get a marriage license. He told me when their firstborn came the child was real dark and the Melungeon mother had thought it would be white like the father and so she choked her firstborn to death. I never believed that story. There were a lot of stories floating around over Cantwell County; some I could believe, but too many were impossible for me to believe. I knew Deutsia had heard all these stories.

"Why are you so silent, honey?" I said.

Then Deutsia turned to me and smiled. Her violet-blue eyes were misty with tears.

"You still love me, don't you?"

"Oh my, yes. I'll always love you, Dave."

"Then why are you afraid of me?"

"I'm not afraid of you."

Then there was more silence between us as the wood burned low and left a pile of red embers.

"April returns and I can't run barefooted with the wind and leap streams in the moonlight and the sunlight," she sighed. "Out there tonight the streams are white in this moonlight and they are pouring over the rocks. I used to leap over the streams or, if I couldn't, I found a wild grapevine, cut it, and I swung over across the stream, and I dropped to the ground on the other side. I love the wind on my face. And I love the freedom of the day and night on Sanctuary Mountain. But I don't have it now. I'm confined in this house."

"But Deutsia, you will soon have him and you'll be slender again," I said. "You can run like you've always run. You can be as free as the wild fox on this mountain. Yes, you can be free if I have to stay here at the house and take care of our child while you go." I laughed at my words and patted Deutsia on the cheek. I thought it would make her happy, but it didn't. There wasn't even a forced smile on her face. "Did you hear what I said, honey?"

"Yes, I heard you," she said. "But I can't hunt with my brothers and sisters and Daid and Bass like I used to hunt. I can't course the bees and keep our family in wild honey like I used to do on Sanctuary Mountain."

I hoped it was only Deutsia's fear of losing her freedom that depressed her while she was carrying our son.

26

LOW FLASHES of lightning barely missed the ridge top as they flashed over the dark green earth. By their light I could see white banks of cloud drifting below us. A dark cloud hung over the mountaintop. Thunders rolled like heavy jolt wagon wheels across the sky.

"Dave, it's time. Hurry and tell Daid and Bass to come," Deutsia said.

I grabbed my hat and ran out into the night. This would be the night our son has to come, I thought, as I ran to the Huntoons' shack.

"Daid," I said, gasping for breath. "It's Deutsia. Bring Bass. Hurry."

Then I thought about Fern, forgetting what she had done to us. We had to have someone beside Daid, Bass and myself. I knew that Don Praytor would be the man. He would go after Fern and bring her, if anybody could. I ran to the barn, bridled the mule, leaned astride him bare-backed, and kicked my heels against his ribs before I could get him into a full gallop.

Low-hanging limbs on the white oaks swished my face. But I held on around the ridge road, hoping and praying that Daid and Bass were with Deutsia by now. At the finger of the ridge road, by the light of the lightning streaks, I reined the mule down the path, slowed him at the steeps before I reached Don's shack.

"Don, I want you to get Fern Dewberry as soon as you can and bring her back to our shack," I said. "It's Deutsia. Take the mule and ride him to the mountain steeps. I'll run back to the shack."

Don's wife and children stood in silence as Don grabbed his hat, ran outside and lifted the bridle reins from the palings. He leaped astride the mule.

"I'll fetch her," he said. "And I'll be back soon as I can."

The mule plunged into the light of the lightning streaks and the darkness ahead. As I left Don's shack, I saw his wife's face and his children's faces outlined against the bright window panes. They were looking into the darkness the way we had gone. Thoughts ran through my mind as swiftly as the lightning streaks flashed in the black mountain night. I thought that Deutsia might die. Women had died in childbirth. When I reached the ridge road, I ran faster, for now I wasn't running uphill. Then I came to the little path that led to our shack.

"Anything happened?" I asked as soon as I opened the door.

"No," Bass said, standing in the front room smoking a cigar.

"Is Deutsia in bed?"

"Yep. Daid's in there with her."

"Take it easy," Bass said. "Baby might not be born before morning."

I wiped away streams of sweat from my forehead.

"I was like you are now when Deutsia was born," Bass said. "I remember that night like it was yesterday."

"But Deutsia is in pain," I said, listening to sounds coming from our bedroom.

"That goes with childbirth."

"But if she'd gone to the hospital—"

"The hospital," Bass said. "Why did you want 'er to go to a hospital? She's not near death's door. You must be a skeery man."

"I am a scary man when it comes to her, Bass."

"Sit down and take it easy," Bass said. "No use to walk the floor."

"If I could only have got a doctor."

"He's never been on this mountain in his life," Bass said. "He's too good for us."

"But Fern will come, won't she?"

"Yes, Miss Fern will come, if she can get here and knows about it."

"Don Praytor's gone after her."

Only now and then did I hear Deutsia moan in pain. I wanted to share her pain. I filled one pipe of tobacco after another and smoked it quickly. But Bass sat in a chair and smoked calmly.

Daid opened the door.

"Dave, she wants you."

When I hurried into the room, Deutsia reached out her hand. I stood by her bed holding her hand and I could feel the pain surge through her as she gripped my hand. I watched her face fill with agony when pains struck her, and when the pains left, she would lie quietly and look at the walls of the room.

Daid walked around on the other side of the bed and held her other hand.

"It's a shame we can't get a doctor up on this mountain," I said.

"I've seen a lot of this in my day," Daid said, her face showing as much pain as Deutsia's face.

"Daid," Deutsia said.

"What, my child?"

"When will it be over?"

"Take it easy, my child," Daid said, tears streaming down her dark face. "It will soon be over."

Bass opened the door. "How is she, Daid?"

"She's getting along as well as can be expected for her firstborn."

"Do you suppose I'd better go after Ma Madden?"

"You'd better fetch 'er, Bass."

"I don't want Ma Madden," I said.

"We must have help, Dave," Bass said. "Ma Madden's delivered a lot of babies in the last forty years."

"Fern will be here," I said.

"She won't come in this storm," Daid said. "She won't leave the valley in a storm like this."

Bass left Daid and me holding Deutsia's hands while she writhed in pain.

Deutsia was gripping my hand, her fingernails tearing into my flesh.

"Listen, Dave," Daid said.

Above Deutsia's groans we heard wind-waves of rain sweep over the shack, beating over the clapboard shingles, beating the window panes and the walls.

"Bass is caught in a storm," Daid said.

"What about Fern Dewberry and Don Praytor? They are somewhere on the road."

"Miss Fern isn't," Daid said. "She's never started on a night like this."

"I believe she has, Daid," I said, wanting to believe that she was on her way with Don, that they had reached the top of the mountain and that she was riding the mule while Don walked in front, leading the mule up the lonely lightning-lighted path.

"Valley folks are afraid of these storms," she said.

Now Deutsia's pains had left her and she lay perfectly still, with her dimmed blue eyes fixed on the ceiling.

"How're you feelin', honey?" Daid asked.

"It's awful, Daid. I feel like I'm in a skiff crossing the Clinch when the water is swift and I'm holding onto the oars."

"Fern Dewberry will be here in a little while," I said.

"Miss Fern?"

"Yes, she's coming, honey," Daid said. "Don Praytor's gone after her."

Deutsia's eyes were closed. She gripped my arm, screaming in pain as Daid and I held her.

"Be patient a few more minutes," Daid said. "This pain will soon leave."

"But another one will come," Deutsia said.

"Tomorrow you'll forget these pains, honey," Daid said. "You'll look at your firstborn and smile and forget you ever had a pain."

The heavy wind carrying great sheets of rain shook our shack down to its foundation. I heard the front door swing and I thought the wind had blown it open. While Deutsia was at ease between birth pains I ran into the front room.

"Bass. I'm glad you've come." Bass had opened the door and his clothes were soaked. Water spewed from the lace holes of his shoes when he stepped.

"Bad luck," he said, taking off his wet hat and shaking his head. "Ma Madden's gone on a sick call."

"I was afraid of something like this," I said. "I have an uneasy feeling about Deutsia."

"All young fathers have when the firstborn comes," Bass said. He was trying to make me feel easier but I could tell by the clouded expression on his face that he was worried, too.

"Pains are getting worse," I said. "And they're coming more often now."

"That's the natural course," Bass said.

"There's only one chance left," I said, as he started to the room where Deutsia was.

"What's that?" Bass asked.

"For Fern Dewberry to get here."

"She'll never make it through that storm," Bass said. "Not one chance out of a hundred. She'd be risking her own life to go out on a night like this."

"She wouldn't risk her life for one of us," I said. "Ben wouldn't let her."

Bass took Deutsia by the hand while Daid held the other. I couldn't stand to see her suffer any longer. I went back into the room and looked at the fireplace. My eyes were fixed on the spot where we'd watched the flames on winter evenings, drunk our wine and dreamed our dreams.

Now there was a wisp of cold gray ash left where once there had been flame.

Voices, I thought, turning my face toward the door. Could it be voices or the sound of the wind and rain? Could it be Bass and Daid's voices getting louder? I was hearing voices, along with Deutsia's screams behind the closed door.

"Open the door and walk in." I knew Don Praytor's voice.

I ran to the door and opened it wide.

"Fern, hurry to Deutsia; she needs you."

How had she ever climbed up the Sanctuary Mountain path, over the cliffs, in a storm like this? Had God spoken with an inner voice and told her to go?

"How is Deutsia?" Fern asked between panting breaths. "Is she having birth pains yet?"

"She's having horrible pains," I said. "I couldn't stay in the room with her any longer. I had to come out."

Fern took her raincoat off in a hurry. Don followed her through the door. Then Ben Dewberry came in behind Don.

"It's good to see you, Ben," I said. "I'm so glad you've come. Give me your hat and coat."

"I had to see that Fern got here on a night like this. Sorry you're havin' all this trouble. But this comes to a man when his wife has a baby. I've been with Fern on so many calls lately, I'm beginning to be quite a doctor myself. And I'm beginning to feel and understand about the sufferin' of people on this earth."

Before Ben had finished these words Fern was in the room with Deutsia.

"You didn't expect Fern to come and I am sure you never expected me to come with her, did you, Dave?"

"No, I didn't, Ben. I didn't expect anybody to climb to the top of this mountain on a night like this."

"I've been thinking a lot since I married Fern," he said. "She's been thinkin' a lot, too."

Then there was silence between us. After living in a shanty in the woods with Ben for years, I knew his nature. I knew he had more to say and I waited for him to say it.

"You're right, Dave. Marryin' Deutsia Huntoon. You married the girl you loved. Let bygones be bygones," he said softly.

"We'll shake on that, Ben," I said. "I'm sorry now for all I ever said to you."

"I deserved it." I felt the strong clasp of his hand on mine. "A man or a woman should be free to choose. You love Deutsia and I love Fern. We've been accepted by the people in the valley, and on the mountain. You and Deutsia haven't. People can be cruel or kind, and either way, life on this earth isn't always pleasant."

"The Melungeons love your Fern, Ben. She's the only one who will help us up here. Look, tonight, getting up here through this storm. I just can't understand why she hasn't been friendly in Oak Hill. She's good at heart."

"She's outnumbered down in Oak Hill," he said. "Put yourself in her place: what would you do, Dave?" He spoke softly. "Fern's never been against the Melungeons. If she had, do you think she would have delivered the babies and doctored all the chills, fevers, bellyaches and snakebites on Sanctuary Mountain?"

"Now let me tell you something," he added quickly.

"Fern and I have talked this over. We're going to let our hearts guide us from now on. We're a-goin' to act the way we feel; we're a-goin' to be as strong-willed as you've been. Maybe we'll have to leave the valley, and build a house up here and live beside you."

I reached for his hand to shake it again.

"We're on your side now, Dave. There is too much trouble in this world for us to be divided."

"Just a minute, Ben," I said as I ran to the room where Deutsia was. "Do you need me for anything?" I asked Fern.

"You just keep your shirt on," Fern said. "Go back in the front room and wait until we call you."

Bass came out of the room as I did. He pulled a cigar from his vest pocket and lit it. "Guess it's starting all over again. Thought I was through with this when Cress was born," Bass said.

"Bass, this is Ben Dewberry."

"I've heard Dave speak of you, Mr. Dewberry," Bass said, shaking his hand in a friendly welcoming manner. "I'm glad to know Miss Fern's husband."

"I'm glad to know you, Bass."

"You married an angel—an angel to us on the mountain," said Bass.

"It's a bad night out there tonight for my angel wife."

"And it's a bad night, Dave, for your boy to want to come into the world," Don Praytor said. "But this is the kind of night a boy likes to come. There is an old saying on Sanctuary Mountain that when a child is born in one of these storms, he has dreams and imagination."

He takes after Deutsia, I thought, but didn't say it. She has no fear of a storm.

"Did you hew the logs in this house, Dave?" Ben asked me, looking the room over.

"I did."

"I thought you had," he said. "I believe I'd know your work with an ax any place. Never saw a man as good with an ax. It's a fine home you have here."

There were a lot of things I wanted to talk to Ben about, but I couldn't do it now. When I heard Deutsia's screams in the other room, I stopped to listen, but Don, Bass and Ben talked louder than ever. They talked loud enough to drown her screams. Then all at once the whole place was very quiet except for the storm outside. The storm had quieted down too, and there was only the sound of rain pattering steadily down on the clapboard shingles and against the window panes.

I heard a different sound.

"Listen," I said. "He's here!"

"Easy, easy," Bass said with a smile.

"But he's here," I said. "He's come at last!"

"How do you know it's a he?" Ben asked.

"Deutsia said it was a boy." I ran over and knocked on the door.

The door barely opened and Fern put her face out to the crack.

"A boy?" I asked before Fern could speak the words her lips were shaping to speak. "And how's Deutsia?"

"Yes, a boy," she said softly. "But you cannot come in now."

"A boy," I said, turning to Bass, Ben and Don. "A boy!"

"Congratulations," Ben said, shaking my hand.

"Glad for you," Don said.

"Shake hands with Grandpa," Bass said. He was as happy to be a grandfather as I was to be the father of a son.

Then I filled my pipe. Ben, Bass and Don laughed at me when I struck four or five matches before I got a light. I puffed clouds of smoke as I walked proudly over the floor. Life has been good to us, I thought. We've overcome everything that's been put before us. We have won our fight. And now Deutsia will not feel depressed. She'll be happy.

I cannot tell you the thoughts I had as I walked the floor waiting to go inside to see my son. I thought of a name for him. I thought of calling him Bass. But I wouldn't call him that. I couldn't think of a name good enough for him. And I thought about the days ahead when he'd go to the woods with me. He'd follow me along the path as I had followed my father, and what a time we would have together! I couldn't see him as a little baby but only as a small boy wearing little overalls and a blue shirt and a straw hat.

I could hear him cry and I could hear Daid cooing words to him. And I heard Fern talking. I listened to hear Deutsia speak, but I never heard her. No wonder she doesn't talk, I thought, after all she's been through. She will have to do a lot of resting. She will have to take it easy for some time. I'm not going to let her get out of bed and put out a washing like some of the women on this mountain. Deutsia had told me about a Melungeon mother's working two days after a baby's born. I'll see to it that Deutsia doesn't, I thought. Daid and Bass will stay tonight and Meese will come and stay with Deutsia until she's able to be up and about. And I'll help with the work then. I was thinking these things while Don, Bass and Ben talked.

Fern came to the door, "It's Deutsia," she said . . .

"What's wrong?"

"Come, Ben."

Ben jumped up quickly and ran into the room.

"No, no, Dave," Fern said. She stopped me at the door. "Not now!"

"But Deutsia . . ."

Fern, Ben, Bass and Daid were gathered around her bed.

I stood at the door. I looked in. They didn't have to tell me. I knew. She was hemorrhaging. The bed was red. Deutsia was lying pale and lifeless on the bed.

Fern injected warm salt water in Deutsia's veins. The wintry looks on Deutsia's face flashed in my memory now as I saw her lying there while Fern, helped by Bass and Don, worked to save her life. Her blood—once so highly condemned, was spilled in childbirth. So much blood was spilled that warm salt water could not replace it.

Daid was holding on to young Huntoon. Huntoon was the name that flashed in my mind more than any other. And Huntoon was the name for our son. I looked through the open door at their faces, while they whispered something to each other that I couldn't understand. Then I saw the tears running down Daid's face in the yellow glow of lamplight.

If anything happened to her, could I ever forgive the people in Oak Hill? Yes, I'd forgiven my old friend Ben. He's a real friend, I thought. And there was Fern. I'd once hated her. But I didn't hate her now; I'd never hate her again! I watched her fighting to the last to save my Deutsia. If Deutsia went, then what was left for me? Our son.

I couldn't let myself hate as I'd hated. I'd hated until I could have fought any man, over my wife. Our Creator had made us all of one blood, I had to believe. I knew the blood was life itself, and without blood there would be no life. And now, they stood . . . they just stood beside her bed. . . . They acted like helpless people! Yes, God forgave! I had to forgive too.

Daid let out a scream and Bass, shaking and sobbing, leaned against the wall with his arms around his face. Don stood sobbing, with his hands over his face. And, now, poor Fern! She stood stone-still and her face was real white. Tears flowed freely down her cheeks and they looked bright in the glow of soft yellow light. Fern put her handkerchief to her eyes. It was all over. They'd done their best. It was midnight and my Deutsia had breathed her last breath on Sanctuary Mountain.

God, I forgive them, I thought. I know You're forgiving and You have already forgiven them. God, You have received her, and You'll be kind. She went in childbirth. You question not the color of her blood, no more than a nation questions the color of blood from its sons that has been spilled in battle to save their homeland. It's awful, God, to think about this! I'm all shaken, God, and I'm not thinking right, maybe, but why should this happen to us when we've been so happy together? Why is it, God? Tell me! I've faced hunger, storms and challenges in my lifetime, but I've never had to face anything like this.

I felt myself leaving the room and Ben and Bass trying to hold me. But I went out into the storm that was raging over Sanctuary Mountain. Ben and Bass were not strong enough to hold me, a terrified and a raging man, for I had a superhuman strength.

27

❧❧❧❧❧❧❧❧❧

NOW thirty-six years have passed, but I can still remember when I ran from our house into the dark night. The weight of the storm clouds pressed heavy upon me when I looked toward Heaven, where no stars looked down. I lifted my face and I prayed. My loss was so heavy I didn't think I could bear it. I believed that night, and I know this is true now, that a man has only one great love in his lifetime. My love was Deutsia Huntoon. And when she went that stormy night, the best of me went, too. It left me never to return.

I remember how Bass and Ben came out into the storm after me.

"It's the Lord's will," Bass said. "It was for a purpose. She was so kind. She never hurt anyone. She couldn't look at another person without smiling."

Then Bass shook like the raging winds were shaking, bending and tearing the trees apart on the mountain. He sobbed like the distant ebbing of low thunder.

When they led me back inside our home, I remember how Daid, good mother that she was, was holding our son in our arms. "My son, my son," she said. "He must never leave his people on Sanctuary Mountain. And there will be a young David Stoneking on the mountain."

"No, no, Daid, not David," I said. "He must be named Huntoon Stoneking." While I fought with every ounce of strength I had to get hold of myself, Daid was speaking about our son's never leaving the mountain.

Thirty-six years have been a long time to be away from Deutsia and Sanctuary Mountain where my love and my youth lie buried. But my memories are strong and deep. I'll never forget how old Mort and Hezzy came to my aid. That was one coffin I couldn't have made, and I think Deutsia would have wanted me to make it. But Mort and Hezzy made it, out of wild cherry, lining it with cedar. They made it in Skinny's barn. Ben and Fern stayed in the house with me until it was over. Had it not been for Fern and Ben I don't know how I would have managed. Fern saw to it that Deutsia was buried in the dress she loved, the one with the daisy figures that I'd bought her in Oak Hill for a Christmas present. Daid and Meese were giving all their time to our son Huntoon. Hezzy, Mort and Ben had to look out after everything. They took charge of digging Deutsia's grave. Now, when my heart was full of trouble, they were beside me.

I saw a funeral larger than Sylvania's, the largest I'd ever seen in my life. When the coffin was made, it was brought from Skinny's barn to our house and Deutsia was dressed and laid out for burial by Fern and a few Melungeon women who helped her. She was carried by relays of pallbearers from our house to the Sanctuary Mountain graveyard and buried at high noon, on the second day after her passing. I saw to it that her hands were crossed and that Brother Dusty, minister of our people, preached her funeral sermon and had charge of the services.

That day was the first time I locked our house on the mountain. I went home with Daid and Bass to stay a few days and to make the biggest decision I ever had to make in my life. The decision didn't come easy. I'd had dreams of our son going with his mother and me to the woods at night and walking the paths and leaping the streams in the moonlight. I wanted him to grow up as his mother had grown up in the freedom of Sanctuary Mountain. I wanted him to know the changing seasons, to know the powers of the sun, the magic of the moon and the taste, smell and feel of the wind. I wanted him to interpret the sounds of the wind as Deutsia and her people had done for a century. I wanted him to know and love the night as his Melungeon ancestors did.

I had carried pictures of our son in my mind, when Deutsia was carrying him and had first felt life. I could see him following at my heels along a path as I had followed my father along the mountain paths in Wise County, Virginia. I knew that someday I would make him a little bow and arrow and I would make him a little wooden plow. I'd make him a hobby horse of wood like one I'd seen once in Wise. I'd get down on all fours and let him ride on my back when we played horse and rider just like my father had done for me. I had good memories of the way my father had treated me when I was a little boy. I had all these dreams for our first son, and for other sons and daughters I had hoped we might have. Now all of these dreams had ended.

Fern had come and had helped Daid with the baby's feeding. Seeing the loving care that Daid, Meese and Alona gave little Huntoon under the supervision of Fern, I knew it took women to care for an infant. I knew more about cutting timber than I knew about how to care for an infant.

"He must never leave his people," Daid said a dozen times a day.

At night, I got out and walked under the full moon on the mountain paths, trying to make a decision. Maybe Daid knew already that if he stayed with them and was raised in the tradition of the Melungeons, he would be hurt less than if I took him with me. Maybe Daid was afraid I would take him among my fair-complexioned people where he might feel prejudice. Could I take my son to my father's home? I wasn't sure. What if I did take him and he grew up dark? Where was the better place for him, with Huntoons or with me? My parents were now getting older and my mother would be worried trying to care for an infant baby.

All my better judgment pointed to my leaving our son with Deutsia's family. I knew that I had had my one love, and that I would not marry again. I was broken in body and spirit. I knew that I would leave Sanctuary Mountain and go back to the land of my own people. I would go back to my father's and my mother's home and all I would take back there would be my clothes and my toolkit.

On the fourth day after we had laid Deutsia to rest I was ready to go. I still had plenty of money left to buy my bus ticket home. Ben and Fern had climbed up Sanctuary to go back with me to Oak Hill. Hezzy and Mort came over and joined the Huntoons in the house I had built. It was the last time I ever saw that house, the house where Huntoon was born and where Deutsia breathed her last.

After I'd looked over the rooms for the last time, I gave Daid the key.

"It is yours," I told her. "Everything belongs to you. All I want is my toolkit and my clothes."

Daid, with Huntoon in her arms, wept bitterly. Meese had to take him from her arms.

Then I held Huntoon, our son, in my arms for the first time. He looked, I thought, like his mother.

"He'll be as handsome a man as his mother was beautiful," I said. "Deutsia will never die as long as he lives. He is our son."

"Goodbye, Huntoon," I said as I gave him back to Meese. "Goodbye, our son."

Bass, Pribble, Force, Cress, Alona shook my hand. Meese wept and Daid threw her arms around my neck.

"Oh, how could it happen?" she said. "I've asked God in my prayers. But it is for a reason she died! It is for a reason! It is for a reason!"

Mort and Hezzy turned their faces from me and wiped their eyes with their bandannas. Ben picked up my toolkit and Fern carried my turkey of clothes. Each brother-in-law and sister-in-law gave me a bouquet of wild spring flowers. It was an old Melungeon custom to give flowers to a departing guest. Ben, Fern and I moved slowly out of the house and down the path. I looked back and Huntoons were gathered there, Meese still holding Huntoon while Daid leaned on Bass' shoulder, watching us go.

About the Author

Jesse Stuart—poet, short-story writer and novelist—is one of America's best-loved regional writers. He has written over twenty books, all, with the exception of *Daughter of the Legend*, set in his native Kentucky hill country. He has taught and lectured extensively both here and abroad. One of his most famous novels, *Taps for Private Tussie*, was a Book-of-the-Month Club selection.

Jesse Stuart and his wife Naomi live on a farm near Riverton, Kentucky. They have a grown daughter, Jane.

Tendencies of the
Modern Novel

TENDENCIES OF THE MODERN NOVEL

by

Hugh Walpole
Hamish Miles
Milton Waldman
Jacob Wassermann
V. S. Pritchett
D. S. Mirsky
Luigi Pirandello
Erik Mesterton

Essay Index Reprint Series

BOOKS FOR LIBRARIES PRESS, INC.
FREEPORT, NEW YORK

First published 1934
Reprinted 1967

PREFACE

THE essays which appear in the present volume were originally published as a series in the *Fortnightly Review*. So far at least as the novel in other countries is concerned, they are intended not only to indicate the lines along which the younger writers of fiction have been working since the War, but also to serve as a guide and introduction, for English readers, to their most outstanding work. So far as possible an effort has been made to indicate those works of foreign authors which are available in an English translation.

CONTENTS

ENGLAND

Hugh Walpole

I. ENGLAND

SOME ten years ago it would have been a comparatively simple thing to write about the contemporary English novel.

In the first place a group of names quite definitely asserted itself, practically without challenge. Those names were: Thomas Hardy, Joseph Conrad, John Galsworthy, George Moore, Arnold Bennett, D. H. Lawrence, H. G. Wells, Rudyard Kipling, Virginia Woolf, E. M. Forster. These were, in 1920, quite clearly the leaders of the English novel (and throughout this article when I say English I mean British).

Ulysses, James Joyce's vast work, had not yet penetrated the consciousness of the interested reader.

And now—in 1934—what has happened to those names? Hardy, Conrad, Galsworthy, Moore, Bennett, Lawrence—these are dead; Wells is interested now in sociology and not at all in the novel, Kipling writes only an occasional short story, Virginia Woolf is moving more and more completely into a world that is the poet's rather than the novelist's, Forster has not published a novel for ten years. And to these, what men have been added—added, I mean, in this assured and separate class? James Joyce is writing now in a language that is, to one of his admirers at least, quite unintelligible. Somerset Maugham has published one amusing and witty novel in *Cakes and Ale* and some admirable short stories, but has never approached the dignity and size of *Of Human Bondage.* For the rest, it may be said that there are many, many novelists, that the general standard of accomplishment is quite remarkably high, but that, at the top, now, there are great empty windy spaces, that there is no English novelist alive (save possibly the old Wells and the ancient pre-war Kipling) to be named in the same breath as artist with the German Thomas Mann or the Scandinavian Sigrid Undset. And there is certainly no one in America.

Yet one cannot doubt but that the novel in England has during the last thirteen years shown great liveliness and an almost "kicking" vitality. It has been a period, however, of novels rather than of novelists, and the reasons for this are worth examining. When we look back across the distance novels spring up and confront us—*The Good*

England

Companions, Juan in America, The Fountain, Without My Cloak, Broome Stages, Magnolia Street. These, we instruct our inquiring foreigner, he must read if he wants to know what has been happening. But must he, in general, read Priestley, Linklater, Kate O'Brien, Louis Golding? Ah, there we are more ignorant. We scarcely know what to say. It may be that this foreigner visited England last in 1920: he looks at his note-book and rediscovers a few questions that at that time he was asking. The Sitwells—what have they been doing? The author of *Howards End*—surely he has been a great influence. Conrad—has not every one, since then, been Conradian? And we must tell him—no, very oddly, nothing has happened as he might have expected. The Sitwells no longer rouse much interest, save the most brilliant of them, Sacheverell, and he is one of the best poets in England. The author of *Howards End* has published only one novel, and that, indeed, a remarkable one; but now, for a long time past, he has told his inquiring friends: "I have nothing more to say."

And there has been no Conradian influence—no, simply none at all. The foreigner then, naturally, inquires what the influences *have* been and so brings us into the heart of the matter.

We offer him four names—James Joyce, D. H.

Lawrence, Virginia Woolf, Aldous Huxley. These are the writers who have been supreme influences on the English novel in the last ten years.

Influences in what way? The situation will become the more obscure to the inquiring foreigner when he discovers that James Joyce is interested in language rather than the novel: that Lawrence in his later years was interested in his philosophy and not in the novel at all: that Virginia Woolf does not consider that her works *are* novels in any accepted term; that she would, if she could, find some new word for her art: and that Aldous Huxley does not care whether he is a novelist or no.

It is perfectly clear that this at least has happened in the last ten years—no one in England has known what a novel is except that the Higher Critics are resolved that it is something unintelligible to the Common Man, and the Lower Critics are resolved that it is nothing that the Higher Critics *call* a novel!

Before 1914, in England at least, this was quite definitely not so. In 1910, Hardy, Conrad, James, Moore, May Sinclair, Bennett, Galsworthy, Wells were novelists. There was no question about it. Wells might be interested in sociology, but he wrote *Tono Bungay*, and that was a novel. George Moore might write a lovely language, but *The Brook Kerith* was a novel. Why were these books novels? Because their authors created characters beyond their own autobiographical experience and engaged in some kind of a narrative. Uncle Ponderevo, the Baynes girls, Nostromo, the wicked butler in *The Turn of the Screw*—these were born of their creators' personalities, but they were at the same time definitely alive beyond the experience and characteristics of Wells, Bennett, Conrad, and James.

As early as 1910, however, there was someone who did not agree that the thing produced by Wells, Bennett, and Conrad *was* a novel at all. This was Henry James, who, in his *Notes on Novelists* and in his quarrel with H. G. Wells, wanted to know *what* these men were after, and why they thought that their simple nursery-like productions merited any serious consideration. "Poor Conrad!" he cried, lifting his hands over *Chance*, one of the most complicated and intricate of all Conrad's novels.

Before the 1870's the English novel received scarcely any general critical attention at all, and it was not until the early 1900's that people began to talk about it in solemn whispers as an Art that only Artists should be allowed to practise. This attitude of specialist cerebrality has grown and grown, and to-day the whole quarrel about the novel centres round this question—is the novel *only* a special lovely exotic rare fruit produced in Cambridge greenhouses for a small group of intellectual horticulturists, or is it still a rather common wayside flower which almost plants itself so prolific is it, and sometimes plants itself with quite splendid and magnificent results?

That it *was* once a jolly friendly flower, bright for every one's picking, is quite certain: Richardson, Fielding, Scott, Jane Austen, Dickens, Thackeray, Trollope, Stevenson, Hardy, have been plucked by almost everybody, and large packets of seedlings of the Dickens flower are at this very moment being sold, very cheaply, at the doors of the newspaper offices.

Henry James disliked these vulgar wayside blooms. A number of ladies, Mrs. Edith Wharton, Miss May Sinclair, Miss Dorothy Richardson, disliked them, too. Then the war made all private passions common and mean; Mr. Joyce, after writing an easily understood masterpiece about an Artist, threw Mr. Bloom on to the world, Mr. Lawrence was banned by the Police, a number of ladies and gentlemen went to live in Bloomsbury, Mrs. Humphry Ward's nephew lashed his aunt's predilections with scorpions—and confusion has reigned ever since!

For it is a *real* confusion. Were right quite plainly on either side we would know better, whichever our camp, how to abide the issue. But whatever the stalwarts may say there *is* no clear issue!

Mr. Harold Nicolson, about a year ago, gave a series of Wireless Talks about the New Literature, and, in regard to his listeners, he told them that if they did not read Mr. Joyce, Mr. Lawrence, and Mr. Aldous Huxley they were lost indeed. He was right to give them fearlessly his own opinion, and, in my opinion, the director of the B.B.C. was in the wrong when he so sternly objected. But Mr. Nicolson, alas, did his own side much damage, for many, many listeners at once sent to their booksellers for copies of *Antic Hay* and *Women in Love*. They read these works, and, in many cases, were so sadly puzzled and affronted by them that henceforth, instead of reading Mr. Priestley and Mr. Brett Young as they had done, they read Mr. Frankau and Mr. Warwick Deeping.

Then a lady, a Mrs. Leavis, of Cambridge, published a work on the contemporary English novel and the general bad taste of the reading public, in which she limited the possible English living novelists to five alone—to Virginia Woolf,

Aldous Huxley, D. H. Lawrence, E. M. Forster, and one of the Mr. Powyses. She even gave George Moore a hasty rap on the knuckles.

"Oh, dear!" moaned the ordinary intelligent reader, wanting to be in the right way. "This confines me, at the most, to five new novels a year—really three, because Mr. Forster has ceased to write and Mrs. Woolf says her novels *aren't* novels!" Then D. H. Lawrence died, and now he has, year in and year out, only Mr. Huxley and Mr. Powys to cheer him—and neither of them are exactly cheerful writers!

Then it happened that something really important occurred in the exactly opposite camp—this was the publication and quite phenomenal success of a novel called *The Good Companions*, by J. B. Priestley. No such general popularity of any novel has been known in England since the days of Hall Caine and Marie Corelli. And the event in this case had elements of very real importance. For it was not, whatever Mr. Harold Nicolson and Mrs. Leavis (who have, in all probability, never read *The Good Companions*) might say, a success of vulgarity. Mr. Priestley had already written the best critical work on George Meredith (with the exception of Mr. Trevelyan's study of Meredith's poetry), some of the best essays of our time, and a brilliant book of general criticism. *The Good Companions* was the work of a man of letters. It created, as few contemporary novels were able to do, a character, Jess Oakroyd, who could take his place, without shame, in the true gallery of English characters. Moreover, Mr. Priestley showed that he could not only be witty but also funny, a trait that is to-day, alas, almost solely Mr. P. G. Wodehouse's prerogative. Also he could do what very few novelists of to-day *can* do—he could keep it up. He could write a long novel that tires very seldom and never, in spite of its eight hundred pages, dies altogether.

But—and this was the signal for battle—he appealed quite deliberately to the Plain Man. His ideas are the ideas of the Plain Man, his world the Plain Man's world. Secondly—and this was a worse crime than the other—he dares to be un-flinchingly cheerful.

This, in the judgment of the very serious artists, condemned him altogether, for how could anyone in these grim days write cheerfully and pretend to paint life as it is? It is true that Mr. Priestley followed *The Good Companions* with *Angel Pavement*, which was a very serious novel indeed, but even here "cheerfulness would keep breaking in." Then that very difficult and very ancient question

21

as to "What *is* Truth" began to be asked once more, for the Plain Man stood up and said that so far as he could understand them the stories of Mrs. Woolf, Aldous Huxley, and D. H. Lawrence weren't true at all. It could be definitely proved that members of Concert Parties and Yorkshire working-men often had their cheerful moments, but the Plain Man had never known anyone who was alternatively male and female as was Mrs. Woolf's Orlando, nor did his wives and daughters go mad over the "dark urge" as did the heroines of Mr. Lawrence's novels, nor could he see that Mr. Huxley's characters were anything like real life. Here, I think, the Plain Man and the Plain Critic went a great deal too far. Their determination *not* to read what they called by the horrible phrase of the "Highbrow Novelists" deprived them of some of the finest work of their time. It has been, in my opinion, the great crime of the superior critics that they have frightened the ordinary intelligent man from so much that he would otherwise have enjoyed. It is one thing to proclaim loudly that you care only for the very best, but the superior arrogance of that cry has its dangers, and especially in the case of the novel which, as Mr. Wells once said, is intended to do everything and anything except be boring.

22

England

The beauties of Virginia Woolf, for instance, are as easily understood as the ironical sentimentalities of Sterne, and when Mrs. Dalloway walks through a London Park on a summer day, when that last voyage is taken to the Lighthouse, when the Elizabethan world blazes on the frozen Thames, beauty is added permanently to English letters. So, too, the brilliance of Aldous Huxley's dialogue is no ordinary matter, and D. H. Lawrence's genius of perception and descriptive prose no repetitive sexual agonies can dim.

The principal danger of this group of writers, however, lay not in themselves, but rather in their influence. Their example was dangerous because it was so easy to follow.

It was tempting, obviously, for the young novelist of 1926 and 1927 to copy those serious writers who were most frequently noticed and praised by the more serious critics. Moreover, these serious novelists were plainly contributing something new to the novel, while novelists like Mr. Priestley, Mr. Brett Young, even Mr. Somerset Maugham were content with the old methods and the old straightforward narrative. It was possible, in fact, to be clever, lazy, and daring all at once. Joyce had shown that all you needed was "to look in yourself and write." Never mind what you found there—how-

23

ever untidy, however minute, however shocking, out it must all come!

This incoherent autobiography was very much easier *and* very much more modern than the old weary business of inventing a narrative and creating characters *outside* yourself. Moreover, as every novelist knows, it is very much simpler to be gloomy than cheerful, to write about lunatics rather than sane men. We are all, so Freud has told us, sexually mad, hopelessly frustrated, potentially imbecile. The novel, if it is to survive at all, must move forward.

The subjective autobiographical method has, however, one very serious drawback—namely, that it can become very boring unless you happen yourself to be a very exceptional person. Exceptional persons are rare, and I venture to doubt whether, if you omit from them what was almost their whole stock in trade, their creative zest, Fielding and Jane Austen, Thackeray and George Eliot were in themselves very exceptional persons. But creative zest is the very thing that the new subjective autobiographical novel forbade because above all else it must tell the truth, must avoid excess, must fear sentiment like the devil (far more indeed than the devil) and limit itself to minute and unchallengeable detail.

England

The result of this was that the English novel found itself checkmated. It could not move in any direction with safety. Novel after novel appeared that resolved itself into a clever analysis of frustration and an intensely bitter revelation of nothing.

Every link with ordinary suffering, patient, and often humorously courageous humanity disappeared. Humanity was, of course, in a bad way, but it had been in a bad way before. At one of the most dangerous and despairing moments in English history some of the Elizabethans produced the most courageous and defiant literature in the language, but to read most of the clever novels published in England between 1925 and 1930 you would imagine that this brave Island was inhabited only by waiting gnats and blindly agitated ants.

This attitude of negation could not, of course, endure for long. Rebellion against it was inevitable, but the danger of that rebellion was, and still is, that the benefits to the novel of these post-war experiments might be lost.

One thing at least is certain: that however the Plain Man and the Plain Critic may exclaim and protest, may appeal for a return to "the heartiness and exuberance of the Victorians," the English novel can never be the same as it was before

Joyce, Lawrence, and Virginia Woolf experimented on it. And this is true, especially, of the sexual freedom and frankness that Joyce and Lawrence brought into it. While it is certain that there are other things in life beside sex, it is also certain that both modern psychology and modern life make the old reticences and taboos as absurd as they are old-fashioned. The Victorian novel assumed quite falsely that marriage was the best possible haven for its more virtuous characters. We have changed all that in our lives as well as in our novels.

On the other hand, the assumption of the post-war realists that there is no haven anywhere and that a condition of happiness is an impossible sentimentality is as absurd as unreality. What has happened, therefore, is that the novel in the last three years has begun to expand in a new and more romantic direction. This new romance is very different from the old, which was a very simple manifestation of cloak-and-sword narrative, often full of zest and excitement, but ending as completely in nothing at all as the examples of minor post-war realism.

One characteristic of the new romantic novel was the sudden appearance of long family histories. Just when it had seemed that the novelists were content to write very cleverly about nothing whatever, they began to write defiantly about everything.

Phyllis Bentley in *Inheritance,* Clemence Dane in *Broome Stages,* Louis Golding in *Magnolia Street,* Francis Brett Young in *The House Under the Water,* Mazo de la Roche in her *Jalna Chronicles,* the vast works of John Cowper Powys, *Wolf Solent* and *A Glastonbury Romance*—these, in spite of the wailings of the reviewers, have been among the prominent successes of the last few years.

All these novels may, in one form or another, be called romantic, but, at the same time, there is no one of them that does not show the influences of *Ulysses,* of *The Rainbow,* of *Mrs. Dalloway.* Whatever may be said about these novels critically, we may at least sigh with relief because we have escaped, when it almost seemed that we were doomed, from sexual trivialities, sexless auto-biography.

One further element there is in the new English novel that must be mentioned—a fresh interest in the things of the spirit. The leader in this is Charles Morgan, whose *Portrait in a Mirror* and *The Fountain* have had a quite astonishing success. I say "astonishing" because these grave, quiet, very carefully written books would not, one would have supposed, have appealed to a large public.

27

But they have insisted that man does not live by bread alone, a doctrine that had been absent from the more intellectual English novel for nearly twenty years.

In the work now of all the more interesting younger writers there is a new spirit, very far indeed from the defeatism of ten years ago. Men like L. A. G. Strong, William Plomer, John Collier, Francis Stuart; women like Rosamund Lehmann, Marguerite Steen, E. Arnot Robertson, Kate O'Brien, Helen Simpson—to name only a few— look on life, however perilous it may appear, with humour, courage, and wisdom. We have broken away, it seems, from pessimism and artificiality, and, in this new world of adventure, new genius should be born.

Best of all (and here I return to the interrogation mark at the beginning of this article) the novel is once again beginning to be a novel, it is once again experimenting both in narrative and the creation of character, the two achievements for which this beautiful and exciting art, more than any other of the arts of writing, is especially adapted.

FRANCE

Hamish Miles

II. FRANCE

I

I own to a distrust of the word "tendencies." To the artist, whether he be novelist, poet, or painter, a "tendency," or a "technique," is generally a quite natural attribute or process of which he himself is seldom consciously aware, a descriptive classification provided for him, often very surprisingly, by outsiders. He is apt to be suspicious of it. And not without reason: for a "tendency" is often a pattern arbitrarily imposed on the outward scene by a critic more anxious to find that pattern than truthfully convinced of its existence. As a form of literature, the novel is probably the most tempting to generalize about. Generically regarded, the novel is like one of those insect's eyes which, endowed with (is it?) eight hundred and eighty lenses, duly reflect eight hundred and eighty pictures of the earthly scene. But with the novel the separate lenses, the individual novelists, are all different; and the pictures are no less diversified. Sorting them out, one might find in the novelists' pictures of life certain resemblances, and group them in classes accordingly. But on the whole the spectacle of the novel, like the spectacle of life, from which it draws its sustenance, is too complex to seize at a glance. As in watching an ant-heap, the eye soon falls back on the individual worker, and by watching that seeks clues to the activity of the whole.

France is the most individualist of Western countries. And it is not surprising that the novel, a highly individualistic form of writing, should in France offer singularly good opportunities of observing through its medium the currents and forces of contemporary French life. Even in its less important forms, the novel of entertainment or distraction has its significance in this aspect. Not long ago, for instance, I was told by a French friend that the type of "forbidden" fiction read *en cachette* by the schoolboy of to-day was of a totally different type from that which he and his contemporaries had smuggled into the *lycée* in pre-war days. Then, it was Octave Mirbeau or Pierre Louÿs, erotica more or less veiled; now, it is the *roman policier* (or such weeklies as *Détective*) which feeds the adolescent craving. And he linked this up with the general shifting of the old preoccupation with sexual interest which marks modern French fiction in general, the vanishing of the morbid glamours of adultery in a world where the older standards of sexual morality have become lax.

That is by the way, but it points to one very characteristic feature of the post-war novel in France, which is worth observing, as it explains, I think, how fundamentally uninteresting a great deal of fiction has been during the past decade and a half, or even longer. In general, I mean the absence from most modern novels of that element of *conflict* which gives intensity of significance to most of the great novels of the past. Most novelists can no longer present in the characters of their creation the conflict of the human with the divine law, nor the clash of men and women in ordered love, because, lacking an apprehension of divinity or a sense of clear-cut standards in the conduct of love, the element of conflict no longer arises. The classic figure of Emma Bovary, to go no further back, for all the clarity of Flaubert's drawing, is blurred to the modern eye (in the more limited sense of "modern") by the supposed unreality of her conflict. The anecdote is told of a young woman lately reading *Madame Bovary* and complaining to a friend that, although it was *très beau*, she could not understand what all the fuss was about. *"Ah, mais vous savez,"* replied the friend, *"c'était un péché dans ce temps-là. . . ."* On a less lofty plane of literature, a popular novel like Ohnet's *Maître de Forges* is nowadays of significance only as a record of class distinctions which have, for better or worse, lost their validity. This flattening trend in the novel as a literary form is not, of course, exclusively French; neither *Tess of the d'Urbervilles* nor the dramas of Hall Caine could be written in the nineteen-thirties. But it is conspicuous in the most important contemporary fiction in France—especially, perhaps, because it has moved side by side with a lessening of the artistic sense of *form* which has always characterized French literature—and it shows clearly the interactions of life and letters in the social organism. François Mauriac, a novelist in whom the old sense of conflict has never been atrophied, has pointed out that the absence of these moral or ethical conflicts has not only been a matter of indifference to many writers, but has even become the positive and essential theme of their writing. He cites the characteristic figure of Paul Morand, whose earlier work showed an unvarying series of "men and women, of every race and every class, seeking each other, taking each other, leaving each other, meeting each other again, unaware of any barriers, slaves of momentary instinct, and made more incapable of pleasure because the sole law known to them is that which forces them to a perpetual process of refining their own sensations." Morand's pitiless skill in the portrayal of these men and women will stand as a ferocious commentary on the years which followed the war of 1914–18—a kind of Goya's *Disasters of War*— but fundamentally it is monotonous and empty; for, as Mauriac remarks, "the story of an amorphous society cannot be endlessly written and re-written, as our predecessors wrote and re-wrote the conflicts of spirit and flesh, of duty and passion."

II

Marcel Proust died without progeny. Nobody has tried to repeat the unique creation of a unique personality and life. But, although *A la recherche du temps perdu* was essentially the culmination of the nineteenth-century novel of analysis rather than the pioneer work of a new age, his perception and presentation of life have had profound influence. He crystallized, if he did not originate, certain habits of thought and vision peculiar to our time. He was one of those novelists who are read because their vision of life provides those who read with a mode of life. André Gide has been another such; in England, to some extent, D. H. Lawrence was also one. The Proust-taught eye learns to catch a sublimated significance, now dramatic, now poetic, in every hour of everyday life. He looked for reality in the hidden animating forces of men and women, not in their moments of extraordinary experience or crucial decisions. But that is a process which, coupled with the Proustian sense of the mobility and flux of the ego, the deliberate abandonment of any examination of morality, the assumption of a standpoint of knowledge-for-its-own-sake, accorded well with the new temper of the nineteen-twenties. He has been a master, if not a model, to many novelists.

Proust's mode of vision, for all its apparent exactness, was in some ways related to that spirit of vague but profound disquiet which marked most of French fiction between 1918 and 1930. It was the fashionable malady, and its connection with the frustrated romanticism of the War and Wilsonian idealism is easy to trace. In the Dadaistes the sickness took its extreme form, in their apparently silly, but really quite significant, denial of all accepted validities—the social structure, verbal meaning, intelligence, literature. They saw an escape from despair in acclaiming the total

supremacy of spontaneous inspiration, in denying
realism and logical intelligence. In the work of the
group of "adventure" novelists, of whom Pierre
Mac Orlan was the chief, another line of escape
was indicated—escape through wild adventuring,
or through a world of fantasy which has generally
been foreign to the pure French genius. It was
followed by Montherlant, by Cocteau, by Morand,
by Soupault, by Crevel, and even by Duhamel,
in books of very varying character, but having
this in common—that their personages are misfits
in the life of their time, men to whom actual life
is less real than the life of their desires, their invention, or their imagination. The hero of Soupault's
A la dérive, for instance, was a perfect example of
this class, of "*le hamletisme de nos jours*," as it has
been styled. "*David ne pouvait s'attacher à rien. . . .
Il ignorait volontairement les liens, les attaches, les
clairières. Très jeune, il comprenait cette impossibilité
impérieuse comme une vocation. . . . Le regard de ces
hommes impitoyables qui ne peuvent admettre aucun
souvenir est semblable à celui de ces bêtes fauves en
cage, regard qui va plus loin que le décor proche et
qui cherche là-bas une étendue inconnue et solitaire.*"
Is he not a pure example of self-conscious, intro-
verted romanticism? Does not that last sentence
ring with the true Baudelairean echo?

III

Turn now to individuals.

It is not easy to choose them. A few have been mentioned in passing, and the novels of many more conspicuous writers have attracted attention and left a mark on the consciousness of the past decade: Gide, with *Les faux monnayeurs* and *Si le grain ne meurt*; Jean Giraudoux, with *Siegfried et le Limousin, Simon le Pathétique, Bella, Adorable Clio*; Pierre Hamp, with his documentary pictures of industrial life; Valéry Larbaud, with his curious studies in the *monologue intérieur*; Drieu la Rochelle, as typical as any of the generation which was plunged into war at the university age; Jean Giono, with his simple, seemingly ingenuous pictures of the primitive peasant life of Provence; André Maurois, who, as a novelist, moved forward from his half-playful performances in the Bramble and O'Grady books to the exquisitely finished *Climats* and *Cercle de Famille*; Léon Daudet, a veteran, the greatest living polemical journalist, who has turned out half a dozen novels still throbbing with the vitality of the *furor politicus*; André Malraux, whose elaborate pictures of revolutionary China (notably *Les Conquérants* and *La Condition humaine*) are surely unrivalled in their vivid presentation to the Western world of the profound significance of the changes in the contemporary East; Eugène Dabit, whose *Hôtel du Nord*, a study of a back-street hotel, was the rallying-point of the so-called *populiste* school a few years ago; Mauriac, the most important of the Catholic novelists, who can present so vividly (his orthodox critics say so dangerously) the battle of the spirit and the flesh; Georges Bernanos, who likewise writes with stunning prolixity of spiritual agony, and portrayed, in *Le Soleil de Satan*, a modern saint with grandeur and passion.

The catalogue could be expanded. But at the moment I should like to look more closely at the work of two writers: one unknown as a novelist until his first book appeared; the other a dramatist and man of letters with twenty-five years of consistent work behind him, but both characteristic of their time. The first is Louis Ferdinand Céline, and the second, Jules Romains.

Voyage au bout de la nuit,[1] the novel with which Céline abruptly broke into the rather circumscribed field of French literature, is one of those books which cannot be labelled and pigeon-holed. Even if it is opened with the cautious scepticism which the experienced reader tends unconsciously

[1] Published in English by Chatto & Windus.

to emanate when he notices "250ᵉ *édition*" on the cover, it takes the breath away. Little is known of its author. He is said to be a doctor in a Paris suburb, so little aware of literary practice that, in submitting his vast mass of manuscript, he offered to pay for its publication. (And in France, be it remembered, writers on the whole form a professional corporation more than they do in England.) But, instinctively one would say, Céline has summed up the moods and experience of the age that followed the war and seems to precede an undefined revolution with more intensity and passion than any comparable writer.

The novel is as hard to describe as to label. It is written in a style and language which to most foreign readers, and to many French readers, will seem difficult, haphazard, and uncouth. It is rambling and, by all the accepted rules, ill-proportioned. It is excessively long; but one feels that Céline, like Pascal, might retort: "*Je n'ai pas eu le temps de la faire plus court.*" But it seizes one's whole attention, imposes itself on one's imagination, with a force that few novels do. It is too soon to say that Céline has written one of the enduring masterpieces; the strength of *Voyage au bout de la nuit* is probably to a considerable extent dependent on the contemporary mood and experience;

it lacks, I suspect, the essentially timeless quality of great fiction.

The story centres round the experiences, during and after the war, of a young man, Bardamu; and the first few pages hint at, and then suddenly clinch, the awful fatality of circumstance which falls upon him, and, by extension, upon his generation. He is caught up in the machinery of war: *"J'allais m'en aller. Mais trop tard! Ils avaient refermé la porte en douce derrière nous les civils. On était faits, comme des rats."* And from that instant Bardamu was caught in the most tragic currents of our time. His journey into the uttermost places of misery is more than the record of a personal experience; it is symbolic of a disintegrating civilization. From the stricken areas of Flanders he escapes—into a lunatic asylum; from the Paris of the peace he ventures into the interior of Africa, the obscure agent of a trading company, as surely doomed as any front-line infantryman; from Africa he plunges into the America of Ford, and his adventures as a slave, in the new style, become grimly fantastic in chapters which are perhaps the most virulent satire of any on the most specious materialism of our time. Returning to France, he becomes a pitifully ineffective doctor, and his attempts to practise in a squalid faubourg of the capital, culminating in his complicity in crime, enable Céline to pour his corrosive acid on another cluster of plague-spots. Thereafter the novel tends to concentrate more on the personal drama of Bardamu and his friend Robinson; but if it loses some of its universality of vision, the sense of drama is heightened, and the violent climax of Robinson's death is magnificently treated. As the imaginative anatomy of a stricken, uncertain, unstable civilization, the novel is in its kind unmatched.

Jules Romains, on the other hand, is an experienced writer, who knows exactly, almost too exactly, what he is doing. The development of his work, from *Mort de Quelqu'un* or *Les Puissances de Paris*, forward to the opening volumes of his projected series, *Les Hommes de Bonne Volonté*, is disciplined, scientific, deliberate. A few years ago he published a trilogy—*Lucienne*, *Le Dieu des Corps*, and *Quand le Navire* (just published in an English version by John Rodker: *Boriswood*), in which he analysed with extraordinary subtlety the mysticism of the sensual life. And he has now embarked on a greater task, one for which his earlier work as the prophet of *unanimisme* has been, he declares, his apprenticeship. Of this, *Les Hommes de Bonne Volonté*, a goodly number of volumes have by now appeared—several have appeared in English (translated as *Men of Good Will* by Warre B. Wells: Lovat Dickson)—and he promises an undetermined, but not indeterminate, number of volumes which will fulfil his purpose of a giant novel with Paris as its background and its hero. Choosing the morning of October 6, 1908, as the centre, he slices a cross-section from the living flesh of the city, and dissects its living nerves, its veins and arteries, the substance of its tissue. Men and women of every class move to and fro across the pages, their paths impinging, meeting, parting again, in an intricate but beautifully controlled pattern. Romains, in the spectacle over which he leans, sees "myriads of human activities scattered in all directions by the indifferent forces of self-interest, of passion, even of crime and madness," and apparently destroying themselves or becoming lost in the void. In this turmoil of life he sees a whole, which looks as if its chosen mode of progress were "a series of clumsy jolts." Yet, after all, in that confusion and clash of wills, there must surely be some "of good will." And to extract these, and by his art to muster them, would seem to be his objective. How far he will, or even can, succeed—who can say? But the opening stages are astonishingly interesting.

Tendencies of the Modern Novel

And if only because of their ambition, their search for a certain grandeur of conception, the one instinctive, the other willed and almost scientific, these two novels of Céline and Romains have a special significance. For they offer a compensation for what the novel has suffered in vitality by its loss of the element of moral conflict.

AMERICA

Milton Waldman

III. AMERICA

It is, perhaps, easier to discover tendencies in contemporary American than in English or French literature, because so much of it, and that largely of the best, has been clearly tendencious. One has the impression in England and France of widespread confusion in aim, with so much of the best talent in recent fiction devoting itself, out of a mixture of weariness and uncertainty, to experiment in both subject and form that have little apparent relation with the classic novel in either country. This tendency has already been ably analysed by my predecessors in this series, and I mention it here only by way of contrast with the post-war development of the novel in America.

Up to and including the early years of this century the American novel was a branch of English literature; truly a branch in that it sucked its nourishment from the same roots and gave forth a similar foliage. Washington Irving might fashion into narrative the native folk-legends, Hawthorne

the effect of Puritan political hegemony on New
England soil, Melville the intercourse of the mariners
of the Eastern seaboard with distant oceans, Mark
Twain and Bret Harte the comedy and drama of
frontier life; yet, though the setting was American,
and hence to an Englishman strange, there was
nothing essentially unfamiliar either in the matter
or the form. The dialect might be strange, but
certainly no stranger than is Thomas Hardy's outside Wessex. As for the substance, the writers were
in their outlook, their codes of values, their charac-
teristically English preoccupation with conduct
indistinguishable from their fellow novelists in the
Mother Country.

Towards the turn of the century, however, a new
and definite note was heard in growing strength and
volume. Henry James and William Dean Howells,
Edith Wharton and Theodore Dreiser, different as
they were in most respects, found it increasingly
inevitable, every time they took up pen, that they
should ponder such questions as, "What is an
American? What distinguishes him, *qua* American,
from other folk, from an Englishman or a European?
What are the peculiar conditions of his life, what
has Nature contributed to his corporate being that
differentiates him from them?" Howells and Mr.
Dreiser tried to answer these questions by putting

their characters against their native background, James and Mrs. Wharton by placing them against the background of European society and culture, but all four were definitely conscious of a difference. Already there was an American problem—almost like a Polish or Irish or Jewish problem—except that it was social instead of political.

Howells and Mr. Dreiser were, as novelists, less accomplished than the other two; yet the ground they ploughed seems to me more fertile than the plots so elegantly cultivated by Henry James and Mrs. Wharton. For how a man lives out his life against his own background is more important, as far as it goes, than how he conducts himself against an alien one, be it ever so rich, subtle, and spiritually satisfying. But the most important thing of all, I take it, is for the novelist to reveal that something in the soul of man which is independent of all background. The social setting of his story may provide a sense of reality, a foil for his characters, a *décor* interesting or beautiful in itself, but it cannot assume a position in a great novel of equal importance to the human beings with whose fate he is concerned. Yet I feel that the novelists descending in a line from Howells and Dreiser have in another way limited their goal and consequently their attainment. They were so largely occupied with background

49

that they were at least as much critics of men in mass as creators of men as individuals.

This search for and concentration upon a single broad and elusive thing which may be referred to —unsatisfactorily—as Americanism had, however, its good as well as its bad consequences. It provided significant material, organic form, coherence. Mr. Walpole says that the period since the war in England "has been a period of novels rather than of novelists . . ." and he is probably right. But the statement could not be made of the same period in America. Sinclair Lewis, Joseph Hergesheimer, Willa Cather, William Faulkner, and at least as many others are novelists as distinguished from authors of stray novels. No one would take the work of any one of them for that of anybody else; what each has to say in one book is merely an extension of what he says in all his others, and not a different or unrelated thing; nor did any of them remotely exhaust his creative impulse in any single work.

The appearance of Mr. Sinclair Lewis's *Main Street,* about a year after the war, was a portent, and quite as much for its extraordinary and instant popularity as for what it had to say. His direct forerunner, Mr. Dreiser, had until then been unknown except to a small public and various meddlesome bodies of unofficial censors. *Main Street* was a far more direct and vigorous onslaught on America's crudeness and smugness than were *Jennie Gerhardt* or *The Financier* on its conventionality and corruption, yet it found a thousand readers for every one of theirs. The explanation is not to be found primarily in the quality of the novels themselves—if Mr. Lewis writes better prose than Mr. Dreiser (and that is not saying a great deal), there is far more humanity in Jennie than in the heroine of *Main Street*. The reason for the enormous success of the younger author and the neglect of the elder was simply that the former struck the mood of a public arrived at self-consciousness. It was ready, even eager, to hear about itself, to be told, in its own current slang, "where it got off" in the eyes of the author, to learn how the life it had created compared with an ideal or even with that of other societies. Mr. Lewis and those who thought with him (amongst whom Mr. H. L. Mencken, though not a writer of fiction, stood easily first) surveyed America, found her manners, customs, and ideals unworthy of the astounding opportunities with which Nature had blessed her, and said so in an unmistakable voice.

A whole school of literature of this sort sprang up, most of whose members are to-day nearly or wholly forgotten. They had in common a tremendous earnestness, a passion for political and economic reform—many of them, including Mr. Lewis, had at one time or another been disciples of the formidable Mr. Upton Sinclair—and a distaste for the canons of orthodox English prose.

This last deficiency was not altogether a bad thing, in so far as it rose from their desire to report accurately the raucous, uncouth, monotonous noises of the civilization they were castigating; and to that extent it represented a search for truth. These writers also, in their zest, disdained the timorous craving for that tepid uniform good taste in their houses and personal appurtenance which was so provoking a feature of the lives of the classes that rose to luxury; and there was certainly at least more health in the rude, jerky prose poured out by those prophets from the prairies than in the bloodless decorum of the Fifth Avenue Interior Decorator or the guaranteed impeccability of the Chicago mail-order house. Later, however, this prose was to grow self-conscious in its turn and experiment on itself.

Head and shoulders above the mass of social critics who wrote so large a part of America's fiction in the 'twenties towered Mr. Lewis. With all his irrelevant indignation (irrelevant to fiction, that is) at the abuse of the poor by the rich, for all his ungainliness of style, he was a true artist capable of rising to great heights when the poet in him was roused. For he penetrated then beneath the ugly surfaces, which as social novelist he was exploring, and discovered human beings, whom he loved even while he chastised them, as every great satirist does.

He was annoyed because Gopher Prairie failed to resemble architecturally an undefiled Georgian village; that was childish, and in his heart he knew it, for he knew as well as any man that those Georgian villages would never thrive again, even amidst their native wealds and moors, except in the picture books. But if the appearance had gone, the reality might be created anew in a different form. For this the novelist yearned; and he knew that unless it were so Gopher Prairie would drive the last trace of those villages out of the world, to the eternal calamity of the conqueror as well as the conquered. He states his case in a passage which contains an astonishing amount of his essence, his vision as well as his *naïveté*, his awkwardness together with his eloquence:

But a village in a country which is taking pains to become altogether standardized and pure, which aspires to succeed Victorian England as the chief mediocrity of the world, is no longer merely provincial, no longer down and restful in its leaf-shadowed ignorance. It is a force seeking to dominate the earth, to drain the hills and sea of colour, to set Dante at boosting Gopher Prairie, and to dress the high gods in Klassey Kollege Klothes. Sure of itself, it bullies other civilizations, as a travelling salesman in a brown derby conquers the wisdom of China and tacks advertisements of cigarettes over arches for centuries dedicated to the sayings of Confucius.

Such a society functions admirably in the large production of cheap automobiles, dollar watches, and safety razors. But it is not satisfied until the entire world also admits that the end and joyous purpose of living is to ride in flivvers, to make advertising pictures of dollar watches, and in the twilight to sit talking, not of love and courage, but of the convenience of safety razors.

These critics of America naturally drew their vision of civilization from the past—from Attic Greece, from France and England before industrialization, and by these standards they measured the deficiencies of their own. Yet, paradoxically, what they desired for America was, not that she become less American, but more; they believed that her salvation lay in discovering her essential self through self-examination and a proper appreciation of her past rather than in imitating other societies, whether better by virtue of their age or no. For the United

States did have a past and in many respects a splendid one. Ultimately this school became so fired with its new nationalism that its authors and reviewers began to ask of a new literary product not "Is it good?" but "Is it American?"

This declaration of literary independence was naturally directed against the country from which political independence had originally been achieved. The language in which novels were written, the traditions upon which they were based, the laws and largely the conventions and customs by which their characters moved, were all English; and so for a considerable time it was felt by a large body of writers that the diminution of English influence and English traits was essential to the attainment of a truly American novel.

This liberation was difficult to arrive at, however, for the most experimental, the most revolutionary writing, like experimental and revolutionary government, must have a starting-point even if it does not know where it will in the end arrive. Here, I think, lies the explanation of much that has puzzled the ordinary English reader in recent American fiction; the authors, turning their backs on the recognizable models merely because they were English, dug eagerly for roots that were *not* English. A great many of the younger American novelists passed their literary apprenticeship in Paris, and it was there that they discovered the alternative influences on their taste and style. France, as in 1778, assisted in the Struggle for Independence. Only this time it was France at one remove, for no writer of fiction in one language can ever really discover a dominant influence in another. Proust, of course, had his effect, as he had on nearly every eager young novelist in the Western world, but the peculiar fascination was exerted by older writers in English who had so long worked and quarrelled with tradition in the French capital that they had evolved types of experiment peculiarly their own—Mr. James Joyce and Miss Gertrude Stein. There was something invigorating and refreshing to young people who had something to say, and were convinced that the traditional significances and associations of the English language were inadequate for saying it, to discover two eminent seniors in letters who were demonstrating that new nuances and combinations were possible with the old words.

The effects of this influence were not only marked in writers who had been directly exposed to it— writers so diverse as Mr. Ernest Hemingway and the usually orthodox Mr. Louis Bromfield, who had long lived in Paris—but spread to others who, like Mr. William Faulkner and Mr. James Cozzens (*vide* his recent novel, *A Cure of Flesh*), have, so far as I know, passed nearly the whole of their lives in the United States. What that effect is will be recognized only by those familiar with the Proust substance *cum* Joyce or Stein method—that sensation of looking at characters a great way off, whose voices and gestures seem remote, yet who are brought physically close to us by a powerful glass which serves simultaneously as a screen between their and our reality. This method is not conducive to popularity, particularly where the personages and the scene retailed are otherwise unfamiliar; and I am inclined to think that one of the most important of contemporary American novelists, Mr. Faulkner, has failed of wide appreciation in this country because so much of his work produces that particular sensation.

Mr. Faulkner has published five novels, all of which are laid in the Southern states, a setting much less well known to English readers than the Eastern or Middle Western. The first impression that these books convey (apart from their eccentricities of language, to which I shall revert later) is of an intense violence and a close sectionalism. Drunkenness, the most brutish lusts, lunacy, and every conceivable crime of blood make up the action of these novels; and one is never permitted to forget that all this passes in one small and restricted locality in the lower basin of the Mississippi River.

Yet, out of violence that is at first sight incredible in its horror and variety, and with characters as grotesque as those of Dostoevsky, Mr. Faulkner has contrived to fashion novels that are as genuinely works of literature as they are unmistakably American. Somehow one believes that all the bizarre sequence of idiocy, incest, suicide and greed of *The Sound and the Fury* are natural to a decadent white family like the Compsons, nurtured on the hatreds and the ruin of the Civil War. All the nightmare of rape and murder in *Sanctuary* is conceivable in a community whose rulers descended from the carpet-baggers. The same is true of *Light in August*, the latest and, I think, the best of Mr. Faulkner's books, for in it many of the crudities of style and of factitious melodrama are ironed out, leaving a novel which is notable for the clarity and subtlety of its narrative and for the unsentimental brooding pity that lights it from within. And in *Sartoris* he shows that he is capable of other moods, a feeling for heroic family memories (such as the reminiscences of the gallant cavalry general Stuart and of the glamour of pre-Rebellion days) which Miss Cather herself could not have surpassed, and of the ability to draw a woman of wit, nobility, and breeding in Miss Jenny, one of those characters whose presence in it justifies any work of fiction.

In sum Mr. Faulkner, with less social consciousness and perhaps less absolute genius than Mr. Lewis, has advanced further toward the pure art of the novel which is to be grown in the soil of America. His sectionalism is a virtue rather than a vice—Dickens and Hardy were none the less English for being so narrowly occupied with their respective small corners of England.

His style exhibits a queer mixture of influences. Much of the dialogue is negro, and that part seems to be excellent, including the effect of negro dialect on the speech of whites, both cultured and ignorant. But apart from dialogue he frequently adulterates his own narrative style with solecisms derived from negro speech. Over and over he uses "like" for "as if" in a way to make one shudder: "He continued that thick movement, like he could neither stop it nor complete it." He invents compounds like a German—"frictionsmooth," "womenvoices." And every now and again he writes a passage which distinctly echoes Miss Stein.

While one school of novelists was subjecting America to a merciless scrutiny and trying to bring her to an understanding of herself, another and equally conspicuous one was withdrawing further and further from the ugliness and turbulence which so fascinated the first, in order to create worlds of romance all their own. The most famous and talented of this school is Miss Willa Cather. Mr. James Branch Cabell and Mr. Joseph Hergesheimer were pursuing similar ends, the one in fable, the other in history, but both had reached their maturity earlier. Miss Cather enjoys in her own country a reputation and affection equalled by few novelists in their own lifetime. Her earlier works, *My Antonia* and *One of Ours*, though laid in the Middle West where she was born, showed little of that impulse toward social analysis which was to characterize the novels of that section a few years later, but did already display the acute delicacy of understanding and the exquisite prose which was to distinguish every line she wrote. Perhaps she herself felt that her powers were unsuited to the immediate world about her; at any rate she dedicated them henceforth to the past, and from *The Lost Lady* onward—that little classic of the building of the West—she produced a series of small masterpieces, now laid in the period of the missionaries in the South-West, now in the period of the French domination of Canada, now in the New York of what Miss Wharton calls the Age of Innocence. No American writer of this generation has been more, or more justly, esteemed in England; none is more likely to live.

Yet one cannot help being disturbed by certain symptoms in her latest work. The artistry is still intact, the content becomes ever more ethereal. In these studies of those enchanting men and women that are gone, of beloved causes that are dead, these recreated fragrances of forgotten sentiments and societies, there is a feeling as of the silver waning of the twilight. The texture is growing thin as an old brocade, though the colours on it remain bright as ever.

If this were true of Miss Cather alone, one might say that it is the natural relaxation of the artist who has passed her prime. But when one recalls the teeming vitality of Mr. Thornton Wilder's *The Cabala* and *The Bridge of San Luiz Rey* and compares them with *The Woman of Andros*, which was equally lovely in language but appreciably lighter in substance, or remembers the inability of Mr. Oliver La Farge to repeat the success of *Laughing Boy* or the gradual decrease in the specific gravity of Mr. Robert Nathan's delightful fantasies, one begins to wonder. . . . May it not be a law of literary being in America that the novelist, if his strength is to flourish, must seep himself in the whirling, raucous life about him and go hunting in all possible directions for a means of saying what he feels, no matter how bizarre or ungainly the forms which call him?

Yet, there must always be room in any civilization for the pure artist whose imagination is tempted by the remote in time and space, and whose style is the heir of the best traditions of his mother tongue; and though it would appear that the tough excogitator of the here and now will have the greater influence on the American novel of the future, yet those lovers of the past have already left that future a precious legacy.

GERMANY

Jacob Wassermann

IV. GERMANY

In giving some account of the contemporary German novel I feel unexpectedly hampered by the circumstance that I belong myself to this category of German writers, as may be seen by a mass of work ranging over thirty-five years. It is not for me to judge whether or to what extent my own work has contributed to the development of narrative literature in Germany. And there is another difficulty related to the first: how shall I, living and working in our time—and as one who cannot and will not deny active participation—attain to that unprejudiced judgment which is requisite in any such review and survey? For obvious reasons I must, throughout, put myself out of court and consider my contemporaries, and those who started writing after me, not, like a literary historian or professional critic, ranging them under certain headings and in so many schools or groups (for which task indeed I have neither the courage nor the Olympian calm), but seeing in them living persons like myself, visualizing each one of them in his spiritual climate following his destiny; striving sometimes with and sometimes against me, forging ahead or hanging back, maybe accompanied by success or maybe unheeded by the public, just in the way things do happen in this world of ours, and particularly in the sphere of art.

I see no other way of avoiding this dilemma than by restricting the mention of any names to the indispensable minimum and, instead, by devoting myself rather to a consideration of general tendencies; to explore intellectual roads rather than describe personal deeds. Such a course, anyhow, must commend itself, since a real synthesis of the achievements in novel-writing would otherwise be impossible without going into a maze of detail.

At the time when I began to make my bow to the public, in the last years of the nineteenth century, that literary *genre* which is described in England and America as "fiction" was quite unknown in Germany. Neither convention nor tradition recognized it. We had "high" literature (*belles-lettres*), the classical or would-be classical drama, also the classical lyric with all it derivatives and offshoots. Even the epic poem was still in vogue, making up in pretentiousness what it lost by diffusiveness, and, boring though it was, always appeared as the *obbligato* birthday and Christmas gift. But the so-call "serious" man would have considered it *infra dig.* to bother himself with such productions. (As a matter of fact, I doubt very much whether the "serious" man would ever have read a poem by Hölderlin, or would know anything else out of *Faust* except certain trite quotations; a genuinely artistic culture was a rarity in such circles, indeed anywhere, for among the *élite* art was only a kind of superstition.) Then from these respected and sometimes shyly admired literary works, both genuine and spurious, one was reduced, without any transition, to reading the trash of the publisher's market, rose-tinted love stories, the romantic historical novel, trivial comedies, grim studies of social manners cut to a pattern with characters like lay figures. That was the position only a decade or two after the death of Dickens, Flaubert, Turgenev, and Dostoevsky, and at the very time when Zola and Maupassant in France, and in Russia Tolstoy and Chekhov, were creating their master-pieces of narrative.

The differences between the English and German story-telling of the nineteenth century is extra-ordinarily characteristic and significant. You had in England a high average and a number of individual outstanding figures; within this average a secure and continuous tradition; a sure grasp of the appropriate and fitting, social life mirrored in all strata of society; an inexhaustible wealth of types; and finally breadth and ease of manner (to me, Thackeray appears the high-water mark with his peculiarly Victorian humour). Whereas with us in Germany there were only a few achievements by individuals such as the incomparable composition *Die Wahlver-wandtschaften*, a treasure like Achim von Arnim's *Kronenwächter*; a monumental work like Immermann's *Overhof*; a profound epic writer like Adalbert Stifter or the attractive and original Gottfried Keller; a creature of genius like E. T. A. Hoffmann, the wonderful Eichendorff, the portentous Conrad Ferdinand Meyer. None of these, however, had any real following, they left no visible traces on the spiritual life of the nation; each of them created a world but not one of them a tradition; great individuals they were but without any of that strength that inspires the common touch, each was as it were ruler in his own satrapy (with the exception of Goethe, whose novels, after all, have never penetrated to the people).

There you have the explanation of the steep decline from those heights, and the absence of any surface affinities; besides the fact that there never was in Germany a "society" as there is in England

and France. The novel needs, however, a surface, a certain agreed basis of forms, of social custom, and of living racial tradition. When, as a young man, I opened a book of Balzac's and read the word Paris, that was not for me just any city you like, it was a definite symbol, the vital centre of a nation prefigured already in countless images. With us in Germany it was never so. There was nothing like that. For this reason those who, thirty years ago, set about creating the German novel came up against wellnigh insurmountable difficulties, difficulties which were much greater than those that creative writers of other nations have had to face. The *Buddenbrooks* of Thomas Mann was a piece of good fortune, an exceptional case; as the scion of a Hansa city with century-old ties here was one author who had, so to speak, a century-old social background. All the same, he had to forge for himself the form of his novel and that *could* only be a personal accomplishment. (Incidentally he may be said to have succeeded by spicing it with irony, and irony, to my mind, is tantamount to an evasion of artistic form.)

As for the rest of us, what did we find? I am not speaking of the political, economic, or social situation, I am not referring to the fact that at that time the man of letters in Germany, if he were not actually

receiving Court patronage or in some way had been
officially sponsored, was looked upon as a person of
dubious character—he still incurred something of
the odium of the lewd fellow, such as a century
previously was the lot of the actor. And here I am
referring to the general intellectual position round
about the year 1890, when the first swingings of the
naturalistic movement foreshadowed a kind of
renaissance. I am thinking of books which were
widely read at that time, such as those of Friedrich
Spielhagen, of Paul Heyse's *Kinder der Welt*, the
refurbishings of antiquity of a Georg Ebers, all these
great ones renowed in their time but belonging to an
epoch which is manifestly of the past; indeed, to-day
you cannot even get access to the mausoleum where
they lie at rest. True, it should not be forgotten that
such a notable descriptive artist and narrator as
Theodor Fontane and such a quaint artificer as
Wilhelm Raabe, both men of sixty, had already
produced their own most important work. These
were, however, very little heeded by *le grand public*,
indeed they were appreciated much less than they
really deserved; it was only when the literary revival
set in that they were borne along with it and their
names became generally known.

The renewed animation of which I am speaking
—to some extent it may be termed a spiritual

Germany

revolution—was based first and foremost on the influence of the great Nordic and Russian writers; the quiet poetry of a Jens Peter Jacobsen had paved the way, then came the great rebels and prophets, Ibsen, Tolstoy, Strindberg, Björnson, Zola, and their fiery breath was a powerful inspiration to us. The world took on a new complexion. I can still well remember the excitement provoked by Tolstoy's *Kreuzer Sonata*, a book that sent the blood rushing to the head, a straightforward prose narrative reflecting in immediate and model form a violence of life which bore the stamp of truth, yet treating of the inmost affairs of Everyman. Here was no philosophy, here were no scientific discoveries, no public scandals, but the record of human souls, nay, the spiritual pilgrimage of ordinary individual men, who, though but creatures of the author's mind, inflamed one's spirit and tugged at one's heart-strings.

It was something unprecedented, something that unquestionably had revolutionary effect. We seemed like people rudely awakened from our slumber, first with only a dull sense of all the noises that make up the daily round and unable to distinguish individual sounds. And among the voices then to be heard there was one speaking to us in the accents of our own language, one which though belonging, at the

71

turn of the century, to no living person, possessed, nevertheless, the most insistent appeal, and compared with which the sound of all the other voices seemed to be merely a faint chorus. Yes, the truth is that Friedrich Nietzsche was the real awakener of the young generations of Germans round about 1900. But that is philosophy over again, it will be said. I reply, Yes and No; for his mission measured in terms of time and spiritual importance was more that of a critic and educator than of a thinker; he induced agitation and not contemplation.

If in the Bismarckian era there was a general disposition to look down upon the novel, an attitude which goes back to Schiller's lofty dictum that the novel-writer was the half-brother of the poet, within a decade a remarkable change had set in—though indeed the reading public at that time was surfeited with a flood of inferior products of the *genre* trashy novels with a purpose, chitter-chatter of every conceivable kind, or manifestations of erotic love of a frankly exhibitionist and sensation-mongering character. These were, however, only the luxuriant overgrowth of the exuberantly thriving plants. Simultaneously you had the *Buddenbrooks*, already famous; you had Knut Hamsun, fêted almost as if he were a native poet; Gerhardt Hauptmann's *Emanuel Quint;* while Hermann Hesse, Arthur

Germany

Schnitzler, Henrich Mann, Eduard Keyserling, and the writer of this article also came on to the scene.

I regard the decisive intellectual event in the narrative literature of those days to be the break-through to reality. When I say reality I mean the fusion of character elements with the sensuous truth of an experience, and consequently a definite turning away from pedestrian portrayal of types no less than from vague creatures of idealism; avoidance of the indefinite subjective creation, as of the self-centred, lyrical effusion, clear delineation and grasp of the artist's sphere, simplicity and sobriety of presentation and, as goal, a distinctive, i.e. inimitable, word-picture. Such art requires strict discipline, a profound spiritual intentness, an intellectual determination to avoid every romantic diversion and to derive all the possibilities of self-development from simple human experience.

With the field ploughed and fertilized this way, the younger writers who came after had an easier task. Reality in the artist's sense is always something created, it does not exist *a priori*. And what I term intellectual tradition is the sum of the realities thus created. The very same process, a conquest of reality, is observable during the last decade in American literature. Whether the result in this case will be a solid achievement of tradition it is too

73

early to say; in any case it would be a unique occurrence. For us in Germany there always develops in time a fateful vacuum which, in its turn, has to be overcome, and at every attempt of this kind all our resources are needed. The building up and the destruction of a tradition frequently follow one another immediately. That is patently a waste of strength and likewise a continual using up of capital, and as such it is plainly shown in the various phases of our literary evolution. The same is true of the individual work. No one likes to feel that he owes anything to anyone else, each one of us obstinately goes his own way, and then, so as to delude himself about it, adheres to some watchword or slogan which may, so to speak, cover him and give him an inward assurance against the reproach of a lack of tradition. Thus the generation after the war hoisted the verbal flag "Expressionism"; ten years later it was *neue Sachlichkeit*. In either case it was really a flight from the essential.

Fortunately, however, single achievements are not determined by the stream of tendency in which they float. In those years just after the war we do perceive an abundance of young talent at work. A great number of the finest characters among our youth, it is true, fell on the battlefields; while those who came back, wearied of action, longed for

74

the contemplative life, and the *élite* of them yearned to mould into form their experiences and their impressions. Their life-material in itself had all of a sudden grown to immense proportions. There was an inexhaustible supply of material stored up in each one of them. It required no particular artistic bent to awaken the desire to testify to what one had seen and felt, and in so doing to relieve the pressure of mental distress. Society, State, family, economic life, presented a completely changed appearance; where the old still prevailed it seemed to challenge destruction. That was the time when innumerable war-novels appeared; works glorifying war were still rare, actual truth which had been lived through was stronger than the atavistic impulse to romantic soldiering. Call it humanitarian conscience or anxiety as to the survival of civilization, or even merely reaction against murder and horrors, there was sincerity and passion in books like Ludwig Renn's *War* or Remarque's *All Quiet on the Western Front.* And that was why they exerted such an effect on people's minds, though their artistic and literary importance certainly failed to come up to their importance as polemical writings. The real epic of the world war is still unwritten, and I do not believe it can be written within the next twenty years. Combustible material cannot be wrought into

75

shape. Artistically important experiments like Hans Carossa's *Rumanian Diary* (Secker), or portrayal of the struggles for a more extensive national area like Hans Grimm's *A People without Space* are no more than the prelude to a mighty drama.

Before that drama can come into being this polemical tendency must be overcome, for under its inspiration artistic products of a higher nature have been already nipped in the bud. The incursion of political life, of the party-epithet, and particularly that of Marxist ideology has wrought havoc. Perhaps we should once and for all recognize that our age is no time for the pure work of art. But is the novel in this sense to be regarded as a pure work of art? Do we not rather expect from it a picture of conditions at a given time, a spiritual narrative of that time, internal and external developments, the conditions of existence, the conflicts of ideas, the pattern of fate in all its warp and woof as affecting the characters, either raised to the plane of types or presented as symbolic? If there are any laws to which life and art have to conform this is one of them.

And if I do not conceal my doubts as to the likelihood of a new efflorescence of the novel, those doubts are directed above all to the intellectual radicalism of the younger generation, which not

Germany

only stifles all tradition, not only exposes the artist's trade as such to any casual intromission, but also veils the horizon, distorts our picture of the world and switches moral responsibilities on to the wrong lines. Such a state of affairs leads to paradoxes and convulsions, of which the general onslaught on "psychology," the abuse which has been hurled at all the established and recognized authors, is one of the most devastating. All at once the idea was that "psychology" was taboo. To the extent that this revulsion applied to the atomization of the soul which had been carried to a pitch of virtuosity there was nothing wrong in it, it was high time to do away with disclosure of the most secret intimacies which was a sheer outrage of decency and the ruthless post-mortem examination, as it were, of the figures portrayed, instead of creation and synthesis.

The general public was weary of this dismal perfection, the more cultivated turned away and sought something new. They thought to find it in the works of James Joyce, in the volumes of Marcel Proust. About the year 1924, the year when Thomas Mann's *The Magic Mountain* (Secker) appeared, a work which was not so far removed from this trend, the influence of these two writers was notable. Novels such as Döblin's *Alexanderplatz* or Hermann Broch's *Sleep-Walkers* (Secker) are inconceivable without them. In general, however, the confusion they spread was greater than any beneficial influence which they may have exerted. By transferring into the sphere of art the scientific knowledge of Freud and Jung, very often with the fanaticism of the disciple, we have, as regards the much-maligned psychology, fallen from the frying-pan into the fire; things were fashioned in accordance with the most up-to-date principles, but they betrayed their essence and their origin all the same.

The essence of all narrative, of any description of facts, of any portrayal of life at all, is found in the movements of the soul, and without communication of the spark from soul to soul there can be no visible record, no tangible happening, no figure in which you or I can be mirrored, no fate that really stirs our emotion. There is, it is true, something rather mysterious about the revulsion against "psychology"; a certain joylessness in a pattern which had presented itself too often and too slickly to have any further power of attraction; mistrust, too, of feeling, but no less mistrust of intellect. Just as the tendency was in music to abandon melody, and in painting to give up representing the objective, so in the novel the idea was to have no more finished actions. In its repudiation of reason and experience this tendency was a mystical one, in its deliberate aversion from the traditional technique and the suppression of conventions it was, on the other hand, a product of rationalism. There is one author of genius in whom all these characteristics are united, Franz Kafka. His work is extraordinarily German in the widest sense.

This German was, as it happens, a Jew. The fact cannot be passed over in silence here that a strikingly large number of modern novelists are Jews. The names of many of them have been carried beyond the frontiers of Germany, men such as Alfred Döblin, Stefan and Arnold Zweig, Franz Werfel, Max Brod, Lion Feuchtwanger, Hermann Kesten, and Josef Roth, whose *Job* and *Radetzky March* (Heinemann) are works of genuine poetic quality and who, I think, has a great future as an author. Jews have always been intellectual pioneers, the protagonists of every new art and new doctrine. They were the first people in Germany to do homage to Richard Wagner, the first to spread the fame of Nietzsche, and their passionate interest in literature has had in the last fifty years the effect of a driving force. A thousand years of oppression had stored up in them powers and cravings which were now surging up with elemental force; an intoxication it was, indeed, and the results necessarily of a hybrid character.

Tendencies of the Modern Novel

That the sons and grandsons of a section of the nation which had been so long and so insistently restrained from active participation—whose allegiance to their chosen home had, notwithstanding this repression, become a feeling of love—should now throng into the field of artistic creation, for which they were entitled to feel qualified by virtue of their fresh, unused energies and their peculiar and manifold original gifts, is too natural a process for me to try and explain it. I do not wish to say any more about it.

If I were compelled to make a tally of the contemporary and the up-to-date authors I should be very much embarrassed. With the super-abundance of production it is scarcely possible. It suffices that I have indicated the direction of the various tendencies. For the time being no great achievements are in sight, but on the other hand there is a certain collective striving which may, perhaps, lead to intellectual and social clarification. It is perhaps also preparing the soil for a new communal tradition, which is, nevertheless, as opposed to the spirit and essence of art and free characterization as that barren individualism which has brought the form and civilization of Europe to the edge of destruction. Who will save us from it?

SPAIN

V. S. Pritchett

F

V. SPAIN

THE similarities in the relation of Spain, Ireland, and Russia to the rest of Europe make a fascinating and tempting material for misleading generalization. Each is outside the main current of European culture, each is an isolated and "backward" country, and each has passed through violent political upheaval since the war and this upheaval was the conscious aim of the writers of the generation which preceded it. But, stripping away all dubious resemblances, the main fact which emerges is that there are two kinds of society in Europe: the modern, mechanized and irreligious, possessing an international economic homogeneity; and the less powerful, non-mechanized society which is only at the beginning of the struggle of its values and traditions against the machine, and is still nationalist in tendency and essence.

And as there are two societies in Europe, so there are two literatures, one in the main European current and the other outside it; and the latter, like a secure and hidden mountain lake, is visited by pilgrims from the former in those frequent times of spiritual drought which afflict the people of the mechanized plains. Soon, we suppose, the pipe-lines will be laid and the lake will be brought into organized unity with the modern world.

Spain and Ireland still belong spiritually to the old peasant and feudal cultures; or, rather, we should say that they have not yet shown what the effect of social upheaval upon their life will be. In Ireland where nationalism is synonymous with religion and the land, the impulse at the moment is to isolation; in Spain, on the other hand, the movement is towards Europe.

This break with the long isolationist tradition of the Spanish decadence is a matter of great interest, for the Reformation and the French Revolution had been rejected. The conflict vaguely known as the struggle between Africa and Europe in the Spanish mind has entered a new phase. After spending two-thirds of the last century in civil disorganization and strife the Spaniard had seen liberalism—which meant Europe to him—eclipsed in the fall of the first Republic; and later he had seen the exuberant Bourbon restoration punctured first by the Colonial disasters of the war with the United States in 1898, and latterly by the Moroccan failure of the 'twenties of this century. Both catastrophes were decisive; the first provided the inspiration which was to break into action after the latter. Students of Spanish literature are familiar with that much overworked caption: "the generation of '98." It would be more accurate to put down the Spanish intellectual renaissance to the pervasive educational movement of which Don Francisco Giner de los Rios was the leading figure. But it is true that in '98 a mood of pessimism, introspection, and realistic self-scrutiny engrossed the best minds of the country, a desire to prick the bubbles of patriotic rhetoric and to discover what Spanish facts really were. Regeneration, Europe, and realism became the intellectual watchwords of the day.

There is no need to discuss the "generation" in detail, for we are concerned only with the novel; it is enough that every writer of mark was influenced by its ideas. Then Spanish individualism asserted itself and each writer took his own course. But the irony of it is that the only writer to attain an assured European reputation is the one who has most eloquently declaimed his antagonism to the European idea. When Miguel de Unamuno cries in his Basque voice from the wilderness of Salamanca, "I feel within myself a mediaeval soul," that part of Europe which is weary of European culture—middle-class culture and Unamuno's "false god"—reads his *Tragic Sense of Life* with applause. It is indeed a great book. When, however, we turn to Unamuno's novels, such as *Niebla* (translated as *Mist* in an American edition, a novel highly regarded in Spain), for some sight of the life from which the mystic has sprung, there is disappointment. Unprophetic, Unamuno sinks to the garrulous, the Chestertonian, and the merely ingenious.

His only contemporary to win an English audience was, inevitably, Blasco Ibañez. There is no doubt about the vigour, the narrative power, competence, and panache of Blasco Ibañez, but his reputation abroad lies not in his early studies of Valencian peasant life, but in his gaudier cosmopolitan melodramas. We need not linger over him; except to note that the more vulgar side of Parisian influence has a fatal fascination for those Spaniards who throw off tradition and restraints entirely, in order to cut a figure. The mass of quasi-pornographic Spanish novels published during the past thirty years, which have been the reading of the small, non-intellectual middle-class, show clear traces of the non-inoculated intellect with the worst of France.

We are left with two or three excellent novelists

who, though translated in the United States, have been little heard of in England. Gabriel Miró and Valle-Inclán both stand apart from the modern world. Miró has died recently, and his death has removed the most fastidious and individual writer of prose in this generation. He has portrayed the pagan Catholic peasant of Alicante. Valle-Inclán is a man of the Renaissance who has survived into modern times. He also is admired for the sumptuous music of his prose style and the utmost refinements of poetic artifice. It is not far-fetched to compare him in this respect to George Moore—Galicia has many resemblances of scene and race with Ireland—and, except that his sensuality is suave and exotic dreaming, with the more fiery d'Annunzio. But both Miró and Valle-Inclán are delicate wines which do not travel well. Miró, particularly, is essentially of the peasant twilight.

The intense regional nature of the various Spanish genius has not diminished in spite of the move towards Europe. It is the source of the Spanish novelists' vitality and, for want of a better word, his sweetness. It is also the characteristic which frequently gives him a difficult provinciality from the point of view of the foreign reader, unless he knows the Spanish environment well and can identify himself with the native temper. How

is it, the English reader finds himself asking again
and again, that an author who has entranced him
in the Spanish disappoints him in translation?
Once the sound of the "lordly language of Castile"
has been poured away there is so little left. Was
his pleasure merely a form of self-flattery at his
ability to read the language? Was it that in Spanish
sound and sense are more peculiarly entwined
than in English? Was it that a nostalgia for the past
worked like a transforming and insidious wine in
the veins or that the revolutionary sounded more
revolutionary in a foreign language, the devotional
more devout? Was it that, absorbed by the nostalgia
in Azorin's evocations of the decaying Castilian
towns, we did not notice his debt to certain French
stylists since out-moded? In short, once the thing
is in plain English before us, do the wheels of that
movement to Europeanization creak, and, although
we may find comparable dissatisfactions with our
own Aldous Huxleys, are they not easier to gloss
over because they are also ours? Furthermore,
remarkable as the contribution of the "generation
of '98" is, it received its spiritual death-blow at the
hands of the Great War, and having begun in
almost puritan nationalism at the beginning of the
century there remained for it only to gather
the bouquets of revolutionary triumph with the

Spain

establishment of the republic. Since the war politics have become an increasing preoccupation, and as novelists the older generation have had little new to say and the young no time or wish to say it. Putting aside Pío Baroja and Ramón Pérez de Ayala, the two outstanding novelists of the last thirty years, perhaps adding the name of Benjamin Jarnés, there are none of like stature among the young as far as a foreigner may judge. They are absorbed in politics, and neither stability nor disillusion has yet released them. When it does we may expect a number of political novels of the kind our English Communists pray for but do not get. One such novel is worth noticing, more because of its subject matter than because of its writing, which is very unequal and rather commonplace. It is an agglomeration of material inadequately differentiated. *Siete Domingos Rojos* (Seven Red Sundays), by Ramón Sender, is contemporary political history intelligently reported. It describes the men of the Syndicalist, Anarchist, Communist, and Socialist movements, their meetings, intrigues, secret organizations, their processions, their acts of sabotage, and their clashes with the police, with a heavy bias against the "bourgeois" republic. It contains some good descriptive writing, and it gives an interesting, if long-winded, account of working-class ferment. The book is worth reading, and certainly surpasses in interest most of those German novels on civil strife which have been recently translated into English. Behind the laconic and caustic realism of Pío Baroja's work, behind the intellectual brilliance of Ramón Pérez de Ayala there could always be detected an atmosphere of idyllic innocence and sweetness. The kind of literature which may be deduced from *Siete Domingos Rojos* has replaced this by a naïve, Soviet poster-fed lyricism of physical fitness and the novelties of exercise. This apparently is the only refreshment the revolutionary puritan is to allow himself.

Until the political spate begins Pío Baroja must stand as the only notable revolutionary novelist, and he began writing thirty years ago. In fact, although with apparent perversity he early transferred his interest to the past in the innumerable novels called *Memoirs of a Man of Action*, which deal with the intrigues of the Carlist wars, he seems to me to be the revolutionary novelist *par excellence*. Firstly, because he is the novelist of the streets; secondly, because his central preoccupation is the young man of anarchic, wandering disposition, at odds with society, moving from job to job and from town to town.

Spain

He is unable to fit into the stupid and barbaric life which surrounds him and his end is a stoical despair. He is petulant, melancholy, hopeless, a man foiled by the stupidity of the world until the spark of a new adventure catches him. Such a character, given his head, is ruinous to the construction of a novel, and since, as he has confessed, Pío Baroja finds difficulty in invention, his novels tend to become a string of episodes. This is the picaresque tradition in liaison with the Naturalists.

Open any of Pío Baroja's novels and you are looking at once at a street down which every kind of street-haunting character drifts, stops to talk for a while, and then passes. Now it is an aged beggar and his daughter, now a doctor—Pío Baroja began life as a country doctor, ran a bakery later, writing his novels in the account books— a prostitute, a penniless political hanger-on, an agitator, a youth living by his wits, a priest. The stream is endless, and the grey inertia of the streets is upon every one. As in the life of the streets these people also suddenly break into sporadic activity. Often the author follows the passer-by to his home—some crumbling place in a provincial town, a room in a boarding house, a Ministry, or a slum, and in a few words he can sketch the essence of a man or woman's life with unforgettable

91

vividness. Pío Baroja's knowledge of the way the poor and struggling genteel classes live in Spain is unsurpassed among his contemporaries. He is a bitter anti-clerical, abrupt and perfunctory in his contempt. His temper is epitomized by the title of one of his novels on the rag-pickers of the Madrid slums—*La Busca* (The Search). And he answers our tacit inquiry with the Selah which runs through *Paradox Rey*, a kind of Peer Gynt fantasy: "Parece que busco algo pero no busco nada" ("I seem to be looking for something, but I am not"). He is not. He has this perverse humour. He moves on from scene to scene, an intellectual and spiritual anarchist sharp-tongued with the pessimism of '98.

Whatever his defects as a novelist, Baroja has drawn the life of his country with a variety and acuteness of observation equalled only by Galdós among the moderns. He is like a traveller of sad eye passing from town to town and province to province, putting down the chance words of the journey and the main notes of the landscape.

He is a prolific novelist. His early trilogies of Basque life—*El Mayorazgo de Labraz* must be read—of the sea, the cities, and the struggle for life, are more attractive to foreign readers than the *Memoirs of a Man of Action*. In these he seems

to have been inspired by the *Episodios Nacionales*
of Galdós. The intrigues of the Carlists and
Liberals in Bayonne, the secret traffic of the frontier,
and the character of Aviraneta, a soldier of fortune,
Liberal spy, and Baroja's kinsman, are the kind of
material to which he can escape from the boredom
of modern life. In England there is a preponderant
middle-class who are comfortable enough to put
themselves at one remove from the more urgent
facts of the struggle for life, and they may therefore
refine upon their sentiments and discuss on a full
stomach the finer issues of psychology and
sociology. In Spain this security is less secure—
I doubt, for example, whether, in spite of his fame,
Pío Baroja has ever been able to earn enough to
live by his writing—and his novels are steeped in
this atmosphere of the fight for security and
subsistence which is written on the faces of the
people.

As a Basque Baroja has the frigidity of his race.
His lack of geniality (though not of humour), his
deficiencies in the racy and robust, leave him with
the superficial traits but not the warmth one
expects in a picaresque writer. For this genial
quality one turns to the work of a younger man,
an apostate from the teachings of the Jesuits, a
more polished and more intellect-ridden anti-

93

clerical than Baroja—Ramón Pérez de Ayala.
He is the most brilliant of contemporary novelists,
a complete European but rooted in the Asturias,
his native province, where the scene of most of
his novels is laid. Some of his books have appeared
in American translations, and last year *Tiger Juan*
(Jonathan Cape), his latest novel, was published
in England.

Ayala first made a reputation as a poet, and in
his love of fantasy and the fantastic metaphor the
poetic tension is on every page he writes. The
Spanish have frequently been reproached for an
excess of originality, for an ability to strike bizarre
attitudes and to perform astonishing isolated feats,
a failure to sustain their effort, and a lack of discipline. They are the enemies of organic form, and,
as in government so in literature, they prefer the
grandeurs of individualism, being quite willing
to resign themselves to its monologues and
longueurs. As in their life, they drift along to the
blank interior monody of their self-isolation,
limp, and apparently without will. One sits in the
café listening to an interminable conversation
about everything, and one is the only person
listening. Each of the others is conducting not a
conversation (which implies criticism, discipline,
and suppressions) but a monologue. Suddenly an

Spain

incident occurs, an idea is thrown out, and every one
has gone up like a rocket and a passionate brilliance
is in the air. The minds flash, and then, as suddenly
as it all occurred, they go; and instead of rockets
in the air one is aware of the ring of empty sticks.

Applying the test of this experience to the work
of Ayala one finds a writer on the contrary who is
brilliant all the time. Ayala is the chameleon of
Spanish novelists. Opening his novel with perhaps
a description of the huddled houses of the Asturian
town of Pilares, he moves from the sardonic
humours of his picturesque manner, which delights
in the fantastic and grotesque, to a swifter and
robust picaresque realism, thence to the novel of
discussion in which intellectual Aunt Sallies are
put up and knocked down, and on to idyllic scenes
of innocent love. His humour is broad and lively.
Restless, excitable and witty, he cannot resist a
fantastic theory, a strange metaphor, an exaggera-
tion of character or a passage of dialect, so that
one might be meeting Synge, Fielding, and Aldous
Huxley, and on the same page. His novels are fairy
tales which have lost their innocence and have
gone to the university, the fantasies of a mind
electric with ideas, rascally, and malign, but which
is capable of a pure and limpid sentiment. In
modern English literature pure sentiment has

become not only unfashionable but impossible. The techniques of psychology have acted like an acid on sentiment and have split it into its component parts. Psychology has moved the stress in feeling from the passive to the dynamic, and we now have characters which leap into passion and then have to worry their way out of it. Sincere sentiment, in our preoccupation with mechanism, has gone. It survives only in degenerate state in mediocre fiction. It has become a sham antique. In the Spanish novel and theatre—one recalls the plays of Sierra and the Quinteros—this decline of sentiment has not yet taken place. The Spanish mind has not yet been mechanized. It dwells in a world in which the machine is still the servant and not the master, and is treated with that lack of respect with which a Spaniard treats his animals. The master is still the mediaeval Catholic childhood, and the current of sentiment flows through even the most tortured or most emphatic Spanish agnostic writer and refreshes the divided paganism (which is a common result of the Jesuit education) of such a writer as Ayala, like the springs and green streams of his Asturian mountains. This sentiment has not the pantheistic associations which it has had in England; we must turn indeed to Irish literature to find anything like it. Its existence in

garrulous intellectual fantasy is puzzling to the
modern English reader.

Tiger Juan is the most ambitious of Ayala's
books, the most conscious, the most subtle and
elaborate piece of writing; and, while it is not in
my opinion his most successful, it is a rich book.
As writing, it has the monotony of its own brilliance. It is a theory put into fiction, and its theme,
the purgation by fire and suffering of a typical
Spaniard from the evils of the seventeenth-century
doctrines of honour and his transformation into
a modern man with a sane understanding of the
relations of the sexes, is of less interest to English
than to Spaniard readers. The story moves slowly,
and the character of Tiger Juan, quack, market
vendor, public letter-writer, fuming about his
honour at his stall, seems too grotesque and archaic
a figure to bear the brunt of the argument. But the
people who move about him step with the grace
and life of truly imagined creatures—the soldier,
type of the romantic lover; the commercial
traveller, who is Don Juan brought up to date;
the women. These lovely beings are allowed to
appear when the author has thrown off the load
of intellectual conflict, and then he is the superb
poet of a picaresque ballet. Again and again in the
more limpid pages of *Tiger Juan* one thinks of

Alarcón's *Three Cornered Hat,* but with a northern
pathos and tenderness added to the intrigue.

Realism and mysticism, mutually responsive
poles, are the great Spanish contributions to
literature, the one perfectly balancing the other.
The Jesuits have effectively destroyed mysticism in
Ayala; at least, a mingling of sophisticated rationalism and a Celtic nostalgia has replaced it. In
Belarmino y Apolonio—his best and least translatable
book—he has soared into an air where these
elements have attained a delightful equilibrium;
and again in the short stories *Luz de Domingo,*
Prometeo, and *La Caida de los Limones.* Ayala
has experimented more than any other Spanish
novelist, and *Tiger Juan* contains a great deal of
technical interest to the foreign novelist. The
climax of this book, a Midsummer Night's Dream
of transfiguration, is one of the best things he
has done.

But, like most of his contemporaries, Ayala is
now deep in politics; he believes that the revolution
of establishing the republic is enough to go on
with, and that it must be firmly established.
Literature in the meantime waits, and at the moment
his position as the most European of Spanish
novelists is unchallenged.

RUSSIA

D. S. Mirsky

VI. RUSSIA

THE Russian Soviet novel has passed through three stages which correspond in the main to the stages passed by the country since the end of the civil war. In the first stage, Soviet literature was chiefly dominated by writers who did not belong to the proletariat or to the Communist party.

In the civil war novel, to which their work is devoted, the writer is either a passive onlooker thrilled by the grandeur of the spectacle and intent on expressing his personal attitude to it in as individual and original a way as possible; or else he is a blind atom that has lost all sense of will and personality in the impersonal (and equally blind) revolutionary force; or, again, a helpless but fascinated victim, both dreading and worshipping the Juggernaut of the revolution. Hence the dominant features of the novels of those years— the absence of individual characters, the dominant rôle of masses, crowds, communities, armies—a fatalism in the presentation of the oscillations of victory and defeat, as of the individual fates of that helpless atom, individual man—and, on the other hand, a fierce insistency on the author's originality, a desperate desire to write as personally and as originally as possible.

These features will all be found in various proportions in the works of the most representative non-Communist novelists of those years: in *The Bare Year*, by Boris Pilnyak, the earliest success of the Soviet novel; in the Siberian stories of Vsevolod Ivanov; in the early work of Leonid Leonov; in the consummately condensed stories of *Red Cavalry*, by Isaac Babel; and in Artem Vesely's epic, *Russia Washed in Blood*.

The last named may be taken as the summing-up of all this phase of the Soviet novel. It appeared in its full and final form only in 1932, long after the phase had passed, but all the main parts were written in 1923–27. The impersonal, mass story is given pure and simple. The novel consists of two disconnected parts which deal with two distant parts of the country, the North Caucasus and the Middle Volga, and have no link except a unity of atmosphere, and the one impression left is that of a seething maelstrom of struggle, horror, and heroism.

The second stage of the Soviet novel is the early proletarian novel, which is almost the exact opposite of the novel just described. The term "proletarian" does not so much imply the individual origin of the author in a working-class family, as his general political and ethical attitude. The proletarian novel took form chiefly in the end of the nineteen-twenties, but its first steps were made at the same time as those of the non-Communist writers, and its earliest productions may be regarded as, in a sense, an answer to the works of writers like Pilnyak and Vesely. The individual novels sometimes actually preceded in time the works to which they are an answer. Thus, nothing is more illuminating than a comparison of Vesely's *Russia Washed in Blood* with the first great achievement of the proletarian novel, *The Iron Stream*, by Serafimovitch. Serafimovitch is seventy, and Vesely not thirty-five. *The Iron Stream* appeared in 1922, and *Russia Washed in Blood* in 1932, and still *The Iron Stream* is a step further than Vesely's novel, and an answer to it, in about the same sense as *Joseph Andrews* was an answer to *Pamela*.

Serafimovitch's novel is a story of leadership, of effort of revolution, a story of how the Bolshevik leaders of the Taman Red Army saved it from demoralization and disintegration, and led it to victory. In style and manner *The Iron Stream* is reminiscent of much pre-revolutionary literature, and lacks many of the features of the mature proletarian novel. But the main feature of the latter is present: the approach to the story, as to a problem of leadership, education, and victory. For the main subject of the proletarian novel is the political education of the rank-and-file by the conscious revolutionary, and the education of the revolutionary himself on practical work with the masses.

The masterpiece of the proletarian novel was *The Nineteen*, by Alexander Fadeyev. It is also a story of the civil war, the story of a commander of Red Guerrillas in the Far East. The story is written in a manner strongly influenced by Tolstoy. This Communist novelist is primarily interested in understanding the human material by which Socialism is being fought for, to appraise the real value of every individual fighter, to know what to expect of him, and how to get the best out of him. Two characters of Fadeyev's novel are particularly memorable—the commander of the fighting group, Levinson, and the young intellectual, Meychik. Levinson is the first adequate character of the Communist in imaginative literature; steady, unspectacular, utterly reliable, unassuming, brave and patient, capable of gauging the value of every man under his command, and with his quiet, persevering energy keeping up their energy and resolution, even after a seemingly hopeless defeat (the Russian title of the novel actually is *The Defeat*). Meychik, the individualist, the young man brought up on "human values," dreaming of abstract heroism, but afraid of blood and incapable even of keeping himself tidy in bush warfare, or properly looking after his horse —an ineffectual individualist, who from sheer discouragement and offence becomes a traitor.

Novels like these changed the face of Soviet literature in the later nineteen-twenties, and must be regarded as the fountain-head of the Soviet novel of to-day. But in the interval developments took place which changed the face of the country and affected literature most profoundly, making of Soviet literature something fundamentally new and different from other literatures both past and present.

Here is not the place to give an account of these changes, which began in 1929–30, and which amounted to the advent of Socialism, that Socialism which had been a distant goal for so many generations, and the foundations of which the Soviet Government had been steadily and unostentatiously laying ever since the moment of the October revolution. Outside the Communist party, this coming of Socialism was almost unexpected, and the mind of the intellectual was strongly impressed by the new developments.

The intellectual always imagined that Socialism was a noble dream, a distant and delusive ideal. He suddenly realized that it was a more efficient practical proposition than capitalism.

An important effect of all this on Soviet literature was to do away with the existing distinction between proletarian and non-proletarian writers, and to merge all in one army of Soviet writers equally concerned in the great work of Socialist construction, and to give Soviet literature a unity it had not hitherto possessed. This political background has to be brought out before we can understand the new tendencies in the Soviet novel. They are entirely conditioned by the social upheaval of those years. The key to the Russian novel and to all the Soviet literature of to-day is the will to help in building Socialism. Literature has become a conscious part of a common effort; a function of the social organism closely and consciously co-ordinated with its other functions, which all converge towards one common purpose.

The two new characteristics of the new Soviet literature are its conscious purposefulness and its conscious co-ordination with a collective existence. This has to be grasped before anything can be understood in the novels that are being written in Russia. To understand what it is the Soviet novelists are doing, the non-Soviet reader must make at least some step towards understanding the new Socialist civilization that is growing in the Soviet Union.

First of all he must get rid of the individualistic aesthetic ideas that are dominant in England and other capitalist countries about literature being the "expression" of an individuality, and about its producing an independent world of "value." A "willing suspension" of all acceptance of the ideas of Benedetto Croce, Bertrand Russell, and Middleton Murry is an act of goodwill required of the person who intends to understand Soviet literature. If he approaches it as just another "national" literature, comparable to German, American, or French literature, he will find himself in the ridiculous position of a biologist who would study a bird from the point of view of its adaptiveness to the life of a fish.

It may be useful in this connection to say a few words of the attitude of Soviet literature to the literature of the past. It would be wrong to regard the former as *solely* a growth of the new social conditions, with no roots in literary tradition. The recognition of the great importance of the cultural

heritage left to Socialist civilization by the civilization of the past is an essential point in the
Communist outlook. A great interest in the classics
of the literatures of the world is a striking and
essential feature of literary life in the Soviet Union.
Translations and books about them are numerous
and widely read. My last work before sitting down
to write the present article was an extensive essay
on Smollett, to serve as an introduction to a new
translation of *Peregrine Pickle*, which is shortly to
appear simultaneously with *Tom Jones*.

Of all the writers of the past, the two that are
to-day most on the lips and under the eyes of the
Soviet man of letters are Shakespeare[1] and Balzac.
In the present connection it is the latter with which
I am most concerned. We recognize him as uniting
in a supreme degree all those features which in
the novel of the past are most actual and instructive
for the Soviet novelist. Balzac, you will say, was
neither a particularly purposeful writer, nor had
he any sense of being part of a great army working
at a common task; but these qualities are precisely
what the Soviet novelist has no need to learn from
the past. He gets them direct from the time and
place he is living in. What he can and does learn

[1] Two Shakespeare plays, *Hamlet* and *Twelfth Night*,
have been running recently in Moscow.

from Balzac is the art of seeing society, of seeing and showing history in its uninterrupted flow, of giving historical forces, classes, and social entities individual life in characters of unsurpassed convincingness and reality. Balzac was a greater historian of his age than any professional historian. His art was knowledge, and the Soviet novelist regards his art as an instrument of knowledge.

Balzac's knowledge, however, was not applied, it was not placed at the service of a great common cause. In this respect the Soviet novelist has nothing to learn from Balzac, and everything to learn from the scientific Communism of Marx and Lenin.

The Soviet novel of to-day wants to be an instrument of knowledge applied to the great tasks of the time. It wants to be a picture of its vast collective effort and a study of the men and women engaged in it, of the changes operated in them by the new conditions created by themselves, and of the further possibilities contained in them. Purposefulness, co-ordination with the social whole, and an approach to imaginative work as a form of knowledge—these are the three main characteristics of the new Soviet novel. Their combination is defined by Soviet criticism as Socialist realism.

The reality which the Soviet novel of to-day

reflects is the Socialist reconstruction of a vast country, according to plan and directed by one conscious collective will. The vast scale of this reconstruction gives the literature that reflects it a scope that may be called epic. The Soviet novel is an epic of purposeful effort. As a rule it has no definite plot in the traditional sense of the term. It is the story of a series of successive engagements in one and the same campaign, every hard-gained victory raising new tasks and demanding fresh victories. "The fight goes on" is the refrain that ends every novel. It was the refrain of Fadeyev's *Nineteen*, which ends with the defeated irregulars, who has been dispersed in their last encounter with the Japanese, gathering together and rallying for fresh battles. The new Soviet novel usually ends on a victory, but a victory which demands new exertions in order to gain new victories.

These words of "fight" and "battle" and "victory," and these analogies with the war novel of Fadeyev, must not be interpreted too literally. The fight is not necessarily a fight with lethal weapons. It is, on the one hand, of course, a political and economic fight against the last of the propertied classes, the village bourgeoisie, but it is also a productive struggle with the reluctant forces of nature, and a fight with the servile and indolent mentality bred in the people by generations of subjection to bosses, an educational fight to bring up a Socialist mankind.

The most characteristic novels of these last two or three years are all connected with one of the two main problems that had to be (and were) solved by the political leadership of the country: the problem of turning the rural districts from a world of isolated petty properties into a system of collective Socialist farms, and the problem of turning a backward agricultural country into a country of advanced industrialism. The examination of these two problems in their respective fields is the subject matter of what we may call the *kolkhoz* (collective farm) novel and the industrial novel.

We may take as specimens of these two types of novels two which were probably the outstanding successes of the winter of 1932–33: the first volume of *Broken Earth* by Michael Sholokhov, and *Forward, Oh Time!* by Valentin Kataev.

Sholokhov is a Don Cossack. His first novel, *And Quiet Flows the Don*,[1] is a vast chronicle, constructed somewhat along the lines of *War and Peace*, relating the stories of several Cossack families from the period preceding the war to after the civil war. This vast scale is typical

[1] Published by Putnam.

of the modern Soviet novel: it tries to take in as much as possible of life and to follow the unfolding of history in all its varied detail. But if *And Quiet Flows the Don* is a story of the recent past, *Broken Earth* is a story of the present. It is typical of the Soviet novel to come out in parts, without even the author sometimes knowing what will be in the next part, because the events that he will have to relate have not yet happened. The *kolkhoz* novel which shares the first place with Sholokhov's is Fyodor Panfyorov's *Bruski* (of which the third and by far the most interesting volume appeared a few months ago), another instance of such a chronicle. It is the history of a whole rural district, from the end of the civil war onwards, which can be continued until the final victory of Communism.

Sholokhov's book is the history of a village of Don Cossacks during the crucial period of the campaign for collectivization, the early months of 1930. It is the story of the fight between the Communists and the rural bourgeoisie, led by ex-officers of the Tsarist Cossack forces, as to who shall win the main masses of the working Cossacks. The plot is unfolded simultaneously in the two hostile camps. Davydov, a Communist workman of the Putilov works in Leningrad, arrives in the village to direct the work of collectivization. He acts with the support of a very small number of local Communists and of the village poor, and soon succeeds in winning over the "middle" Cossack, and in establishing a *kolkhoz*. But the inexperience of the Communists in this entirely new field of work leads to exaggerations and excesses: they insist, for instance, on socializing even the poultry. These exaggerations give fuel to the reactionary propaganda of the officers. A Cossack officer lives concealed in the house of his former sergeant-major, and succeeds in winning over a considerable number of "middle" Cossacks. They get ready for an armed insurrection. Davydov loses ground—he narrowly escapes being lynched by a mob of women, but his steadiness and resoluteness win through. By degrees he acquires the experience he lacked at first. Then arrives the news of Stalin's famous article (March 1930) condemning and cancelling the exaggerations of the local Communists. The middle Cossacks swing back to the Soviet side. The officers' plan collapses. Davydov is brought to trial before the district party committee, but succeeds in vindicating himself, and shows himself an admirable organizer during the first "sowing campaign" of the new-born *kolkhoz*.

This bare outline will give an idea of the extra-ordinary richness of Sholokhov's book, of the wealth and variety of characters, and of the wonderful colour and vividness of every scene. Least of all is the story a mere strategical account of the moves and turns in the struggle. Davydov acts in a complicated atmosphere of political and personal relations; and his love affair with a Cossack woman plays a prominent, though not dominating, part in the latter part of the novel.

For wealth and truth of detail, for variety of characterization, Sholokhov has nothing to fear from a comparison with Fielding. The principal thing in his novel is the characters, characters which are the best instance of the Soviet novelist's ability to unite the general with the particular. Davydov; the Cossack officer; Polovtsev, the ex-N.C.O.; Ostrovnov, who is the officers' agent in the *kolkhoz*; the Cossack Communist and civil-war veteran, Nagulnov, who has never been outside the Don Territory, but whose fondest dream is to see England a Soviet republic; the absurd and naïvely selfish old pauper Shchukar, are figures that hold their own by the side of the greatest in the portrait gallery of Russian literature. They are, at the same time, searching studies of the social forces at work in the Soviet Union, and an invaluable contribution to the practical work of understanding and directing them.

Forward, Oh Time![1] is a very different perform- ance. If Sholokhov's novel is a chronicle like *War and Peace*, Kataev's, like *Ulysses*, is the story of twenty-four hours in one town. The town is Magnitogorsk, or rather the site which has since become Magnitogorsk—for at the time described by Kataev not one of the plants was ready, and the whole place was doing nothing but building. Kataev is a brilliant and sparkling writer, who conveys his characters with a marvellous lightness of touch through their gestures, through the accent of their voices, so that, as in real life, one sees them as sensuous images before one perceives them as natural agents.

The story turns on the rivalry of the three relays of workmen engaged in a particular part of construction; which of them will work better and hold the red flag. The issue is, how many mixtures of concrete can be made in an hour. The story is told with extraordinary *brio*, and reads like the most exciting novel of adventure, or rather perhaps like a sparkling comedy.

Kataev is a less central figure in Soviet literature than Sholokhov. He approaches his subject from

[1] Published by Gollancz.

the outside, and not without a certain levity, but he succeeds in conveying the atmosphere of Soviet industry with extraordinary vividness.

I have not room to analyse in any detail any other novels. Their variety is great. Nothing, for instance, can be less like *Forward, Oh Time!* than the industrial novel of Marietta Shaginyan, *Hydro-electric Central*—a thoughtful and searching study of the main motives of the Socialist worker and engineer, and of the spirit of collective work. Again, a very different variety is presented in *A Man Changes his Skin*, by Bruno Jasienski—the story of the building of a great irrigation system in Central Asia near the Afghan frontier, where the characters of Socialist realism are paradoxically, but successfully, blended with the technique of the detective novel—the story turning round the discovery of a plot to wreck the enterprise.

An entirely different type again is the book which was the most successful first novel for several years—*I Love*, by Alexander Avdeyenko. As a literary production it is not typical of the Soviet novel, but of all books it is perhaps the one of which one may most confidently say that nothing like it could have been written outside the Soviet Union, and before 1930. It is unlike the

Russia

typical Soviet novel, for it is what usually that is not—the expression of a personality. But what a distance from anything in those literatures where the expression of personality is the one accepted object of literary work. The novel is autobiographical. The hero is born in a miner's family about 1905; the family, exposed to all the miseries of a proletarian existence, falls to pieces and dissolves. The boy becomes a waif, and develops into a thief. After many years of anti-social existence he is taken into an educational settlement. There he learns to work, and learns the pride of work. From there he goes to Magnitogorsk as an engine-driver. Avdeyenko's Magnitogorsk is very different from Kataev's, but both are permeated with the same spirit—the pride of work, the pride of the Socialist working for no bosses but for his own class. Avdeyenko is young, and his education was casual. His work is distinctly immature, but no one has yet expressed this new pride which is bred by Socialism with the same force.

Avdeyenko is very representative of the mentality that is growing up in the new generation of Soviet workers, but as a writer he can hardly be regarded as typical, for he lacks what is, after all, the dominant feature of our literature, the attitude towards imaginative work as a form of knowledge.

Among other things, this attitude finds expression in a tendency to break down the boundaries separating imaginative literature from other forms of knowledge, especially from social science and history. In this connection a highly symptomatic development is the *History of the Factories*, a tremendous enterprise inaugurated by Gorki and directed by L. Averbakh, for which the active support of thousands of factory workers and engineers and hundreds of professional authors has been mobilized. The *History of the Factories*, of which two volumes have already appeared, aims at being a scientific history of the individual plants which together form the vast army of Soviet industry. Without surrendering a tittle of scientific rigour, it aspires at producing at the same time genuine art, "the great epic of the Soviet proletariat," as Averbakh puts it, and thus bringing together these two essentially cognate forms of knowledge.

The very nature of the *History of the Factories* makes it a collective work. A still more novel experiment in collective literary work has been attempted in the book, just out, on the White Sea Canal. The book was written by a group of over thirty writers (also presided over by Gorki) and welded into one in such a way as to form a single seamless whole. The group describes itself as the first literary *kolkhoz*. Being myself one of the group, I will venture no opinion on the result, all the more as the book is not, in any strict sense of the word, fiction.

ITALY

Luigi Pirandello

VII. ITALY

Francesco de Sanctis, the illustrious historian[1]
and critic of Italian literature, who was exiled for
his opinions by the Bourbons of Naples, considered
Manzoni's *Promessi sposi* (The Betrothed) to be
the basic work of Italian narrative literature. In
the *Promessi sposi* the humanitarian idea is completely freed from the Biblical, Christian, religious
idea, and is made more humanly dramatic by the
fact that the vast plot has its centre in two peasants.
In these lowly peasants is embodied the sense of
human dignity that had emerged only recently,
and was to form the foundations of the history
of to-day.

This Manzonian idea, of love and consideration
towards the humblest, with all the concepts,
spiritual, moral, and social, that sprang from it,
and all the warnings and feelings it implied, has
given our literature a fundamental quality that has
found development more or less near to it, and

[1] *The History of Italian Literature.* Oxford University
Press.

artistic results more or less appreciable, in works such as Ippolito Nievo's *Confessioni d'un ottuogenario* (Confessions of an Octogenarian), in Emilio de Marchi's *Demetrio Pianelli*, in Fogazzaro's *Piccolo mondo antico* (The Little World of Yesterday),[1] and in the novels of Edmondo de Amicis. All subsequent writers, in one way or another, are linked to this group.

In almost direct descent from it is Marino Moretti, a cautious writer, of delicate and savoured intimacies, with a pervading tone of humility, yet combining sudden outbreaks of caustic wit. Among his numerous novels must be mentioned *Il sole del Sabato* (Saturday's Sun), *La voce di Dio* (The Voice of God), *L'isola dell'amore* (The Isle of Love), and *L'Andreana*.

Giovanni Verga, in the mighty works of his maturity, is also linked with it—but in another sense. On one side he is specifically artistic, on the other ideological, in direct contrast to his contemporary Fogazzaro. Verga is not romantic, nor psychological, nor yet idealistic, though his work is in the stream of literature that flowed from Manzoni. His world is humble and human, of lowly people who are instinctively religious. But

[1] Published by Hodder and Stoughton under the title of *The Patriot*.

religion, instead of consoling them, leaves them disconsolate. And the art of Verga is denuded of every ornament, of every grace of literature or allurement of humour—his art, as it were, is anti-artistic; it is stark and bare, the mere representation of things.

This starkness, this system of pure representation, this reducing of things nearly to their origins, gives Verga's work a true epic quality, more especially in *I malavoglia* (The Slothful) and *Mastro-Don Gesualdo*,[1] which are his masterpieces.

These works appeared during a violent literary reaction, which had started with Carducci against the Manzonian idea. And, partly perhaps through lack of understanding, this new and great art of Verga was treated with abuse and contempt, or ignored. But Verga's values were of course to reappear, and not merely as a fashion or affectation, as was the case with his first disciples, de Roberto and Capuana, but as the beacon and guide of the new generation. Not all of these followers, of course, had the purity of Verga, who strove unceasingly for art with devotion and sensibility. But the more the years pass, the greater becomes Verga's influence on the new writers; his art is an authentic stream running through the whole

[1] Published by Jonathan Cape under the same title.

of our narrative literature. It is found (with the
differences, of course, that come from difference
of stature and variety of quality) in the works of
the famous Grazia Deledda, the woman novelist
who won the Nobel Prize, and in those of Bruno
Cicognani, Federigo Tozzi, Rosso di S. Secondo,
Mario Puccini, Corrado Alvaro, and Alberto
Moravia.

Carducci, properly speaking, does not belong
to this article, for he was not a novelist. But
besides being a poet he was a great critic and
prose-writer, and was occupied, in his way, with
the problems of our prose. His reaction was a
natural evolution in our literature, and arose
especially from the rejection of two great streams
in literature, of Giacomo Leopardi in poetry, and
of Manzoni in prose. With Leopardi and Manzoni
both poetry and prose had been purged, and at the
right time, of the excess of scholasticism, the
academic stiffness, of the rhetoric and formality
that had arisen from the exterior cult of antiquity.
The reaction of Carducci was not only in forms,
but also of the spirit. In place of the Manzonian
idea—religious, Christian, Catholic, of love for
the lowly, of meek resignation—it put forward an
idea that was pagan and heroic. This new humanism
was founded on culture. Carducci had a hot

temperament, so his outbreaks of anger in his writings were genuine, and for that reason found true and lively expression.

The fruits of his reaction, in ideas and forms, were extremely varied. Writers seized on it from different sides, developed one aspect to the exclusion of others, each taking what suited him individually, so that the consequences deduced from it might seem contradictory without being so in reality.

The vital works, the historical, political, and social works, of Alfredo Oriani, were on the lines of this reaction. His non-fictional works are alive and breathing. But as a novelist he was linked, unfortunately, with a determinism that his spirit never wholly accepted—hence the weakness of his fiction. And other writers, often extremely gifted, remained in their novels artificial and unformed. The fermentations in the reaction, both in spirit and in form, were too many and varied; its followers took and attempted to develop more than they could assimilate.

But the fruits of greatest splendour, by far the most important of the whole reaction, are unquestionably the works of d'Annunzio. He took the reaction from its formal side; he never allowed its spiritual complications, or its moral values, to quench for a moment his living sensibility, the most rich, refined, and acute that can possibly be imagined. His works, more particularly his novels, mark the highest point of the reaction. While linked always with Carducci in forms and in spirit, he maintained a position of free independence. A great part of our fiction to-day derives in some way or another from d'Annunzio.

While the work of d'Annunzio was developing with a splendour and opulence truly amazing, and a prestigious skill that made many of his followers, and himself too, pronounce it to be bordering on æstheticism, his free attitude of independence made him wander from the straight line that together with humanist culture was the basis of Carducci's reaction. Among his disciples and the younger writers came cleavages. We will mention but two of them—Guido da Verona and F. T. Marinetti—as complete a contrast as could well be imagined: Guido da Verona with his rich colouring, his rampant sensuality; and Marinetti with his clear self-confidence, his boldness and impetuosity. Marinetti is the leader of the Futurist movement, which, however, has not taken root as an intellectual formula.

A writer of vast output who has never sacrificed clearness in thought or in style, but gives an exquisite grace to both by his modesty as artist

and man, is Alfredo Panzini. In a period of confusion in society and in politics he saw the ill and
proclaimed it, and at the right moment. This he did
in his novel *Il padrone sono me* (I am Boss), a work
of high originality. And in his *Viaggio d'un povero
letterato* (The Journey of a Poor Scholar) he had
the quickness of spirit and self-confidence to
prophesy the Great War before anyone had thought
of it. His works without exception have harmony
and style, but these qualities are found most
abundantly in his novel *Santippe*, written with a
clean brevity, and with profound and rich sentiment.

Contemporary with Panzini, but influenced on
different sides by d'Annunzio and Oriani, as also
by the Russians—more especially Gorki—is the
novelist Antonio Beltramelli, who in his *Cavalier
Mostardo* foresaw the confusion and ferment of
to-day.

Corrective of the wanderings from Carducci is
Riccardo Bacchelli, the author of *Il diavolo al
Pontelungo* (The Devil at the Long Bridge);[1]
corrective, but not arid. On the contrary, he is
rich and copious, full of warmth and savour.
Corrective, too, in their separate ways, are two
writers who died young—Fausto Maria Martini

[1] Published by Longmans, Green.

and Umberto Fracchia. Martini is intimate and delicate, with passages of lyricism. Fracchia is romantic and pathetic. The vast panorama of his canvases, as, for instance, in his *Angela* and *La stella del sud* (Star of the South), give him, perhaps, a sort of likeness to Dickens. Corrective, also, in his fashion, is Aldo Palazzeschi (a highly original poet if ever there was one). His recent novels, carefully written, are clear and lucid. Yet he managed to leave his mark on the Futurist movement with his famous novel *Il codice di Perelà* (Perelà's Code). Among this group there is also Giulio Caprin, a refined, delicate writer, whose novel, *Quirina e Floriana*, has been put into English.[1]

But far more important, complex, and significant is the position of three writers, all of them in the first rank—Giovanni Papini, G. A. Borgese, and Massimo Bontempelli. Borgese, besides being a novelist, is renowned as a critic of contemporary literature, not only of Italy. His masterpiece of fiction is *Rubè*, a work of torrential force, almost like a rushing fire, that puts in dramatic relief an obscure spiritual complex amid the turbid passions that marked the period of the war and armistice.

Giovanni Papini is the author of the *Storia di*

[1] Published by Jarrolds under the title, *Bohemian House.*

Italy

Cristo[1] (The Story of Christ), which marked his conversion to Catholicism. But his conversion has not checked his output, nor devitalized his art, which continued as before in the stream of Carducci. His greatest novel is *Un uomo finito* (A Man—Finished), one of the fundamental works of the modern fiction in Italy. Papini's influence has been immense. His proud spiritual impulses, his restless ardour, his wealth of new and provocative ideas, and his crashing judgments, have been a strong stimulus to the younger generation, and have drawn to his side, if only temporarily, even writers of real independence.

So the reaction of Carducci, in spite of its errors, did, in fact, enrich our literature. It plunged it into a long travail of forms to be renewed, of problems to be solved, of needs to be satisfied, of styles to be applied and imprinted, not merely on art, but also on life. The results of this travail, more especially in regard to forms, can be seen in the works, clear, capricious and witty, of such writers as Ugo Ojetti in his *Cose viste* (Things I have Seen),[2] of Emilio Cecchi, Guelfo Civinini, Vincenzo Cardarelli, and Bruno Barilli—writers with a kind

[1] Published by Hodder and Stoughton.
[2] A selection from these essays has been published by Methuen under the title of *As They Seem to Me*.

of humour and whimsicality that had already been an element of some parts of our literature.

Among the younger generation of to-day there is a group of writers, not novelists, nor indeed preoccupied with fiction at all, but who are intent on man's duty to the State, his spiritual wholeness, who meditate on political facts as moral pledges. They, too, are a result of the Carducci reaction, and for that reason I will mention them briefly. Of this group there are two writers very much to the fore —Nino Savarese and Enrico Pea. The first started in the stream of Verga, but later became occupied with style. The second is fantastic and extravagant, flitting between heights and depths as in a dream. Both live in a world of fantasy that they treat with extreme seriousness, arriving at poetry through a dry nudity of facts.

In the recent works of Bontempelli we get the highest degree of life and actuality. He has renewed the values of Carducci in a way not thought of; he has dug them, as it were, from their dry river-bed and, with limpid clearness and an intelligence that is truly prodigious, set them on a new and flowing stream. His works are most personal—impossible to conceive him as influenced by anyone, or of taking the ideas of any school whatsoever. He is free and independent, living in a world of his own creation, which he describes as "verismo magico," in the sense that truth creates itself in the poetic imagination of the writer. And he does it with incomparable style. It is difficult to say what we admire most—his logical daring, his rapidity, lightness, and complexity of sensations, his luminous clearness in rendering the most imponderable things, almost in their musical essence, his transforming of the probable into the absurd and the absurd into the probable, making everything so real that we accept it unquestioningly. He is one of the most original of writers, not only of Italy, but of the world. In fiction his masterpieces are *Eva ultima* (A Latter-day Eve), *Il figlio di due madri* (The Son of Two Mothers), *Vita e morte di Adria e dei suoi due figli* (The Life and Death of Adria and her Two Sons), and *La famiglia del fabbro* (The Blacksmith's Family). Of non-fiction his best is *Verismo magico* (Magic Reality), absolutely inimitable, which has attracted to his orbit a group of very young writers, "The Twentieth Century," so-called in the hope of enriching their own works. But Bontempelli is privileged and unique. He has reached maturity through long experiments, and has attained not only to a conquest of style, but also, and above all, to an organic and individual conception of life.

To conclude, there are novelists of various tendencies, some belonging to groups, and some isolated. There is Italo Svevo, famous for his *Conscienza di Zeno;*[1] and the poetess Ada Negri, who in fiction is the author of *La stella mattutina* (The Morning Star). And there is a group of writers, still young, who will certainly give us larger works, more complex and important than hitherto, such as Giovanni Comisso, G. B. Angiolotti, G. B. Titta Rosa, and Bonaventura Tecchi. An authoress of standing is Sibilla Aleramo, who began as a naturalist, but is now becoming an aesthete. And there is Achille Campanile, very popular for his fantastic, buffoonish plots, who all the same is a sensitive writer. Others of merit are Arturo Loria, Giacomo Stuparich, and Quarantotto Gambini. Of the romantic novelists with a large following the best are Guido Milanese, Salvator Gotta, Virgilio Brocchi, Lucio d'Ambra, and Alessandro Veraldo.

In the rich vein to which the new generation is returning, as to something secure and solid, we have Bruno Cicognani, whose first novel, *La Velia*, is a work that deserves to be remembered in the history of our literature. It has an admirable

[1] Published by Putnams under the title of *The Confessions of Zeno.*

style, very sure and direct, and a well-handled plot of close texture. The events are described with implacable reality, the passions developed with inexorable truth, and the whole is so convincing as to be almost irrefutable.

A writer not entirely in the tradition of Verga because of a certain exuberance both in spirit and forms, yet substantially and intimately true, is Rosso di S. Secondo. Closer to Verga in style and material, describing as he does the lower and middle classes minutely and with stark simplicity, is Mario Puccini, a writer who by now has a considerable output. But the novelist of by far the most importance in this connection is Federigo Tozzi, who died very young about ten years ago, in the first maturity of his creative genius. His *Tre croci* (Three Crosses) is a real masterpiece; others not far behind it are *Il podere* (The Vineyard) and *Con gli occhi chiusi* (With Shut Eyes). In *Tre croci* the influence of Verga is unmistakable, but his sobriety and starkness are so intimately transformed by Tozzi's creative powers as a writer that they seem instinctive, so natural they are and spontaneous. In him there is an astonishing richness, an absolute novelty of sensation, as well as an exalted spirituality. In his life Tozzi was neglected, his books were abused, or ignored;

but immediately he was dead he was proclaimed universally as a great writer. And certainly his *Tre croci* is one of the best of our contemporary novels.

We have now arrived at the most recent tendencies of the novel in Italy. On one side we have "magic realism," on the other an artistic consciousness that goes deeper and deeper into life, into its very roots, growing always richer and more complex. Among the best of this school is Corrado Alvaro, a very serious and solid personality. His short stories are admirable, but his short novel, *Gente in Aspromonte* (People of Aspromonte), is undoubtedly, up till now, his masterpiece. But Alvaro will go far. Impossible to set limits to his achievement, for he is never satisfied, is always moving forward, searching, experimenting, with a creative gift that seems inexhaustible. Though his narrative is held close to reality, minute, verifiable, exact, there yet arises from it a breath of authentic poetry. He explores the new culture, the new relations between society and the individual, the origins of our life to-day and the presentiments of the new reality that is maturing.

A young writer from whom much is expected is Alberto Moravia. Very young in years, he is fully mature artistically, as is proved by his first novel, *Gli indifferenti* (The Trimmers), a work that was deservedly acclaimed from the beginning. It dissects with cruel impartiality a sadly corrupt and vitiated element in society to-day. His *Mariagrazia* is unforgettable. She is shown, as it were, in the round, with a truth and consistency that make her almost symbolical. Moravia, in the handling of his characters, shows the gifts of an acute psychologist.

SCANDINAVIA

Erik Mesterton

VIII. SCANDINAVIA

AMONG the few recent periods that can be regarded with any confidence as having importance in creative literature is surely the nineteen-twenties. In the Scandinavian novel a number of interrelated tendencies come to clearer expression in these years; but running through them all has been some attitude towards the temptation to escape from the problems of an industrial civilization. The means of evasion was offered in the convention of regionalist literature, which has bulked so large in modern Scandinavian fiction. What the more living writers have tended to react against is decadent regionalism, implying devotion to the *idyllic*; the cultivation of those secluded moods and interests which give relief from the less welcome aspects of life; as well as the exploitation of the picturesque. The idyllic peasant novel may have a slender justification as a store of anthropological facts; as a picture of life it is false, since it presents as peacefully existing an order of things which in reality is already destroyed or disintegrating. The fact of this disintegration is evident in Sigrid Undset's work, although she fails to come to grips with the process. She alternates between two planes: her early studies in urban realism, to which she has lately returned, and her mediaeval novels —two planes which are unrelated except in their common insistence on traditional values in individual and family life. The spirit of the Swedish 'nineties in its reliance on a great national past and its themes of heroic effort and sacrifice finds its belated Norwegian counterpart in her mediaeval family sagas. She, however, in contrast to the 'nineties stands firm on her Catholic feet: she has the pride of the past and the sense of the historical picturesque, but not of historical process and decline. A Danish example of the historical novel is J. V. Jensen's *The Fall of the King*, treating a period from the great past of Danish hegemony. But Jensen focuses upon the idea of a fatal crisis of national history, whereas Sigrid Undset sees only the stability of a past order. The theme of decline is the undoing of a free peasantry by autocratic government.

A recurrent theme of the peasant novel is that of the prodigal son: the man who leaves his birthplace in the country and returns again after sojourning in the industrial wilderness. This study of the *déraciné*, homesick for his land of childhood, even if not explicitly avowed, is the underlying motive of regionalist fiction. In Sweden, with its more advanced industrialization, it is more interestingly revealed in the later vogue of provincial town novels than in the devitalized rustic tradition. Two themes may be distinguished: the contrast between the emigrant's idea of industrial America and the idyllic Stockholm of pre-war days, and the opposition between urban mechanization and the idealized small town. Superficially realistic, the tone betrays the falsity of attitude; the provincial idyll is of the past, and these writers can afford to be charmed because they are safely out of it. In France, for instance, the old order is still very much alive, and the atmosphere of tension, conflict, and acute dissatisfaction infects the French novel of family life (*vide* Mauriac). The title of one of these Swedish novels, *Home from Babylon,* with its obvious reference to the prodigal's return, testifies to the endemic mood of nostalgia.

In Norway, too, the peasant novel is a major form, and has shown greater possibilities, especially in its psychological insight. An interesting development has been the school of dialect writers; one of its most prominent exponents being O. Duun, who, in a many-volumed saga, uses the common material of "change in the village"—the struggle between tradition and the encroachment of urban mentality. In opposition to the usual family chronicle of decline and degeneration, his theme is progress. This, however, he can only achieve by concentrating on the dramatic values of one character who sums up in himself the qualities and aspirations of generations.

The pursuit of the idyllic—in the sense of a dream world of placid contentment—is a tendency worth mentioning, not only because it has exercised a considerable *influence par réaction,* in André Gide's phrase, but as evidence of a state of mind from which it vainly attempts to divert attention. Ultimately, it is an indirect expression of a complex attitude which is the essence of post-war mentality and which has its direct and complementary expression in the experience of desolation. In Sweden and Denmark, the open expression of desolation is the mark of the generation for which the Great War came as the crucial experience of maturity. The incarnation of "post-war" sensibility is the Swede Pär Lagerkvist. The initiator of Expressionism in poetry and the drama, he was also the first to rebel against the traditional novel. With *The Eternal Smile* he evolves a new form related to, though not derived from, the "subjective" or "poetic" method which appears elsewhere in the European novel: a rhapsodic narrative, built up with short episodes, sometimes superficially unrelated in mood, round a number of controlling themes: among others the isolation of individual experience; and the protest against a meaningless existence together with the recognition of the value of the mystery. *The Guest of Reality* comes nearer to the straightforward story, but the characters, instead of being three-dimensional, are rather units of feeling, symbols of significant experience. Confusion and disorder, which in his early work were projected on to the external world of post-war chaos, are now realized as being subjective, a state of soul. But the essential experience of adolescence is for Lagerkvist that of *violence*. This theme comes to its fullest expression in his latest work, *The Hangman*. The method employed here shows affinities with the mythical method of Joyce and Eliot in the juxtaposition of past and present, linked by the symbolical figure of the hangman, who is both the expression and the victim of the eternal human lust for violence. As in *Ulysses* and *The Waste Land*, the nostalgic intention of historical contrast has been transcended in Lagerkvist's identification of mediaeval and contemporary reality. The old order of stable relations has now lost all value as a refuge of security: it is presented for the sole purpose of enforcing the identity of *l'immortel péché* in the permanent make-up of the human being.

In the Danish Expressionist movement the double theme of the idyllic and the desolate is also pervasive. The shock of realizing one's desolation lies behind the attitude taken up here towards the bankruptcy of bourgeois ideals: that of the bohemian *enfant terrible* whose revolutionary zeal is appeased by exasperating the philistine with modernistic pranks and calling the universal bluff by exercises in sardonic satire. Escape to the idyllic is found in romantic travelling to the far away, presented in a hot-house vocabulary whose exotic colouring has proved extremely fugitive. All that remains of the period is Kristensen's *The Arabesque of Life*, an exhaustive stocktaking of social corruption which is saved from futility by a genuine note of desperation.

A tendency not yet prominent in England is marked by the proletarian novel, which in Scandinavia has an importance probably unequalled anywhere outside Russia. As a critical term proletarian literature in the accepted sense has a wide connotation. First referring to writers of proletarian origin who in their work more or less relied on their experience of proletarian life, it has also been made to cover the social document novel when applied to the conditions of the working classes, as well as the propagandist novel of class war—three occasionally overlapping but distinct types.

In Sweden, the most influential proletarian novelists are Martin Koch and Dan Andersson. The first named gave the prototype of the novel of social (and Socialist) indignation, deriving from, but far surpassing, his American models of the "muck-raking" school. His subject is the Stockholm underworld, his intention is to lay bare the functioning of the lower organs of metropolitan civilization. The *milieu* of the other master, Dan Andersson, is that of the rural proletariat, and this accounts for his susceptibility to the romantic free-life-of-nature element in Hamsun, his nomadic love of the wilds and backwoods of the North; a preference for the primitive, which implies the rejection of the settled community of the old order as much as of urban civilization. For him there is no idyll, either past, present, or future; what replaces it is an agony of desire for a complete change, a miracle that can hardly be conceived except in terms of a New Dispensation.

Tendencies of the Modern Novel

The novel of class war found its finest expression in Denmark with Nexø's saga of modern Labour. The book is too well known to justify discussion here: it is enough to point out an obvious comparison. *Pelle the Conqueror* is the antithesis of Andersson's homeless proletarian Individual, so deep is Pelle's sense of an historical mission. Equally striking is the contrast to Duun. Nexø is able to develop his history of a human progress without suppressing any essential aspect of the process of contemporary reality: for him the progress of the individual is indistinguishable from that of the social movement with which his hero's destiny merges.

Only one other Scandinavian has treated a fundamental movement in the modern world as a theme of progress, the Swede, L. Nordström, He has gradually evolved from the pre-capitalistic to a post-capitalistic idyll, that of an imagined World Town in which the whole planet is integgrated as an urban unit. In his aggressive acceptance of mechanization and its implications he had a predecessor in Jensen who first came out as the prophet of the machine age. These writers, though both affected by the post-war awakening of the national spirit, have reacted very differently as an inevitable result of differences in their social background. The progressive theme of Nordström's saga of the expansion of Sweden into the growing world town has the support of a real industrial future, whereas Jensen, in responding to the revived sense of national values, is thrown back on the regressive theme of the Danish countryside as a secluded idyll. Nordström is further significant because he illustrates the difficulties of the contemporary writer in attempting to fuse his sensibility as an artist with his concern for ideas. His concrete experience and his sociological theory exist side by side, unrelated except in the form of abstraction. In Nexø we find a fusion between the two: we can trace the growth of both interests— in theory and in emotional life—since he has a living personal relation to the movement embodying the idea, whereas in Nordström the relation is the purely impersonal one of the spectator.

Nordström stands isolated in a generation which established the novel of realistic narrative in Sweden, devoted to the reporting of topicalities, and excited by the latest ideas. For this type of novel even at its best, when presenting accurate knowledge of a social background, international importance can hardly be claimed. Its pre-war originators have now the position of the grandfather generation to *les jeunes*, and it is interesting to observe a certain similarity between them on points which differentiate them both from the post-war generation. Both have the desire to achieve an "acceptance of life." Eyvind Johnson's *Farewell to Hamlet* makes the representative gesture of "liquidating" the maladjusted post-war hero, the young man of literary ambition with shattered nerves and a distaste for regular hours. Where the older generation was preoccupied with the problems of will and energy, the young find no adequate satisfaction in the idea of individual striving, and offer instead the ideal of open receptivity and an almost religious insistence on the value of the impulsive human being. Instead of the would-be energetic grandfather and the sincerely desperate father, we have the son dreaming of a new super-man, not intellectual and sophisticated, but the "young god" of primitive instinct. This primitivist school, an offshoot of the proletarian movement, has for its central doctrine the recognition of sexual love, not as possessive, but as a state of spiritual plenitude and a condition of any real contact with life. Of the group Eyvind Johnson is the most interesting figure, endowed as he is with a brilliant destructive gift unequalled since Strindberg. In his work the need for positive values is felt almost as a craving, but it is clear that for him

Scandinavia

none is to be found in actuality. In his most
ambitious achievement, *Bobinack*, he attempts for
the first time to create an ambiguous character
representing both the anarchic principle, destroying
a corrupt and impotent civilization, and the
heretical divinity of fertility and spontaneous
vigour, in one complex symbol.

The novel of adolescence had been one of the
chief literary forms of the 'twenties, when not
only the theme but often also the implicit standards
of evaluation are those of adolescence. In Sweden
the wave of autobiographical fiction includes
Andersson and Lagerkvist. Less obviously adolescent in feeling, but nevertheless having affinities
with this movement is an autobiography of G.
Hellström, informed by the tragic recognition of
the limitations of an adolescent temperament which,
one feels, the author can realize but not transcend.
The most disturbing contribution made by a
younger generation in this genre is Agnes von
Krusenstjerna's *Tony* trilogy, which marks an
advance in the treatment of early development, not
in profundity, perhaps, but in range of experience,
notably sexual experience. The attitude is neither
that of revolt nor acceptance, but rather a wondering
submissiveness before the awakening of sex, set

off against the onset of hereditary insanity, with which it is intimately bound up. The more recent novels of adolescence have tended to become media of self-exploration and revision of experience rather than expressions of immediate feeling. Examples are to be found in the novels of the Dane, J. Paludan, and in Norway in Sigurd Hoel's latest work.

The psychoanalytic novel has been a late growth in Scandinavia, though vague glimpses of the new psychology have furnished commercial fiction with attractive novelties. A genuine impact of Adler's psychology is to be found in Hellström's auto-biography. A more detached use of psychoanalysis is seen in the work of Hoel, whose *A Day in October* is the most finished product of the type. It confirms the rejection of post-war metaphysical pessimism; the pessimism that remains is conditional, and one is allowed to entertain the possibility of psychological and social control. Technically, the book breaks away from the traditional approach to "character." Instead of the three-dimensional figure, Hoel introduces a new interpretation of character as a sequence of responses conditioned by circumstances. A similar conception of character also marks Aksel Sandemose (a young author of

Scandinavia

Danish origin now writing in Norwegian), and is evident in his first Norwegian book, *A Sailor Goes Ashore*. In his later work, however, he returns to a more subjective expression of emotion in the form of phantasmagoria.

The abandonment of the post-war mood proceeds very differently in Denmark. Here a number of writers have taken up active attitudes in face of the collapse of standards—partly following the lead given by Paludan. The most noteworthy of these is M. Lauesen, whose chief work so far, *Waiting for a Ship*, gives no complete evidence of his sincere and troubled search for positive values. It is a variation of the family chronicle, recording decline, and in its traditional preoccupation with the details of everyday existence it has nothing to contribute to the development of contemporary sensibility, except in so far as it succeeds in suggesting an atmosphere of impending change and its necessity.

To complete what is necessarily a brief sketch of the modern Scandinavian novel a word is needed to emphasize the position of the writer who, in isolated superiority, represents the real greatness of his age in literature—Hjalmar Bergman. In illuminating contrast to that of most of his contemporaries, Bergman's work is untouched by the malady which has vitiated so many of their most ambitious undertakings: the dissociation of thought and feeling referred to in discussing its most notable Swedish victim of the same generation, Nordström. In manipulating both regional and urban materials, Bergman shows full awareness of the break up of the idyllic order and the disintegration of industrial civilization. For him, however, the process of human decline is never the nominal theme, it is suggested wholly within the psychological texture of personal sensibility. He is as free from parasitic explanatory theory as from nostalgic sentiment. His positive values are only present by implication, as intimations of possibilities of living of the same order of intensity as the suffering and frustration which are the overt and dominating themes of his best work. In his masterpiece, *Grandmother and The Lord*, Bergman shows us the destruction from within of the family idyll, by laying bare the working of the possessive instinct —as conditioned by the demands of an acquisitive society—preying on love and affection and distorting them, until they defeat their conscious aim, finally making both communication and self-knowledge an illusion. Bergman, however, sustains the tone of serenity: his attitude is not that of "pessimism," but the acceptance of the knowledge of life, of the conditions imposed on the "Naked Man," the unchanging human being.

In Bergman we find the terrifying honesty of the pure creator as defined by T. S. Eliot in his essay on Blake. He alone was able in his greatest works to "exhibit the essential sickness or strength of the human soul." He belongs to the small company of writers who, like Joyce and Eliot in England, offer justification for the belief that the nineteen-twenties will eventually take their place as one of the great creative periods of art.

INDEX

Index

Tendencies of the Modern Novel

Index